TRAITORS' CREED

BOOK I

LAUREN PARKER RHODES

WILDFUL WRITINGS

NSW, Australia

Paperback ISBN: 978-1-7637346-9-2

eBook ISBN: 978-0-6454523-1-0

ALSO BY LAUREN PARKER RHODES

Access Lauren's other books here, or at:
www.laurenparkerrhodes.com/books

DRIARN DUOLOGY
The Wife (short story prequel)
Amber Wolf
Blue Pointed Star

WHEN SECRETS BECKON

TRAITORS DUOLOGY
Traitors' Creed
Traitors' Promise

Author's note: Each of these books, with the exception of Traitors' Promise, were previously published by Lauren Searson-Patrick and have been republished, with permission, by Lauren Parker Rhodes. Traitors' Promise has only been published by Lauren Parker Rhodes.

CONTENT WARNING

This book is intended for adult audiences and contains mature themes and relationships. There is a threat of, and attempted, sexual assault of a side character and discussion of sex trafficking and child abuse. This book is the first in a duology and ends on a cliffhanger.

For my brother, who is always encouraging us to look a little closer.

PROLOGUE

I *met with him today – the boy we raised. Although it was you, really, that did most of the raising. A fact I am infinitely grateful for. Sometimes I do wonder what it would have been like if we'd chosen a different path. Stayed home. Stayed small. Stayed ... silent. I know, of course, that life wasn't ever ours. But it doesn't mean I don't wonder.*

He was impressive today, 'our' boy, although I don't know how much of me he remembers. I would like to think his ability to sway you from your fervent focus on bloodshed to a longer, more strategic play had something to do with me. But, the truth is, I think it was all him.

He tells me they are feeling the loss of their head of intelligence, a fact that hurts my heart immensely. I will do what I can to ease her suffering from where I am. They had a semblance of a plan on how to manage if one of them was taken, and it's that plan we are now moving to enact. Thankfully, he is still focused on the future. Whatever the outcome of their – our – recovery mission, there are a number of other issues that can be dealt with at the same time. Only time will tell how those cookies crumble, so to speak.

To help ensure we're set up for that future, I have been observing one of my team here. Her time here is coming to an end and she would be a natural in the place where we most sorely need some inside intelligence. She's smart but unassuming, and has a background in academia focusing on social issues that I can't help but think will form the foundation for her and the things she will come to understand. She just doesn't know it yet.

I will ease her into that new role, help her peel back the layers to see what's beneath, and continue to do what is required of me.

There is a way to go my friend, but this phase will see some true penance being paid.

I remain hopeful it can go all the way.

I cannot send you this letter, I realise. I write now more out of habit and as my own personal outlet than with any real thought that we'll be able to talk openly again – there is too much at stake for us to be friends in the daylight anymore.

I am unsure when my next update will be but I remain, as always, loyal to our goals.

Placing the heavy black pen down slowly, I stare at the words, accustomed now to the hollow feeling writing these letters that go nowhere brings. But I take heart in the things I have been able to release – even knowing they will simply be swallowed in a void of silence – and in the meeting I had today, knowing the series of events that will come from it.

The metal bin scrapes lightly on the carpet as I pull it from under the ornate timber desk with my booted foot, holding the letter over it and grabbing the lighter from my bottom drawer. I take a moment to run my thumb over the engraving, my chest warming a little, before I flick the lighter to life and let the corner of the paper catch. I pinch the corner of the paper until it's too eaten by heat and flame for me to hang on to anymore and I drop it into the empty bin and watch it burn.

When I'm satisfied any evidence of my only partly censored thoughts has disintegrated, I take the bin to the window and tip the ashes in the night sky.

CHAPTER ONE

The prisoners are restless.

They always are before a new intake – desperate to see who will next come through the ever-revolving doors. Would they know them? Had they worked together? What events brought them here?

Their murmuring, along with irritable glances, echo between the stone walls as I monitor the group. The teams of concierges move effortlessly through the space – its high ceiling, along with the stone, make it feel like something from an elegant dream – quietly offering food and drink to the prisoners from laden gold trays. I nod at any who glance tentatively my way, looking for a reassurance they're on the right task. We've been through this process countless times during my five years here and I know they will execute their duties well.

The prisoner closest to me, Miana, grips the stem of her long glass like she wants to snap it in two, her red painted lips fixed in a false smile. It doesn't take long for one of the other concierges to notice and top up her drink.

I'd felt ill when I heard the whispers in my National Duty cohort about our destination. We'd all heard the rumours – prisoner and concierge alike – that those who come to the prison-island never return to the Nuntainia mainland the same. If at all.

But that's as far as our similarities go. Putting our dress code aside, there is some undefinable *thing* that clearly sets the concierges apart from their charges.

Outwardly, dressed in all manner of finery, the prisoners try to maintain an appearance of civility – or maybe it's professionalism they attempt to keep. Whatever it is, it's clear they are always unsettled about the changes that inevitably come with a new batch of inmates joining their cohort. But they always settle again. The new prisoners find their own rhythm and space up here and the existing ones adjust to the changes in dynamic.

Back when I was assigned to my duty and arrived at the distribution hall on the mainland, I didn't know the truth – just as the new prisoners who arrive on the island don't know for sure until their feet touch the marble receiving plane – that there are two prisons on this island in the sky. The notorious Vana, and the one where I was allocated and have served for the last five years. While both prisons inhabit the same island, the work we do in mine is very far from the torturous halls of Vana. A truth that makes me feel both infinitely grateful, and, if I think about it too long, heavy with guilt. Because I've seen the people that do their duty at Vana, seen how their spirits are dampened, broken, just because they were sent to the other side and I wasn't.

I've never laid eyes on the prisoners there. I stifle the shudder that starts to rock across my back. Nor do I want to. I've heard enough stories from the workers to last me several lifetimes. Nothing that happens in that place is something I want to experience.

Twisting the floral table arrangement before me, gently shifting the low hanging greenery on the silk tablecloth, I try to force my shoulders to relax as I brush out the imaginary creases in my dress. Because, while the prisoners and their attendants at Vana endure goodness knows what, I am currently overseeing a welcome banquet for our newest inmates, preparing to soothe their jitters with the best available food, drink, and entertainment. Something I need to look like I enjoy. And I do, mostly – even if it's something that, at first, I struggled to comprehend.

Our concierge contracts mean we can't voice the fact they are actually more like esteemed guests in a luxurious resort than prisoners to anyone that doesn't reside on the island, even if we were allowed to talk about the details of our duty. But, up here, this is our normal. Guests or prisoners, they're off the mainland, out of sight and out of mind; even if the public assumes that means they're in Vana ... at least the so-called prisoners they know about.

Swallowing the thought away, I do another visual sweep of the room, noting the appropriate cleanliness of the coloured, high-pile rugs. The usual undercurrent of tension is there but, so far, tonight is going without a hitch – a point I hope will make its way back to the Prime Minister's office. But I don't let my hopes get too high; the well-connected prisoners in the room before me are far more likely to use those connections to complain than compliment.

That's supposed to be the upside for us concierges – commit several years to the country in a service of the Nuntainia Government's choosing and, if done well, get a recommendation to move straight into a better role on return to the mainland. Which would be wonderful ... if I knew what role I wanted a recommendation for, what sort of life I should try and build after my time here.

I let my fingers trail the pale silk cloth again as I search out Blossom in the milling crowd. She moves gracefully around the grandroom as I mentally walk through what else I need to do for tonight – which essentially boils down to making sure all the people who have not been sent here to work have the best experience possible.

Bloss's tight brown curls bounce after her as she offers drinks. The short glasses crowd the gold tray, condensation dripping from the sides and ice clinking gently with her expert balance. She smiles politely as one of the male prisoners takes a glass from the tray and winks at her. He's been hoping she'd get transferred to the playroom his entire stay, but the Warden never sends anyone there against their express wishes.

And Blossom is nothing if not clear in her wishes.

The soft, billowy fabric of our dress code floats through the room in various parts of my vision as my team go about their work. All different colours, but all intended to invoke a sense of calm for everyone here, including us. It's hard to feel anxious or irritable when everything is so beautiful.

It's also easy to feel contained.

'Luka,' the Warden says softly, breaking into my thoughts, 'a word.'

Soundlessly, I turn to follow him from the low light of the room, nodding gently at Blossom on my way and leaving her in charge. I can't help but suck in a full breath of fresh air when we reach the white and gold hallway, the moonlight that streams through the open roof glinting on the balustrades.

'How are we looking for the rest of this evening?' he asks, his voice gentle, respectful. The deep navy of his uniform is striking against his rich, dark skin.

'We're ready,' I confirm. 'The kitchens are preparing the last of the food – Koko's new enchantments in the chocolate balls will not disappoint. And I've just listened to the final music rehearsal.' He nods along as I talk, his thick brows furrowed as he ticks off his own mental list.

'Seating is appropriate?'

'Yes, sir.'

'Very good. Bring me the final run sheet for the evening,' he says.

I don't have to fake the smile on my face. The plan is perfect, I checked it myself. But I'll go over it at least one more time before I give it to him, just in case.

When the feast finally starts, I begin to unwind my nerves. A slow detangling of the edges that have frayed over the lead up to tonight. The terse words from prisoners, the assessing study of the Warden, and the trembling lips of the newest members of the concierge team – those who arrived separately to the prisoners, and now begin their duty. All of which add up to the weight that is my own service to the nation of Nuntainia.

I turn my attention to the quartet who are just about to count in. The new lead violinist looks in my direction as he lifts the yellowing timber to the side of his chin. When it meets his skin, the black pad sparks to life. Three sparks of white light race from beneath his jaw, around the edges of the woodwork and along the strings. He smiles gently to himself as he positions the bow just a touch above the instrument, gaze now glued to the conductor.

As one, they begin and the sound seeps into the room. I close my eyes briefly and get ready to let it wash over me. Opening them again, I find the tiny sparks that illuminated the instruments as they multiply and carry the music throughout the heavily decorated grandroom. The warm yellow of the bass tones dance just as nimbly as the white light of the treble. Each light shimmers between the warm and the white as their respective instruments duck and weave through the notes only they seem to know.

Soon, the room is full of glittering lights that soften and dim into the background, the chatter of voices and clinking of glasses becoming the dominant sound. Judging by the wink of the violinist, my observations don't go unnoticed. My cheeks heat and I glance away.

He's cute. If I had a next time here, maybe I'd wink back. Biting down on my private smile, I move to find Blossom.

'Are you sad this is your last one?' she asks, ocean blue eyes surveying the melting pot of prisoners.

'Mostly that it's my last with you,' I say, looking across the room myself in case anyone needs us.

She scoffs, only half jokingly. 'I wasn't asking you for real,' she says. 'You don't get to be sad – you get to go home. I still have two years left.'

I smile, mostly because it's what I am expected to do here. But, the truth is, I don't know what awaits me at home. A new start. But what will I be starting when I am so far behind? I certainly don't have my academic career to go back to. Letting my mind come back to tonight, I focus on what I need – another uneventful evening as the final step to a glowing recommendation from the Warden.

Bloss's piercing gaze swings my way and I purposefully keep my attention on the small group of prisoners starting to dance in front of us. Some are awkward, a couple are gently suggestive, and I know some will be downright sinful before the end of the night. The prison has its own societal norms as the prisoners embrace their time here.

'You know the worst bit for me?' she asks. A breeze kicks up, blowing through the stone archways that line the grandroom, the scent of jasmine floating on the wind. Our skirts shimmy around our legs and ankles.

'You won't get to see my smiling face every morning?' I ask, said smile still in place, although they are almost always genuine where Blossom is involved.

'Hardly, you scowl hard enough to break glass in the mornings.'

I stifle a laugh.

'No,' she continues. 'I will not miss your morning wrath. I'm pissed I won't get to see the mysterious Nix when he comes to collect you.'

I smile wider, my cheeks aching from the giddiness at the thought of seeing him again. But it's also tinged with worry. He's been my best friend since childhood, but the letters we've exchanged over the last five years have felt ... different. They started out so normal, and I treasure them over our less frequent texts, but Nix's increasing sadness, and sometimes anger, have grown palpable even through the ink on the pages over that time, and I'm almost desperate to see him again.

'He's not so mysterious,' I say. 'You just haven't met him.'

'Precisely. Your *other* best friend is literally coming to this island in the clouds and I will be barred from meeting him.'

Davorous, the prisoner that favours her, approaches Blossom and she groans just loud enough for me to hear. I note the genuine unease that sits underneath it.

He holds out his pale, well-manicured hand as an invitation to dance and she accepts it politely – as she must, at least in such a public domain. I watch them spin around the room, some of the other prisoners looking on with disdain on their faces. They might like to use us when we're in the playroom – and sometimes out of it – but we are still the help.

The Warden meanders through the crowd, his keen observation missing nothing, making sure everything is in place. Then he finds me. I'm in place, too. The warm and spicy scent of the small bites of food passing before me makes my stomach grumble, but I don't reach for one. A sparkling drink or two is okay, getting my face or hands dirty with food is not.

'You've excelled yourself tonight,' the Warden says as he approaches, taking Blossom's position next to me as we watch.

The warm, deep timbre of his voice wraps around me. He's been Warden the whole time I've been here, and for a long time before. There's a certain tiredness that has brought to his features, but it clears when he looks at me. Mostly.

'It will definitely be an adjustment – not having you here,' he says. 'I've come to depend rather heavily on you, Luka.'

I don't look up at him as I swallow back the gentle emotion that rises at his words.

'You executed your duty almost beyond compare,' he says.

I don't miss the 'almost'. It's that part my heart won't let go of – that reminds me of my old self – even as my head tells me that's unnecessary.

'You will be able to get just about any role you'd like when you return home.' He looks at me. 'My recommendation comes highly valued.'

I nod. I know, the same as my father's could have – should have. Until he decided not to give it. But it's not just the Warden's recommendation I've strived for all this time. It's his genuine appreciation as well, and I think he knows that.

'Thank you, sir,' I say as he takes a tall glass of Koko's signature cocktail from the concierge that passes by. A small sound of appreciation leaves his lips as he takes a sip – Koko definitely knows how to use her Clayti abilities to manipulate natural resources for our enjoyment.

'Is there anywhere in particular you'd like me to write to?' he asks.

I think of the school I used to work in – was supposed to run one day – until the 'almost' that seems to always accompany me meant the role was offered to someone else. Not even my father's reputation as Nuntainia's premier magic historian and social policy expert was enough to put that 'almost' aside, not without his recommendation.

'No,' I say after a beat. 'A generic referral would be perfect, please.'

I sip my own drink, a vibrant purple that compliments my soft lavender gown. My worries about what to do when I get home fizz in my mouth along with my drink. I haven't visited once during my five years of service at the prison – none of us do – and I can't contemplate how the world has changed since then. I do know I have no idea where I fit there any more. Wherever it is, I know it's not to be second or third place in an institution I built from the ground up.

The Warden is still looking at me when I turn back to him, a contemplative look on his face. As if there's a secret he's considering sharing.

'I should like to work with you again,' he says carefully, 'if we have the opportunity.'

I pause. Working with the Warden is a joy I didn't expect from my duty but ... after five years, I don't think—

'Not here,' he says quietly, his tone snagging in my mind and I frown at him. 'Somewhere ...' he sighs. 'You've got a good heart, Luka. In another life, I could use it elsewhere. If you were willing.'

The Warden takes another sip from his drink as Kasera, one of our longest serving prisoners, approaches us, her gaze fixed firmly on his tall form, flicking momentarily to his mouth. He holds his mostly full glass to me with a meaningful look I don't understand, and I take it without question, quietly observing the tilt of Kasera's chin as she waits for me to be gone. Like she's impatiently waiting for someone to clear the dust out of the corners of a room before she enters it.

'You should take the rest of the night off,' he says as he walks towards Kasera, sweeping in to kiss both her cheeks. 'We'll talk more about what's next when you fly the nest.'

He throws me one last, long look before returning his attention to the prisoner. Her two-piece mulberry suit shimmers in the flickering light, the matching sheen on her cheekbones sparkling like dawn.

Fly the nest, he said. It's a phrase I feel too old for – I flew my nest a long time ago. At the same time, though, it feels so accurate. My life has been on pause these last five years, my only focus during my time here: Finish the duty. Get a recommendation. Leave. Although, we *are* currently living in the clouds. Perhaps 'fly the nest' is actually spot on. Or it would be, if there was a chance I'd have Karaylia abilities and grow wings but – even without the dampener – that's highly unlikely.

I stare after him, wondering what was lying underneath his words. More than that, though, is the sharp pang of knowing how much I will miss working with him, too. Because coming back here isn't an option for me. After five years on one of the most confidential duty allocations and no option of even a leave of absence in that time ... I'm done.

So I carefully tuck away the possibility of working with him again. I've given myself a week once I get home to settle back into my townhouse, get my things back in order, and then work out what I will do next.

I take a moment to soak in the atmosphere of the room, the scent of the jasmine filling my nose, and hair tickling the back of my neck in the breeze. The lights of the music play around me, spinning on the top of my shoulders and running down to my fingers. I open my hand and they jump on my palm as I twist it in the air. I will miss some of this, too. Not the prisoners. But the concierges, the music. The island itself. This ... being in the sky. But I'm ready to be free – whatever that looks like.

The recollection of the Warden's words creates a lightness in my chest. I might not know what I should do when I get home, but he will. Even if managing the expectations and disappointments of my father will be up to me.

The concierge wing is quiet as I arrive. I pad down the carpet-lined hallway to my apartment and my lace up sandals are the first thing I remove as I enter the soft, gentle space I will only call home for a few days more. A space that's filled with the life Blossom brings to it. I'd been coasting through my service until she arrived and brought an abundance of genuine joy to my time here.

My phone gives a muffled chime in the pocket of my gauzy dress and I dig it out, tossing it on the bed as I undress and wash. I'm hopeful it's news from home – and not the Warden forgetting he needs me for something – and I want to savour the anticipation of it.

By the time I get out of the hot shower, smother myself in thick body cream, and pull on my gold night dress, there are three more notifications.

Akira: Three more sleeps, babe! Are you excited? Tell me you're excited?!

Zale: Of course she's excited. Isn't Nix collecting her? About time he COLLECTED her...

Akira: If I wasn't shacked up already, I'd let Nix collect me.

Zale: You and me both. Just don't tell Teddy, she's got her heart set on us joining some cause – if she thinks I'd be taken care of by Nix, she'd probably leave without me!

I grin even as I shake my head. To hear their banter face-to-face – none of which would be surprising to Nix, despite how much they like to try and stir our very platonic, almost sibling-like, relationship – will be the best possible balm to all the missing them I have done over the last five years.

Being unable to really tell them anything that happens here because of my contract makes our conversations quite one-sided at times and … none of my possible updates feel like mine, anyway.

My smile dampens as I remember it will be Blossom I miss soon. And I'll have two years to wait until I can introduce her to Akira, Zale, and Nix. Outside of Nix, and his quietly protective older brother, Akira and Zale are my best friends in the world. Sisters when I had none of my own, and I know without doubt they will accept Blossom into the fold.

Luka: My FRIEND Nix is collecting me, yes. And I am definitely excited for the girls' night you have secretly planned for me.

Akira: Zale! Did you give us up already? Traitor!

Zale: I'd suggest we're just predictable, A. Must be what motherhood does to us.

I place my phone in the drawer next to the bed, ignoring the slight tightening in my gut at the mention of their new lives, and take out Nix's last letter instead, focusing on his scrappy handwriting. It's dated some weeks ago, but that's not unusual – his own obligation to Nuntainia, whatever it is, keeps him from writing often and access to his phone patchy at best. The details are scant, the magical contracts required of our confidential duties making it difficult to share what the government doesn't want others to know. But it's clear just how much he's also looking forward to it being done. He has another year on me; his service requirements longer for his designation – partly because he can take leave – and I sigh at how obviously that makes me out of sync with him, too.

I cannot wait to see you, Luka, there is so much to tell you. Don't be late to collection. I can't bear another minute longer than absolutely necessary.

I'm ready for a taste of home.

CHAPTER TWO

The sun soaks into my pillow as the last tendrils of sleep leave me. I untangle my legs from the sheets with a groan as I readjust my night dress and replace the thin strap back on my shoulder. Dragging myself from the cloud-like bed, I can't help but sigh as my feet meet the cold stone, the chill of the mist encasing my bare arms as I make my way to the balcony and take in the view of the sun as it paints the sea of clouds around me pink and gold.

This morning ritual is one I will miss immensely. The sensation of being part of the sky so seamlessly, where I can literally reach out and touch the heavens, will forever be etched into my memory. Zanteera Island might be feared by those on the mainland because of the reputation of Vana prison, but they're not all aware of what's actually up here. For me, now that I've seen it – lived it – this being part of the sky and *not* having any ties to Vana, I wonder again how hard it will be to adjust back to life in the city below.

A city full of people, and towering buildings with lights that never turn off, and the silent transport pods that aren't actually silent but leave a quiet ringing in my ears every time they go past. All of that ... pressing up against other people's lives. Compared to the witnessing, supporting, and ... watching from afar I do from up here. Sometimes I'm desperate to be back in the middle of it all, and others I dread the day I have to give up this quiet.

But that doesn't overtake the nervous excitement that's starting to gain traction. A gentle tingle under my skin at the options that are now opening up to me. The compensation for my duty has been reasonable and, with no family to send it back to, I have enough put away to give me time to work out what I want to do.

For a long time, I resented that thick, cream envelope that arrived under my door. The one that said, in no uncertain terms, I had been randomly selected for national service by the government of Nuntainia. Not long after, so were Nix and River. But never Zale or Akira. Given they'd started families before me, I was relieved for them to not be selected. But it didn't stop the pinch behind my ribs that wondered what my life would have been like if I wasn't selected, either.

'Luka!' Blossom calls from our shared living space, and I push aside the vastness that seems to be my future before it's too overwhelming.

She's always up before me and prepares our morning tipples. That's her routine – her way of starting the day in a fresh, focused frame of mind.

My glasses are lined up on the white stone bench that marks our small kitchen space. They're barely the size of my thumb, and in no particular order other than what Blossom reached for in the cupboard first. The first one – the contraceptive tonic – makes me hesitate a fraction. Not because I don't want it, and it's mandatory for all that serve here anyway, but for the tiniest moment it makes me wonder what could have been if I'd had a family at the same time as Akira and Zale.

If I am now edging towards too old to consider such possibilities – the time it would take to find the right person and …

The tonic tastes of berries and cinnamon as it goes down in one go, the gold-rimmed glass clinking heavily as I place it on the bench and pick up the next one. This is the rhythm. Up, throw back, down. Clink. Up, throw back, down. Clink. Three times as I take the contraceptive, an immune boosting agent, and magic dampener.

It's the magic dampener that's the most bitter and I ponder, after the best part of five years, why I take it last.

But I know: it's a reminder that serving my country costs me, too. For whatever pride I have in fulfilling my duties so well – for excelling in this service I was selected for, and making the Warden proud like I was never able to my father – there is an everyday reminder of what I have given up. The government – the Prime Minister's Chief of Staff, in particular – told us it was simply a pause. A pause in our own magic, in which time we would serve the country of Nuntainia and grow in different ways. But, for many of us, we were, or are, not only at a peak time for families, but for our magic to properly manifest.

For those who were lucky enough to have it before they came, the dampener does just that – softens it into remission until they go home and stop taking the tipple. At which point their magic will flare back into life. But for those of us, like Blossom and me, whose magic hadn't yet come in before we were sent here, there is a high chance we are tricking our bodies into forgetting what they were made for.

And we will never know what that was. Something that would have – will – devastate my father.

Over time, Blossom has started to follow the same rhythm with her tipples, and she pulls a face as she swallows and looks at me. Her brown curls are squashed on one side where she's slept, her freckles all the more prominent with her clean skin.

I prefer her like this.

I prefer me like this, too.

Our required dresses are pretty and our faces and hair are always done to perfection but, after a while, the novelty of that perfection wears thin.

And Blossom and I each crave for others to see us as we truly are. I think that's part of the reason we became such close friends so quickly – we saw each other.

'I still think it would be better if they let us see if our magic would come in before we leave,' she says, eyeing me. 'It would make the transition home easier. What if it would help us decide what we wanted to do? Would you do landscape design or become a mining magnate if you had Clayti abilities? Or take cooking lessons from Koko? Or use your Arkanan magic to heal—'

I pin her with a look. 'I will *not* be a mining magnate and Nix is a strong enough Clayti for all of us.' But I still can't help but sigh. 'It does feel like I don't quite know myself,' I say slowly, not that this is news to Blossom. 'The Warden will give me a recommendation for almost anywhere, but you're right. I don't know how to choose that when my magic is unknown. I keep trying to tell myself my magic – or lack thereof – won't define me ... but I'm not sure that's true.'

Blossom is silent for a beat. 'No, magic doesn't define us. Love does,' she says, lifting a shoulder. 'And loving someone, including ourselves, sometimes means ... accepting the things we can't yet see – however much we might wish it was different.'

A shadow crosses her face and I know she's thinking of her husband, but she shakes it off before I can even take her hand.

'None of that today,' she says with a faint sniff. 'Today, your future starts and, magic or no magic, I know it will be one filled with the most wonderful surprises for you. Now, shoo, you need to get ready for your last intake.'

'Any moment now,' I say to the line of concierges before me who wait for the new arrivals. For the first time, I won't be allocated any prisoners and a tiny hollowness starts to burrow under my ribs.

'Smile,' I say. Their faces sparkle just as I know mine does. Even the platinum blonde braid I have pulled over my shoulder glitters in the sunlight.

The receiving plane is a broad expanse of grey marble with a white vein on the roof of the prison. Being up here used to make my stomach churn as the island around me seemed to disappear into nothing underneath the stone platform. It still does, somewhat, but the need to drop to my knees to steady myself has all but subsided, replaced by an almost giddying freedom. Up here, I don't belong to the prison or to the home I left behind. I lean into the sky – perhaps I am leaving one prison just to find myself constrained in new ways and I will yearn for these small tastes of liberty.

Wind tears at my dress, the skirt and sleeves threatening to rip away, reminding me I do still belong here. Just for a little longer. The portal lets a soft scream into the sky as the seam of the world is torn slightly and the prisoners stumble out. As high profile and educated as they are – they are the only sort of prisoners we get here – it's still unusual for many of them to have travelled by portal enough to be used to the sensation.

And most of them have never been delivered into the sky before.

The Warden steps forward as the portal sighs closed and the wind drops back to a gentle breeze. He assesses the twelve prisoners that stand before him. Each dressed in a sickly green pantsuit with their hands magically bound at their front, the vines that twist around them cutting into the skin.

Before even a single drop of blood can mark the marble, the Warden taps his fingers against his thigh and the vines disappear. The wounds swept away with them. The prisoners, nine men and three women – not an unusual ratio – stare at him. Most of them draw their spines up straighter. One of the men sags in relief.

They've heard about our prison, I'm sure, through the whispers that weave their way through the circles of the elite, but nothing more. As part of our service contracts we are barred from talking about the prison when we return, our tongues unable to form the words. But those in high places always seem to be able to find ways around the laws that govern the rest of us. The only thing they truly seem to be barred from up here is accessing their magic.

Yet, there was a sliver of doubt; it's clear even in those who now look down their noses at the Warden. They didn't know for sure if the rumours were true that more than one prison exists on the island.

The Warden motions them forward. The prisoners file across the expanse of stone, led by Emeris, in his cream pants and white, sleeveless vest that leaves little of his sculpted chest to the imagination, only to balk at the end. Emeris maintains the lead and the rest of the concierges, me included, slip in between the prisoners so they each have a personal assistant to help get down the stairs that cut into the side of the building. Clinging to the balustrade set into the grey stone brick walls that hold the marble aloft, the prisoners are a mix of tears, sweat, and snot as they navigate downwards. The action going against all of their instincts – as it did mine the first several times.

The open side drops away from the building and slides down directly into the sky, beckoning to any who might slip. We have lost more than one that way – a difficult situation to explain to the Chief of Staff. But, for whatever reason, the platform remains the destination of the arrival portal.

Perhaps it is their first and last punishment for whatever got them sent here.

Today, we make it to the bottom without incident and into the receiving hall, where each new prisoner is attended to by a team of concierges who spend the allocated hour helping them wash, dress, and generally feel once more themselves.

I wait patiently with the Warden, watching each of the closed doors off the receiving hall.

He lets go of a heavy breath and I glance over at him.

'Long night?' I ask quietly.

'Paperwork,' he says with a slight shake of his head. 'In all my time here, there has never been so much unnecessary shuffling of papers.'

I press my lips together to hold back a soft laugh at his regular complaint. He's so committed to his role, I'm not sure any amount of paperwork could tarnish it for him.

He glances across the receiving hall and its pale tiles to the arch window and the blue sky beyond. 'Traelen will be here shortly to announce them.'

I nod. Traelen, the Prime Minister's Chief of Staff, is a regular to the prison. The Warden is in charge up here, but it's Traelen who calls the shots from below, who manages the prison on behalf of the Prime Minister.

'I've almost completed your recommendation,' he says quietly, and I glance up. There's something in his features that sparks the tiniest flicker of doubt and I think back to our conversation in the grandroom. He remains focused on the closed doors but keeps talking. 'I should like to suggest you take a position in Parliament.'

A slightly strangled noise leaves me and I cough to cover it up. The slight twitch of a smile from the Warden tells me I was unsuccessful.

'I—'

'It's rare to get the required recommendation, I know,' he says, dark eyes finally finding mine. 'But you'd be a great asset there, Luka.'

I can feel myself frown. 'So why the "should" then – you can recommend me for wherever you like.'

'Not all duties end with a recommendation of choice, but I believe people *should* have choices in these matters. And Parliament, despite its potential personal benefits, can be … an adjustment. Politics isn't for everyone – neither is working with politicians.'

I look back to the doors, none of which have opened yet, and wonder how naive the Warden thinks I am. But as I think over the scheming and plotting I have seen even here, where the inmates are so far removed from their usual arena, I can't help but think he's right.

'But you want me to do it anyway?'

He's silent for a long moment, the time heavy with something I don't understand.

'I do. You have many other options, though, and I'd like you to consider them all. But, if you choose to let me recommend you for Parliament, I would like to stay in touch during your time there – would you allow that?'

'Of—'

I break off as Traelen's tall, slim form takes shape in the entrance from the hall. The only sign he's descended the outdoor stairs is a single lock of straight, deep-gold hair that's fallen over his left eye.

Sweeping it from his face, he strides towards the Warden, his attention flicking only momentarily to me. We've met on multiple occasions, but he never shows any signs of recognition. I must be one of hundreds of concierges he's seen over the years – from memory, he has been the Prime Minister's longest serving Chief of Staff.

'Traelen,' the Warden says in greeting.

'Claudius.' Traelen stands next to the Warden, impatience billowing from him as the first of the prisoners emerges from one of the small rooms.

Would the Warden be recommending I work directly with the Chief of Staff in Parliament?

One of the new prisoners, now dressed in a deep purple ensemble with knee length shorts – his large, pale calves bulging out underneath – and a crisp white shirt cuffed tightly around his wrists and ballooning out and up to his shoulders, steps out. Why anyone would choose that particular outfit, I have no idea. He nods curtly to Traelen, whose gaze sweeps across the other doors, as if he's impatient to get this done with and return to the real world.

As soon as the last prisoner has rejoined the group, Traelen clears his throat.

'Alderson Finch,' he says, and one of the women steps forward. 'Minister for Play and Recreation, board member of several esteemed charities, and Principal Adviser to the Prime Minister on special projects.'

'Emeris,' the Warden responds. Emeris steps forward, offering her his elbow to take her for a tour and escort her to the room she will spend her stay in.

'Zenaton Blake,' Traelen says and the next prisoner steps forward. 'Decorated war veteran with numerous missions completed.'

I take in Zenaton and I can see it there – the military service in his stance, so much like the Warden's – and I wonder what horrors he has seen. And I say a silent thank you that our government managed to withdraw Nuntainia from the conflict between Tae and Coprath.

As Traelen introduces the prisoners, most of whom are from the very Parliament the Warden has mentioned, I mull over his thoughts on my recommendation. Without one, I will have nothing to show for my time here, but are these the sort of people I really want to spend my working life with? I don't know what they are sent here for, but it's clearly nothing so terrible that warrants them going to Vana prison instead. All I know about them is the outrageous, and sometimes obscene, personal requests they make while they're here. And working in Parliament would give me a status and compensation that would truly allow me to help Akira and Zale and their families as they need. To help Nix, to be a safe landing place for Blossom when her duty is finished.

My heart swells a little with what I could contribute to their lives even as I work out what to do with mine. How I could watch their children grow into their magic. I haven't been able to see their early childhoods, but I could see which of the four lines was their dominant. If they'd throw towards the earth-wielding Clayti, like Nix, or healing Arkanans like his brother, River – it's unlikely they'd have Shaide or Karaylia affinities, but stranger things have happened, and they could have elements of more than one. The fact River is also Karaylia was surprising enough.

At the same time, I will finally be creating my own life. Making my own choices on what to do with my time and what impact I want to have on the world and the people around me. And working in Parliament would give me both more time and an opportunity to stay connected to Claudius.

Traelen and the Warden follow this call and answer pattern until all of the achievements are voiced, and the concierges allocated, before Traelen nods again at the Warden and leaves without further interaction.

'Are you ready for your collection?' the Warden says to me when we're once again the only two people in the receiving hall.

'Yes, and thank you for the recommendation to Parliament,' I say. 'I'm very grateful for the opportunity.'

He assesses me for a long moment, and I almost think he's going to take the offer back.

'Thank you, Luka. It will be with you when you get back to the mainland, once Traelen has signed off on it. Remember, the brighter the opportunity, the greater the potential risks. But you will always have access to help.'

CHAPTER THREE

The clothes I put on feel foreign. And tight. The dresses I normally wear as my concierge uniform are floating and ethereal, and the black, slim-leg pants I now wear threaten to cut all circulation from my stomach down. My favourite old t-shirt is a comfort, in a way, but I don't recognise the person it used to belong to.

'Holy ...' Blossom trails off as I leave my bedroom, my running shoes squeaking slightly on the tiles. Her deep blue eyes are wide as she blinks at me.

'I do not know what I expected,' she says. 'But that ... I just don't think that was it.'

I grin. 'Me neither, actually. And I am seriously going to have to lose this button.'

Blossom snorts a giggle as I lift my shirt to show her the straining waist of my pants. 'Do it – ditch the button.'

Breathing a sigh of relief, I pop the fabric open and adjust my t-shirt. Laughter bubbles from my throat as I think of Nix's reaction at collecting me as I bust out of my pants. Just as suddenly, it disappears as I look at Blossom. I will be reconnecting with one best friend, and saying goodbye to another.

'Stop overthinking,' Blossom says.

She strides to me before I can respond and grips me in a tight embrace. I cling to her and bury my head in the crook of her neck, her curls tickling my nose.

'You promised to write to me,' she says into my hair. 'Don't you dare get so carried away with your new shiny life and your fuckable best friend that you forget about me.'

I shake my head, not only at the 'fuckable' bit. 'Never.'

She pulls away too soon, this goodbye feeling horribly similar to the one I shared with Akira and Zale. Two people who promised to never change in my absence, and then did exactly that. As they should have – it was inevitable. But the sting of being left behind still exists. At the same time, there's a soaring in my chest that now, finally, I will get to do the same.

'I love you, Luka.' She's solemn as she looks at me.

'You too, Bloss. Be good here. Just keep doing what you're doing and soon enough I'll be back to collect you, okay?'

There's only one collection every year – only one time the government schedules a Shaide to create a portal between our prison and the Nuntainian mainland – and the world would have to end for me to miss Bloss's. Her husband should have been the one to collect her at the end of her service, but he passed away in her first year here. It's a loss I know she'll never recover from, nor the guilt of not being with him when he went to the next world.

She looks down, sweeping her hands down her front as if brushing away some imaginary dust.

'Bloss,' I say, tipping her chin back up. 'I *will* be here.'

She nods and smiles, blinking to clear the tears that have started to gather. 'I know.'

She walks me to the departure room, a space neither of us have ever seen the inside of. Blossom still won't, not yet – those who continue to serve are not allowed in. Apparently it reduces the temptation for a concierge to tell a collector things they have seen and done here – assuming they could find a way around the contract. But perhaps being in the same place the bans apply to is a weakness in the magic. Whatever the reasoning, the organisation of our collections is much the same as how we get to our designated duty destinations – secret. Not even the people collecting their loved ones will know where they are coming to, only the room itself.

The timber door in the far hall is unassuming, despite it being a one-way path to my next chapter. Excitement begins to tingle in my fingertips until my stomach joins the celebrations. I swallow.

'Live hard, my friend,' Blossom says, nudging me away. 'Now get in there before you miss it and you're stuck here for another year.'

I give her one more long look and push the door open, but I'm unable to meet her gaze as it closes. There are three other concierges going home today, and they all look up expectantly at me when I enter. Ciltra flits around the room, positively beaming.

'I can't tell you how much I am looking forward to today, Luka. We're done!' She waves her hands in the air before racing forward and throwing her arms around my neck.

I laugh with the others, my nerves quickly being consumed by their happiness as well as my own. There is no one in this room I am concerned about leaving behind.

Just one who's coming for me. One I have waited a long time to see again.

My heart beats faster and I begin to sweat. Brushing my hair back off my face, I tuck the stray strands behind my ears before wiping my palms on my thighs.

The sound of a portal opening to my left snags in my ears and I feel like my whole body is trembling with anticipation. The smile on my face sticking to my teeth, I lick my lips and watch the pale blue wall swirl into something else, a gentle breeze spinning through the small room.

An older woman steps out, holding her hand to the wall to steady her entrance. The long, white dress she wears is thicker in fabric than we wear up here, the temperature at home a fraction cooler than ours. She scans the room quickly but a shriek rings out before she seems to quite find who she's looking for, and one of the younger men sweeps her up into his arms. She cries – and laughs – in time with him, and I can't help the happy tears that run down my own cheeks.

He looks back at the remaining three of us once before he steps into the portal, hand in hand with the older woman.

My fingers press into my lips to suppress the giddy sounds that make their way forward, my mind in free fall that it's today. A day I have waited for every moment since I arrived.

An attractive man is next through the portal and he spies his concierge immediately. They embrace hard, their mouths coming together almost angrily in their desperation.

Then it's just Ciltra and I left. We share an awkward smile but there is a current that runs between us. The last two who have served our time and are ready to go home. The depth of the missing we've felt for our friends and family is now beyond words, and we each look back at the wall and wait. More than ready to see our loved ones again.

'Mummy!' A little girl races out of the portal straight into Ciltra's open arms. I gasp as Ciltra drops to her knees and grips her child. I had no idea she was a mother. She sobs audibly now, her young daughter bouncing on her toes in her arms, jostling them together.

Ciltra looks over her shoulder at me, her brown eyes shining. She stands, taking her daughter's hand and steps through the wall.

I blow out a long breath. Nix is coming. I'm going home. Now.

My *life* starts again. Now.

I grin as I recheck my t-shirt is covering the partially open waistband of my pants – all good. I can't wait to laugh about this with Nix.

The breeze starts to subside a little and I watch the wall, ready for Nix's broad form to step through. At least he *was* broad, I imagine he's broader now. I wonder if his hair has lightened at all in the work he does, or if it's the same dark auburn it was when I last saw him? I close my eyes and imagine his champagne ones smiling back at me, their slight almond shape curving up as he smiles.

I wonder if he still looks how I remember? If his life has changed as much as Akira's and Zale's?

My eyes open again to the portal, the breeze stilling further. The stutter in my heart kicks up a notch.

The portal starts to recede.

No.

'No!' I scream, racing for the closing portal. It's only open a fraction when I reach the wall and I slam my arm in, trying to hold it open. But my fingers meet the wall, bending back on themselves, and I cry out.

Ignoring the biting pain in my left hand, I run them furiously over the wall.

'No, no, no.' My stomach heaves but the portal doesn't return.

The pounding of my fists makes no difference.

Slowly, I sink to the floor, staring at the wall that was supposed to contain my future, and try to will life back into it.

It doesn't return.

I don't know how long I sit there, dialling and redialling Nix – long enough that the pale blue textured wall in front of me blurs. The feeling has gone in my legs from the way I'm crouched, and I force myself to get up and shake it out, the blood starting to burn as it recirculates in my limbs.

Looking back at the wall, where the portal Nix was supposed to walk through was, I brush away the tears that have fallen. Then, I make myself turn my back and walk out of the room. Blindly, I meander the halls, oblivious to the concierges and prisoners I pass. The excitement I'd felt just this morning has turned to something heavy and bitter in my stomach. Someone grips my elbow and drags me into a room. I don't resist; at least they are giving me some direction.

'Luka?'

It takes me a moment to place the voice of the Warden and I stare at him without really seeing.

'I—' he says. 'What—' He drags a hand over his face. 'How are you here?' he asks.

I look at him properly, the concern pulling at the corners of his eyes.

'I wasn't collected.' Saying it out loud makes it suddenly real and I gasp a shuddering breath. 'Um ... I – wasn't collected,' I repeat, my voice starting to wobble. 'I was supposed to go home.'

He takes each of my upper arms in his hands and looks down at me. Dimly, I note he looks a little more frazzled than normal; he curses softly.

'We'll get you home, Luka,' he says, but I think it's a reflex response to my current circumstances.

I shake my head. 'Collection is only once a year,' I say, my voice hollow, telling him something he already knows. 'And I'm not supposed to go on my own. I–I'm meant to be collected. He was going to—'

The hands that hold me grip harder as he searches my face. 'Luka, I will find a way to get you home. You've done your time. You have so much to offer – you were supposed to—' He pulls in a deep breath. 'I *will* get you home and in to position in Parliament. I just ... need to work it out.' Straightening, he stands to full height, tugging me in against him in a way he's never done before.

I cling to him like a life-raft, even though I know the rules say collections only happen once a year, and he shushes me as I cry. Just as my father once would have. When he wasn't working on correcting the social imbalances of Nuntainia.

'I haven't filled your room,' he says against the top of my head. 'I thought Blossom might need some space before someone new joined her. Let's get you back there.'

I nod my thanks as we make our way back to my room, the bag in my hand dragging my shoulder down. Blossom is out when I get back, tending to her duties, and the Warden leaves to do his with a final squeeze of my arm. I dump my belongings on the floor of the room that now feels so much more like the prison it supposedly is, curl up in my bed, and let myself succumb to the quiet tears.

'What the fuck?'

Blossom's voice breaks into the darkness I've created with the pillow over my face. She yanks it off as if she can't wait any longer to confirm it's me. As if the pants I half wear wouldn't do that for her.

She stares at me as I carefully open my tear swollen eyes and blink into the light. The bed depresses as she perches on the side but she doesn't ask.

I sigh, almost choking on my thick throat.

'He didn't come.'

Nor has he answered any of my calls or messages.

She visibly deflates and a wave of concern pulses over her features. I can see it there, the thought I have been trying to avoid since I was left in that room. Instead, letting myself get washed away in the idea that perhaps he changed his mind about collecting me.

But, the truth is, I know he wouldn't do that. He'd never do that. As far as I'm aware, the system tries to make sure this never happens, as well.

Which means the alternative is far worse. And recent.

Blossom hovers around me for the rest of the evening, bringing me enchanted wine that warms my mouth and insides and feeding me my favourite food – including Koko's latest chocolate ball creations – and insisting I change out of the clothes that feel so strange and constraining.

Unless I am filling my mouth with the things she brings me, I sit on our pale, cushion heavy couch with my head in my hands. Going over and over the possibilities, so many of which I don't know. Just as Nix doesn't know the detail of my service, I don't know the detail of his. Except it's dangerous. And it made his anger and sadness palpable in his letters.

My phone chimes and I pounce on it, desperate for word of Nix.

Akira flashes on the image that's projected and I brace myself.

Where are you babe?? Tell Nix I have a Flaming George waiting here for you! If I must, I'll buy him one too ... he can't keep you to himself all night.

I want to be happy at her remembering our go-to drink in our younger days. But the fact she obviously hasn't heard from Nix either makes it harder to breathe. My fingers clench around the small device in my hand and I snooze its message, the image disappearing from the air. I know I shouldn't delay telling them – postpone the questions that will come – but I don't even know how to form the words to myself.

Something has happened to Nix, and I'm now trapped on an island in the sky.

'Telling them won't be easier in the morning,' Bloss says gently, looking pointedly at my phone.

It takes me three goes to write something comprehensible that doesn't show just how high my desperation feels like it's running.

Luka: I'm still here. Nix didn't arrive. I've tried to contact River, too, but I haven't heard anything from either of them. I don't want to talk now in case they ring. Sorry about tonight, I'll let you know.

Zale: Oh Luka, I'm so sorry. Please tell us as soon as you hear. I'm sure he's fine. Focus on finding out what happened to him, and then we'll work out how to get you home. Akira and I are headed to his house now – he was on a short leave of absence to get you, right? We'll see if he's there. Will let you know what we find. Stay strong. Breathe. We'll find him.

I throw the phone on the white couch next to me and it bounces as it lands. I watch it, again willing something to happen, but a deepening sick feeling in the pit of my stomach tells me silence will be my only answer.

'I need to find the Warden,' I say, standing up and walking to the door. 'I was too stunned to ask him earlier, but he has to be able to help me find out what happened. How to get me home ... he was going to find a way.'

Blossom doesn't respond, just joins me on my way out, her brows pulled into a furrow – probably unsure how to tell me there is no way home outside of collection. Not even the portal-creating Shaides can go beyond the wards around the island without coming through the collection room, the marble plane, or the Warden's private residence on an approved schedule.

The Warden's office is just beyond the receiving hall, close to being under the outdoor staircase, where he has incredible views of the sky. If you peer out of the window far enough, you can just make out Nuntainia below; but there's a better view of it on the other side of the island – from near the actual prison.

Voices filter down the dark hall as we make our way towards his office. Much of my prison is asleep at this time, aside from the night teams, but I know the Warden will still be up – it's the only time he gets to his paperwork. I glance at Blossom as a male voice continues rising and she frowns deeper in question at me in return. We slow slightly as we creep closer, pressing against the soft cream wall, being careful not to disturb any of the gold framed paintings.

'—not coming in here,' I hear the Warden say.

'We don't have a choice.'

It takes me a moment, but then the voice registers. Traelen. I whisper as much to Blossom and she nods in agreement, still creeping forward, just ahead of me now.

'You know I can't get them there from here without alerting the Prime Minister and we'll have a riot on our hands if anyone here finds out where they're supposed to be,' Traelen says. 'I just need some time to smooth it over internally and work out what happened.'

Bloss reaches the doorway to the large receiving room, where it is now clear the voices are coming from, and peeks around the frame. Pulling herself back against the wall, she stares at me.

'Prisoners,' she whispers and shakes her head. 'But I don't think—'

'Keep them here,' Traelen continues, voice low, 'treat them as you would any others, and I'll try to organise a quiet transfer as soon as I can. Assuming I can get the Vanan Warden to cooperate.'

I tug Bloss's arm and we switch positions at the door so I can take my own quick glance inwards. The Warden and Traelen talk with their heads close together, each of them carefully watching the prisoners at the other side of the room. Blossom's right, they are very clearly different to any of our usual inmates. They're bigger, dirtier, and their hands are still bound.

My heart races.

I pull back for a moment, taking a long breath, processing the pinched look on the Warden's face, the raised voices. The bindings that haven't been removed.

They're meant for Vana.

The prison for murderers, and rapists, and people who do indescribably horrible things that lie beyond my comprehension.

Their voices have lowered again and I can't make out what they're saying. Sneaking another look, my blood curdles like the last tipple I take in the mornings as the net of the prison tightens around me.

Before the Warden stands Nix's older brother, River Kilroy.

And Nix.

CHAPTER FOUR

Blossom marches me back to our room and I don't fight her. Not because I'm in a daze like I was when Nix didn't turn up and I didn't want to think the worst. But because the fire that's starting to lick in my veins is chasing me, too.

Nix isn't dead. But he's here, intended for Vana prison.

That's not a huge step up.

The door to our room closes quietly, far more quietly than the protesting that's currently rampaging through my body. There is no way, *no way*, Nix has done something to warrant him ending up in that prison. We hear stories of it here, but we're not allowed to go. It's beyond the forest at the back of our prison and any interaction with their prisoners or the workers – they don't get the title 'concierge' – is strictly forbidden. That doesn't mean there hasn't been a gathering, or several, in the forest between the two groups, but it *is* forbidden.

What is also true, if what I learned of Vana before my duty is to be believed, is that if Nix steps foot inside that place I'll never see him again. There have been no successful appeals to a sentence to Vana that I'm aware of, and the attendants have confirmed there are no visitors, just like here. And I realise, while I am absolutely confident in my belief he hasn't done anything to deserve a sentence there, I will save him and River even if they have.

I just need to work out how.

Blossom tracks me as I pace our living room. She also hasn't sat down and, instead, watches from the white kitchen as she prepares us a drink. The iridescent blue liquid she pours is not intended to soothe me, but to focus me. Bring clarity to my thoughts.

The Warden has been good to me, almost fatherly – a mentor of sorts – but he's also loyal to his job and prides himself on his execution. Asking him to free Nix also implicates him in a way that would tarnish him beyond repair. I don't even know if he has that power.

I start at a knock on the door, giving myself a shake as I try to steady my racing thoughts until the drink takes effect. The brass door handle is cool in my hand and I use the sensation to ground me before I find the Warden on the other side.

His uniform is as pristine, as usual, but there's still that tiredness to him I noticed earlier.

'Does anyone else know you weren't collected?' he asks softly, as the door closes behind him.

'Just Bloss. I don't know who else has seen me still here but I've only told her.'

He nods before taking a long drag of the steaming tea Blossom made him, the dainty, pale pink cup too small in his hands. He looks between us.

'I'd like you to keep it that way. Our story is that your duty was extended at the last moment, and your collection has been delayed. There's no confirmed end date as yet, but it could happen at short no-tice – that should help a bit when you seemingly disappear before next year's collection. An exemption,' he says. 'We'll say it's an exemption to the collection dates because of the unknown tenure of your extension.'

Blossom and I nod even though I've never heard of there being exemptions before. She's perched on the couch next to him, keeping a polite distance, and I sink myself into the sole tan leather armchair. It creaks a bit as it takes my weight and I tuck the emerald-green, velvet cushion against my stomach as I sit.

'As for your collector, have you been able to get in touch with them? It was your friend Zale, I think?' he asks and there's a lurch in my stomach.

'No,' I start, the front of my mind dusting with confusion, 'I haven't … but it wasn't going to be Zale – there's been a complication.' I glance at Blossom, who gives me a reassuring nod before looking back to the Warden and, briefly, I question if I should tell him. But there's nothing about his kind, honest face that I don't trust – not that I have any other option.

'My collector is here.'

He stills, teacup part way to his mouth. 'How is that poss—'

'We saw you,' I say, 'in the receiving hall with Traelen.'

The Warden's face pales. Something I've never seen it do before. His mouth opens slightly but no sound comes out as I watch the pieces come together behind his eyes.

'Who?' he asks, his voice barely audible.

'His name is Nix Kilroy.' I press my fingers into the ache that's started in the side of my head. 'He's a good man, Warden, I—'

'I know,' he says, putting the teacup down carefully on the coffee table.

Blossom's brows lift and I'm sure I misheard.

Clearing his throat, the Warden rubs at his breastbone. 'This timing isn't ideal, but it's what we have to work with,' he says, almost to himself.

'What timing?' Blossom asks. 'I'm afraid you're going to have to fill us in – we seem to be missing a few things.'

Slowly, his gaze lifts to both of us before landing again on me.

'If you *ever* repeat this,' he says, 'I will not only deny it with my dying breath, but that breath will be the cost.'

I glance at Blossom, her ocean-coloured eyes a stormier shade than normal.

We both nod.

'Tell us,' I say, a strange tightening taking a tentative hold between my ribs.

'I was expecting that cohort of prisoners as a departure from their scheduled destination of Vana. Traelen was not.'

We let the words settle in the room, but I still don't understand them. If the Warden was expecting Nix and River – and expecting them to come *here* despite a sentence to Vana – but didn't know Nix was the one that was coming to collect me … what was he expecting him for? How does he even know about Nix if he was supposed to be going to Vana?

'I was hoping you'd be in Parliament before their arrival,' he says. 'But it appears our timing has been moved up. With it … some adjustments will need to be made.'

Parliament. Where my next chapter was supposed to start. My brow furrows as I consider that, by 'adjustment', he might mean I need to stay. That he won't get me home.

'I've done my duty, sir,' I say when he doesn't continue. 'Five *years* of duty. I-I'm done.' I lift my hands and let them drop back onto the arms of the chair. 'Parliament or no Parliament, I want to leave. That's how this is supposed to work. But now—'

But even as the words leave me, I know how much more complicated it is now. Before, I was leaving with a plan – a plan for me, and a plan for Blossom. Now, with Traelen making sure Nix and River find their way into Vana, too many parts of me are trapped up here.

The Warden shifts forward on the couch, the cushions collapsing around him, and presses his palms together between his knees, steepling his fingers towards the floor.

His voice drops to a whisper. 'I'm sorry, Luka.' A thick quiet fills the room as the Warden holds my gaze. 'When we talked about your recommendation to Parliament you said you'd be happy to still work with me.'

It takes me a moment to find my voice, my mind still swirling with the arrival of Nix and River. That Claudius – the Warden of my prison and very much *not* the Warden of Vana – was *expecting* them.

He waits until I nod in agreement. A tendril of uncertainty starts to weave its way through my chest.

'I think I am,' I say. 'But it doesn't really feel like a priority right now.'

'No, not yet, I can understand that.' He pauses for a moment. 'Even if the things I ask you seem unusual, would you be prepared to help me with something from here instead?' he asks.

I open my mouth to respond but I don't know what with.

'I'm asking you both if you trust me,' he says.

Yes, my brain responds immediately. My voice confirms it a little later. Blossom does the same and the Warden's shoulders drop a fraction.

'There is a prisoner – on the other side of the island.' My throat thickens. 'She is one of the few whose portalling abilities fully developed before she got here – a highly talented Shaide. I need you to make contact with her, get her to trust you. You will be able to contact her more easily, and faster, than Nix can as a guest of this side.

'She will be the way out for him and River if they can avoid a permanent transfer to Vana – we don't need more people on the inside of that prison. She is also the one who can get you out before the next collection if you're not already gone – if your extension hasn't concluded.'

I blanch. That doesn't sound like helping, it sounds like putting us on the wrong side of the law. I will help them both, regardless of what they've done, I know that. But it doesn't mean my nerves don't skitter under my skin as I wonder what in the world has meant River and Nix have ended up here – with the goal of getting off this island again with the help of a Vanan prisoner.

'Are they not fed dampener tipples over there?' Blossom asks.

The look he gives her is sombre but a tiny bit relieved. 'That bit, Cortane manages on her own for now. She's far too strong a Shaide for their tipples to have enough of an effect on her portals yet – something the Nuntainian government doesn't know – it's the wards that keep her on the island. The longer she's there though, enduring the malnourishment and torture of the Hunters stationed there, the dampeners will start to win. But I can't be seen anywhere near there, even the boundary walls. You will need to convince her yourselves that you can be trusted. And she has other priorities.' He looks solemnly at me. 'She'll need things from you. Information.'

'Hold on, how dangerous is she?' I ask, so many questions exploding in my mind I don't know where best to start. 'Are you suggesting we get her to open us an illegal portal? What if she escapes with them?'

'I'm counting on it,' he says.

I blink. 'What?'

But he only shakes his head, his short black hair not moving even slightly with the action. 'I can't tell you everything now, Luka, I'm sorry. River has the details of how to get in touch with her.' He glances to the door. 'Gain her trust, and it *will* work.'

'What will work, exactly?' I ask, trying to keep the rising hysteria from my voice. 'I'm supposed to be getting *off* Prison Island – not trying to be sentenced to Vana for life.'

'There are things afoot in Nuntainia, things that have taken years to put in place. Things I can't risk by betraying them now. But our Government has gone unchecked for too long and I promised to be ready when the time came. That time is now.' He stands and I stare up at him. 'I know you – I trust you – and I need you to do the same of me. Get Cortane what she needs and she will help you get off this island, along with the others.'

I stare at him. What exactly is the Warden suggesting I get involved in? What is *he* involved in? How does it implicate Nix and River?

'That's why you're helping,' Blossom says. 'Instead of just telling Luka she needs to wait another year – this is your opportunity for something else, too.'

He tugs at his open collar, the navy-blue fabric of his jacket absorbing the light, and a flicker of anger crosses his face – something so foreign for me to see on him. I glance at Bloss as an icy feeling trickles down my insides.

'I don't think either of you should still be here at the next collection,' he says quietly. Firmly.

'I—' I start, completely unsure what to ask for any of this to make sense.

The Warden was expecting River and Nix, even if it wasn't now. And he has connections to a prisoner in Vana that he wants me to … build on? I glance at Blossom. She's right, whatever he's involved in, he wants – needs – it done before the next collection, and he needs me to help. But what with, exactly?

'Claudius'—calling him 'sir' right now feels unusual given how far outside our Warden/concierge relationship this conversation has gone—'I just need to understand—'

'I'm sorry,' he says, 'Traelen is expecting me to talk him through the room allocations.' He glances at his phone. 'I'm already late. I just needed to confirm no one else knew you weren't collected. They'll know the timing was tight, but the extension story will be enough for now – I will take the heat for doing it so last minute.'

'Claudius,' I say, stepping quickly after him, 'please—'

The Warden looks back when he gets to the door. 'Cortane is someone important to me, important to what I believe in, as are you. But I can't contact her to know what gaps remain in her own tasks and knowledge of how to get back to the mainland – not without compromising us all. I need you to be a conduit for her. To get her what she needs to get herself, and those boys, out.'

His whole body thrums with tension and I can only blink at him. 'You will need to be careful what you say, particularly outside this room.' He moves as if to reach for the handle but pauses, sadness fracturing his features and a lancing spike of hot worry runs through my chest. 'Just before dawn, you will be able to find the final room allocations in my office – Traelen and I will be done with our call by then. I'm sorry, Luka,' his voice is heavy, 'time is no longer our friend and this has become a bit of a mess. But, if you trust me – trust her – and get her whatever information she still needs, you and your friends will be home soon. And, hopefully'—he gives me a searching look—'you'll have taken up your recommendation.'

I didn't sleep a wink after the Warden left and, judging by the particularly squashed and frizzy curls on Blossom when I find her in the living room, neither did she. This time I throw the tipples back – not missing the fact there is still enough for me – without registering the rhythm, nor that it's far earlier than I would normally take them. Wake up, take the tipples; some habits are hard to break. She's in her exercise clothes and I give her a thin smile.

Neither of us talk, my mind still whirling through our conversation with the Warden last night and the hours after Blossom and I talked it around and around trying to understand everything he was trying to say. For the past five years, I have done everything in my power to fulfil my duty to an exceptional standard – a standard my father might finally be proud of. Now, it seems I am being asked to risk having all that hard work thrown away. Or, do nothing but my duty and watch my friends disappear into Vana?

We share a quiet breakfast of fruit and pastries, despite it still being nighttime really, before I quickly tug on my own gear and we sneak down the stone stairs off the end of our balcony. The balcony itself only has room for a small, two-person table and chairs. The external wall to our apartment and the balustrade are made from the same brown-grey stone bricks that make all the arches around both the outside of the immense building and the internal hallways.

These stairs though have guard rails on the side that are open to the sky and there is far less distance to fall. At the bottom of the three-storey drop is the beginning of the sparse but lush concierge gardens – a place where more than one raucous party has been held, the sound warded from the rest of the prison lest we disturb any of the prisoners.

I'm slightly out of puff as we weave our way down, our running shoes landing in the soft grass. It's a touch wet underfoot and the surface gives a little, the sensation comforting after the hardness of the stone stairs. I glance back up at the prison, each of the concierge staircases running along and across the side of the wall like stone roots climbing up from the grass below. Their shapes are almost otherworldly in the near dark, the space lit by tall, gold posts dotted around the garden. The balls of light at their tops held only by gold cages.

'We've got about three hours until breakfast,' Blossom says. The breakfast that's put on for the prisoners. The one Nix will be at.

After I've found what room he's been allocated.

The Warden's office is in a separate wing to the concierge residences and accessing it from the outside will be the easiest option to avoid questions from other concierges. A guilty warmth moves across my collarbones, but I try to remind myself we're not doing anything wrong. At least not as far as the Warden is concerned. A fact that makes my head spin. I don't let myself think about what laws we might actually be breaking if we do make contact with the Vanan prisoner.

The staircase to the Warden's balcony snakes up the wall the same as ours, but is much closer to the edge of the island. From the upper part, it's almost tempting to try and fly into darkness. I close my eyes as the abyss of the dark calls to me, asking me to float away with it. Blossom pokes me in the behind and I take the next step.

Shimmying open the far left window – the one that doesn't quite catch – we ease ourselves in. It's darker in here than outside without the garden lights and the stars that decorate the sky, and Blossom takes her phone from her bra, a tiny ball of light leaping from the screen.

I make straight for his desk. Forcing myself to go carefully, slowly, I make sure everything I touch goes back exactly how it was but come up empty-handed.

Blossom trails the bookshelf, running a finger over the spines as she goes. 'We should read more,' she whispers absently.

The drawer of the large, pale timber desk moans fractionally as I pull the brass handle and slide it out.

'He's got books on all sorts of magic in here,' Blossom continues as she walks, taking the light with her.

I squint at the papers sitting in the top drawer. They're clearly marked 'Guests' and my heart leaps.

'Here's one about Karaylia – I've heard their wings are incredible in real life. Have you ever met one of them?' she asks, a wistful tone in her question.

'Bloss, light,' I say, taking my own finger and running it down the list. 'My father was obsessed with Karaylia,' I whisper absently. 'River is Karaylia, actually. And, yes, their wings are incredible.'

She hums absently before walking on silent feet to join me and the list comes properly into focus. It's short but clear, and perhaps stupid – River and Nix share a room. Depending what they've been accused of, I don't think that's a strategy I would use. But I won't deny it makes life easier for me. Having them together was obviously a deliberate choice of the Warden's. And Traelen didn't object, it seems. The Warden must have been particularly convincing.

'Room 18,' I say, unable to keep the smile from my voice.

CHAPTER FIVE

The halls are still quiet as Blossom and I sneak out of the Warden's office and down the hall.

'Are you sure you don't want to go back to our room?' I'd asked Blossom just before cracking the door open, and she'd given me a mock stern look.

'Firstly, I'm not going to miss out on meeting this *friend* you're going to a hell of a lot of trouble for, and'—she'd pointed a finger at me—'the Warden has now involved me too. So, no – not on your life, lovely.'

I gripped that finger and pulled her into the hall.

I still hold her hand now as we take the open hallway that wraps around the upper levels of the internal courtyard and creep towards the prisoners' wing. In hindsight, we probably should have changed into our uniforms. But our running shoes are quieter on the stone than the sandals we normally wear. It's not at all unusual for concierges to be visiting the prisoners' wing, but out of uniform would encourage questions – innocent, legitimate questions – but ones I don't know how to answer just yet.

The thumping in my chest reverberates through my whole body as we reach the entrance to the wing. Room 18 is towards the end, on the right-hand side. The trip down feels like an eternity and yet, before I can really comprehend, we are staring at the large, brass numbers on the door.

I take a deep, unsteady breath and ease the door open with my concierge key, slipping us both inside before Blossom shuts it again, and we both blink into the darkness. A faint, sharp whisper is the only sound I make out before I'm pressed against the door, something cold against the side of my throat.

Blossom squeaks beside me. A faint light comes up towards my face and the blade slowly drops away.

Fierce, baby-blue eyes lock onto mine and I release a fast exhale, my shoulders sagging a bit on the door. 'Nix,' he calls quietly, 'you'd better get out here.'

River's stare has grown more intense since I last saw him and I scan his face for a sign of his gentler self. Slowly, he takes a step backwards, giving Blossom – whose hands cover her mouth – a quick once-over.

Tucking the knife into his pants, River reaches behind her, swiping his hand along the wall. 'Lights,' he mutters, and the apartment blooms into view.

'That's some fucking welcome, Riv,' I say, staring at Blossom before glaring at him.

He quirks a smile, turning back to her again like he didn't see her properly before.

'You've got to be fucking kidding.'

Nix's voice is just how I remember, deep and a little gravelly, and I spin to the second bedroom door where he strides across the living room. I know the prisoner rooms are more opulent than ours, I've cleaned them enough times, but the layout is similar. Still, I can't focus on the details of this one when Nix, broad and stocky Nix, is so close after all this time.

My feet unfreeze themselves and I launch into the arms that stretch out to greet me. Crushing me against him, Nix's smell envelopes me. A musky wood scent that lies underneath the soap he's used.

'I thought I'd never see you again,' he mutters into my neck, his voice cracking and driving tears to my eyes.

His normally dark, auburn hair is damp – from the shower, I assume – making it even darker. But it's his slightly curved eyes that make my heart somersault over itself with memories and the deepest sense of home I've had in a long time. That deep, sparkling gold soaks me in when I pull back slightly and take his face in my hands. He and River are the personification of my childhood. But there's no joy in his expression as I pull myself out of his arms.

'What are you doing here?' he asks, brows pulling together.

'Me?' I ask, blinking furiously as he remains silent. I glance at Blossom whose eyes are narrowed on Nix and River almost to the point of slits. 'Well … I was waiting to be collected from here … by you.' The confusion in my voice is clear even to me.

River lifts his chin in a way that makes me think something has just dawned on him. Nix rubs his face.

'They didn't tell me no one else came,' he says. 'Fuck, I gave them *all* the detail.' His gaze finds mine, the gold of so many of my memories now clouded. 'I would never have left you here, Lu. They said you'd be collected by someone else, I assumed Akira or Zale. I-I didn't even know you were assigned here.'

I look between him and River, overwhelmed by their closeness and a desperate desire to know everything that's happened since I last saw them. But the question of *why* they're both here screams the loudest.

Until I register what Nix is saying: he thought someone else was going to collect me.

Meaning something changed and he didn't tell me.

Didn't check to confirm that I wasn't going to be left here.

'Don't look like that, Lu,' Nix says, his voice strained - a dead give away he knows exactly why I might be hurt.

'Like what, exactly?' I ask, lifting my shoulders in what feels like a very false show of nonchalance. 'Like I thought my best friend didn't collect me because something awful happened? Like I haven't been worried sick since you didn't show? Like I am now stuck in limbo in a life I don't *want* because you didn't show? Like my best friend *decided* to leave me here?'

My voice rises with each question I don't leave space to be answered. At the same time, Nix's shoulders drop lower and lower until he looks almost defeated.

'Not to mention that something terrible must have happened for you to be sentenced—' I cut myself off.

He – they – *decided* not to get me. Possibly so quickly he *couldn't* tell me.

The Warden was expecting them.

Nix is clearly unhappy with the prospect of me staying here.

My head starts to spin.

'How—'

'The how doesn't matter now, Lu,' River says, cutting me off with a firm look at Nix before letting his gaze slide to Blossom's again. 'Are you going to introduce us?'

My cheeks tremble with the effort of holding back on demanding Nix tell me everything. That is one tactic that has never worked, and trying to force it with an audience will only make him clam up tighter. River holds out a hand to Blossom, his face full of suspicion, and she looks at me instead, eyes wide and questioning.

'Sorry, Bloss ... this is River,' I say, barely sounding civil. 'And he doesn't normally hold knives to people.' I glare at him again and he pulls an apologetic grimace.

Blossom walks past his outstretched hand and takes a seat on the large couch. Nix takes my elbow and I reluctantly let him lead me to sit next to him. I don't bother introducing Nix to her, she'd have worked that out by now, but I do tell him and River who she is. Nix gives a tight smile even as the worry in the small crease between his brows doesn't dissipate.

'I've heard a lot about the "friend" you have here, this is her?' he asks in a clear attempt to help River shift the subject along.

I nod slowly. We're not allowed to name any other concierges in our letters or texts. My heart warms at having them in the same room, despite the circumstances, and I try not to resent the fact that Nix always wins me over in the end.

'I need you to explain what's going on,' I say, looking between the brothers.

They share a look.

'There's not a lot we're able to explain,' River says, looking sideways at Nix. 'The ... magic they used on us before we came is not unlike what they do with the service contracts – the sensitive ones anyway. We can't tell you why we're here.'

I lean back on the couch, tiredness starting to take hold as my sleep deprived mind tries to understand what's happening here.

'We already know you've been sentenced to Vana and Traelen – the Chief of Staff – is investigating how you ended up here instead. Yet, somehow, the Warden *knew* you were coming here instead,' I say quietly. They stare at me, neither confirming or denying, and I wonder if Claudius organised the shift in destination himself or is working with someone who did. 'I also know I don't believe you actually did whatever you've been accused of to get you sentenced to Vana.'

I drag myself forward on the couch, too restless to stay cocooned in the luxurious cushions that suck me in. Watching Blossom glance out the window at the lightening sky, I know we don't have enough time here.

'You're in on this, too?' River asks Blossom.

She gives him a long look. 'I was ... until you shoved a knife at the throat of my best friend.' There's a hint of steel in her voice and I wince. Not quite the introduction I was hoping for.

'Shoved,' River says evenly, 'is a bit of stretch. Preparing to defend my brother and myself from two unexpected intruders is just common sense.'

He leans back on his part of the couch, resting an arm atop it, and folds one leg over the other. I look at where his ankle meets his knee. There's a strap there and the glint of another blade.

Yesterday, I would have said I had no idea how they got them in here. Today, I am wondering if the Warden had a hand in that, too?

'And it won't happen again,' I say on his behalf. 'Nor will they hurt anyone else here Bloss, I know them. They're not violent.'

She doesn't look convinced.

'What was your plan, Lu?' Nix asks, shifting in his seat next to me.

My brows shoot upwards. My plan?

'Well,' I start hesitantly, the details feeling slippery in my mind, 'on my way here, I was thinking I'd get you off the island by leveraging the Warden's contact, and have your charges cleared.' The three of them just watch me with variations of the same, expectant, expression. Nix's face starts to creep into a grin as he seems to wait for me to come to the right conclusion. 'Now, I'm realising there is something more that I'm not understanding but it seems you can't – or won't – tell me what that is.' As the words leave me, the temperature of my blood seems to start rising. Nix *left* me here Wand he can't even tell me why?

River looks sadly at me as Nix laughs. I bristle at the sound.

'Correct,' Nix says. 'We can't – and won't – tell you anything, and you know nothing, which means you have no plan, Lu. No reason to be here. And every reason to return to your duty as your *country* requires of you.'

I feel more than see Blossom slowly look at me, as if she's waiting to see how I take that comment, or if I will.

'*No reason to be here*?' I ask, staring at Nix's irritatingly smug face. Something else simmers underneath it, but he is not getting out of this so easily. 'How about the next year of my *life*, Nix? Is that reason enough? No. How about two of the people I'm closest to have been sentenced to fucking *Vana*! Tell me you'd sit back and watch that happen to me?'

I exhale and I cross my arms. 'Actually, you'd decide to leave me to it. But River wouldn't,' I say, looking at him instead, silently daring him to contradict me.

River sighs heavily, so much like he used to when he'd be stuck in the middle of Nix and me. 'Lu, there *are* no charges that can be cleared,' he says. 'We either do what we came to this...establishment for and get out; or end up in Vana, current sentence or a new one. So Nix is right, that's equivalent to no plan for you. You will have no part in what we're doing here and neither of us will share anything that will endanger you, you know that.'

I search his face. There's no joking there, not that I expect there to be. These two have always protected me, almost to the point of exclusion. I try not to dwell on that right now – not when it's the first time I've seen them in years. I look across to the other lounge where Bloss wrings her hands together. I'd promised I'd help her start again when her service was finished. That's two years away. And mine has been extended ... indefinitely. My stomach falls as the idea of going home seems more and more like a dream. However Nix came to his decision to leave me behind, I know it wouldn't have been lightly – even if I am still so mad at him I feel like screaming. And neither he or River seem to be in a hurry to get off the island. Quite the opposite. There is a determination in both of them to do 'what they came for'.

Something I know from experience after experience I will not be able to talk them down from. The same as I wasn't able to convince them jumping from their three-storey house before River's wings were fully grown was a terrible idea.

The room is quiet for a moment and my mind fills with space. Space for more questions than answers.

'How do you know the Warden?' I ask them.

'A connection from a previous duty,' River says, his features full of meaning that feels just outside my grasp, but it doesn't mean I don't want to know.

'So you know the Warden,' Blossom says when River doesn't continue, 'and he was expecting you here, but you also need to do something at Vana before he can try to get you out again.'

She doesn't pose it as a question and neither of them confirm. But there's something in their faces that tells me she's right. The pieces floating around in my mind were heading in the same direction. Blossom turns to me.

'Their task at Vana is the same as ours – the Warden said as much. But that it would be faster and easier for us to do it now,' she says.

Nix blanches. 'You're not to go anywhere near that place.'

'Are there other things you're supposed to do here, in addition to making contact with the Vanan prisoner?' I ask, ignoring him. I can't imagine what else they could be doing up here, as if trying to break out one prisoner isn't enough. But he doesn't answer which makes me think, yes, there's more.

'We know what's required for Vana,' I say slowly, reinforcing Blossom's statement and swallowing away that it's against all my instincts to do it. 'We can help with that part – I can likely give, or access, information that prisoner needs to ... fill in any gaps.'

Nix sighs heavily and takes my hand. 'Lu,' he says gently, 'we talked about this in our letters. You're supposed to be at home, living your life.'

Tears spring to my eyes unbidden and I try to blink them away.

'Did you get your recommendation?' he asks.

I sniff quietly. 'The Warden said it would be ready for me after I was collected ...'

'I'm so sorry,' he says, pulling me closer and tucking me under an arm. The words strike home, feeling like they're for so much more than my recommendation.

'Where was it for?' River asks.

'Parliament,' I say into Nix. His grip on me tenses and he curses.

River mutters something and I sit up, watching Blossom assessing us all.

'I'm going to take a leap and say you were supposed to be their contact there – after you were done up here,' she says to me.

It makes sense – that's why the Warden wants me to find the Vanan prisoner. In addition to whatever reason he wants her out for, he wants me off the island to take up my recommendation in Parliament so I can ... I don't know. But my vision clears and I sit a little straighter. In all my time here, the Warden has never asked me for things I couldn't, or wouldn't, do. And he's certainly never put me in a position to compromise myself. If he feels that taking up my recommendation in Parliament is the best place for me – a place I can help him – I will do whatever I can to get there. Even if one of the suggested means is a bit more unusual, I trust his intentions.

The four of us look at each other for several moments until Blossom breaks the silence and stands. 'We need to get to work.'

I blow out a breath. The thought of going back to my duty now, after I thought I was done, is ... depressing. And now so much more complicated.

'We're not done here,' I say, looking at Nix and River. 'The Warden gave Blossom and me the task of working with Cortane, and he's processing my recommendation. I intend to follow through with both of those things. I don't know how well you know him, but I know him *and* the two of you. Claudius is finding a way off the island for me, and I know his plans for you will work, too. There's no way he brought you here without something in place to get you out. As for the two of you – I know you're not going anywhere until whatever else you came here for is done. So ... you need to focus ... and I'll get Cortane to trust me as quickly as possible.'

And I will hope like hell they're – we're – not now all mixed up in something even more dangerous than Vana.

River and Nix look carefully at each other – a look they used to share when they thought I needed to be shielded from something. But I push the unease away and breathe into my faith in the Warden. He's going to help us. I'm going to help the boys. We'll be fine.

'Outside of the people in this room,' Nix says, 'the only person you trust is the Warden, okay?'

Slowly, I stand with Blossom and look down at Nix. Something sad flashes across his face but I can't quite tell what before he looks up at me.

'I really don't want you mixed up—'

'It's best we don't let on that we know each other,' I say across him. 'The less attention from the other prisoners, the better. If Traelen has any sense you're causing a ... disruption here, he will accelerate the transfer to Vana.'

As Blossom and I wander to the receiving hall where another small transfer of prisoners has arrived, my eyes feel gritty as I look at the prison in a new light. I wasn't supposed to be here anymore and I've found, overnight, the admiration I'd had for its beauty is starting to slip. I wonder if there is something that happens in one's mind when they have finished the time they'd been given and it just refuses to accept a moment more.

I look up at the painting nearest to me, it's one that often catches my eye on the way to the hall. A woman, draped in white fabric and lying on an almost equally white chaise lounge, gazes off into the distance. She's probably meant to look serene. I can't help but think she's dreaming of all the other things she should be doing, could be doing.

There are only five prisoners in the receiving hall today. One of our smaller intakes, but not unusual given it's only been a few days since the last official one and they are often months apart – and less than a day since Nix and River arrived. There has been a slight increase of the number of prisoners arriving here over the last year or so, but that's not completely unusual depending on the political landscape and priorities at home. And sometimes they just need a break from the public eye.

The team that greeted them on the portal platform scatter, only three staying behind for the allocations, along with Blossom and me. Traelen scans the group, now dressed in their chosen outfits – a mixture of casual and more formal, but all opulent – and clears his throat.

'Porter Mills,' he calls out, and a man in a pale-orange, open-neck shirt steps forward, 'instrumental in driving wealth creation for future generations and implementing Nuntainia's first retirement reserves for all eligible citizens.'

'Allysia,' the Warden responds. Allysia nods politely to Porter and leads him from the hall.

'Finn Archt,' Traelen says, 'recognised for special services to the Prime Minister and cross-border negotiations.'

'Luka,' the Warden says. His expression is warm when he looks at me but the tension that was apparent when I last saw him is still there, gently simmering under the surface, and I make myself turn away before Traelen notices as well.

I smile a welcome to Finn, a tall, very fit man with skin the colour of a night-time sky and hair to match. Deep charcoal eyes blink down at me. He doesn't smile, but there's no hostility there, either. Just assessment of one kind or another.

'This way,' I say as I walk him out, and back down the hall with the lounging woman in her gold frame.

'I'll take you to your room first,' I continue, trying to sound as if all my attention is on him and not still whirling through my last proper conversation with the Warden and Nix and River. 'Your belongings will have been delivered by now. You'll have about thirty minutes there, and then I will show you the rest of the facility. Do you have a preference for what you'd like to see first?'

I glance sideways at him but he still doesn't seem to react, just soaks in the surroundings. I let my own gaze travel over the stone hallway that runs above the internal courtyard and up to the open sky. It's particularly blue today, with a smattering of fat white clouds. It's not different to what it looks like most days but, when I take the time to take it in, it's still breathtaking. Even if it feels a little tighter than it did yesterday.

'Just my room is fine,' Finn says.

I try not to jump at the sudden sound of his soft voice. For the first time in a while, I wonder why he's really here. My first few prisoners intrigued me to no end, to the point I would dream about why they were here and the inability to ask them directly was torturous. Then they just became a blur of prisoner after prisoner and I let the duties of my role take focus, counting down to my own future instead of fixating on their pasts.

But Finn is different to others I've had before; he's quietly self-assured, graceful, but without an ounce of obvious arrogance.

Not to mention the reason for Nix and River being here sits as an uncomfortable question at the forefront of my mind.

'Of course,' I say as we reach the prisoners' wing.

Leaving him in his room, taking care not to look at Nix's door, I head to the concierge breakout room. Until I can get more information on the Vanan prisoner and understand the Warden's plans to get more than myself back to the mainland outside of a scheduled collection I need to fill my days with work again. Which means I have to get a handle on where things are up to and what needs doing.

On the back wall of our breakout room a large, glass board takes up most of the space. It's filled with prisoner names, their allocated concierge and room number, as well as all manner of requests they have made and things that are outstanding. It also tracks the facility's management like maintenance, and cleaning, and what events and activities we have planned.

I sigh as I scan the information on the board. It tells me so much, yet so little. I know every moment of the prisoners' movements and whims while they're here and yet I know almost nothing about my own situation. Like why the Warden wants me in Parliament? Who is this Vanan prisoner to him that he wants to get her out badly enough to risk everything? How does he know Nix and River, and what did they do to end up destined for Vana? And why did the Warden arrange for them to be here instead? Something Traelen will be actively trying to rectify.

How did Claudius do that?

How do I get myself into a role in Parliament outside the collection cycle without marking myself as 'wanted' if I take some sort of unsanctioned way home? And how do I do that without condemning Nix and River to end their lives on the other side of the island? Not to mention what would happen to Blossom?

Playroom request: Blossom reads the board next to Davorous – the prisoner she danced with at our recent feast.

My gut turns over at the repeated request. I have every faith the Warden's position on moving us to the playroom will hold, but Davorous takes the denial less well each time.

Someone runs into the room and I spin, their fast pace startling me. Its presence in the serenity of the prison is very out of place.

'Emeris,' I gasp at his paling form. 'What is it?'

His white vest hangs limply.

'The Warden – I think he's dead.'

CHAPTER SIX

Silence roars in my ears.

Emeris finally stills at the bottom of the raised platform I stand on, with the glass board at my back. We stare at each other a moment, his skin has gone pasty underneath the sun-kissed tones.

'What – what do we do?' he asks. Pleads.

I close my eyes for a moment, pressing my hand to my chest. My breasts flatten a fraction under the pressure and distantly I think what a strange thing that is to notice when our world might be about to fall apart.

Has started falling apart.

'Where is he?' I ask, my voice quivering. 'Are you sure?'

Blinking, frantic eyes are set in Emeris's otherwise blank face.

'Um ... in his office.' His voice is weak.

I stride from the room, desperately hoping Emeris is wrong and trying not to break into a run. But the shock on his face is clear – he knows.

Smiling at the prisoners I pass has never felt more fake than in this moment, and I push away the thoughts of what we will have to tell them, the insensitive questions they will ask, of what comes next – that, despite my desperate desire to go home, I am the most likely person to be asked to run the prison in his absence. At least temporarily.

Arriving at the Warden's office door makes me pause.

But I only let it last a moment, just in case Emeris is wrong. The white-panelled door opens soundlessly into the handsomely decorated office and I glance to the window Blossom and I snuck in last night as if I could go back to that moment.

But, slumped on his desk, is the Warden.

Only the top of his head is visible from here but I can already tell his back doesn't seem to be rising with his breath.

Swallowing, I cross the floor and press my fingers into the soft part of his neck, under his jaw.

Nothing.

I prod harder.

Please.

My throat thickens as I wait, imagining him sitting up and smiling warmly at me. Just like he did when allocating me Finn, my last prisoner.

There's a tightening between my ribs. *Please.* Please, just let me see your kind, dark eyes. *Look at me.* Tell me this isn't real.

But there's nothing.

Just silence.

Stillness.

No marks, no sign he's hit his head, or some other explanation for what's in front of me. Nothing that the coldness starting to emanate from his skin doesn't already tell me, despite how badly I want otherwise.

A spinning sensation takes root behind my temples.

Emeris's face is starting to clear as I look back at him, but he's still silent. I watch as I think through what we need to do: action. That's what he would have expected of me.

There has been the occasional death on the premises before, but that's normally a matter of notifying families and Traelen's staff making the arrangements. The concierges would pack their belongings for the families but it never affected the running of the prison.

But this is ...

Claudius.

A sob catches in my throat and I cover my mouth, shaking my head a little to try and clear it.

The prison *needs* running.

I'm supposed to be going home.

He was going to help me with Nix. And River and Blossom.

He was like my—

My head swims with the things that will need to be managed on the Warden's behalf even as a sharpness takes root in my chest. He was my friend – my mentor. A man who wanted to help me create a good life for myself after so long serving here. The person who was going to help me understand why Nix and River are here, and exactly how to get us all home. And now ...

'Luka,' Emeris says gently. 'We will need to tell Traelen, but first I need to find Janly.'

I nod. It makes sense to have her – the concierge next in line, behind me – to help with whatever comes next. Neither of us will be able to take on the role of Warden permanently, that's normally reserved for people with senior military backgrounds, but it will be the two of us who need to run it while that role is ... vacant.

But before I can ask why Emeris would bring Janly in here right at this moment, he's left and I am alone. With the Warden. The walls seem suddenly closer but I make myself turn away from the door and look back at him.

'What happened?' I hear myself ask him, as if he could tell me why he's gone. How. Where.

Staring at him, if it wasn't for the slight cold in the air surrounding him like an aura, something that feels like just the beginning of how cold he's going to get, he could be sleeping.

If sleeping on the job was something he did.

A heart attack? A stroke, maybe? Would those things leave any signs? Wouldn't there at least be some disturbance on his desk if something like that happened?

Instead, it looks like he tidied everything away before he lay his head down and died.

But why would he do that?

Slowly, I make my way to where he lies over the desk and kneel before him. Silently begging him again to open his eyes as tears prickle in my own. I'd been torn about my duty when I was first selected for my service.

Knowing how much I was going to miss out on in my own life was a weight I couldn't avoid, despite understanding the government makes decisions on what is best for the country. It was the Warden that helped me come to terms with what I was having to give up – with how much I was actually doing in a different way.

And I'd thought, with every part of me, that he would be there to help me understand the next stage, too. How to execute the recommendation he'd given me for Parliament, and serve my country even better. How to *get* there without spending another year of my life here.

I gasp as a thought hits me. Did someone not want him to not be doing that? Did someone know he got River and Nix here? Know he was clearly involved in something … other than what it appeared?

I let the tears spill gently as I draw back to standing, one hand on his shoulder. The sun streams in the window and catches something shining underneath his collar. Carefully, I pull his shirt away a fraction.

For those that prove— is written on his skin. It's a tattoo I didn't know he had, and I press his collar back gently before I read the rest. If he'd wanted me to know about it, he would've told me and reading now feels … invasive.

But it fires something in my blood all the same. Because I know, even with him gone, I will prove to him I can do this. I can find out what happened here. I can get to Parliament with the recommendation he started. And I can fulfil whatever goals he had for Nix and River. And me. Because, as evasive as they're being right now, they forget how patient I can be. I *will* find out.

'Oh, Claudius,' Janly says quietly as Emeris shuts the door behind her.

I stand with Emeris while Janly says her goodbyes to the Warden, crouched where I was a moment ago. The sound of her whispers are like soft waves, but I don't try to make out what she's saying. The Warden was a special man to many of us here, and it's clear he may have helped Janly as much as he did me. The affection in her voice wraps around me.

She gives his hand one last squeeze before joining Emeris and me at the low table on the other side of the room.

'Traelen will need to know,' I say.

'And the concierges,' Janly adds, her voice dull, eyes lined with red.

'Did he have family?' Emeris asks.

'Some,' Janly says.

I look between them until they each look up at me. It feels strange to break this moment, to let anyone else know of what's happened here and who is gone. But there are events, and prisoners, and schedules, and reporting to the Prime Minister's office that need to be done.

And I now also have my own agenda – help Nix and River, find the Vanan prisoner, and find out what happened to Claudius. All while doing my duty so I can go home – something that now Traelen will probably play an even bigger role in.

I draw a breath that's tight with the knowledge of what I will now need to lead and manage. Because, even in death, I will never let him down.

'Ready?' I ask, trying to hide the trembling in my fingers.

I pick up the gold, antique looking, phone on the Warden's desk. There's a curled, shimmering cord that connects its two pieces that's always intrigued me. It's cool in my hands as I hold it up to my head.

'Traelen,' I say softly into the metallic finish.

There's a faint chime I register distantly, watching Emeris and Janly as if we are part of some elaborate dream, grounding each other in the uncertainty that's starting to whirl around each of us.

'Warden,' he says in greeting.

'Traelen, sir,' I respond. 'It's Luka, we – um – we've met ... here be—'

'I know where you're calling from. You're the one whose duty Claudius extended – I remember. How can I help you, Luka?'

I note the comment he makes on the Warden being the one who extended me. Up here, the message was going to be that I was extended from below. But I let the uncomfortable knot of two conflicting stories go and focus on what has to come next.

'We, um ...' I take a cooling gulp of air, dragging it deep into my lungs and letting it out in a rush.

'We have a situation sir,' I say. 'The Warden has died.'

Silence greets me from the other end and I don't know how to fill it.

A moment later, Traelen's voice comes back.

'Can you keep him from view of the prisoners?' he asks.

'He's in his office.'

'Good. Lock the door and wait for me there.'

The line goes quiet in a different way than it did when he wasn't talking, and I put the speaking piece back in its cradle on the desk.

'We wait here,' I say to the others.

My mind spins with everything I didn't know about the Warden – his family, for starters, that Janly is obviously aware of. I steal a look at where she now sits on the couch in front of the desk. There's a weariness in the set of her shoulders but no shock in her features like there was in Emeris's – I can't imagine the incomprehension on my own face – and the tears that gently roll down her cheeks seem almost resigned.

Traelen thinks I've been extended.

Now, not only can the Warden not tell him when I'm done, there's no way I can tell him I wasn't collected because Nix is *here*. That whatever substitute – and illegal, I assume – method they thought they'd organised for my collection didn't work. Which means the only timeframe I am now working to is Traelen's.

The most obvious thing would be for Traelen to leave me here until the next collection. But if anyone can organise an unscheduled portal back to the mainland, it would be the Prime Minister's Chief of Staff. An uncomfortable tingle breaks out across my chest and I rub at the exposed skin at my dress's neckline. If Traelen does what he thinks Claudius wanted – to get me off the island after an extension, not at the next collection – how will I make sure Nix and River have done what they came to do before he gets them transferred to Vana? Including what is now my job of forging a relationship with Cortane?

Shit. What does happen to all those plans now Claudius is dead?

Me, a small voice at the back of my mind says. I happen. Between the academic school I established and ran, amongst all of the challenges in an industry filled with individuals with their own agendas and the fundamental belief that their way is the only way, and my time navigating the wants and needs of Nuntainia's politicians up here, I can do this. Claudius trusted me. And ... I need to trust me.

I jump in my place on the beige settee as the door handle jiggles slightly. Leaping to the door, I peek out to see Traelen in the light-filled hallway. Ushering him in as professionally as I can when there's the body of someone I love on the desk, I shut and relock the door.

'I'll deal with this,' he says, waving at the Warden and eyeing me critically. 'Luka, you're in charge until I appoint another Warden – I have something in train, but there are a few remaining sign offs to get before his arrival. Until then, you will report directly to me.'

I swallow. It's nothing less than I expected to do on my own, but I didn't realise Traelen would know how integral I was to the Warden as his unofficial second-in-command. But there's also a flicker of recognition of doing what I do best – executing roles to an impeccable standard, but only temporarily. Never well enough to actually do the role on my own. Permanently.

'It's only temporary and should be quite short at that,' he says, his voice a fraction softer than before and I register no surprise at his confirmation I'm never a long-term option. 'Organise and host his send-off, keep the day-to-day running in the meantime, and then I should have a replacement.'

My mind starts to fill with all the things involved in that, but I nod through it.

'Family,' I say, my mind finally grabbing on to something. 'I believe he may have some family who should be there?'

'Leave that to me.'

He looks at Emeris and Janly, who haven't said a word as yet.

'You will assist Luka with anything she needs in this time.'

They nod, though Janly doesn't meet his gaze.

'Thank you,' Traelen says, looking directly at me. His pale-pink suit is too much for the conversation we're having. 'He spoke very highly of you, and I have every confidence in your ability to shepherd us through this transition phase.'

I watch his back as he walks from the office, the long jacket he wears hugging his shoulders perfectly.

Transition phase. The coldness of those words leaves a chill down my spine.

Emeris stands, walking to me to take my hand in his.

'We can do this, Luka,' he says, squeezing my fingers. 'We've got this.'

I hope so, I think. But first, I need to find Blossom, and tell Nix and River. If Traelen is going to be here with a new Warden sooner rather than later, their timeline for transfer to Vana just got even tighter.

Nix and River seem almost at home in my apartment, even if they do have to sneak in from the garden side so other prisoners – and, ideally, concierges – don't see them. If Blossom feels any unease at having them lounging on our couches long after dinner has finished, she doesn't show it. Not any more than the distrust they've already planted in her, anyway.

This was something I'd forgotten though – just how much room the two of them can take up.

'You don't seem surprised,' I say, holding Blossom's hand in my lap.

River sighs heavily. 'I suppose we're not. Not really.'

I drop Blossom's hand and press my fingers into my temples, a wave of nausea rolling through me.

'What the fuck is going on?' I ask, the events of the day weighing on me. 'Literally everything was normal until you'—I look at Nix—'didn't show for my collection, and now nothing makes sense. He was in the prime of his life—' I break off and close my lips tight around the strangled sound that wants to escape.

'You weren't supposed to be part of this,' Nix says gruffly.

'Of *what*?' I grind out. 'Perhaps if you'd collected me when you were supposed to, I wouldn't be! And he—'

'There are things you don't understand,' Nix says, a mix of anger and resignation soaking his words.

'So *help* me,' I say, throwing my arms wide.

'Lu,' River says calmly, raising a hand in my direction. 'Take a breath.'

I cross my arms. Fucking River. Always the sensible one. I do one, audible, inhale and exhale through my nose as I glare at River. 'I know you're both smart enough to work around the contracts – even if you have to talk in broad terms. Tell me. Now.'

Blossom watches the brothers impassively as they glance at each other, some unspoken message being passed back and forth. But I don't miss that her hands are so tightly gripped in her lap that her knuckles are white.

'It doesn't leave this room, understood?' There's a bite in River's tone I haven't heard in a long time.

But I nod once.

'We're soldiers, Lu,' Nix says.

I look between them, trying to listen to what they're not saying. Nuntainia has no active conflicts and hasn't for some time.

'Former or current?' I ask.

'Current,' River confirms. 'For now. Our service would be terminated automatically when – if – we officially set foot in Vana Prison. Right now, we have a few ... outstanding tasks.'

'And these tasks came from the Warden?' Blossom asks.

'Yes and no,' Nix says. 'He knew our commanding officer.'

I turn it over in my mind. 'So your commanding officer and the Warden worked to get you here ... and the Warden wanted me in Parliament as a contact ... he also said Traelen didn't know about you. So I assume that's true and having you here is not Traelen's plan? Only Claudius's and your officer's?'

Nothing.

'What happens to your – their – plan now he's dead?' I flinch at Blossom's question.

'Nothing,' River says. 'Claudius got us here and now we continue – there are others counting on us to succeed.'

Letting a breath leave me, I sink back into the couch as I think on the reality that we all have the same intentions – to follow through. And I can't help but glance at Nix as I do so, at the way there seems to be permanent creases beside his eyes. Whatever has got him and his normally happy-go-lucky demeanour so ... fractured, hasn't changed that at least.

'Claudius thought the Vanan prisoner could get you off the island once your job was done,' I say. 'Can you make sure you're not actually imprisoned there before they have a chance?'

Nix shifts in his seat on the couch opposite Blossom and me.

'Lu,' he says, gently gripping his knees. 'I promise, if we do this right – and you're really going to contact Cortane – we're not going to the other side.'

'And there's nothing more you can tell us?' I ask, knowing the answer will be no.

'You already know about the Vanan prisoner,' he says, sounding almost defeated. 'I assume you know what she can do. Honestly, it's better you don't know more than that. And sorting out the new Warden will keep Traelen occupied for a time, at least enough for us to get started on what we came to do. Then we'll go back to the mainland.'

I notice him look at Blossom as he says that, but he doesn't comment on how not seeing out her duty would throw her life into turmoil as well. But Claudius also thought she should be gone before the next collection.

Fuck.

What none of us have voiced is that breaking out a prisoner from Vana, using them to get an unsanctioned portal to the mainland – in the wake of who knows what River and Nix will have done – would make us fugitives on the mainland. But Nix didn't use the word 'home'. He knows that's no longer an option for us, too.

'And in the meantime,' I say, 'I'm supposed to just run the whole prison, get a new Warden up to speed, work to bust out a criminal, make sure you fit in here well enough that Traelen forgets you're supposed to be in Vana while you do your *tasks*, and wait until Traelen releases me from the *extension* he didn't order and organises me a sanctioned portal, while also finding a way for Blossom to get out *before* her duty is up?'

Can I do that?

Nix smiles grimly. 'That would be great.'

CHAPTER SEVEN

Dozens and dozens of people stare up at me as I take the podium at the edge of the island, the sky that envelops us softly blue. As if it knows we need to be treated gently today. The crowd before me are dressed in a mixture of the weightless dresses, and pants and vests, of the concierges, and the more vibrant and varied clothes of the prisoners. The forest around us is sombre. Its glossy dark green leaves bowing to the earth as if they, too, are under the weight of the emotions that run through the clearing.

My fingertips tremble and I fight the urge to press them to my numb lips.

I am but one of a number of speakers, chosen to represent the staff in my case, but the honour of doing so is not one I'm sure I will live up to. The Warden was almost a father-type figure to me, someone who didn't seem to share the same disappointment in me as my own, and he certainly eased my transition to this life far more than any other would have. It was so natural to me that he would help me get off the island and move into the next phase, and now ... I clear my throat.

Claudius had a view of service being an honour but it's hard to feel that way about it when it strips you away from everything you know. Yet he never judged me for my struggles and helped me perfect my mask of calm, hone my ability to focus on the rhythm of my tasks instead of the doubting in my heart.

And it's that ability I need to draw on now. Perhaps it's that mask that made him think I'd be good in Parliament?

I glance at the ornate urn where it sits on its own pedestal next to me. Surrounded by a carpet of white flowers that pick up the glare of the sun that streams in from behind me, trying to pierce the forest through the clearing. The cloying scent of the island's jasmine is almost suffocating as the image of him slumped on his desk, the colour drained from his face, slams into me.

Bringing my hands together at my front and linking my fingers, I grip them hard enough for my nails to dig into my skin. Pulling me back to the present and the small sea of people in front of me. Mostly concierges and prisoners, but there are others I don't recognise.

And, of course, Traelen.

Traelen looked after all the security for today and Hunters are dotted inconspicuously around the meadow on the edge of the island, their presence needed so people from the mainland could be here without realising where they are. Traelen told me one of the Claytis he has on staff will be obscuring the edges of the island so the Hunters are to make sure they don't wander too far. All they will know is this clearing and the room for the celebration of this life that comes after. Which, as far as they will be concerned, is somewhere secure on the Nuntainia mainland. Dimly, I wonder how much the Hunters are here to watch our engagement with the visitors as well – to make sure no unnecessary information is shared.

I'd wondered if it would be easier to bury him below, on Nuntainia, but the Warden was clear in his last wishes – he wanted his service here, and then ...

Traelen offers me a small nod and I clear my throat.

'Claudius,' I begin, trying to project my voice, 'was a man deeply respected and admired by all who knew him.' My gaze lands on Nix and River as I talk, Nix smiling gently to encourage me on. A look that bolsters me. 'And I was no different.'

My mouth knows how to form the words I practised last night, and I concentrate on keeping my breathing steady and the tears from falling. Blossom nods at me as I go. She listened to me practise, helped me refine what I was to say.

'One of his favourite games was to pretend he didn't know of the parties we'd have in the garden, until dropping incriminating tidbits of gossip with a sly grin,' I say. My focus dances over the crowd, my voice coming to my ears as if it belongs to someone else. 'A tradition we hope – at least the part about ignoring our celebrations – continues in his absence.'

A stilted laughter moves through the concierges.

The wind whips up suddenly and I press my dress back to my sides, willing it to stay in place. The generous amounts of fabric in the skirt wave like a flag towards the crowd until the breeze settles again and it stirs mildly around my ankles. And yet, I keep talking.

A few people dab their eyes. Emeris, standing with Bloss, wraps an arm around her shoulders and she leans into him gratefully. Janly lifts her chin and stares, resolutely, at the urn. I find a tall man with dark-brown skin and a black mark on his neck at the back of the crowd.

Please don't be his family, I think as I look away and back to Nix, who's still smiling softly as I talk.

But I find my awareness pulled back to the man at the back. He doesn't smile.

Just stares intently at me.

Despite the intimidating strength of his watchful gaze, it settles my nervous heart and I deliver the rest of my tribute to the Warden – carefully worded to be genuine and not giving away any details of how, and where, we worked together – while locked in silent communication with this stranger, his stare keeping my feet rooted to the spot.

'My mentor,' I say, my voice growing softer as I reach the end, 'was one of the best men I've ever known.' I swallow thickly. 'I will forever treasure his belief in me, and in my friends,' I try to stifle a loud sniff. 'I wish you nothing but joy and peace in the next world, Claudius.' My voice breaks on the last bit and a tear slips my defenses.

'Go well.' They are the last words I can get out before I know the torrent will come.

I slip off the stage in the silence that follows and Traelen takes my place.

My feet almost trip over themselves in my urgency to get away, the tears flowing harder now. But I won't let the others see me break down, I can't.

I owe it to the Warden to keep it together, to 'steer the ship easy into the night', as he would say.

Walking as quickly as I can, back down the path that led us to the clearing, I breathe deeply into the cool and shadowed forest, leaving the ceremony behind me. But I don't want to go back to the prison, either. Going back means completely taking on everything he left behind. Just when I thought I was going to be starting to live my life to the full, I will now be trying not to be caught breaking Nuntainian law.

I stop in the middle of the path, looking both ways, my heart pounding at the decision.

As I study the ground, an angry heat rising on my cheeks at my hesitation, I notice a slightly worn path through the trees and I take it. Relief to be moving again washes over me, but not more than the knowledge I now won't be found until I want to be.

Only a few minutes in another small clearing appears, large enough for me to see the sky again, and I sigh. The short path I followed was cool, a place where it was harder for the sun to shine her warmth, but I have grown used to being able to see the sky. More than that – feeling at one with the sky. Her soft, gentle blueness caresses my senses and I calm my pace as I circle the space.

The silent tears fall freely now, taking all the energy I have to stand, and I sink into the soft grass. A carpet of scarlet flowers scatters out from my knees and I pick one, caressing its velvet petals between my fingers. The rhythm and the smoothness of petals beneath my fingertips helps soothe my heaving tears and they settle into a steady, but slower, beat down my cheeks and into the grass.

I've seen these flowers on the island before and I vastly prefer them to the white that surround the prison, particularly the jasmine, and I wonder if Claudius did, too. There's something jarring about the purity of white around our walls. Despite not being able to know the prisoners' sins, I know they must be there.

Lifting the almost palm sized flower to my nose, I close my eyes and inhale its vanilla-like scent before spinning the now short stem in my fingers. My thumb and index fingers rubbing together as I watch the petals whirl. They look like I imagine the inside of me does now, as well – ordered in its chaos, but ready to stop.

'Are you okay?'

I practically leap out of my skin, dropping the flower as I jump to my feet and spin to face the deep voice.

The man from the back of the crowd stares back at me, as still as if he'd always been standing there. I blink furiously and wipe the tears from my cheeks. It's pointless to pretend I haven't been crying, and I take the time to gently press the length of my fingers under my bottom lashes to catch any remaining tears.

'I'm fine,' I say, giving a shaky smile as my heart rate attempts to regain its rhythm.

He doesn't respond, his steely gaze raising the hairs on my arms. I glance at the trees around us and back to him.

'How did you know him?' I ask to break the silence.

Eyes that match the forest around us flick over my face.

'In a number of ways,' he says, not entirely answering my question, and I find I don't care. Instead, I feel lighter at the thought of avoiding that false conversation we seem to have with everyone at a mourning. Relieved, almost, that someone has seen the pain I feel at losing the Warden without asking me what comes next.

He walks towards me slowly until he's within arm's reach. My body thrums as it wars with itself to run, but unsure of which direction – away from, or to, the man in front of me.

I let my eyes travel his chest and neck where I realise the mark I'd seen is a tattoo. It shimmers in the dappled light of the clearing and I can't make out what it is. As I follow its trail down into his shirt, I find myself staring at his broad chest again. His black, high-collared shirt straining ever so slightly across his breadth.

He dips to a crouch before me and my breath hitches as I watch him.

Collecting the flower I'd dropped from the grass, he holds it out to me as he stands. I look between the flower and his face. My fingers brush his brown ones as I reach to take it, so much darker than my own pale skin, and our gazes slowly come back to find the other's.

We stay like that a moment, our hands joined by the flower, my heart hammering, completely unable to look away.

'I'm sorry for your loss,' he whispers.

'And you,' I say, finally taking the flower from him.

I glance around the clearing, realising I no longer know where the path is but I feel steadier about returning to the prison. There are people relying on me there.

'Would you like me to walk you back?' he asks, and my insides warm a little at his kindness.

I nod slowly.

We walk, side by side, at a careful distance from each other back through the forest until we get to the main path. It's quiet here still, but I can hear the soft murmur of voices along both ends of the path – of those still in the clearing and those headed back towards the prison. People slowly scattering in the quiet aftermath of the mourning ceremony. Even if many of them will still be hemmed in by the Hunters, even though they don't really know it.

I look back to where the Warden's ashes will have now been scattered over the side of the island – one final nod to freedom – and decide I'm ready to go back and find Blossom. Nix, too, but he didn't know the Warden like Bloss did and, right now, I don't feel up to worrying if I will get gentle or angry Nix. As soon as I think it, a pang of guilt presses in behind my ribs – there was nothing but support in his face when he watched me give my speech.

'I should—' I break off, gesturing towards the prison that can't be seen from here. The one he can't know about other than the room he will be taken to via the special portal I know Traelen arranged somehow.

He inclines his head.

'Thank you,' I say, lifting my flower weakly.

'It won't necessarily get easier,' he says gently. 'But it helps to believe everything happens for a reason.'

'Does it though? Did this?' I blurt.

The corners of his mouth tug up in a half-attempt at a smile. 'I don't know. I said it helps, not that I can do it.'

I laugh softly.

'I should let you go,' he says after a moment. 'I'm sure you have people you'd like to be with at this time.'

Yes, I think. *And a huge job to wrap my head around.*

'Thank you for checking on me.'

'I found I couldn't help it,' he says. 'Your speech was very moving. I'm sure he would have been honoured.'

I hope so. Just as I hope I can follow the path the Warden laid out as he intended.

'I'll give you a moment.' I watch him walk away and towards the clearing before I head in the direction of the prison.

After three steps, I'm unable to stop myself turning around.

The path is empty.

'Hey,' Blossom says when I get back to our apartment.

The day is fading and we have a dinner in honour of the Warden I will need to make sure we're prepared for soon. But, right now, the weight of the loss and the day is starting to drive me into the ground. My face feels swollen and my eyes sting from too many tears. Normally, we'd get a day off a week but I have no doubt that will be a thing of the past in my running of the prison – the thought of that alone adds to my exhaustion. Despite my personal reactions to always being second to *something*, being Warden of this prison was never on my wish list. Not that it would be expected of a concierge to aspire to that anyway – concierges don't make Wardens.

'Hey,' I reply as I sink into the couch beside her, placing my blood-red flower on the glass table.

I hoist the layers of my ivory dress up and over my knees and lean forward to undo the ties on my sandals. They wind around and around my calves and my skin all but exhales as I loosen and finally remove them completely. Rubbing my thumbs into the soles of my feet briefly, I collapse back on the couch cushions.

'How are you traveling?' I ask, turning my head to Blossom.

She stares out at the sky.

'I don't know,' she says heavily. 'I'm sad for the Warden. He clearly had … unfinished business here.' She turns her own head on the couch to look at me. 'But I'm mostly sick to my stomach about how far you will go to work it all out now Nix and River are here, without him to help you.'

I look away, back out across the balcony. It's true – right now there doesn't feel like there is anything I wouldn't do to understand the bigger picture here, or make sure Nix and River have a way off the island before being forced to go to Vana. But that feels easy to say when I have no idea where to even start.

'I don't have to involve—' I start, pushing against the memory of Claudius telling us we should *both* be gone before the next collection. A whole year before Blossom's duty is up.

'Bullshit. I'm already involved. But I'm not worried about me, Luka. I have nothing to go back to, anyway. Nothing but time to work it out.'

The heartbreak in her voice chips at me.

'But I do worry about you throwing away your future,' she says. 'You know I want to ask you to let them manage themselves, right?' My chest constricts. 'If they end up on the other side for any reason, you can't go there too, Luka.' Her voice is a touch gentler now and I know she doesn't mean to chide me. The worry is real.

'He's not just anyone, Bloss. Neither's River.' I don't know how else to explain that I'd give it all up to keep them safe. 'They were my brothers before I even thought to want them. Claudius wasn't just anyone, either.'

She studies me for a while and I can see the thoughts whirling behind her eyes. 'No … that's why I'm going to help you with three things: managing the prison and keeping Traelen onside – meaning you need that recommendation and a *legal* way off the island, regardless how those brothers leave – understanding exactly what the Warden wanted from you, us, and making sure those boys are done with whatever … mission they're on as soon as possible.' She inches her hand across the space between us and grips mine in hers. 'But my priority is getting you through all of this unscathed, do you understand?' She squeezes my hand without waiting for a response. 'You don't have to be their contact, but, being in Parliament will give you options you need to keep open.' She pauses for a long moment, seemingly warring with something. 'Do you know exactly what the role is? The actual one you were going to have to show you were doing, not just that Claudius wanted you as their group's contact.'

I shake my head. Understanding what role he was going to recommend me for feels like an important part of the puzzle.

'Traelen will,' Bloss says. 'But he doesn't know you as well as the Warden. He's going to be much more involved now, at least until there is a new Warden. So *your* priority is making sure he knows how good you are at this. We don't want any hiccups with your recommendation.'

My stomach sinks a little. I should have thought about that already – the … former … Warden was highly regarded, but I imagine there is only so far a dead man's recommendation can go. But, for me, his requests can't go unanswered.

'I'm not sure what I did to deserve you, Bloss,' I say, turning my head on the couch to look at her. 'Do you have any thoughts on where we start? 'Breaking out a prisoner from Vana might be tricky,' I say. 'It's not like we can waltz in.'

'At this point, there are only two people we can ask without fear of repercussions,' Blossom says carefully, as if she only half believes it. 'But, first, we finish Claudius's send off.'

CHAPTER EIGHT

The Warden had as soft a spot for Koko's enchanted chocolate balls as I do, so there's every variety imaginable on the long white table in the grandroom. The kitchen staff organised them into colour blocks so a rainbow shimmies on the table cloth.

A number of the guests, including the concierges who also wished to celebrate the Warden's life, have helped themselves already. For some it's very obvious they've indulged and their lips match the colour of the treat they ate. Or soft bubbles emerge as they talk, drawing giggles from them and their companions – it's impossible to talk about anything sad when bubbles sprout from your tongue. Others have sparkles erupting from their fingers as they wave them around.

But I love the ones that pop in my mouth and fill my nose, making me sneeze, and tears come to my eyes. It's ridiculous, but so fun.

I don't feel like one today.

Instead, I move to where the Warden would come and stand next to me to watch the proceedings and take a glass that fizzes with silver bubbles in rose gold liquid. I can only assume it's another of Koko's creations but I don't care what's in it, or what it's called, today. Emeris spots me from across the quiet room of concierges, prisoners, and strangers, and nods. Everything is going to plan.

I look to the quartet who are about to begin their next arrangement and the violinist gives me a sad smile. I'm staring back at him when Traelen joins me.

'You've done very well, getting us to this point and organising today, Luka,' he says, hands behind his back and reminding me much of the Warden. But I don't ask if he has a replacement. The prison has really run itself while Emeris and I prepared for today, but I find I'm not yet ready to hand over the responsibility to anyone else. If I look after it, I can pretend there won't be a permanent change for just a little longer.

Pretend there's not a countdown on Nix and River being here and not in Vana.

I look down for a moment before surveying the people who start to smile a little wider as the lights of the music wraps around them. There are more people here than normal and the room feels full but not bursting. Although it's still a bit claustrophobic with Traelen's security – the Hunters – lining the walls. Anyone who doesn't live here will be escorted off the island together and provided with a palatable story about where they were and who they saw – the details of which only Traelen knows. But, even still, I can't see the man from the clearing and something compels me to keep looking.

Just for a moment, I imagine myself slipping out with those who will return to the mainland tonight. How would that feel? But, despite the slight quickening in my chest, I know that single thought is as far as I will take it.

'He will be missed from here, I can see,' Traelen says, his voice heavy with something I can't place. I can feel him looking at me, and I glance at him politely.

'Yes, sir,' I say. 'He was an excellent boss ... and an incredible man.'

He nods, smiling at one of the prisoners who makes her way past us, her hair towering over us all.

'His replacement will be here soon.'

I look sharply at him.

'I'd like you to assist him. At least for the first few weeks.'

'Yes, sir, of course.'

'I'd like joint check-ins from you, each week. And I expect our prisoners to be back to their normal schedule from tomorrow. Claudius and I didn't get a chance to talk about the length of your extension, but we can do that with the new Warden once he's comfortable.'

He doesn't wait for my agreement before he walks away, my heart sinking a little at the inevitable removing me from running anything. Then the actual reality of what he's saying hits me and I swallow thickly as I fold my fingers into fists. I'm good at what I do – something I need to maintain so Traelen doesn't change my recommendation if there is to be any chance I will leave the island at his will and ... not with the prisoner I will be releasing. If I could even bring myself to do that. If I can work out *how* to do that. But if the new Warden finds me so useful in the transition he doesn't need me long, where does that leave me to do everything else I'm now personally committed to?

Eventually, long after Traelen has started mingling, I decide I can leave my post and I weave through the crowd. Most of them talk of things other than the Warden now, but I don't begrudge them for it. While many of them didn't know him like I did, there's only so long we can talk about our own grief with others.

I look around again for the man from the forest but I only half-heartedly think I'll find him now; the edges of the room are too dark as the light outside fades and I don't want to investigate every nook. What need would I have to talk to him again anyway? Other than the little flurry behind my ribs that seems to start up when I think of him and the intensity with which he regarded me.

Something sours a little in my stomach at the knowledge I will never know who he truly was to Claudius, and I mentally add it to the things about my Warden that will now never be answered.

I'd picked up the flower the stranger gave me from the table in our living room and placed it beside my bed before I left tonight. My mind seemingly unable to stop trailing back to him since I left the clearing. I appreciated that he came to check on me, found me at a very low point, and didn't judge. But he also struck me as someone who would grieve in private, and so I force him from my mind. Pressing my lips together as I scan the room instead, searching for something I could – should – do.

Nix reaches for me as I pass by him and River and I almost find myself wanting to be swept up by him, consequences be damned. It's been so long since we've been together and the events of the last few days have happened so quickly, we've barely caught a breath between us. Instead, my pulse rate kicks up at the thought of those consequences – the fact that Traelen is in this very room and *nothing* can draw his attention to them. The only thing that could have done so more than them being inconspicuously in this room, would be their absence.

*Treat them as you would any other*s, he'd said.

So, I step aside gently so his hand falls away. He frowns slightly and then seems to remember we can't be too familiar here. Traelen hasn't spoken with me about them, even in the aftermath of the Warden's death, and probably particularly not with a new Warden on the way. Perhaps it will be a secret he won't share at all. But that's a theory I don't need to test.

'You were great today, Luka,' he says, his gold eyes pale and sad as they hold mine.

'Not something I want to repeat. Ever, ideally,' I say quietly.

'We all die someday,' River says, somewhat solemnly, and I look up at him. His face gives nothing away.

'Ever the optimist,' I say slowly, a sharp sting of regret about my actual father flashing across my torso.

'The realist you'll find, Lu,' he says.

Nix remains silent.

'I need to sneak out for a moment,' I say. 'I'll be back. Try the plain chocolate balls, they're my favourite.'

I duck down the stone hallway to the nearest concierge bathroom. It's not the closest one to the grandroom but we're not supposed to use the prisoners'. The now night sky sparkles over the internal courtyard as I wander down its long side, the music fading the further I go.

The bathroom is empty when I arrive and, after relieving myself, I take in my appearance to check everything's in place before I return, taking the isolation of the bathroom as it is – the only reprieve from the needs of others I will get in a long time. A moment just to be on my own. The ivory dress I wore for the ceremony still looks fresh and I absently thank the crease-resistant fabric. Strands of my platinum blonde hair fall around my face. They weren't designed that way but I think I prefer the softness they create when my hair is pulled partially back off my face.

Digging through the layers of the skirt on my dress, I find the tube of soft pink lipstick and reapply what wore off as I drank my silver drink. Taking one last look, the toes of my golden sandals poking out beneath the dress, I sigh. This is as good as it's going to get, and as long as I'm going to get – I should go back, make sure I am seen in the room, supporting the prisoners, supporting the staff. And soon to be supporting the new Warden.

But, instead of going back where I should be, I drop forward and brace myself on the sink, the weight of saying goodbye to Claudius too heavy, too close to the things inside that make me work – make me breathe. My lungs feel tight. I can't fall apart now.

My phone bumps against my thigh gently as I stand and stare myself down in the mirror, deciding on my next action. Steeling myself to go back into that room.

Reluctantly, I take my phone out of my pocket as well – it's been too long since I told Zale and Akira I wasn't collected and they will be worried for both Nix and me.

Luka: I received word that my duty has been extended which explains Nix's absence. I'll let you know when I do about my new end date.

I don't look at myself in the mirror as I lie. The phone buzzes in my hand.

Zale: Oh wow. I'm not sure what to make of that, but I'm relieved it means Nix is okay – we alerted the Hunters to his being unaccounted for but we haven't heard any more from them. That will be why. Teddy was ready to join that bloody vigilante group she's heard of to try and find him – they call their leader the Rebel Prince, can you believe it? To say I'm relieved I talked her down from that is an understatement!

Teddy – Zale's wife who I barely got to know before I was sent here. The weight of my phone as I slide it back into my pocket mirrors the heaviness that's taking up residence between my ribs. But I agree with her, having Teddy running off chasing some 'rebel prince' sounds ridiculous in the extreme.

Making my way back to the grandroom, the music no longer plays and the quiet is loud. My pace picks up a little, reflecting the skittering in my stomach.

Traelen's voice filters down the hallway.

I can't quite make out what he's saying but I know what it will be – he never makes speeches at these events, and he already addressed the Warden's passing at the service.

He's introducing the new Warden. 'Soon' obviously meant 'now'.

Shit.

I scurry along the hallway, trying not to get too winded and pause at the door to the grandroom to collect myself and smooth my hair, steadying my nervous breathing. The room is strangely silent, reverent almost – at least from this side.

Placing a hand on the door, the room breaks into a gentle applause.

I missed it.

Fuck.

Gently pushing the doors open and slipping inside, I find the guests starting to mingle once more. As they part, I find my vision blocked by something else and a small gasp escapes me.

A large pair of storm-grey wings, utterly still, fill the space. The back they come from is broad and covered in dark clothing, but I can't drag my attention from the wings.

There is only one person that it can be.

We have a winged Warden – a Karaylia.

Not that it matters, I suppose, feeling my brow furrow at myself. It's just not often I see wings like that up close. Despite endless family history lessons from my father about the different abilities in our line, wings were just one more interest outside of me that occupied him. For River, though, his wings were a source of pure joy and entertainment he shared with Nix and me as they were coming in.

I clear my throat, steeling my reserve to introduce myself and walk properly into the room.

Less than three paces away, Nix grabs my wrist.

I spin into him.

'What are you doing?' I whisper urgently.

'Don't go near him,' he says, his voice dangerously low and rough.

'What?' I pull back where he holds me.

'I don't want you anywhere near him,' he says. I blink in confusion, but the conviction on Nix's face is clear.

I take my other hand and use it to push his off, glancing around at the other prisoners. 'It's fine, Nix,' I whisper. 'I've been here a long time and I still have a job to do. What am I going to do, ignore my new boss?' I give him a pointed look and turn back to the wings I can nearly touch, thankful the music will have drowned out my hurried conversation with Nix.

Nix makes one last, sort of subtle grab at me and I skip a little as I get out of his reach.

Only to collide with the wings.

A sharp sting cuts out along my stomach where I come into contact with them. Staring stupidly, I realise the wings are no longer storm-grey feathers, but thousands of blades. Changed in less than a blink of an eye into something deadly.

A warmth spreads along the top of my underwear and down the front of my right thigh.

I glance down.

Oh.

Red petals bloom from my centre and down the front of my dress. My head feels fuzzy, like it's suddenly full of my dress fabric, and the room starts to spin. The winged man turns towards me, the tattoo on his neck sparkling but blurry. The people around me talk on, their voices droning in my ears.

The grandroom starts to go black at the edges and the last thing I see is Nix's face.

Almost stormier than the wings.

CHAPTER NINE

Consciousness wrests back control and the night sky fills my vision. The stone walls of the prison hallway reaching out towards the stars. But it's blurry and I can't hold the shape of the sparkling lights. The sting in my stomach has turned to a dull burn that radiates across my abdomen and down my leg.

My head bumps against something hard and I peel my eyes open again, the night sky still spinning above me. But there's something else and I turn my head into it to get a clearer picture. It's round, and slightly shiny. And so *close*.

I squint.

A button.

I push back, only to hiss in pain at the movement. So I take the coward's way out and curl into the person that carries me, my cheek resting on the firm expanse of their chest.

I close my eyes and try to expel the pain on my exhales.

Eventually, I'm jostled slightly as the person – man – lies me gently on a high surface and I struggle to prop myself up on one elbow and look around, holding my stomach with my other hand.

The wellness centre.

Its roof isn't open to the sky here, being on one of the lower levels, but the large arch windows set into the walls normally let in a lot of light. At this time of night it's lit with only the soft bulbs that run the perimeter of the room.

A man, the one I assume carried me here, stands at the bench that lines the wall of windows, his back to me. I glance around again, waiting for the healer on call, but when they don't appear my gaze travels back to the man. The shape of him is broad and strikes a small note of recognition, but I can't place who he is – either prisoner or concierge.

I watch his back as he washes his hands in silence, an unusual, but welcome, sense of quiet falling over my mind with the rhythm of his movements.

As he turns to face me, I notice the dark mark on his neck, just above his right shoulder, and a flickering tendril of a memory sparks something in my stomach – strong enough to paint my cheeks with warmth.

Just like the green of the forest is inky in the night, so are this man's eyes as he looks at me. The hard lines of his face turn harder when he focuses on the hand I still have clutched at my stomach. Slowly, he approaches where I half sit, half lie, on the bench.

'Can I have a look?' he gestures to my middle, and I swallow.

Giving myself a moment before I take my hand away and look at myself. The ivory fabric of my dress is now sticky with an expanse of blood larger than my hand, the fabric cleanly sliced. It sticks to my leg where blood has run there, too.

My palm and between my fingers are wet.

I swallow the bile that starts to rise, the room beginning to spin again. 'Easy,' he says, taking my shoulders. 'How about you lie down?'

I try to nod but my head slumps forward instead and he moves me himself, placing a hand behind my head as he lies it down on the bench.

'I'm going to take a look,' he says, and I groan my consent.

Keeping my eyes closed, promising myself I will not be sick, I feel him tear apart my dress a bit further. Exposing more of my skin, but giving me the dignity of not raising the dress up my legs. I wince as he gently prods around my stomach, palpitating the soft tissue there.

A sudden loss of warmth prickles my side and I open my eyes to find him gone. Scanning what I can see of the room quickly, I find him opening and closing the overhead cupboards on the walls that run back towards the door.

The deep brown skin of his arms is the same as when I met him in the clearing, but the shimmering on his neck is all but invisible in this light – as if I have imagined it and am trying to will it back into existence.

I watch him as he approaches me again – also watching me but saying nothing. A warm cloth drags on my skin as he clears away the blood and around the wound. Then he holds his hand there, a grounding weight just inside my hip. He pulls himself up short as if he's just remembered something.

'I can get you a professional healer if you prefer? Or a magically gifted one?' he asks softly. 'I assume you have very talented Arkanans here.'

'Do you know how to do it well?' I ask.

He nods. 'But manually. Mostly.'

'Okay.'

I close my eyes again and listen to him breathe in and out, imagining the creases I now know exist at the corners of his eyes and not really understanding why I didn't request one of the magical healers I know. Perhaps because Blossom and I got drunk with one once. But we do actually have very talented healers – Arkanans – here. Or if it's because, for some unidentifiable reason, I feel like I can just be me in this moment. I don't need to have all the answers or make the calls, and he won't judge me for it. I don't need to be the unruffled concierge. Nor the second best option for everything.

A little voice wants to scoff at me that I don't actually know this man, but I drape an arm over my face and push the thought away. If I don't have to look at my stomach again, I will take whatever help I can get.

'I will use some numbing gel and help it along myself, but this still might sting a bit,' he warns.

A moment later a cold and, yes, stinging sensation burns its way along my lower stomach. A heartbeat later it's tingling instead.

'I'm going to stitch it, okay?'

'Fuck,' I mutter as my gaze flies open to see if he's serious. 'Do you have a drink?'

He grins and my heart just about stops.

'You won't need it for this, promise.' He looks at my middle and then back up to my face. 'How about after you get through it?'

A small smile tugs at my own mouth and I pretend it's because of the hot tingle on my stomach and nothing at all to do with the weight of his hand on my middle. Or the dimple in the left side of his face when he smiles. Or the deep green of his eyes.

Nothing at all.

A gentle, but slightly uncomfortable, pulling starts in my lower stomach. Towards my belly button, but also near my hip. The tugging seems to be everywhere and in a single place all at once. And it brings a swell of nausea stemming from wherever it begins and up my throat. I slam a hand over my mouth and swallow hard.

'Breathe through it,' he says, his voice gentle and rough at the same time. 'There's not too many, I'm almost done.'

Tears leak down my cheeks at the discomfort and I inhale and exhale deeply, as instructed, through my nose because I don't dare remove my hand from my mouth.

Several minutes, and countless breaths, later he announces we're done and gives my stomach a final wipe that I can only partially feel. My hand is small in his when he takes it and helps me sit up, lifting the top portion of the tall bed for me to lean against.

Just like in the clearing, our hands stay linked for no apparent reason.

He looks down at where I sit on the bench, towering over me. A ripple travels through the green of his eyes and into the set of his shoulders.

'I'm sorry,' he says. 'About the cut.'

I look down at the blood on my dress, still not quite believing how it got there. I frown, why would he apologise?

The shape of his shoulders as I watched him in here starts to overlay with what I could see in the grandroom. Behind the massive grey wings.

'Oh,' I say as a weighted uncertainty starts to take the place of the jitters that have been dancing under my skin. 'You're the new—' I start, but realise I have a better question and look him straight in the eye. 'Why did you do that?' I look at my stomach again. '*How* did you do that? You *cut* me.'

He looks genuinely pained. 'It was … a reflex. I don't normally have them out when there's no direct threat. But I was ordered that they be … on display.'

He drops my hand.

'But it shouldn't have happened. I-I wasn't expecting anyone to touch me. I'm sorry.'

He doesn't look away as he apologises for the second time and the intensity in his stare burns into mine. As it did at the mourning ceremony. And in the meadow when he came to check on me, gave me the flower.

My stomach does a strange little flop as that look of his calls to something in me.

'How bad is it?' I ask, unable to break his gaze.

'Ten stitches,' he says solemnly. 'It will heal neatly but you will likely have a small scar. I'm—'

A small laugh escapes me and he stares at me, brows lifting ever so slightly.

'Sorry,' I let out a final, breathy laugh. 'That's just … not as bad as I was expecting, given how much blood there was. I thought I might have been ripped in half.'

It's his turn to laugh in surprise. 'I do have *some* self control, you know.'

'The next time I'll try to remember I won't be severed and not pass out on you.'

Seriousness descends, darkening his features.

'It won't happen again,' he says. 'I don't make a habit of hurting innocent people.'

I nod and the room falls quiet as we watch each other, my mind starting to swirl with the implications of a new Warden. Of *this man* being Warden. That, on one hand, I will be working to make sure his takeover of the prison is smooth and, on the other, working to directions by his predecessor – ones that put me in direct contact with a prisoner from Vana and crossing the forbidden line between our prisons. I swallow.

'Given we'll be working closely together,' I say slowly, 'I think that's a good thing.'

He cocks his head in question and my tummy spins under the cut as I follow the action. Remembering that we didn't introduce ourselves in the meadow and he has no idea who I am or what my role is here.

'Are you not the new Warden?' I ask, the doubt clear in my voice and the pulling of my brows I can feel.

'I am, and you are Lu—'

'Luka, yes.'

His face lightens. 'I was told about you. Now I understand why it was you who spoke at his send off.' He smiles slightly and my stomach continues its merry-go-round at the dimple that tries to appear. 'I think you've just made this job a bit more interesting, Luka.'

His dimple is a little too captivating and I slide off the bed and stand, a fraction shaky, and he grips my elbow to keep me upright.

The door to the wellness centre flies open and I flinch, the new Warden pulling me into him slightly.

'Luka!' Blossom says as she runs into the room, her hair flying everywhere. 'I've been looking all over for you.'

Her mouth drops open when she joins us, her focus bouncing between the new Warden – even as she appears to not quite be looking straight at him – and the blood on my dress.

'What the fuck—'

'I'm fine, Bloss,' I say, fixing her with a look. 'The new Warden fixed me up.' I frown at her and then look back at the new Warden taking Blossom in as he lets me go. 'Did no one else notice?'

'I think it happened faster than you realise,' he says. 'Anyone who saw you probably thought you'd just had too much Silver Sparkle.'

'Oh.'

'Exactly what *did* happen?' Blossom asks, her eyes narrowing and subtly trying to move closer to me.

He looks at me, ready and waiting for me to tell her. Almost as if he's waiting for my open condemnation. Which seems ... a little excessive.

'An accident Blossom, I'm fine.'

'It was my wings,' he says, surprising both Blossom and me. 'She bumped into them and—'

'Your blades came out,' she finishes for him.

He nods.

'Okay,' she says slowly. 'Makes sense ... I suppose. I know how sensitive you Karaylia can be.'

Karaylia. That does actually make sense, my father would have been mortified I hadn't thought about that detail when evading Nix's reach. River, too. He was so proud to have that magic line surge through his system to the surface. Even if I did worry my father would use him for some kind of research. She looks at me again and lifts her perfectly arched brows. 'I assume your aversion to blood didn't make this any easier?'

I grimace, remembering being carried by the new Warden. 'Possibly not.'

She looks between us, visibly exhaling but still carrying tension in her shoulders. 'I'll give you a moment to finish up while I call off the search party.' She points at me before flicking him a pointed look. 'And then I'm taking you home.'

I wait until she's left the wellness centre before I turn back at the new Warden and find him already looking down at me with a searing gaze that seems to strip me bare. Is breaking the law under his nose something I will be able to do? I'm not even sure I *want* to go against everything I have been trying to support in my service. But, at the same time, the thought of leaving Nix and River here without me – at least without their own exit firmly in place – claws at my mind. And I trusted Claudius, I just can't believe he would tell me to do something so wrong if there wasn't a really good reason. I just wish I knew what that was.

'It's going to be strange calling you Warden,' I say. 'The other one – he was—'

'Don't call me Warden,' he says. 'I'm Quillian.'

Blossom watches me intently as I leave Quillian in the wellness centre and walk with her down the hallway.

'I need to swing past Nix's to let him know I'm okay,' I say.

'*Are* you okay?'

There's an angry sort of uncertainty in Bloss's tone I don't hear often and I brush a hand over my cut, gently touching where Quillian has stuck a white gauze bandage.

'I truly am,' I say. 'It wasn't his fault. I was behind him and, as Nix reached for me, I overcompensated. I wouldn't have wanted to touch them even when they were feathers, but it might have been handy to remember they're lethal on a hair trigger as well.'

She laughs, but it's a little grim. 'You need to stop ignoring all you know about magic manifestations, even if we are on dampeners.'

'What's wrong?'

A loud exhale leaves her lips. 'I ... don't like that you got cut, even if it was an accident.'

'Bloss,' I say in a placating tone. She has a low tolerance point for the mistreatment of women - something I greatly admire but I don't want misplaced. 'It was an accident. I would tell you if it wasn't.' I almost want to smile at the knowledge I now have a team of people here with me. 'I'd even let Nix and River at him if he'd done wrong by me.'

I glance sideways at her and her shoulders lower a fraction at that statement. But looks sideways at me, an unspoken acknowledgement that she's not particularly happy with the knife situation, either.

We arrive at Nix and River's door, knocking this time as we glance back down the hall. Although, now that other prisoners and concierges have seen Nix and River are here, and Blossom and I are together in our uniforms, I feel a fraction less worried about being seen here. It's not unusual for concierges to be visiting the prisoner rooms for all manner of reason, but I don't want to make it obvious that this one holds particular significance.

The door all but jerks off its hinges as Nix answers the knock. His hair is on end and his mouth agape as he looks at my torn, bloodied dress.

'Fucking *bastard*,' he spits, as Blossom and I walk past him and into their living room. My stomach shifts uncomfortably at the fire in Nix's tone.

River sits on the decadent, pale couch and glances between us.

'I'm fine Nix, it was an accident. I came to tell you as much,' I say gently.

'My ass, it was an accident. He *injured* you!'

Blossom stands opposite River and they share a look before returning their attention to Nix and me. The worry in her features is clear – as is her rising anger. I fight the heat that races across my face. The tremble in my fingers that screams this isn't like him – he's protective, yes, but not so ... aggressively so. This isn't what I want her to see. What *I* want to see. But there's no surprise on River's face. Just a ... watchful sort of weariness.

'And he apologised, and *helped* me,' I say gently, pushing away the disappointment in Nix that is spreading. The little bubble that appeared somewhere near where my heart lives when I'd opened my eyes to Quillian is taking the brunt of it. A tiny, happy little bubble.

'I don't want you near him,' he says and I take a step back.

No. Nix might be angry that I have been hurt, but he doesn't get to take it out on me.

'He's my boss, Nix,' I snap, 'and since when do you call the shots on who I go near?'

He presses his lips together and clasps his head in his hands. It's clear there's so much more sitting underneath his anger than tonight. Something that's causing him constant pain. My heart aches.

I sigh, taking his hands. 'Nix, I'm fine. It's fine. I will heal. He helped. End of story. But he's my boss and I need to work with him if I'm to have any hope of seeing out my duty, helping the two of you, and fulfilling Claudius's wishes, okay? What have you got against him, anyway?'

He looks at the still silent River, an unusual thing for him, and nods reluctantly – only answering one of my questions.

I give them both another beat of silence to explain what tonight was all about, one neither of them bothers to fill, and I sigh inwardly. Willing myself to be patient with them. To not press Nix into an even longer standoff for what he will and won't share.

'I'm exhausted,' I say, 'and I have things I need to do before sunrise, including sleep.' I look at the three of them, unnaturally quiet, the weight of spending the best part of the first half of the night in the grandroom, and then the wellness centre, dragging at me. There's an undercurrent between Nix and River, and Blossom is observing them closely. I don't tell them part of my exhaustion is trying to work out all the things they're not saying. 'I need you to hurry this up.'

Slowly, Blossom rises and joins me back near the door. I didn't even get to sit down.

'He's the reason we're here,' Nix says from where he now sits next to River.

River punches him in the arm and Nix curses, but it's nothing compared to the freefall that's begun through my centre.

'How is that ...' I trail off, knowing they can't say. They just watch me, the words unable to leave their mouths. But I don't miss the suspicion in Nix's almond eyes. Like he can see on my face Quillian has had more of an impact on me than he'd like.

'I'll be extra careful,' I say quietly. Unsure what of.

Only that I need to find that woman of the Warden's and find out why she's so important.

Quickly.

'We're going to Vana tomorrow,' Blossom says, looking at me as if hoping I might contradict her.

I nod.

With the Warden's mourning ceremony now over, I will have as much time as I'm going to get to slip away. As soon as Traelen and the Hunters have left the island, I will be heading to the other side. Exactly what I will do there still feels a little ... uncertain. But I will find whatever I can.

The room is silent for a moment, the only movement Nix's hand through his hair. But he doesn't voice any of the objections he clearly has. As if he's resigned to the fact I will follow through with the task Claudius gave me. At least for now. I know him well enough to know this isn't necessarily the end of it. And it's certainly not the end of his views on Quillian.

'That's good,' River says carefully. 'Just before dawn, go to the perimeter – there's a cut out in the wall where you can take cover. It's to the east side. Cortane should be there – she goes as many mornings as she can. She'll meet you there.' A rush of cool relief washes over me even as it leaves a crawling sensation in its wake. Just how much do these two know? 'Ask if she likes strawberries. And do whatever you can to get her to trust you – it will be hard won, but worth it.'

My bed is a sanctuary I can't deny after I've peeled my ruined dress from my skin and washed the remaining dried blood off. I slip my gold sleep dress on and settle myself in. My mind whirls as I think through all the possibilities of what Nix could have meant. What role Quillian had in them being here – was it their sentence to Vana, or their unexpected appearance in this prison he is referring to?

But he doesn't trust him. That much is abundantly clear.

Which means I shouldn't either.

Even still, as I roll over and sleep finally starts to close over the plans Blossom and I have been making to go to Vana following River's instructions – slip out in the night, get across the band of light without being seen, wait in the space he told us, win over the prisoner – the last thing I'm aware of is the red flower beside my bed.

And the memory of the weight of Quillian's hand on my hip.

CHAPTER TEN

The swooshing sound of my curtains being opened startles me from an unsettled sleep and my heart races as I try to locate the sound.

'Time to roll,' Bloss says from where she's exposed the doors that open out to my small balcony. A groan is all I can muster in response as I see the still-night sky outside.

My sleep was fitful after Nix's comments, and every time I thought I'd fall completely into sleep my stitches would pull – not to mention less than a handful of hours is simply not enough for me. But the importance of what I need to do is quick to make its way to the front of my sleep-fogged mind and the apprehension has me rising from the bed despite my exhaustion. Finding and gaining the trust of this Vanan prisoner was the last thing Claudius asked me to do.

Failing him is not something I can live with.

I pull on my exercise clothes, including a lightweight zip-through jacket. The temperature is never particularly cold here, but it does get a little chilly overnight – and it's into the night we're about to venture. Tying my running shoes, I try to push aside the concern that pulses on the edges of my mind that even approaching Vana prison is forbidden, let alone trying to engage their prisoners.

Yet that's exactly what we're planning – to find the Warden's contact at the other prison and ask her not only to find a way to escape Nuntania's most notorious prison-island on her own, but with Nix and River as well. After I have helped them complete what they came here for, ideally. Because I know in my bones they will refuse to go if they haven't. Even more ideally, they should escape in a way that doesn't jeopardise Traelen finalising either my supposed 'extension' and therefore legitimate way off the island – or my recommendation – or implicate Blossom.

And I have no idea what Quillian's position is on people who break rules. I once thought Claudius the most dutiful of men, yet here I am at his request; and River had the route, time, and place all ready to hand ...

We slip quietly down the stairs that run the wall of the prison and back onto the soft grass of the staff garden. Crossing the green expanse at a jog, we ease through the surrounding hedge and out into the forest beyond. Winding through the short forest, the skitter of creatures ripples away from our footsteps. The light provided out here comes from each of our phones – their screens projecting a soft illumination bright enough to catch the tops of our shoes as they stride over the dirt path.

'I'll kill the Warden if she's a total madwoman,' Bloss whispers into the dark.

'Which one?'

'The old one. I'll dig him up and kill him again.'

My laugh feels morbid. 'Tricky to do when his ashes were scattered off the island,' I say.

'Seriously, though. Who was she to him, do you think?'

'I'm hoping we'll find out. But I trust neither he, nor Nix and River, would send us anywhere dangerous.'

'Apart from a prison for the worst citizens of Nuntainia, you mean?'

I let that question hang in the crisp air.

The path starts to widen slightly and breaks into another clearing. The whole island is a collection of clearings and paths in the forest, three of which are taken up by the grounds of the two prisons and the Warden's residence.

But this is as far as we are supposed to go. This is where the prohibited gathering between staff sometimes happens. The middle ground between each of our domains. No one has ever tried particularly hard to stop them, as far as I'm aware, but those gatherings mean there are definitely no wards between the two prisons and our magical contracts prevent any real information being shared. Between the island being populated only with people bound by their duty contracts; my prisoners, who would want to stay as far away from Vana as possible; and the Vanan prisoners, who are walled in, the security on the island is low. At least outside of Vana – it's swarming with Hunters on the inside, from what I understand. Floating in the sky, surrounded by magical wards that mark you for certain capture should you try to escape – if you survive the fall, that is – is a pretty good deterrent to most would-be prison break attempts.

'Sure about this?' I ask Blossom as we cross the clearing.

Her features are ghoulish in the light shining up from her phone, but I catch her nod.

We step onto the forbidden path, the closest we've ever been to this side, and shift into the darker shadows on the left side. Even though I'm sure there are no wards, I still find myself waiting for the scream of an alarm.

Only the sounds of the forest greet us. The quiet hush of the leaves in the soft breeze, the gentle groan of heavy branches. The occasional sound of a cricket.

It feels darker on this side, the trees that line the edges of the dirt track pressing in on us. The scent is fresh though, at odds with what I would expect in a place that's trying to be foreboding. The end of the path appears abruptly and we stop just as suddenly. Staying under the cover of the trees closest to us, we peer out, taking in the huge, brown stone building that looms ahead of us. There's no garden around it like our compound, just a wide stretch of green – like a grass moat.

We pocket our phones, the tiny lights no longer needed in the full lighting of the prison. One of the few things I have heard is that's one of the difficulties of being stationed here – it's almost impossible to adjust to the constant light streaming in the windows and now, as I squint into the glare, I can understand why.

Checking the top of the walls for guards and not seeing any, we make a break for it, racing towards the right corner where River told us there will be a dark alcove on the outside we can slip into. The almost-healed cut on my stomach throbs a little in protest, but I ignore it, focusing on reaching the wall. On the other side there is supposed to be a matching space the prisoner frequents in the hours before dawn.

As soon as we reach the wall, Blossom and I pause to assess where we are. Pressing ourselves against the cold stone, breathing heavily, we stare at each other in disbelief we're doing this.

'Need to move,' Blossom whispers hoarsely. And we take off again, running low along the prison wall, keeping close enough for me to bang my shoulder against it and I stifle a curse.

Just when I think I'm going to have to slow down, the burn of my legs and lungs just too much, the alcove appears. Although it's less an 'alcove' and more a hole hacked into the lower wall. We throw ourselves on to our knees in the shadows of the small space, barely having time to take in the thick bars that separate us from the inside of the other prison before two hands snake through them and forcefully grip the front of each of our shirts, dragging our knees through the dirt as we're pulled further into the alcove.

'Who the fuck are you?' a woman says, but the impact of my face striking the bars makes it sound like it's on repeat in my head.

'Friends of the Warden,' I get out as best I can with my cheek smashed against a cold bar.

'Which one?' she grinds out.

'Clau-Claudius,' I choke.

'Who sent you?' she spits.

'He did,' Blossom says, her voice matching the steel of the bars.

Slowly, the pressure on my face releases a bit and she lets us each go. I rub at my face and head as I watch her, watching us.

She's crouched in the alcove, slightly on her side, so it's hard to tell how tall she is, but the sleeveless shirt she wears shows her strong physique – if the tender spot on my forehead didn't already prove her strength. Her face is made up of hard lines, her lips pressed so firmly together they're almost white.

I try to shuffle myself into a more comfortable position, trying to ease the pinch in my side, and end up half pressed against Blossom in the process, the warmth of her skin seeping through my clothes.

The woman runs a hand over her shaved head – and a large, yellowing bruise – and lets out a huff.

'How do I know that?' she asks.

'Do you like strawberries?' Blossom asks, remembering the instructions from River.

The stranger narrows her eyes.

'What do you want?' she asks, slightly more resigned this time.

'There are things the Warden wanted us to do,' I say quietly, 'including making contact with you.'

Her expression doesn't change. 'That's a big claim.'

Blossom and I remain silent.

'One that will come with a cost should anyone get wind of it,' she says.

'I understand,' I say, keen to be the one who voices our acknowledgment and not Blossom.

She considers us for a moment, her head shifting from side to side as if she's sizing up her prey. My father told me many stories of Shaides in our family line but we haven't had any for generations, their skills so rare. As I look into the cold eyes of the woman staring back at us, I wonder if all people who can tear the fabric of the world to wield a portal are a little ... off balance.

'Claudius really sent you?' she asks.

'Yes,' I whisper, remembering the almost desperate – but trusting – look on his face when we talked about her. 'We worked together. I think he thought we could help each other ... I'm just not totally sure how. Or why.'

A jolt of genuine surprise lights her face. 'I appreciate your honesty. Do you have a name?'

My heart stammers a little harder in my chest. For a moment, I consider giving her a false one, but that could mean she doesn't help. Giving my real one means she could turn us in.

I swallow.

'Blossom.' Bloss holds her hand out to shake the other woman's.

'Luka,' I say quietly.

She shakes my hand after releasing Blossom's.

'Cortane Vixel.'

Cortane. I've turned her name over many times since that conversation with Claudius – it suits her. We look at each other a moment as I wonder what comes next. Cortane's hazel gaze is particularly assessing, even in the slight gloom of the alcove.

Cortane drops her hand from the stone wall, any flicker of softness fleeing from her. 'I don't know you – and I don't trust most of the people I do know. If you're who he wanted to do this, he had good reason. But those reasons are not my own, so you will have to prove yourself to me.'

There's a long silence. The slight rustling of the leaves in the dark behind us, beyond the light, makes my spine prickle with unease.

'What is it you want?' Blossom asks.

'I want the time and date of the next sporting event for the *guests* you serve,' Cortane says. I don't miss the poisonous emphasis she puts on 'guests'.

'That's all?' I ask.

'No,' she says before the question is completely out of my mouth, 'but this is how you start to prove I can trust you.'

Neither Blossom nor I answer. Details of the schedule are supposed to be strictly confidential beyond the concierge team ... but she hasn't asked about a particular prisoner or their movements, which is what is covered in our magical contracts, so we're not bound to secrecy in this case.

'How did you know Claudius?' I ask instead.

She slides her cold assessment to me and I suppress a shiver. 'That's a very personal question for a stranger.'

'Claudius wasn't a stranger to me,' I say, wishing my voice didn't sound so shaky.

Her smile is cold when it slips into place. 'And yet you have no idea why he's sent you here.'

I clear my throat, conscious of Blossom studying the woman in front of us.

'No,' I say. 'He died before he could share all that was relevant.'

The muscles in the sides of Cortane's face ripple, as if she's biting down – hard – on that knowledge, and I can't help but wonder what he could have shared well before now. What he could have done to prepare me somehow. Perhaps Cortane, too.

'We're risking a lot to even see you,' I say when it's clear she won't tell me their history. 'How do we know you're not just setting us up to join you in there?'

She grips the bars.

'You don't,' she spits. 'But Claudius obviously didn't want you in here, and I intend to see that through. If I decide I can trust you.'

At length, I finally say, 'Tuesday at eleven.'

'Come back after that and we'll talk about next steps,' she says, pushing herself up off the bars and leaving us alone.

Just like that, I feel like someone has torn a little portion of me in two and I separate the halves of me into the places left behind. Luka, the diligent concierge, and the other Luka, going against everything I have been taught about believing in the system for just a chance at a life with the people I love.

The run back over the light-moat is harder than the first because the sun is dancing at the bottom edge of the island, ready to take her throne for the day, and we have to move faster.

I shower quickly, washing the slight sweat from my body, redressing what remains of my cut – most of the stitches having now dissolved, leaving a faint scar – and putting on a lilac dress, the first I spot in the wardrobe. It's not my favourite, but I don't have time to be concerned with that now. I need to oversee the handover from the night staff, set the day's teams in motion, and meet with Quillian to take him through the day-to-day ministrations of the prison – all while trying to ignore the gnawing in the pit of my stomach at what will happen on Tuesday.

It's abundantly clear Claudius and Cortane were important to each other in some way. Even if he hadn't told me, it would be obvious now I've met her. But there was a coldness about her that makes me feel uneasy, an unpredictability that sets my teeth on edge.

The concierge room is bubbling with the chatter of people as Blossom and I arrive. The different teams devour the food the kitchen staff have laid out for us. For the day staff, it's a breakfast meeting. For the night, an opportunity for a dinner before they retire to their rooms. It's only the concierges here on these mornings, the Warden normally meets with the kitchen staff separately. Something I would help with at different times, but will now need to introduce Quillian to and see how he would like to manage things going forward.

It's a bit surreal to be thinking about the future operations of the prison when I am actively looking for a way out – an illegal one, at that. At least for Nix and River. Surely Traelen will come through for me when he ends my extension.

Janly is the most senior concierge from night shift and I ask her to brief me on anything I need to know while the others chat.

'Kasera is quite upset about the Warden,' she says, 'or so she claims. I've added an additional time slot to the wellness centre for her.' There's a look of distant distaste on her face but she continues before I can question it.

'The new prisoner, Finn, still hasn't really engaged with the others and only surfaced from his room once last night – sat with me for a cup of tea.' Her deep brown eyes brush over my face. 'He's quite a comforting presence, actually.'

I lift my brows at her and she just shrugs.

'People's true colours come out at night, when they're tired and lonely,' she says. 'He seems like one of the good ones.'

Blossom laughs gently with Emeris to our right, drawing Janly's attention.

'Someone less good,' she murmurs, 'was watching the younger ones carefully.'

'Davorous?' I ask, equally quiet.

She nods, her greying hair bobbing slightly around her face. 'Asking lots of questions about Blossom.' Turning her attention fully back to me she says, 'You need to watch that. I was going to report it to the Warden myself but ...' she trails off. 'Removing Bloss from his team was the right move, but I have a feeling it's not going to be enough. He's not a man to be turned down – especially by the help.'

A painful pit starts to open up in my belly, just beneath my fresh scar, and I look up at the board in front of us. I switched Blossom out of his team weeks ago but it's impossible to be completely isolated from the prisoners, as I should have thought more about when he asked her to dance.

Blossom will be mad at me for interfering, but I'll have to see what Quillian can do. Having Blossom available to Davorous is quickly becoming a hard no. If I was at all tempted to leave her here so she wasn't implicated in my sudden disregard for my service and my duty, the thought of her staying in arm's reach of Davorous makes it disappear in a puff of smoke.

'How's your load?' I ask as I look over the board. Taking in the photos on the left that show each concierge and their charges alongside the schedule. Janly's looks about the same as all of us, but my role has now shifted somewhat, at least temporarily.

'Fine,' she says, almost starting to bristle as if I'm about to critique her.

'How do you feel about having Finn added to you?'

Her hesitant face softens. 'He'd definitely be one of the easier ones you could give me.'

'Traelen has asked me to act as assistant to the new Warden until he's found his feet, so it's just temporary,' I say. 'A short stint, I'm sure.'

She's quiet for a moment, watching me. 'Have you met him yet?'

'The new Warden?'

She nods but doesn't offer anything more, and I wonder if she's feeling a strangeness about the replacement of Claudius.

'He seems nice, Jan,' I say, laying a hand on her arm. 'But Claudius will be a tough act to follow.'

Her sigh is deep in response.

'In so many ways,' she says softly.

The room quiets suddenly and I look over my shoulder to find Quillian has joined us. My body reacts before my brain as a flutter of butterflies takes flight behind my ribs and my cut seems to throb in time with their wings.

The concierges part as Quillian walks to the board, focused solely on me. His tall, wide form grows in my vision until I have to blink to clear my head. It's impossible to look into his dark-green eyes without remembering his gentle kindness in the clearing, his concern and guilt last night.

But Nix doesn't trust him, so I make myself look away until he reaches us. But my mind snags on the things – potentially a *lot* of things – Nix is keeping from me as I do.

'Sir,' I say, 'this is Janly.'

He inclines his head as she smiles in greeting, his short, dark hair swept back off his face.

'Janly primarily does night duty – by choice,' I say. 'I was just getting her thoughts on the shift.' He watches us closely as I talk, hands behind his back. I glance at Janly, wondering if I should continue, and he looks back at me expectantly. 'I've asked her to take my most recent allocation, Finn, but I can take—'

'No,' he cuts me off gently. 'If it's okay with you, Janly, I would like that prisoner to remain on your list. At least until I am up to speed.'

'Of course, sir,' Janly says.

She flicks her dark gaze back towards Blossom and shifts on her feet slightly.

'There is another matter I'd like to raise with you,' Janly says, 'but it's not one we should discuss here.'

Quillian's face doesn't change, but there's a guarded intensity in his stance as he looks at her.

'Luka is across it as well,' she says. 'Perhaps she can fill you in when you each have a quiet moment?'

I nod, taking care not to look at Blossom, and try not to notice the soft question in Quillian's face, the slight lifting of his brows.

The room is still quiet as Quillian steps forward again, thanking us as he moves past and turns so his back is to the board. Janly and I are still close to him, and now in the first row of his audience. I feel the attention of every concierge turn to him and the conversations die away completely.

'Good morning,' he says, lifting his voice so the whole room can hear him. 'I'm ... sorry for the circumstances that bring me to you. I know the previous Warden was a great man, and a wonderful leader.'

He looks around the room.

'I'm not looking to replicate him, but I will do my best to keep your duties here as pleasant as possible during my stay. You may know by now that Traelen has asked Luka to help me settle in, and I appreciate you all helping to pick up some of the load that will leave for others – like you, Janly.'

He looks straight at her and my eyes widen at the blush that rises on her cheeks. Along the crooked row of people, Blossom catches my eye, her lips turned up a fraction at the corner. I glance away quickly before mine do the same.

'I don't want to keep you from your rest or your work,' he says, 'so I will hand it over to Luka. But please, speak freely with me about any questions or concerns you have. I'm looking forward to working with you all.'

He takes a small step sideways, opening up a gap for me to stand next to him, and I slowly take that place. My heart hammers at having to address my colleagues in front of the new Warden. Quillian.

'Thank you, sir,' I say quietly and clear my throat. 'I've spoken with Janly,' I say, addressing the room, 'and the night went smoothly – nothing out of the ordinary to report. Traelen has asked that our schedule return to normal as of today.

'That means all prisoners will return to their individual routines as well. We have aerial yoga resuming in the gardens today, the sport contest on Tuesday, and we'll need to schedule the next evening event as soon as possible. I will leave it to the heads of each of those committees to put the wheels in motion again today. Can you each please report back to me within twenty-four hours?'

I look for the right nods through the group and make sure I don't look directly to my left, where a radiating heat is coming from Quillian. All my nerves stand on end at the knowledge he is watching my every move.

'Importantly,' I continue, 'Traelen has insisted that all the prisoners go back to enjoying their time here. The moment for ... mourning – unless it's a prisoner – in public has passed, I'm afraid.'

I watch the small sea of watchful faces look at Quillian as they absorb this news.

'Which just means,' he says, and I swear he was still looking at me until the moment I turned my head to look at him politely, 'you mourn as a group here, or privately. Please don't let that instruction diminish the different grief I know you will all be feeling. There will be a significant adjustment for some of you, for others less so. But we can be patient with each other.'

He looks expectantly at me but I shake my head. I have nothing further to add. I watch him as he turns back to the room, his kindness sweeping its way through me, and I can't help but think Nix has to be wrong about him, that Nix's constantly simmering, out of character anger, isn't the only thing that's off-kilter about my best friend. Maybe his judgement has suffered somehow, as well.

'Enjoy your day,' he says, and the room disperses, leaving me with Quillian.

'Where shall we start?' he asks.

CHAPTER ELEVEN

Quillian is particularly interested in the prisoners and their concierge allocations as I talk him through the board. I tried to go over the events I'd mentioned to the group, and what Traelen is likely to want to know at different times, but he simply nodded and asked more questions about the prisoners. Given he's now entirely responsible for them, I guess that's probably to be expected.

What I didn't expect was for him to ask me why so many of them were here – or for me to not be able to answer all of his questions.

'And this one?' he asks, pointing to Nix's photo.

It's a smiling one and my heart hitches at seeing it on the board. They only ever give us flattering photos of the prisoners for this wall, something that suddenly seems at odds with the man I am standing next to and his assessment of the 'prisoners'. But I remember the night the one of Nix was taken.

My pulse thrums in my ears as I try, not very successfully, to push away the memory of a night so long ago. When we both had hopes and dreams – none of which included being in a prison, regardless of how luxurious this one is.

Quillian's mouth parts gently, like he might ask a question, and I hurriedly forge on. The table he dragged over so we could sit in front of the board is small and I accidentally bump his elbow as I reach back for my still hot tea – enchanted never to cool down, which I adore.

'I wasn't there when he was transferred,' I say honestly. 'So I don't know what successes were announced when he arrived but,' I look away from the scorching intensity of the man next to me and focus on Nix's photo – reminding me why I have to lie even though the words are uncomfortable to form. 'I have seen him a few times here, he seems harmless. I believe he's here with his brother.' I point to the photo of River.

Quillian looks slowly back to the board. The sunlight streaming in the windows behind the board drenches him in warm light.

'And him?' The last photo he gestures to is Davorous, and I take a deep breath.

Glancing behind me, I lower my voice as I look back to the photo. His hair is a little more blonde in his photo compared to the silvering at the temples he has now. The mostly hazel eyes are a little like Cortane's except with a pale green fleck. But, staring into them now, my stomach churns in a very different way than the unease Cortane gave me.

'He's who Janly and I wanted to talk to you about,' I say, turning to Quillian.

He waits as I drop my gaze to the pale mug in my hands, its gold trim wearing only slightly, but still not good enough for use by the prisoners.

'I can't now remember the successes Traelen announced him with, he's been here about twelve months,' I say, trying not to let my mind linger too long on how Claudius would manage those intakes. 'But I think he's taking a bit too keen an interest in one of the concierges.'

His eyebrows lower. Just a fraction. But enough for me to know this news doesn't make him happy and that I'm right to tell him – he won't condone it.

'He was on Blossom's team initially—'

'Your friend from last night?'

'Yes. But he started to try and get too close. Nothing that warranted any action at that time, but I switched his concierge just to be sure.'

He nods.

'And Blossom has never been interested in the playroom or anything ... extra,' I say. 'So there's no way he could have received mixed signals. But,' I continue, 'Janly said he's been asking an unusual amount of questions of the other concierges about her. And he never fails to be near her when we have events, and I just ...'

I tuck my hair back from face and run the thick, straight strands through my hand as I lay the section over my shoulder before cupping my mug with both hands again.

He tracks the movement and looks back to my face.

'It's a vibe.' I'm struggling not to be self-conscious of my allegations but confident in them all the same. 'I don't think I'm wrong,' I say quietly. 'I don't think he should be allowed near her. Not unsupervised.'

'If I have learnt anything in my time, Luka, it's that you *never* ignore a woman's instincts in these situations. I'll make some amendments to security,' he says, his expression softening even as his eyes darken. 'We'll make sure she's protected.'

The tight ball that was gathering in my chest releases suddenly.

'Thank you, sir.' I lower my mug into my lap, watching the overhead light catch in the surface of the steaming tea. Quillian's large hand finds my forearm and I soak in the difference in the depth of his skin tone compared to mine as his heat warms my arm, willing it not to reach my face.

'Luka,' he says quietly, waiting until I look up at him.

My heart clenches when I meet his serious gaze.

'Please ... just call me Quillian.'

As we leave the concierge room, and I show Quillian around, his demeanour starts to frost over. It's less of a tour than introducing him to the individual teams that run different aspects of the prison: kitchen, cleaning, and maintenance, among others. Each of the concierges greets him politely, enquires after his health, and agrees to keep him informed of anything of relevance.

And each time we talk to the concierges, he is polite in return, albeit reserved.

But as we wander the halls, his expression is flat, and dark, and he doesn't even pretend to smile. Multiple prisoners attempt to engage him in conversation, ignoring me wherever they can, but the most they receive is a short grunt before he indicates to me to carry on.

Outside the library entrance, Kasera walks towards us dabbing at her cheeks.

'Afternoon, Quillian,' she says in her slightly lilting voice. 'Luka,' she says, grey eyes turning to me.

'Kasera,' I say, 'it's lovely to see you.' I glance at Quillian who says nothing but watches us engage. 'How are you holding up?'

She sniffs delicately.

'As well as can be expected, I imagine,' she says. 'But I should like to go home and leave this awful place and its reminders.' She sniffs again and fluffs the wavy, dark blonde hair out of her face, increasing its height.

'It's a privilege you get to go home at all.' Quillian's voice is quiet and lethal when he talks to her. A shiver runs down my spine.

Kasera's face changes colour but she assesses him like an animal of prey, any sadness in her gone altogether. Replaced by something very different. Something harder. I stare at her. What happened to the grieving prisoner?

'You will do well to remember your place ... Quillian.'

I think the lack of calling him Warden is supposed to upset him, but there's nothing that indicates it's struck a nerve.

'Oh, I do,' he says simply, and gestures for me to lead the way, past Kasera.

A fraction of the light returns to his face when he looks at me, my feet rooted to the spot. I watch him blink slowly at me and remember what I need to do.

We don't talk for the rest of the short walk to the music room, but Quillian doesn't thaw. I scramble for what to say but find nothing to fill the space. I glance at him every few paces but, while I feel him looking at me every now and then, I don't catch him and we fall into a companionable quiet.

A stray white light bobs down the hallway to us just before I hear the sound of the musicians practising. We pause at the door of the small room, its walls almost hugging the group and giving maximum listening pleasure.

The room is full of dancing lights and I can't help but sigh as I listen. My mouth wants to draw up into the smile the sound normally elicits from me, but the dark cloud that has been Quillian forces me to restrain myself. Despite the ease of his company, dark cloud or not.

Until I glance at him and find him equally mesmerised.

His gaze latches onto mine when he finds me looking. All the hardness in his face melts away and he smiles softly. The new violinist, whose name I still don't know, catches us watching from the doorway and cocks his head, a grin on his face.

I watch him, forcing myself not to look back at Quillian as the white and yellow lights weave amongst each other, floating towards the ceiling. As the violinist keeps watching us, a handful of lights change direction. I hold out a hand to let one dance on my palm and it scurries along my arm and around my neck, shooting to the sky as I try to follow its direction.

A second light, a bass note, dances before Quillian, just in front of his nose before joining mine at the ceiling. As the musicians reach their crescendo, the remaining lights near us spin around our ankles, the skirt of my dress swaying slightly. Lazily, they spin around the two of us until the violinist winks and a laugh bubbles from my throat.

Quillian smiles broadly at me, the dimple on his left cheek pushing so deep into his skin I have to close a gentle fist to stop from pressing the pad of my finger to it.

The music dies away as Quillian watches me.

'I think it's fair to say they've got this under control?' he asks.

'Agreed.' I laugh, the shift in mood warming me on the inside.

The smile on my face is hard to hide as we make our way to the Warden's office – now Quillian's office. I can't deny Quillian's own dimpled smile has something to do with my lifted mood, but knowing he is now aware of Bloss's situation, and going to help, brings a lightness back to my steps. A lightness I hadn't realised was starting to disappear, even if the weight of responsibility for Nix and River still drags at me.

I hesitate a fraction at the white timber door.

'We don't have to go in if you prefer?' Quillian asks.

But I shake my head, trying to clear the vision of the Warden lying across his desk.

Unresponsive.

Dead.

I blink rapidly.

'No,' I say, clearing my throat, 'it will need to be sometime ... might as well be now.'

I open the door, perhaps a little more forcefully than necessary, and let Quillian close it behind us. My attention lands on the desk and I look away quickly, fighting the sting beneath my lashes.

'So,' I say, clearing my throat, conscious of the watchful study of the new Warden, 'I wasn't really involved in much of the work the Warden did in here. I wasn't actually an assistant,' I add, unsure if he knows I haven't done this before. I let my attention wander the room a little, but it's constantly dragged back to Quillian. It's both unsettling and comforting that, apart from the loss of Claudius and the addition of the man now here with me, it's exactly as it's always been. I wonder what Claudius thought of Quillian. What he would have thought about him taking on this role.

'So,' I ask carefully, 'you knew the Warden – sorry, the former Warden – Claudius. Were you told anything about the ... circumstances of the vacancy?'

His shoulders drop a little but he remains standing in the room, watching me. Assessing me.

'I was,' he says, 'I was incredibly saddened to hear of his passing. He leaves a big hole here to fill, I can see.'

My throat thickens at the obvious emotion in his voice.

'You – you said you knew him in a number of ways,' I say, thinking back to our conversation in the meadow. 'Did he tell you anything about how things work here?'

Quillian cocks his head but there's only warmth in his features. Nothing like the expression he gave Kasera.

'Nothing that would have been outside his contract.'

Of course, I think.

'Okay, how about Traelen?' I ask. 'Perhaps we can start wherever he left off to get you up to speed?'

He smiles at me and my stomach starts to fizz.

'Traelen,' he says, moving towards the couches, 'congratulated me on the role, signed my contract, and told me to find you.'

'Oh,' I say, both disappointed at the lack of answers about Claudius that Quillian obviously has, and surprised at Traelen's apparent complete faith in what I can tell Quillian in a handover. 'I guess ... that just leaves you and me.'

'That's—' he starts but is cut off by the low chime of the gold phone.

'Oh,' I say, 'I can just ...' I step towards the door.

'No, stay,' he says and lifts the smaller part of the phone to his head. His gaze holds mine as he answers and listens, and I wonder if I should look away. Belatedly, I note he didn't seem at all confused as to how to use the Warden's antique device.

'Transfer?' he asks, and I think I might choke. Panic rips through my veins as I make myself breathe and struggle to keep my face impassive.

I knew Traelen could organise Nix and River to be sent to the other side at any time, but I'd hoped it wouldn't be so soon. Not with everything—

'Of course,' Quillian says, still watching me.

'We've got another intake tomorrow,' he says, placing the speaking part of the phone back in the cradle.

I press a hand to my sternum, almost unable to contain the loud exhale that pushes at my lips.

'So,' I say again, trying not to sound strangled, 'I'm not really sure what I can show you in here. Obviously that phone connects you to Traelen.'

He nods and I take the moment to let my heart rate settle. The thought of Nix and River in the other prison – and out of reach – makes me physically ill. Tomorrow night I can go back to Cortane and take the next step forward. As soon as she knows the sporting event has gone ahead when I said it would.

'And I'm sure there are important files and records in the desk,' I say. 'We also have a records room I can show you if you like?'

'Not yet, but thank you.'

I look around, trying to ignore the window Blossom and I crept through. Looking away, I survey the shelves in the room – how much of what they contain will Quillian want to throw away? An old picture frame catches my eye, one the Warden talked to me about once, and I wonder if I could ask Quillian not to get rid of it?

'The tipples,' he says suddenly. 'Do all the concierges take them?'

'Yes, it's part of our contract. Every day, we take the three of them.'

'So no concierges have active magic?'

'Not while they're here,' I say. 'Some may have manifested before they were assigned, but it's not active while we have the dampener, no. There are some other staff that are exempt – our Arkanan healers, and Koko, who uses her Clayti magic to enchant the food and drink are the most obvious.'

We stand awkwardly in the bookshelf lined room.

'Did you?' he asks.

'Manifest?' I ask in return, the surprise in my voice making me cringe a little. I know that's what he meant but my mind stalls for some reason. It seems ... personal to ask about someone's manifestation.

'No,' I say, before he can respond.

'So you don't know what you are?'

The question is blunt but it cuts straight to the core of me quicker than a knife.

'No,' I repeat, a little harder. 'And there's no guarantee I ever will.'

I don't tell him that's not all that's not guaranteed, but also my lack of belonging. The closest thing I have to a home is a prison I now live in temporarily, on an island, totally isolated from my previous home. One my extension will see me leave in some undefined period of time.

'But I know what you are.' My words surprise me as well as him.

He grimaces and rubs the back of his head. 'That's probably not hard, given you've experienced my wings first hand.'

I hum in acknowledgement but give him a small smile. 'Claudius even had a book about your kind in here somewhere,' I say, remembering Blossom's chatter the night we broke in.

A gleam appears in his eyes. 'I can assure you, it won't tell you everything.'

'Who says I want to know everything?'

My palms tickle with the lie.

He moves from behind the desk to lean against the side closest to me, crossing his arms over his chest and examining my face. I stay where I am, a few feet inside the closed door. Watching him from across the small sitting area.

The corner of his mouth lifts. 'I think you've just told me a lie, Luka.'

I curse the warmth I can feel coursing across my cheekbones, but I won't commit.

'Perhaps I do have one question,' I say.

He tilts his head.

'Will I get to see them again?'

His brows shoot up as he barks a laugh. 'Would you want to?' Disbelief drips from his tongue.

He doesn't move but the room suddenly feels so much smaller, something in my chest going taut and trying to drag me over to where he stands.

I can't stop from drifting my hand over my stomach where Quillian stitched me up, recalling the sensation of his on my skin. The hint of a suggestion that he might invite me for a drink at some point. I bite the inside of my lip as a deep flutter seems to settle in the sides of my torso.

'They seemed quite beautiful before they turned deadly,' I say.

He makes a non-committal sound in his throat and his fingers tighten on his arms where they're still crossed. I take the opportunity of quiet, open study to look at the breadth of him and the tattoo that runs up his neck and disappears at both ends. One into his shirt, the other into his short hair line behind his ear.

I still can't work out what it is. A mass of shimmering black shapes, hints of colour teasing me.

'I suppose they can be beautiful in the right circumstances,' he says.

'And what would they be?'

Those deep green eyes move along my body slowly, starting at my toes, covering every inch of me. Prickling until he reaches my face and assesses what he finds there.

'It depends,' he says finally. Quietly. 'But, generally, a Karaylia's wings are very personal. Part of the reason I was on edge was Traelen ordered me to have them out – a show of strength cred authority apparently. Unless they are in weaponised form, or being used for mobility ... they would normally only appear when their owner feels completely themselves, and at ease.'

None of this is news to me. Karaylia might be relatively rare but it would have been impossible for me to not pick at least this much up from my father's teachings – and River's awkwardness as his wings started to come in. But, still, I can't help the wicked smile that graces my face. Or the way my toes want to curl in my sandals at my audacity.

'So ... that's not a "no" then,' I say.

He stares at me so long I don't think he's going to answer. My stomach skitters but I refuse to look away.

'Not a "no",' he whispers hoarsely. 'And that was two questions.'

I throw my hands wide gently, pursing my lips briefly. 'Ask away.'

'Oh, I will,' he smiles back at me, swirling my already spinning stomach. 'I'm just going to save them for when we have that drink.'

My cheeks are positively aching when I leave Quillian's office for the day and head back to my apartment. The last of the day's sun rays are slowly creeping away from the stone halls and the arches are darkening. Preparing to show their views of the stars instead of the sky.

'Lu!' A fierce whisper echoes from the walkway I've just passed and I stifle a squeal.

Spinning on my heel, I find Nix filling the space and my grin falters momentarily before growing wide once more. Forcing myself not to glance behind me like I'm doing something wrong, I walk towards him and find myself alone with Nix in the second walkway. The one that leads to the receiving hall with the painting of the woman. Absurdly, a vision of me draped seductively over a couch enters my mind and I brush it away. No way I could pull that off without looking pained.

'Hey,' I say, still grinning.

'You're happy today,' he says, but his own smile is faint.

'Got to take the joy when you can find it, Nix,' I say. 'It's not ideal that either of us are here, but it's a lot better than having you on the other side of the island.' Now, I do glance around. 'Then I'd have a much harder time working out how to help you,' I whisper.

He takes my hands in his and pulls me closer. 'I've missed you, Luka.' His voice is almost nothing but air. 'I—honestly, I wish you weren't here, though, involved in any of this. These people ... Cortane is as far as you go. Please stay away from everything else.'

The heaviness in Nix's voice presses against my skin and he looks at me, gaze full of all the things he can't seem to say. Tears prickle my eyes as I wonder again what has made him so sad. So angry. I don't miss that he mentioned Cortane's name to me – is that not covered by his contract? But it's clear there is much more pain underneath what he can't say than just his relationship with Cortane.

'This – whatever you're doing here – is it the end of your duty?' I ask him quietly, knowing that I will do anything to ease the hurt that's so firmly under his skin.

'Yeah,' he breathes. 'One way or another.'

CHAPTER TWELVE

I glance up and down the concierge wing as I leave, thankful there is a separate Warden residence on the island, before making my way to the prisoners' lounge. The growing hold Quillian is having on my senses needs some preparation before I see him. Blossom started without me today, my adjusted role meaning I don't have quite the same adhesion to shift hours – I just seem to be always on now.

My normal gold sandals are done up to my knees, criss-crossing my calves and shins as they journey up, only to be mostly hidden by my long uniform. Selecting it had taken me a little longer than normal this morning and I avoided all lilac – that colour really doesn't do anything for me. Instead, I chose a soft sage that plays to my green eyes. Its wide shoulder straps have a second piece that cups the tops of my arms, a small section of my shoulders peeking out in between. It's one of my favourites, almost making me feel more like a guest here than someone serving her country.

I tell myself the extra effort is for my new role in assisting Quillian – and making sure Traelen can see how deserving I am of the recommendation he now holds. It's nothing at all to do with how Quillian's face lit up as we talked yesterday.

The lounge is quiet when I wander in; a small smattering of prisoners drape themselves along the lounges and I swallow a small grin. There is definitely only a certain kind of person who can look good draped on the edge of a couch like the gold-framed painting. And I'm not sure Emeris's charges are it.

Davorous and Finn play chess in one of the window tables which is ... unusual. One, because Finn is interacting with someone, and two, because Davorous's competitive streak means he is normally first in line for all sports and should be preparing for darts in the smoking room.

Until I see Blossom making her way to him with a drink in hand.

Asshole.

As I move towards Bloss, Finn stands, putting himself between Davorous and her, taking the drink himself and handing it to Davorous. Davorous schools his scowl into a thankful grimace as Finn resumes his seat and gestures for Davorous to make his move.

'I need you in the other room,' I say to Blossom when I get within earshot.

She says nothing but walks with me out of the prisoner lounge. We're just about through the door when I look back at Finn and Davorous and both men are watching us leave.

Davorous with a murderous look on his face.

Finn gives me a subtle nod I'm not sure how to interpret. In all my time here, I don't recall a single prisoner going out of their way – subtly or otherwise – to help a concierge. At least not when there wasn't a direct benefit for them.

'I hate that man,' Blossom fumes when we're in the hall that runs the internal courtyard.

'Bloss,' I say hesitantly, 'please don't be mad—'

She stops dead and looks at me.

'You realise starting a sentence like that doesn't exactly make me relaxed.'

'I know, I just – I told Quillian about him.'

'Quillian?' she asks, her tone a touch wary. 'Since when are you on a first name basis with the new Warden?'

I can feel the flush starting to run up my neck and her brows shoot upwards.

'I guess he's quite attractive ...' she says evenly, her face shuttering, and then frowns. 'Although ... you do seem to have a penchant for men with blades. Is that going to be something I have to watch?'

'Blossom!' I yank her to the side of the walkway where it feels more private. It's not, but gives the illusion of it.

Her face is serious when she looks up at me. One of her perfect, brown brows lifts and she sighs. 'Okay,' she says, seeming to make an effort to shake off whatever worry caught her for a moment. Perhaps the thought of me being romantically entangled with a new Warden when we're in contact with a Vanan prisoner. And Nix and River. 'I know it's been a long time since that forest party—'

I cover her mouth with my hand and she huffs a half-hearted laugh, pushing me away.

'Do not finish that sentence.' I point a finger at her.

'Seriously, though,' she says with a sad smile, 'please be careful. He's ...' she looks behind herself quickly, 'he's the Warden and ... close to Traelen.'

I don't know what else I can say to that but, 'Okay.' I know him being Warden is risky given what we're doing with Cortane, that's not news, so I wait. Wait for her to finally address what this conversation was actually supposed to be about.

'Thank you,' she says finally. 'I should have done it myself ...' she trails off.

'You're not angry?'

'No, Luka, I'm not angry.' She all but rolls her eyes. 'You know how I feel about this. It's me now, one day it would be someone else. He can't be allowed to cross any lines.'

She takes my hand and pulls us back into the centre of the walkway. 'At least I now know he won't be at darts. Speaking of, do you think we'll find out why Cortane wanted the timing details?'

'I assume so she can confirm if we are giving correct information and, therefore, trustworthy?'

Blossom hums gently. 'But that would assume she could verify it somehow, how is she going to do that from the other side?'

The hubbub from the smoking room drifts out to meet us and into the sky. I look out at the blue abyss that surrounds us as we walk. Apart from the prison on an island part, I imagine this is how my father spent a lot of his days – in a nice suit, dark room full of haze, talking about every possible theory and philosophy about our magic, our society, our world.

Constantly calculating how to bring some of the most disparate elements of our government services together for the good of the country.

Knowing we are now too close to the smoking room to continue our conversation about Cortane, I let Bloss's question hang. But it bounces around my mind with no particular direction – just another piece of a partial thought I don't know what to do with.

Clearly understanding the same restriction of conversation, Blossom asks what we need to do for the darts session.

'The committee has most of it covered,' I say. 'I just need to check they are on schedule for lunch, and see if Quillian has any questions or changes I need to take care of. This one was set up how Claudius liked to run them, but I imagine any new Warden would like to put their own stamp on things.'

Blossom cocks a brow at me.

'As nice as that might be,' she whispers with careful emphasis for me to know full well what she's actually referring to, 'I think it's best not to ... *blur* anything until we're done here. Until you know *exactly* what everyone's intentions are.'

I glance at her, but there's no jesting on her face. 'There's nothing to blur, Bloss, I know my place.'

But as we continue towards the noise, I realise how much I wish that wasn't true. I want a 'place', sure, but I also want to be free to blur whatever lines I see fit. And as wonderful as it feels to make Quillian smile, my time for that is on the mainland – certainly not with the Warden of my prison.

As for his intentions—

A scream rips through the stone hall.

'What?' Blossom gasps.

We both break out into a run, our sandals slapping on the stone.

The smoking room is full of a fog that drifts towards the ceiling, oblivious to the turmoil underneath. Prisoners scatter themselves to the outer edges of the room, some panicked, others watching greedily. Two concierges, one of them Emeris, kneel over a body near the bar.

One of the young girls, who trained under Janly, starts ushering the prisoners out and sends another concierge away. I assume with a message to the kitchens to get lunch on earlier than expected – at least, that's what I would do.

I don't see Nix or River, and a rivulet of ice trickles down my back as Blossom and I approach Emeris. His lean body obscures most of the top half of a person from view but the legs don't belong to either Nix or River, nor do they wear a concierge uniform, and I can't help the furious wash of relief.

'Emeris?' I say, voice steadier than I feel as we get closer, and he leans back, shaking his head.

Exposing Kasera.

Unmoving.

A dart lodged in her eye.

Cortane, I think as bile charges up my throat.

I look wildly at Blossom, her normally radiant skin paling rapidly. She grips my hand as I think my knees might give and digs her nails in. The room spins around me, the faces of the prisoners and concierges blurring.

The Warden – I should find Claud—

A crushing weight lands on my shoulders. No Claudius. This is my mess to fix.

I try to turn on the spot, dragging on Blossom's hand, but she pulls me forward again.

And it's not Claudius's warm gaze that comes into focus, but a green one instead.

Dark, dark green.

Creases line his forehead above his brows where they furrow.

'Luka?' he asks and, absently, I notice him look to Blossom. 'Are you two okay?'

I don't register her response. Isn't it odd to be asking how we are when Kasera has just had a terrible, terrible accident?

'Luka,' he says again, stepping forward and taking my elbow in his hand. Anchored by Blossom on one side and Quillian on the other, gradually, the rest of the room comes back into focus.

But the bitter taste in the back of my throat remains.

'I'm okay,' I say softly, releasing Blossom's hand. 'I'm okay.' I look sideways at her but she's recovered faster than me and is already peering down at Kasera.

'What happened?' she asks, glancing around as the room empties.

Slowly, Quillian's hand drops away from my arm, and I step forward after Blossom. Kasera's body is lying awkwardly where she's fallen, her long skirt tangled in her legs and one arm high above her head. The carpet is wet where her drink has been spilled, the glass still intact. Blood runs from the corner of her left eye, into her hair and the carpet.

I press my fingers to my mouth as if that will stop the rising wave of queasiness.

'I don't really know,' Emeris says to Blossom. 'One second we were all playing darts, the next she's on the ground. Magnolina always does throw wide, but I–I just never expected this.'

My stomach clenches as the coppery scent of Kasera's blood finds me, and I drop my hand, breathing forcefully through my mouth.

I look up at Quillian, who's now talking quietly to Emeris, his calculating gaze running everywhere in the room but Emeris's face. Every now and then it flicks back to me, as if he's checking on me, and my chest aches at what is quickly starting to feel like a betrayal of him.

Fuck. Could this really be just an accident? If not ... exactly what has Claudius got me into?

'Finn.' Quillian's tone is a command and it startles me that any prisoners are still here, let alone being invited in.

Blossom narrows her eyes at him before she and Emeris each look at me as if expecting me to give some sort of instruction, uncertainty flickering across their features. Finn strolls across the space, not sparing Kasera another glance as he approaches Quillian and Emeris – Davorous nowhere to be seen.

'You two,' Quillian says, gesturing to the two men, 'take her to the wellness centre. The healers there will tend to her body.'

'Blossom,' he says, and she wipes her forehead with the back of her hand before she nods at him. 'Are you able to check in on the rest of the teams and supervise lunch?'

She looks between Quillian and me.

'Yes, sir,' she says.

'Koko will have the food ready,' I tell her. 'Ask her to serve up some special silver bubbles – that will take any edge off for the prisoners.'

'Perhaps ask one of the singers for a performance as well,' Quillian says. 'The violinist is also good at solos, if needed.'

She gives Quillian a long look before turning towards me, her back almost completely to Quillian. 'You okay here?' she asks quietly, taking my hands, Quillian's watchfulness still taking me in over her shoulder. 'I'm not sure—'

I glance up at Quillian. 'Yes,' I whisper, 'we'll talk later. Can you see if you can check on ... the others?'

I'm sure she will understand I mean Nix and River – I already know how Emeris is, and I will check in on the other concierges later when I have to do a debrief with them. I don't have to tell her not to mention our visit with Cortane and the information I gave over, but my mind is whirling with the implications. Claudius told me to make contact with Cortane, give her information. Now, a prisoner is dead.

'Of course,' she says after a moment, giving my hands one last squeeze before I watch her leave, the pink dress she wears trailing after her.

As Finn and Emeris ready Kasera's body for moving, I drop into the closest seat, already thinking of what to say to the concierge teams. Quillian hasn't dismissed me, or given me another task, but I can't bring myself to leave either. My mind is void of any excuses I could have to not be here.

But it's not empty of questions. The loudest being: how the fuck did Cortane manage this? Did she portal here? Is this why she's so dangerous – she just portals where she likes and kills people? Why would Claudius have been happy for me to release her as well? Why Kasera?

I press my fingers into my temples and close my eyes, resting my elbows on the dark timber table, its surface sticky on my skin.

I don't watch as Finn and Emeris carry Kasera away, Emeris grunting slightly under her weight.

'Luka,' I glance up from the table top to find Quillian crouched in front of me. 'Will you come to the office with me, please?'

It seems like the easiest question to answer. So easy, I just give him a shallow nod as I stand, Quillian copying the action a moment later, unfurling to his full height in front of me. I follow him from the room silently. I wonder if he has had to deal with a similar situation before. I certainly haven't, and I have no idea how best to support him through it as the Warden responsible.

'Warden,' one of the newer prisoners – Zenaton Blake, I think, snaps as we cross the hall outside the smoking room. 'What are you doing about Kasera's death? The perpetrator must be punished. It was Magnolina wasn't it?'

Quillian's gaze slides sideways to Zenaton. 'No details are being discussed at this time,' he says, walking on.

'The Prime Minister will be hearing of this!' Zenaton calls after us.

CHAPTER THIRTEEN

Quillian doesn't respond to Zenaton's threat. Just keeps pace with me, a slower one than I imagine is his normal, until we reach his office.

He shuts the door quietly behind us and moves towards the bookshelf. The buzzing sound in my ears rises several notches in the quiet.

I clear my throat a little, remembering I am supposed to be showing him the ropes here. I just didn't think it would involve how to manage a death I caused. I swallow. Walking further in the comfortable room, I head for the small settee.

'You'll need to advise Traelen,' I say, the tremor in my voice now definitely audible. 'Ideally before Zenaton, or anyone else, gets word to him or the Prime Minister first. The ... burial won't be here, so we won't need to organise that like I did for Claudius. Then—' my hands flutter around me.

In three steps, Quillian crosses the space between Claudius's bookshelf and where I sit.

Wordlessly, he hands me a small tumbler full of dark, amber liquid. Our fingers brush slightly as I take it and the contact surprises me. I thought I was numb. His chiseled face is open and kind when I meet his gaze but I can't bring myself to tell him what I've done. Part of me thinks I should pay for my actions. But telling him I met with Cortane, gave her sensitive information, implicates both Claudius and Blossom.

'You're meant to drink it,' he says gently, gesturing towards the cold glass in my hand. 'It will calm you.'

I inhale the heady scent first, trying to clear the smell of blood that remains in my nose, and my eyes water. An actual tear escapes when I drag the flaming hot liquid into the depths of my stomach.

'Sorry,' I say, placing the engraved glass back in his waiting hand, 'I'm not normally the fainting, freaking out type, but that was my second dead body in, what? A week? And there was ... blood ...' I swallow.

'Not normal for you?' he asks.

'Would it be for you?' I ask back before I register it was probably supposed to be a joke.

A flicker runs over his face.

'What did you do before you came here?' I ask, a tiny warning sounding in the back of my mind. A reminder that Nix and River know him somehow. That he put them here. That Blossom isn't distrusting of him, exactly, but ... conscious of him.

'More of the same,' he says.

I scan his face as he sits next to me on the couch, turned completely to me. As if his entire being is focused on me. Very different to how his attention was on every detail in the room as he spoke to Emeris. Assessing every movement, each word spoken around him. Every look. Now the still intensity of that focus is wholly on me.

My skin heats under the attention and I try not to squirm.

'I know this is hard, Luka,' he says and his voice washes over me. 'But ... she wasn't a good person.'

I frown at him. 'How do you know?' I ask, hating the way the weight of the guilt lessens a bit at his declaration.

He studies me so long I almost think he's not going to answer me. But there's a decision happening beneath the surface, so I wait him out.

'Are you not at all aware of why these people are here? It is a prison after all,' he says, watching me carefully. 'Even if it is a fucking joke of one.'

All the words and questions that were previously running through my mind suddenly vacate. I look at where his right arm rests stiffly along the back of the couch, following the limb up to his shoulder and find myself distracted by trying to decipher his tattoo again. There's something about its dancing shapes and colours I want to unpack. But Kasera's death has taken its toll and I can't focus on it and his question as well. As I let myself look back to his face, I realise he's waiting.

Not only for my response, but for my judgement.

My opinion.

'Why do you say that?' I ask.

His shoulders relax slightly, perhaps that I haven't immediately recoiled from his traitorous words as I should – I *should* be defending my service here, yet I'm not. But the tension still runs in his muscles and the fingers that grip the red fabric of the Warden's couch.

'Can I trust you, Luka?' he asks plainly.

My stomach bottoms out. Claudius trusted me. Blossom, Nix and River trust me.

But as I search his face, the way he is openly searching me in return, I know he can trust me. I want him to trust me. And I will do everything I can not to betray that trust.

I just don't know how to achieve that and make sure Nix and River don't end up inmates alongside Cortane.

'Of course,' I say, desperately wanting it to stay true.

His body doesn't completely relax but he shifts a fraction closer to me and drops his elbows to his knees. The navy pants of his uniform rise up at the ankles slightly, his pale blue shirt pulling across the top of his shoulders.

Up this close, I can see his nose isn't quite straight. A short lock of his deep-brown hair falls across his forehead and my fingers twitch with the temptation to reach out and brush it out of the way.

'Traelen, or anyone else, for that matter,' he says, 'would have me imprisoned somewhere far worse than this island if they knew I was having this conversation with you.'

'Okay ...' I say. My response is soft but it doesn't stop my imploring gaze, waiting for more, nor the increasing beat of my heart, begging to be part of this secret.

'You are told of their successes when they arrive. But every one of these prisoners is here for a legitimate reason. Mostly sick, disturbing reasons.' He pauses, watching me.

My mind immediately fills with an image of Davorous watching Blossom.

'Go on,' I prompt, frozen in my seat.

'The only farce is how they are treated up here.'

'Every one of them?' The faces of Nix and River dance in front of me and my stomach starts to churn. But then I no longer believe there was an actual sentence – or a real one – that got them here.

He exhales gently.

'All those who have been sentenced here should be somewhere worse.' He pushes the hair out of his face. 'So don't mourn Kasera like you do the Warden, I promise she's not worth it.'

My heart warms at his concern for me and then I hate myself a little more that it's someone's death that brought it on. But he's right, I've always known there were reasons they were here but, having never been allowed to ask about them, I moved on.

I took the easy way. The route that made my time here easier, serving them easier.

'Can you tell me what she did?' My voice is barely above a whisper and I can't believe the words have actually left my lips. Do I really want to know?

He studies me for a moment.

'It goes no further.' It's a statement but I understand his meaning and I nod. 'She purchased two children and raised them as her slaves. Their conditions were ... not good.'

My breath leaves me in a hurry, replaced by a white-hot fury just as quickly.

'I don't—shit, that's ... awful.' 'Awful' feels completely inadequate, but my mind is spinning.

'Yes. But equally bad is this joke of a punishment.'

He stares at me and I can only hold his gaze in return. The two of us locked in a moment of shared horror, one of us waiting for the other to catch up and ...

'What do we do?' I ask, and his eyebrows almost meet the ceiling.

'You ... would want to do something?'

I frown. Why wouldn't I? 'Of course. That's ...' I trail off, looking for something that will convey what is starting to take shape in my mind. 'If they have all done something that ... abhorrent, I can't—we can't—they can't *be* here.'

Quillian's lips part as he blows out a breath I can feel softly on my face.

'Fuck,' he mutters running a hand down his face. 'No. You,' he says, looking me full in the face, 'will finish your extension and leave. Live your life.'

I continue watching him, pursing my lips as I think over what to tell him. Wondering how much is safe in this moment he's creating by trusting me. Wondering how in the world Kasera ended up here instead of Vana.

'I wasn't extended,' I say, pausing for a moment. 'I wasn't collected.'

We both jump as the chime on the gold phone pierces into the room. He lets it go for a moment longer than necessary, staring at me.

'Quillian,' he growls into the handpiece when he reaches the desk. The couch gently moves back into position next to me, erasing the depression where he sat. 'Thank you. That time suits for Luka and me to give our regular check-in. Though I have an update for Traelen now. Can you please advise him one of the prisoners has passed away?'

There's a pause.

'Of course. Her name was Kasera and the healers are currently preparing her for transfer back to the Zanteera mainland for her family.'

I watch from my position, running the soft fabric of the couch fiercely under my fingernails as Quillian goes through the details with Traelen's office. Somehow, the spinning of my mind slows a little when I look at him.

My next steps are clear. Get through today, confront Cortane.

Quillian replaces the handpiece into the cradle and I listen to its soft *clunk*, not dissimilar to the sound of my empty tipple glasses finding the bench. He walks back to me slowly and holds out a hand. I take it without hesitation and tug against him slightly as I stand.

His focused attention singes my cheeks as I look up at him. He seems taller than I noticed before, but he's not that much taller than Nix. As my heart now aches for the children Kasera has hurt so badly, I find any feeling of guilt has almost completely left me. Did Cortane also know what she'd done?

'What happened to the children?' I ask, not sure how I will cope with the answer.

'They were placed into special care, somewhere far from here. Somewhere they are ... more accustomed to trauma and helping people through it. Their lives will be forever changed now. But it will give them the best chance to move forward. It's not a great solace,' he says, 'but I hope ...'

'It did,' I say. 'I feel ... like I should feel bad about how little I now care about Kasera, but I do feel better.'

Quillian holds my gaze in a way that fills me up with something I don't know the name of. Something quiet and overwhelming. Something unyielding, yet unsure, and I soak it in.

'Unless that's just the whiskey,' I say into the thickness gathering around us, this almost tangible shift in whatever is growing between us with what he's shared.

Quillian's mouth quirks, just slightly in one corner, the hint of his dimple teasing me, asking me to make it appear completely.

'Maybe,' he says, 'I did say it would calm you. But it wasn't *the* drink. I'd still like to do that.' His voice is quiet and there's a question in his features he's not voicing.

'Me too,' I whisper. Even if my chest twinges with what Nix will think. What Quillian will think when he knows I am meeting with Cortane. But there is nothing in me that can find a way to say no.

The hard stare Cortane levels me with gives me a moment's pause, but I don't back down. Kasera was killed – by a dart to the fucking eye – and it's entirely possible, likely even, it was because of the information I gave Cortane. I don't know why the sporting event was significant. Perhaps it wasn't. But Magnolina 'throwing wide' as Emeris claims just feels like far too much of a coincidence to be true. Claudius told me Cortane is a Shaide, that she can portal, said he would make sure her magic dampeners weren't being given – or taken, whatever.

And I told her when the event was.

It doesn't feel like a big leap to think she killed Kasera based on my information. As much as Quillian's claims assuage any guilt I feel about Kasera herself, knowing that I played a key role in her death shifts uncomfortably in my gut.

'I asked you how you did it?' I ask again.

She continues studying me, her hazel eyes narrowed.

'And I'm thinking that's a question people like you don't normally ask first,' she says, her voice as cold as the bars between us. 'People like you normally ask *why*, which makes me wonder if you're more like me than I'd guessed.'

I scoff. But I need to know if she *can* actually portal out of Vana. Because, if Claudius has managed the stoppage of her magic dampener and she can, then we're a step closer to getting Nix and River with her next time.

When I first saw them here I thought there must have been a mistake. Now, however vague my understanding of what they're doing here is, I know it's connected to a picture much bigger than the one I can currently see. One I'm now highly suspicious Kasera is – was – part of. Right now, the best I can do is secure them a way off the island and out of reach of Vana – and hope I can find a way around the wards that surround the island so they don't spend the rest of their lives on the run.

A cold shiver slides down my back as I consider how blatantly I am not only engaging in activities forbidden by my duty contract by being here with Cortane, but how my awareness of the scale of what they're a part of is growing. And growing in a way that makes me want to look a little closer. Deeper.

Two things that put the safe, legal end of my duty at significant risk.

Two things that also, potentially, push me in the direction of Vana if I am found out for being complicit.

'Firstly, I am *nothing* like you,' I say, pushing away thoughts of the inside of Vana and how at ease I am with Kasera's death. 'Secondly, I didn't miss the fact you didn't deny it.'

'Deny ridding the world of a child abuser? Is that what I'm supposed to be apologising for?'

She's more still than anyone has a right to be. My legs still throb from the run across the expanse of grass and quiver underneath my weight.

'I'm not asking you to apologise,' I grind out, wondering if I should be.

The right side of her mouth curls up in a half-grin. One she's giving begrudgingly but there is a tiny spark in her eyes.

'And I'm not missing your lack of shock at what that woman did.' She sits back on her heels in the alcove and lets the grin come completely to her face. 'You have a source. One you believe.'

I stay silent.

She makes a smacking noise with her lips.

'Right answer,' she says. 'Did you learn it from me?'

We watch each other, a tentative release seeping through the muscles of my jaw.

'You need me,' I say, resolute in my belief Claudius wouldn't have sent me here if not. 'I—'

'Don't act like you don't need me, too, Princess,' she snaps.

'I'm no fucking princess,' I seethe.

'You live in the castle in the sky, dressed in the finest silks, eating the best food Zanteera can create. Let me guess, do you bathe in the milk of the gods as you turn a blind eye to everything the *prisoners* you wait on day and night do in broad fucking daylight?'

Davorous's face swirls in my mind, competing with faceless children Kasera imprisoned, and I close my eyes for a moment. Discussing this, now, with Cortane isn't useful.

'You're right,' I say, teeth gritted. 'I need you.'

She cocks her head, watching me.

'Yes,' she says slowly, as if she also understands the need for a truce here. 'Word has reached me of the soldiers awaiting transfer to Vana.'

'So you'll help me?' I ask.

'You're not worried other people will die if I do?'

I let myself sink to the mossy floor of the alcove where I'm perched, kicking my legs out from under me.

'Yes,' I say honestly, leaning my head against the stone. 'But if I don't, those innocent soldiers will end up in here.' I gesture to the prison behind her. Its brown, stone walls so similar to ours, yet draped in hopelessness.

'How much do you know of what happens here?' she asks, genuinely curious.

'Probably less than I should, but more than I want.'

'It's the innocent ones whose screams they delight in the most.' She pauses. 'Also interesting is how quickly the new attendants settle in, learn to be eager to try out the newest techniques. If anyone was to ask me, it's them that should never be allowed home. Exactly what does the Nuntainian government think those people are doing behind closed doors after experiencing all of … this?' She gestures vaguely to the prison that frames her.

I shudder. The clenching in my stomach when I think about letting Nix rot in here, with those kinds of people, tells me I'll never change my mind, but I do hope my own freedom isn't the cost.

'I want to know everything you know about the new Warden,' she says suddenly. 'Including where he stays, who he sees, and how he's adjusting to his new role.'

I stare at her, a poisonous taste forming in the back of my throat.

'Bring me that,' she says, 'and I'll tell you how I help you and your soldiers.'

'Will you hurt him?' I regret the question as soon as it's out and her expression flashes.

'I suggest you don't get too attached to anyone in that palatial prison of yours, particularly not your new Warden, *Princess*.'

CHAPTER FOURTEEN

My phone chimes as I walk back to the prison and I dig it out of the deep pockets of my blue dress. I know who it is immediately – well, one of two – and a pang in my chest is the response. I am fighting to get back to them and yet ... they're not the ones I am talking to about anything.

Zale: Lu, we haven't heard from you in a while. How's your extension going? Are you holding up OK? I don't have any news on either Nix or River, have you heard anything? They're probably just caught up on their duty. I'm sure it's nothing to worry about but please tell me if you've heard from them.

I swallow away the guilt at how much I do now know about Nix and River and haven't shared as I skim through the message that fills me in on how her own work is going, the latest sassy thing her daughter is saying, and her laughing comments about her wife wishing she was part of the vigilante group that still seems to be occupying the news on the mainland. Apparently they are tightening security in key organisations due to the threat of infiltration and the rebels are now being hunted – and her Teddy thinks it would be a grand adventure.

But none of it is anything I have the head space to really absorb now. The regret I can't spare her more thought wraps its way around my heart a little tighter as I pocket the phone again.

The prison – my prison – rises up before me as I make my way out of the forest, leaving the red flowers for today, and back into the concierge gardens.

'How's the murderer you decided to visit without me?' Blossom asks, a bite in her voice, as soon as I appear on our balcony.

I sigh. 'I couldn't risk you going Bloss, not if she—'

'Is the reason Kasera is dead?' she asks harshly. 'Because that's someone you should be dealing with on your own?'

'I am *trying* to keep my best friends from ending up in Vana, Bloss. That happens to include you,' I say. 'If I can secure Nix and River's escape portal and keep you completely out of it – we have a shot.'

She lets out a frustrated noise I hear her make so rarely. 'I know, Luka. I just – please, don't do this without me. I'm already *in* it and I don't want you in this on your own.'

A surge sears behind my ribs and I breathe hard through my nose to calm the tears that want to appear. Cortane told me there'd be a cost and I didn't hesitate. Perhaps Quillian is it. I don't know why that unsettles me. Perhaps because I hadn't expected it would involve other innocent people.

But Kasera wasn't innocent. Does that mean Quillian isn't, either? And why is she another person warning me off him?

Blossom is a turbulent mix of worry and anger and love as we stare at each other across the small balcony, and my desire to keep her safe suddenly feels naive. She's right – I have already involved her in so much. Not keeping her across everything now could be even more dangerous. For both of us.

'Okay,' I agree. 'Cortane ... she wanted more information about times of—fuck,' I mutter. Blossom sighs, but I don't look at her.

'Tell me,' she says and, dimly, I consider the pros and cons of someone knowing me so well.

'She didn't deny it,' I say. I drop my head into my hands for a moment, sinking my fingers into my hair and pulling slightly. 'I think anyone could be next. She told me to ... not get attached.'

'There'll be more?' The shock in Blossom's voice takes it up a notch.

'Quillian,' I whisper. As soon as the words leave my mouth I know I can't give Cortane any details.

Blossom doesn't respond.

'How do I ... I think Quillian's a good man, Bloss,' I say, finally looking up at her and letting the tears come.

Quietly, she takes my hand and leads me through our sheer-curtained doorway and into the lounge room. I watch her as she takes a seat before I join her and she takes my hands.

'You need to stop, Luka,' she says.

I shut my eyes against the words I don't want to hear but know myself anyway.

'You're right, Quillian *seems* like a good man, but we don't know him. And even if he weren't, you're not the person who can decide who pays with their life. Whatever they're involved in, it doesn't end well'—her voice cracks a little—'I *promise* it doesn't end well.'

There's something behind her words – something fuelling them – that isn't just about me and Cortane and it sends an unsettled prickle along my collarbones.

'She's their only out,' I say quietly. 'I can't – I can't risk Nix and River spending their lives being tortured over there, I just can't.'

Tears fall down my cheeks. I know as well as anyone that the only length of sentence in Vana is life. No appeals. No short-term stays. One sentence – or transfer – is all it takes. 'There has to be a way, Bloss, I *need* to find a way.'

Blossom watches me as I regain control of my tears, a tumble of emotions running over her face. Drawing a deep breath, she pins me with a stare.

'I'm not going to talk you out of this, am I?' She shakes her head. 'Fuck. I know I shouldn't even be trying – I know – I just … I can't lose you, Luka. I just can't.'

Tears fill her eyes and worry lances through me.

'What is it, Bloss? What's going on?'

She clears her throat and then her jaw hardens for a moment, as if she's finally made a difficult decision. 'Frank was passionate about making Nuntainia the best it could be …'

She trails off and I frown, not following the connection from Cortane to Quillian to Frank.

'He – we – were going to try and make it better,' she continues. 'He started on his own, mostly from an intellectual – research – perspective, but he wanted to move into politics. Then I came here and he died, Luka.

He *died* before he could do anything and without leaving me anything –
there was no illness, no answers, nothing. Just gone.' Her eyes bore into
mine, like she's willing me to understand something she's not saying, her
hands gripping mine like vices. 'Whatever Nix and River are mixed up in
is not straightforward. Even if they think they're doing the right thing,
poking around under the surface of the Nuntainian government is ... risky.'

The enormity of what Blossom's been through barrels into me and I
don't know how she manages to get through each day without him. I don't
know if I would.

'I'd never be able to live with myself if I let anything happen to them,' I
say quietly.

Bloss closes her eyes and shakes her head with a sad smile. As if she's
heard that same argument before.

'Okay,' she says after a long time, visibly steeling herself. 'But you don't
do a single thing without me, promise?'

I nod and watch Blossom almost physically brush off the last part of our
conversation. 'What if we give her false information about him?' she asks.

A rush of gratitude washes over me. 'Then I think we risk becoming
targets as well.'

'There's nothing to say we won't anyway.'

We're both quiet for what feels like a long time.

'Is it selfish of me to want it all?' I ask. 'My recommendation, to save my
friends, to ... know Quillian?'

To see more of what's behind the mask he seems to have with so many,
but ... far less so with me?

Blossom takes a moment to respond and my heart beats hard, waiting
for her to soothe it. 'No,' she says quietly. 'But I think it's unlikely you will
get it all. This island, this ... prison, what River and Nix and – what they're
all doing – it distorts everything.'

She squeezes my hand. 'Which is precisely why we do it together. But,
this up here and the questions I can see you're starting to ask, it's a false
world and I want you out of it. I like Quillian from what I've seen so far
– if you'd met under different circumstances, I would say go for it with all
your heart ... *and* to give it time. But, at the very least, even if we put aside
how he knows Nix and River, he's now Warden. He has a job to do, and

you have to leave. As soon as you're off this island, I want you so far away only I know how to find you. Keeping the connections you make here, if they're ones that put you at odds with the government, is dangerous.' She sighs. 'At the same time, I want you to be happy.'

Each step I take towards Quillian's office confirms I won't be giving Cortane any details about him. Not real ones. Because, in the face of what I know about Kasera, and what I can't help but feel like I know about Quillian, he doesn't deserve the same fate. Perhaps it's a bias in favour of the Warden role, thanks to Claudius. Or perhaps it's just my intuition. Either way, my stomach turns in knots at the thought of Quillian turning up dead and that is all I need to know about what I can and can't – *won't* – do.

As I walk, listening only to the slap of my sandals on the stone, ignoring everything I can around me, I plan. Plan how I can map out Quillian's actual movements and tell Cortane something different.

Which would work if Quillian had a regular schedule, but we don't have that yet. Not to mention that I am with him so often. Would she kill me, too, if I was there?

Which raises a different set of questions: why does she want to know anything about Quillian? Surely she doesn't want him dead like Kasera? How does she know him? *Does* she want him dead? Shit. Perhaps I should make a schedule for—

I slam into a hard body, a grunt ringing in my ears.

'Hey,' Quillian says, surprise lighting his face.

His hand has found my elbow again, and I soak in the warmth. The warmth that finds its way through my belly, up my chest, and across my face.

'Hi,' I say, unable to stop the small smile that tugs at my mouth. I hope it doesn't look too sad.

There was no doubt in my mind about not giving details about him to Cortane but, if there had been, with the way his gaze darts between my eyes and my smile, it didn't stand a chance.

He's close enough for me to see the soft shadow of stubble on his chin and a faint scar that seems to run along the side of his top lip.

'We should go,' I say, 'we don't want to make Traelen wait for us.' Seriousness shutters over Quillian's features, his shoulders tensing.

Slowly, his fingers slide off my elbow and we walk silently back to his office. It's not until we're there I remember he was on his way out when I bumped into him.

'Are you hungry?' he asks. 'I was just going to grab something quickly before our call.'

A small yawning opens up in my stomach at the mention of food.

'I'd love some, I can—'

'No, that's okay,' he says, 'I'll ask the kitchen to bring it up. It's good you're here early, actually. I was hoping to go over a few things with you before we talk to Traelen.'

I take a seat on the red lounge as he calls down to the kitchen. My stomach skitters a little at the thought of the check-in with Traelen. I never did them with the Warden before. But when I was running the Academy, at least behind the scenes, I always reported to the Board. Until they overlooked me for someone else.

Now, not only do I see him regularly, I no longer have a buffer between me and the man who can make all the calls on my service and how I perform it.

'Sounds delicious, Koko.'

The warmth in Quillian's voice helps thaw the nervous cold that started to creep into my fingertips. Surreptitiously, I glance over at him and find him smiling into the gold phone. My heart does something unusual, a sort of flopping free fall – something I didn't know it knew how to do.

He looks back at me, his left, thick, dark eyebrow quirking when he realises I was watching him first. But I don't look away. I let his deep green gaze remain on my face while my own trails across his shoulders and down the front of his pale-blue warden's shirt, brazenly absorbing everything I can see. The blue is a colour I never gave much thought to when Claudius wore it, although the memory of him in his uniform, in this room, warms me from the inside. But, on Quillian, with his soft brown skin and the shimmering black tattoo, it has an entirely different effect.

He lowers the hand piece slowly and stands there, watching me for a moment.

I hold his gaze. Blossom's wish for me to be happy echoing in my ears – even if it was a little reluctant.

When he says nothing, I break the silence, cheeks burning. 'You wanted to talk to me?' I ask.

He runs a hand through his hair and blinks, looking down at the desk in front of him.

'Um ... yes. Traelen wants an update on the events and ah'—he looks back up at me, his hair a bit crumpled—'I was hoping you could fill me in first. So we're on the same page.'

'Oh, sure,' I say, a small sigh of relief escaping me. This one's easy. 'I spoke to each of the committee leads over the last day and they are all on track for the different programs. The aerial yoga instructor is already here and getting settled in – Traelen organised his arrival and security himself—'

A knock at the door interrupts my update and I pause, watching Quillian move to open it. He moves gracefully across the carpeted floor. If I didn't know he had wings, I wonder if I would recognise there's something different about him anyway.

I glance to the bookshelf on the other side of the office, remembering the book Blossom found. What other secrets could I find in there?

'Please thank Koko again for me,' he says, and closes the door. The bronze tray is full of a small assortment of bowls and plates he balances easily as he takes a seat next to me, placing the tray on the low table as he does.

He hands me a bowl of delicious smelling noodle soup and, between mouthfuls, I tell him the rest of the news from the committees. The soup is hot on my tongue and the noodles drip sauce on my chin, no matter how careful I am to eat elegantly. Quillian smiles but politely looks away as he hands me a white linen napkin and I quickly dab my mouth.

Popping my empty bowl on the table, I quickly scan the rest of the contents vying for space on the tray. A small bowl with a folded note on the top catches my eye.

Shhh ... it says, and I laugh.

'She is too good to me,' I say.

Quillian looks completely perplexed and the strange swirling from deep in my gut starts up again.

'Have you tried these?' I ask, pointing to the chocolate balls Koko has smuggled me.

'Should I have?'

'Most definitely.'

I hold the bowl out to him, two plain chocolate balls bumping each other gently with the movement.

Hesitantly, he takes one of the balls between his thumb and forefinger and I watch him pop it in his mouth. He narrows his eyes at me, suspicious. Just as I see his jaw close around the chocolate, he gasps, almost choking on his shock. His eyes blow wide and he covers his mouth with his hand.

I can almost see the fireworks going off in his mouth and I can't help but laugh.

His dimple appears in full force a moment later. 'That is definitely an experience,' he says, laughing. 'Your turn.' He gestures at the remaining ball.

'I do not need any convincing when it comes to these things,' I say, taking my own ball.

It's thick and rich as it melts on my tongue, a gentle fizzing running the inside of my cheeks.

'So good,' I mumble, just as a burst of scarlet hearts rush from my mouth, exploding in the air around us.

'Oh fuck,' I stammer, a fire on the outside of my cheeks now and more hearts pouring from my mouth.

Quillian's laugh booms around the office, wrapping me in the sound and pulling my own from my chest.

Hearts and all.

CHAPTER FIFTEEN

Slowly, the sound of our laughter dies away and we remain looking at each other. Something like regret dances over the surface of Quillian's face, tinging the angles in sadness, and he looks down at my hands. For one wild moment I think he might take them in his, and they start to itch with the possibility.

But we stay untouching, even if we're close.

'There's another reason I wanted to talk to you before we check-in,' he says softly, 'and it's a bit delicate.'

A fluttering jams itself between my ribs.

'What's your relationship with Traelen like?' he asks.

My eyes remain frozen open, brows lifted, drying slightly in the breeze from the open windows.

'Ah, I don't have a *relationship* with Traelen,' I say, drawing my shoulders back.

He does reach out then, touching the back of my hand ever so softly with the pads of his fingers and leaving a tingle in their wake that travels up my forearm.

'I don't mean like that, Luka.' His voice is quiet but there's a hidden laugh in it, the corner of his mouth lifting.

I exhale.

'Oh, good,' I blurt, 'that could be ... awkward.'

He presses his mouth together, suppressing a laugh. 'Why's that?'

I break out in a sweat all over. 'Just – just because,' I stammer, turning away to hide the burn in my face, and pack my bowl back on the tray.

Clearing my throat, I compose myself before I look back at him, tucking a piece of silken hair behind my ear and off my forehead that's now slightly sticky.

'Why do you ask?'

He looks steadily at me. 'Because I want to know if it's safe for me to ask you not to tell him how Kasera died. To keep our official records of the event clean.'

I stare at him but there's no sign of something hidden. And yet, he obviously has an agenda here – I just don't know what it is. Even still, the thumping organ in my chest tells me to trust him. Trust him, and let him trust me.

'That's safe,' I breathe, even as a tiny voice questions why it would need to be a secret. Questions if I really want to know. 'But Shiloh might—'

'I will see her autopsy report before it goes anywhere,' he says.

'You mean before Traelen sees it?'

He nods and I can't help but think about the Chief of Staff, what I know about him, which is ... pretty much nothing. He works for the Prime Minister, runs a lot of interference between that office and the prisoners on this island as far as I understand. They were powerful people before they got here, and many of them, those who had the connections already, are able to keep their communication with – and influence in – Parliament House during their stay here. But more than that, I'm not sure. For the first time, I wonder what Traelen could be like under the surface. Does he believe in what he's doing? Does he know the things Quillian does? Or is he like me and slowly waking up?

What I do know is that he seems so cold I'm sure I will never be brave enough to see if there's a facade that can be lifted.

Quillian's face doesn't change but his chest falls in what I can only imagine is an exhale of relief. As if he was worried about what I'd say. And that knowledge runs like liquid fire through my veins.

'Thank you,' he says softly, his gaze not leaving my face. 'I wouldn't ask if it wasn't important.'

I believe him.

He shifts suddenly on the couch, breaking the connection that had weaved its way around us since the moment I'd bumped into him in the hallway. Striding to the desk, he lifts the handset and twists the round piece that he'd normally talk into. Something I've never known to do.

A pale, semi-translucent sheet lowers slowly from the ceiling between us. Just before it cuts us off completely, he motions for me to join him. Slowly, I rise from the couch and move to stand beside him, behind the desk, just as Traelen appears on the screen.

A flickering image of a plush, white office fills the space behind him, a striking blue and gold abstract painting. I try to hold my features in a professional mask but I had no idea this was possible from the ancient phone, even though it's not at all uncommon on the mainland, and I can't help but imagine that's written all over my face.

Quillian gently holds the top of the high backed chair, his fingers loose and relaxed as if we're not about to lie about the nature of someone's death.

'Quillian,' Traelen says. His face shows only the faintest flicker of surprise as he takes me in but he acknowledges me politely.

'How are things in the clouds?' he asks.

'Well,' Quillian says. 'The prisoners are back into their normal schedules, and we've taken things up a notch or two to make sure their enjoyment and relaxation levels remain high.' He looks at me. 'Luka has all the events in hand and she's been of invaluable help to me as I settle in.'

Traelen nods, his gold hair swishing softly around his face.

'And the other matter?' he asks.

Quillian clasps his hands together respectfully. 'Kasera's family has been notified and she's awaiting collection in the wellness centre. I think you're seeing—'

'Yes, yes.' Traelen waves a hand dismissively. 'I meant what are the prisoners saying about it up there? My phone has been blowing up all day, a darting accident is quite the discussion piece.'

I resist the urge not to look at Quillian but he doesn't say anything.

'A mix,' I say, and I can feel both Quillian's tension and relief that I've filled the gap. 'They're shaken, of course, and a bit flat, especially those that were close to her. It was definitely a shock for everyone involved.'

Traelen studies me for a moment, the vision of him as clear as if he was sitting in the same room.

'Hopefully that will be the last for a while,' Traelen says. 'Any more unexplained, or unexpected, passings, and I will have to involve the Prime Minister before one of the prisoners does it themselves. I am quite sure they will already be trying to contact him and we don't need that size of a problem.'

Quillian doesn't move as I stare at Traelen.

'There are some financial matters I need to discuss with the Warden,' Traelen says. It takes me a moment to understand I'm being dismissed.

'I'll wait outside,' I say quietly, ducking out of view of Traelen and out of the office, their conversation continuing quietly behind me as I leave.

I peer over the internal courtyard as I wait, my time here still supposed to support Quillian. Pressing my hips into the stone railing, I take in the lush greenery that trails from various heights, before dipping to the stone floor below. Above me is the open sky, a sight I never tire of, and I search it now as if it could put some of these pieces together. Why Quillian didn't want Traelen to know how Kasera died, at least not officially? Why doesn't Traelen want the Prime Minister to know before he can brief him? The second question seems easier than the first. I imagine that's about doing his job well and, perhaps, controlling a narrative. The first is harder to answer. But, worse, is not *why* he doesn't want Traelen to know, but why she died at all.

'It needs to be now.' A familiar voice filters down the hallway to me and I smile.

River. A moment later they appear at the end of the hallway. They both turn to look at me, Nix waving, a grin on his face.

Changing direction, they head for me and I nervously glance back to the door of Quillian's office.

'Here she is,' Nix says, still smiling but glancing to the closed door behind me.

I can't help but smile back.

'She does work here,' River scoffs gently.

The smile falls from Nix's face immediately and he squeezes my upper arm. 'Don't fucking remind me, if I could carry us all away from here, I would. Right now.'

The door to Quillian's office opens beside me and I jump, taking a step back from Nix and his touch.

But not fast enough to escape Quillian's notice.

My skin singes with his attention, a sensation that lingers even as he turns to Nix and River. I expect him to send them on their way, for the coldness that surrounds him when he talks to prisoners to strike hard. Instead, he looks between us, a realisation of some kind descending on his features that sets my nerves on edge.

River looks between Quillian and me, taking a subtle step towards Nix. But instead of hard judgement in his gaze, there is an understanding. Of what, I don't know.

The air around us in the otherwise empty hallway seems to pulse with everything I don't yet comprehend, with the echo of Nix's voice, *'He's the reason we're here.'* Almost imperceptibly, Quillian looks between Nix and me again and nods to himself.

He turns to me, all familiarity gone from his features and my blood runs cold.

'Thank you, Luka, you were very helpful with Traelen. I can take it from here.'

The words fumble around in my mouth, the ones I want to say catching in my teeth.

'Of course,' I hear myself say instead. 'I'll check in again with the committees and leave you to it.'

He turns on his heel and returns to his office, leaving me in the hallway with Nix and River. One all but burning a hole in the door with his glare, the other with sad eyes turned on me.

The concierge room is the most obvious place for me to be now I'm not needed by the Warden. But, the further I go from Quillian's office, the more I feel like I'm walking in the wrong direction. The difference in the moments we shared genuine, soul-warming laughter, and when he left me in the hallway with Nix, is sharper than I could have anticipated.

I scan the board without seeing. I look over the same information multiple times before I register anything. Even then I have to work hard to digest the details, looking for a space I can fill. Without a team of my own to guide anymore, no prisoners allocated to me, more of an 'always on' set of hours as opposed to shifts, and no Warden to assist, I feel strangely adrift.

I don't even have a collection date to look forward to anymore.

Sighing, I force myself to read the board again where the card for the dinner tonight finally breaks into my thoughts. I'm supposed to see Cortane in the early hours of the morning to give her details on Quillian and the thought churns my stomach. Particularly after this morning. I may already know I won't be telling her anything that endangers him, but I'm still scrambling as to what else to give her that would seem plausible. Possibly anything would pass at least temporarily given how well I know the prison and its schedules. But could I sell it to her? What happens when she portals to find he's not where I said?

My vision glazes over, blurring the coloured blocks of text, photos and diagrams on the board before me. This way, it looks so much like my mental picture of what Nix and River are doing. What Quillian is and isn't trying to tell me. Cortane. Claudius. Quillian. Cortane. A dull throb pulses in the base of my neck and I try, and fail, to make those connections and reasons become clear. To make it make sense. ·

I sigh. How badly would the truth go over with her?

Dinner. I let that event fill my mind, pushing out the things I can't solve, and make my way to the kitchen. I move through the halls, smiling as genuinely as I can to all the prisoners I pass. None of them stop to talk, which suits me fine. For the first time in a long while, I find myself wondering what announcements Traelen made when they arrived and, more soberingly, what event led them to be sent here.

Koko beams at me as I trot down the kitchen stairs, her round face splitting in half with the force of her grin.

'Did you like them?'

I blush but the memory now also has a sad tinge. 'I loved them, thank you, Koko. You spoil me.'

'Only you,' she wags a finger at me before shrugging a shoulder. 'And maybe sometimes your friend Blossom ... maybe always now the new Warden.'

She winks and I can't help but laugh.

'We're ready for tonight,' she says, gesturing to the preparations happening behind her. 'That's why you're here, yes?'

I watch the kitchen staff for a moment, working in rhythm with each other. I know more than one of them has manifested but, as far as I'm aware, it's only Koko who's exempt from the magic dampeners in this kitchen. All of the healers are.

She seems so at home here, in this white and steel kitchen, I almost envy her. Not that I can cook. But the sparkle in her eye when she talks about food, when she sees the joy on our faces when we eat her creations, is something I've never had.

My phone chimes and absently I find it in my hand.

Akira: Z, your wife has a death wish. Tell that maniac to stay home, and stay safe. We do not need more vigilantes in this world. Honestly, I'm sure on some level they think they've got an important message but all it means for us is more Hunters on the streets and a harder time for civilians.

I stare at it for several moments until I remember the message from Zale I never responded to, and the slightly acidic taste of guilt simmers a little harder in my stomach. Sighing, I figure there's no time like being in the organised chaos of Koko's kitchen to turn my mind to a response. The weight of pretending I have anything to offer their lives is heavy and I inhale deeply before I begin.

Luka: I don't know, maybe being a vigilante is a bit like being a superhero? Maybe I could go with Teddy?

Zale: If I let you go with her, she responds immediately, *she might never return to me. She thinks you're an elusive mystery she'll never know the answer to.*

Luka: She's obviously a romantic, you should definitely keep her.

I add a little winking face at the end, given I know full well how committed they are to each other. Teddy and I didn't get to spend a lot of time together before I was given my duty; but it was enough to know she was a shining light in Zale's life I hoped she'd never lose.

'Hellooo to Luka,' Koko's voice finds me. Just as I'm about to pop my phone away, River's name flashes on my screen.

River: can we talk?

A weight settles in my stomach.

Luka: Of course. Where are you?

River: your room

Of course he's in my room. No matter it was locked – he and Nix never let doors stop them in our life on Zanteera, why start now?

'Sorry, Koko,' I say, dropping my phone back in my pocket.

'It's okay, you're busy, I know. But you will be at the dinner, yes?'

I stifle a sigh. The prisoners don't always dine on their own, we have to be there to help things along. Even if I'd much prefer to be tucked up in my own room. 'I'll be there,' I promise.

But as soon as it's over, I will disappear to my room for a while and then see Cortane. My palms start to sweat and I make myself breathe, focusing on the fact that I still have a number of hours before I have to meet her to talk about Quillian. Get through dinner first. I can do that.

I take the back door of the kitchen so I can skirt the outside of the prison and go back to my apartment via the concierge garden. Part of me tugs to go back to Quillian's office and explain, but explain what, I don't know. I just know something shifted in that hallway and it's made me uncomfortable. Worse, it's made me sad. Like I've lost something important before I even knew what it was. And I don't want to be on the receiving end of the distance in his eyes again.

Blossom's laugh is hearty when you can get her to do it properly and I'm shocked to hear it through the door of our apartment before I've even opened it. The stain on her cheeks when I enter tells me I'm not the only one that's been surprised by it. River looks at the drink in his hands, a deep red wine that's been brought up from the mainland for the prisoners, a secret smile across his lips. He takes a sip to hide it.

Blossom doesn't look at River as her laugh dies away, looking almost relieved to no longer be alone with him, and my own heart kicks a little harder. She's told me over and over that she could never love anyone like she loved her husband, that he ruined her heart for anyone else, and the future she was to have with him is the only one she wants – despite that now being a complete impossibility.

My heart broke for her every time.

But watching her laugh at whatever River has said sparks a tiny flicker in me. One I will keep to myself. Just like my imaginings of what questions Quillian will ask me. When that drink will be. If there will be time to have it before Traelen confirms my extension is up. If I even should be doing that with ... either him as the Warden, or as Quillian, the man Nix doesn't trust? Not to mention the man Cortane wants information on knows – and shares – things about the prisoners which he shouldn't.

'Hey,' River says, an unsettled flicker in his bright blue eyes, the pale colour almost the same as the sky. 'Thanks for coming, I know you're supposed to be working.'

'It's fine,' I say, 'My timing is a little more fluid now that I haven't had any allocations.'

'I, uh, wanted to talk to you about Nix.'

His gaze is almost apologetic when he looks at Blossom. 'Oh,' she says, glancing at me. 'Sorry, I can go—'

'No,' River says. 'Stay. Please. It's just—'

A knock cuts him off and my sinking heart pauses for a moment. That tone mixed with wanting to talk about Nix can never mean good things.

Janly is standing stony faced in the hallway when I open the door a little, so she can't see River in my lounge room.

'Janly, hi,' I say, trying to keep the surprise from my voice. 'Is everything okay?'

Her dark-grey bob barely moves as she looks up at me. 'We've got another one.'

I frown. 'Another what?'

She clears her throat. 'Another prisoner has died,' she whispers.

A loud whoosh of air escapes me.

'I've got Emeris working with a small team to sort out the logistics but I thought you should know and ... I didn't want to tell you on the phone.'

'Shit, thanks, Jan. Who–who was it?' I ask, an icy sense of dread winding its way around my limbs. Janly looks up and down the hall quickly, and I do as well, half expecting Cortane to appear from thin air with blood on her hands.

'Aiten Gall,' Janly says.

Aiten. My heart sinks – he was one of my charges for a time.

'Are you okay? Is there anything I can do?'

She looks at me almost hesitantly for a moment, and I wish I could invite her in. I can't hear River, but I don't know if he's gone or not and ...

'I'm fine,' she says. 'I'll deal with Aiten but Quillian still wants dinner to go ahead. Can I leave you with that?.'

'Of course,' I say quietly, my mind spinning. 'I'll get Bloss, too.'

Slowly closing the door, I turn back to the lounge room and stare at Blossom, who looks back expectantly, her hands clutched in her lap.

'River,' she whispers in the direction of her bedroom, 'you can come out.'

I let the silence fill the room as River returns, his presence adding a comforting weight to the room around me. My heart rate rising as Janly's words play on repeat in my head.

We've got another one.

We've got another one.

'What's happened?' she asks, her face falling.

'Another prisoner has died,' I say.

She looks desperately at me. 'Who?'

'Aiten,' I tell her, head swimming.

'What's happening?' Her words are quiet and laced with worry.

'I don't know,' I say honestly, finding River's blue eyes, bile trying to make its way up my throat. My mind turns in on itself trying to work it through, wondering how much of this one Cortane is responsible for. What Aiten could have done that made her think he needed to die. But I haven't given her any further information. Not on Aiten, or anyone else. Yet.

The realisation opens a cold pit in the bottom of my stomach. I thought I could control that it didn't happen to Quillian. But perhaps ...

Two deaths.

After Nix and River arrived here.

But also after Quillian arrived here.

I only realise I've started pacing when I stop dead, a snippet of an earlier overheard conversation coming back to me, *'It needs to be now.'*

They're soldiers...

'River,' I say, my voice shaking. 'You and Nix—' But I can't say it out loud. Can't voice that growing suspicion that's suggesting Cortane might not be the only one responsible for people dying in my prison.

Slowly he crosses my living room, skirting around the couch and joining me in the kitchen. Blossom watches from where she's perched on the edge of the couch.

'Lu,' he says, 'I know there are people here you care about. A lot.' He glances at Blossom before looking back to me. 'I promise I will keep them safe.'

I look up into his gentle face. The shape of his forehead and nose is so like Nix's but their eyes are strikingly different.

'How can you promise that? How can you *control* that?' I ask, completely unwilling to ask if he knows we will be safe because we're not on the list of 'things they had to do' here.

'Have I ever let you down?'

CHAPTER SIXTEEN

'A few more moments and then we'll cue the music,' I say to Blossom before I do a slow spin around the room, a smile plastered on my face as I check all the details. Seating. Table settings. Music. Centrepieces. Sheers open. Drinks. Koko. Serving concierges.

But underneath the rote checking of how the evening is set up to run is an uneasy churning in my stomach. I try to ignore the compression in my chest that appears every time I think of the timing of the prisoners' deaths and the arrival of Nix and River.

Soldiers. That's what they said they are.

And soldiers kill.

A sharpness lodges itself under my ribs.

He's the reason we're here.

They didn't know Claudius – at least not well. But their commanding officer did.

Could that be ... Quillian?

But Claudius died before he got here. After Nix and River. So I'm not sure that timing works out.

Could it be because of something Quillian *did*?

The room seems to tilt around me – just a little – and I press a hand to the wall for a moment. Nix and River were clear they had a purpose here. One they didn't want me involved in to protect me, despite the fact I am working around the edges of it anyway. But maybe I also didn't look hard enough, just like I didn't look hard enough at why these *prisoners* are here.

Why Kasera was here.

Janly managed the concierges and the removal of Aiten's body while I focused on calming the prisoners and ensuring the dinner preparations went as smoothly, and quickly, as possible. I haven't even been brought up to speed on all the details yet – my focus being on the rest of the cohort and ensuring their distraction tonight, along with my own. Because what if it was Nix that killed Aiten? My gut twists. The suspicion of it is enough to make me physically ill. How would I really face the possible reality that my best friend's life has come to murdering people?

The prisoners mingle around the grandroom, most of them not even acknowledging the effort that's gone into its presentation. Tonight, it's decked out in floating lanterns that flicker light around the room, creating mysterious shadows. Their white and pink paper cases create an ethereal mood that matches my trailing dress.

Completely at odds with the thoughts rioting through me.

The light in the room continues to dim as the sun dips away, past the bottom of the island. I take a moment to soak in the vivid violet sunset out the arched windows and breathe in the fresh evening air. As if I could also suck in some of its calm. Its clarity.

Turning back to the room, I spot Davorous, dressed in a black suit with a lilac open-neck shirt, as he starts to make his way towards Blossom. A slick grin shows his perfect white teeth and many of the other prisoners fawn after him as they stop him for short discussions. But the whole time, his focus is on Blossom who is making her way to me. Her back is to Davorous and she's unable to see the devouring look he's giving her until Finn steps between them through the crowd, breaking my line of sight – and Davorous's.

He's our most frequent visitor to the playroom and I shudder at what goes on inside those walls. But the concierges that serve there do so of their own volition and can change posts whenever they see fit. Most of them don't offer their services to just anyone, but make their own selections of who to entertain and negotiate any adjustments to their salaries as appropriate. I haven't spoken to Quillian about that practice, and another gnawing of worry starts in the back of my mind. I'm sure he wouldn't treat any of the concierges differently to the old Warden, but better to be sure than to assume.

As if I've summoned him with my thoughts, Quillian enters the wide double doors, his focus on me as if he knew where I'd be standing. But as soon as it seems we're about to make eye contact, he looks away.

'Okay?' Blossom says as she reaches me, and I turn towards her, grateful to have something to do other than let my gaze trail Quillian around the room.

'Yeah, thanks Bloss.'

She quirks a brow at me and I sigh.

'I had a weird moment with Quillian this morning and now I think he's avoiding me.'

Blossom is beautiful, even when she frowns.

'What kind of moment?'

I glance around at who might be listening, but the other concierges are busy carrying out their duties before it's time to take our seats and the prisoners pay us no notice. I watch one of the women, her head thrown back in a laugh as the man next to her leans down and whispers in her ear. There's nothing innocent in the way his lips graze the bare skin on her neck. I'm pretty sure she has a husband back home, but there are no real rules up here.

'I thought we were getting along,' I whisper, and a reluctant almost-smile graces her face.

'Go on ...' she says carefully.

'And now we're not.'

'Because ...' she prompts as if she doesn't want to commit to anything until she knows my thoughts.

I fiddle with my hair. 'I'm not sure. He found me with Nix and River and ... I don't know. I haven't spoken to him since.'

She looks at me for a long time, as if she's making the same connections I've been trying to understand. Or reconcile the fact that I *want* Quillian to talk to me despite her concern about the situation.

'There's more to the three of them than I thought,' I say, taking a quick glance around the sea of prisoners.

'We already knew Nix hates him,' she says.

I nod. 'This just ... felt different. Like more. And now Quillian won't even look at me.'

'Okay, so go talk to him,' she says kindly. 'If you haven't seen him, how do you know there's anything wrong?'

I think of the mask on his face when he looked at me in the presence of Nix and River. The one that's not normally there.

'I just know. Anyway,' I say, looking around, 'I think there's enough here, let's give the signal to the quartet.'

Blossom opens her mouth to say something more but, glancing over my shoulder, she seems to think better of it and disappears. A moment later, I hear the quartet start up and wait for the lights of the notes to begin their way around the room.

'Can we talk after dinner?' Nix's voice is behind me and I turn to face him, subtly trying to survey the room for Quillian. There's no sign of him, but I can't shake the feeling of being watched.

Nix's auburn hair is slicked back off his face, the white jacket he wears fitting his stocky frame perfectly. The prison has the best tailors.

'There you are.' A sultry tone floats across the air to us, as if it travelled here on the lights of the music.

A female prisoner, one I only vaguely recognise – she must have come in the last few transfers I haven't been involved in – drapes a hand over Nix's chest. *Fleur*, that's her name. She's been spending much of her time with Miana, I think.

I look away – this doesn't feel like a moment I need to be part of – to find River watching me as he makes his way over.

He narrows his eyes at Nix briefly before extending his elbow to me.

'Join me for dinner?' he asks.

I smile, welcoming the exit he offers, and slip my hand in the crook of his arm as he leads me to a table. Nix has had innumerable conquests in the time I have known him and my mind is whirling with too many other things to care about one more. He is also a prisoner, after all.

The table we choose is on the edge of the room, close to the arched windows and their sweeping views.

Janly is working tonight and she glides by with a gold tray covered in tall, slim glasses of Silver Sparkle.

'You two look like you could do with one of these,' she says.

Smiling, I pluck one from the tray and hand it to River, taking one for myself, too. Janly studies my face for a moment.

'Maybe take two,' she whispers, ducking away when we've lightened her tray further.

'Do I really look that bad?' I ask when she's out of earshot.

'I think it's safer if I don't answer that.'

I chuckle darkly as River and I clink our glasses together, downing half of my first glass.

'Tell me,' I say, looking around quickly at the numerous people who could move into hearing distance at any moment. 'This ... thing you have to do here ...' He doesn't quite stiffen, but he does seem to use excessive care to place his drink down. 'Do you believe in what you're doing?'

He takes so long to answer, I think I might have struck an unusual nerve. There are very few things River and I haven't discussed over the years.

'I do,' he says finally, looking off into the crowd before us, smiling blandly as though we were discussing the weather. 'I've seen firsthand what I am taking a stance against.'

A rush of relief washes over me. I hadn't realised how desperately I needed him to say that. Nix has been my best friend for a long time, but River has been our anchor. And to have him so sure of their purpose is an undoubtable balm.

'Anything else on your mind?' he asks a few moments later, that knowing grin playing out across his features.

'Ugh,' I say. 'How embarrassing to be so readable.'

River laughs. 'You forget I have known you a *long* time, Lu. I remember your first crush, don't think I can't tell when—'

I elbow him sharply in the ribs, a little bit of Silver Sparkle drink splashing out onto his hand. But I can't help but laugh at the memories of Hugo – the little boy who promised to share his sand bucket with me every day for the rest of our lives.

'So you've become quite the expert have you?'

He laughs. 'You'd be surprised what I notice when Nix is ... settled.' He looks sideways at me. 'Or glaring daggers at your boss.'

I shake my head, unable to stop the slight sinking in my stomach – the bursting of whatever tiny bubble was trying to expand there – at the undertone in River's words when he talks of Nix being 'settled' or otherwise.

'He's got the wrong idea there – as do you. There's nothing to talk about with Q—the Warden.' I take another sip of my silver drink, trying to look at least somewhat like a professional and not a woman talking with one of her best friends.

'Sure there's not,' he drawls, sitting back in his chair with a soft smirk.

'Anyone *you're* interested in?' I ask with a raise of my brow. Bloss might be too raw for me to talk about River, but the reverse isn't true.

He purses his lips, pensive, before taking a long drag on his own drink. 'There might be someone who has caught my eye.'

I wait, but he doesn't say any more so I prompt him. 'And ...?'

'And ... I get the sense that's a delicate situation, would that be correct?'

I look for her in the room and find Davorous only a few people away, his concentration running the length of her. I frown, but a moment later Finn is by her side and a knot winding through my insides relaxes a fraction.

'It would be,' I confirm. I examine my empty glass, the tiny bit of silver swirling in the bottom where I jostle it back and forth. 'Please, River,' I say, looking at him and away from my glass, any trace of jest leaving me. 'Whatever you do, be gentle.'

A chime rings out and I picture Janly ringing the bell for everyone to be seated. She's done it so many times I don't need to look to know that's what's happening. Around us, prisoners and concierges take their seats. Some concierges sit with the prisoners if they have been invited, but most sit together.

I watch Davorous closely and feel River doing the same, but Finn guides Blossom to our table and she takes a seat next to him a little further along. River waits until she's seated before he stops watching but he doesn't seem concerned about Finn's attention, and it strikes me as unusual that the prisoner puts us both at ease when he's with Blossom.

Nix sits at a separate table with the woman who'd stroked him earlier, and I pick up my second drink. A pang of guilt finds me at the extra moment it took me to remember her name, that I can't currently recall her daily schedule and every whim. But any prisoners who arrived after Nix didn't collect me have barely tapped my attention.

River bends his head to my ear and whispers, just as a shadow falls across the other empty chair across from me.

I ignore it, closing my eyes as I focus on River's words.

'I haven't got enough of a read from her but, whatever happens, I'll be gentle. I swear it,' he says. 'But for the record, you've never looked at anyone the way you look at him.'

I jerk my head to look at him. 'Who?' I demand.

Subtly, he inclines his head across the table.

To where Quillian has taken a seat directly in front of me.

'And on his face – that look is completely new,' he whispers.

I elbow him in the ribs and a whoosh of air leaves his lungs, a sound that echoes my deep and sudden inhale. River hasn't known Quillian as long as he's known me, I know that for sure. But how many of the last five years has he spent with him in some way to know his expressions so intimately?

Quillian nods at us politely before taking his seat, and I'm suddenly very conscious of his proximity and the fizz of the drinks running through my limbs. I can see the table Nix sits at from the corner of my eye, and I catch him narrowing his gaze at Quillian even as he drapes an arm over the shoulders of the other prisoner, his fingertips trailing her exposed skin.

The silence at my end of the table is oppressive, and I look longingly at Blossom who's giving me a tentative smile as if encouraging me to talk to Quillian even though she's still getting on board with the idea of us. Finn talks quietly beside her.

River shifts in his seat.

Two lights of the music find our table and hover along the top, making their way up past Blossom and River to Quillian and me, where they dance overhead. I look up at the one above me, conscious of Quillian doing the same, and I silently curse the violinist when the lights start twisting together.

We look down at the same time, catching each other's gaze.

Quillian looks away first and I try to cover my awkwardness with another sip of my drink.

'Sorry,' I blurt out, 'River, have you met the new Warden?'

River looks at me, questioningly, and nods without looking at Quillian. 'Um ... We've met.'

'Great,' I say quietly. 'Returning to my drink.'

The silence stretches so long, I could almost walk its length. Around me the room is full of sound and animated discussion. Yet, I feel like I'm trapped in a bubble of silence, with only the whooshing of my blood in my ears as I look everywhere but at Quillian. Slowly, the room quiets a little – a sign the food is being dispersed – and I drum my fingers on my thigh until Janly appears at our table.

With food – a distraction I've never been more grateful for.

'Thank you,' I say to her, as she pops a series of plates in front of us.

Different prisoners take the spare seat next to Quillian and try to engage him in conversation about everything from the food, to their bed linens, and the weather. I let my attention wander the room, part of me still making sure the evening runs without hiccup. It occurs to me to wonder if I should be worried about Cortane making an appearance? Or taking out another prisoner?

Yet, a large portion of my attention remains across the table from me. I can feel his blistering gaze on me every few minutes but, each time I look, he's engaged in a stilted conversation with someone else. The coldness in his face as if it's never left, and no sign of his dimple.

One of Janly's team brings dessert and I can't help but smile at the small plate of chocolate balls to have with tea.

Quillian catches my eye and holds it, almost as if he's daring me to ignore the fact we've been silently dancing around each other's attention all evening.

The stranglehold I've had on my insides slips, and a small army of butterflies takes flight. Picking up the plate I offer it to him silently, drowning in the depth of his green eyes. The tiny thaw there.

Wordlessly, he plucks a ball from the plate and pops it in his mouth. In moments, his hair is a shimmering electric blue, and River barks a loud laugh.

Quillian doesn't look away from me, a fire starting to forge its way through my chest. Instead, he raises a brow in question – or challenge – that dimple winking at me, and I pick my own chocolate ball.

Deliberately, I place it in my mouth and River stifles a cough next to me. I ignore him as my brows lift and my mouth flames. The popping on my tongue is so delightful it brings tears to my eyes and I grin. I lick my lips as it ceases, using my finger to wipe away any remaining evidence. Quillian's gaze flicks to my mouth as I do, and then my finger that's come away gold.

'Having a good night?' Nix asks as he stops at our table, standing over me from the side. I didn't hear him approach. The tension in his shoulders is clear, and River sighs heavily.

'Leave it, Nix,' he mutters under his breath.

Quillian watches him carefully.

The woman whose side he's been attached to most of the night finds him again, and he smiles at her, seduction replacing all his tension. He gives the three of us another long look before disappearing into the crowd hand in hand with her.

River exhales softly next to me and shakes his head. I don't miss the way Blossom looks between the three men and back at me, concern simmering in her features.

Quillian doesn't look at me again.

CHAPTER SEVENTEEN

Blossom confiscated the last of my third drink before I could finish it – perhaps the rate at which I was drinking, in the awkward lack of engagement from Quillian, was more obvious than I thought. Now, she and River walk me back to our apartment, River a length behind us. Linking my arm in Blossom's as we walk, I lift my face to the night sky.

'You know, I never thought I'd say this so genuinely,' Bloss says quietly, although not quietly enough for River to not be included in the conversation. 'But that Finn ... he seems quite lovely. Gentle, even.'

Gentle. I mull it over for a moment. I wouldn't have described any of the prisoners that way either. They're all different in their own ways, some of them soft. But no, not gentle. So I can appreciate the touch of surprise in Blossom's tone.

'I will forever be grateful he appears when he does. That other fucking man ...' She physically shudders against me as she lets the rest go unsaid.

River's face is stone when I glance over my shoulder.

'Why he couldn't be one that turns up dead, I don't know,' I whisper fiercely. 'Quillian said he was going to increase security around you – him – I'll raise it again. But, for now, you don't go anywhere without one of us, okay?'

It's her turn to glance back at River and a faint blush dusts her cheeks.

But her silent nod of agreement is shadowed in sadness.

River sees us back to our room, making sure the door is locked on his way out. I don't tell him that I'll be sneaking out to see Cortane before the sun rises. Perhaps I could ask her to … dispatch Davorous the same way she did Kasera? Or Nix did Aiten? But would it be easier or harder to watch River or Nix say yes to killing someone? And something tells me that no matter what price Cortane might ask, the cost would still be less.

I sigh heavily, knowing it's literally my duty to seek out Janly and get the full report on Aiten's death. An update, so I can update Quillian, who can update Traelen. A chain of information that's wearing on me simply by being a link in it.

'You really like him, don't you?' Blossom asks, her head resting on the back of the couch, brown curls spilling out to the side. I don't have to ask who she means.

I laugh, the falseness of the sound clear in our quiet apartment.

'What a time to start developing feelings for someone, right?'

Even as the words come out, I know they're not the most important ones. The real reason my interest in Quillian is such a bad idea is because, while I am performing my duty with him impeccably on one hand, I am actively trying to secure a way off the island, and out of Quillian's prison, for two people I care about deeply – people Quillian clearly knows somehow. A way that currently requires me to give a highly dangerous individual information about him. A way that leaves me torn between saving Nix and River and trusting Nix's judgement on Quillian, or trusting my own instincts about him and condemning Nix and River because of it.

Not that he knows I am also trying to save him from Cortane and whatever her interest in him is. The coldness that emanates from her is more than enough for me to know that her attention would be far different from mine.

But I already know I somehow need to tell her I am refusing to give her what she wants.

By now I'd hoped I would have a game plan for the next meeting with Cortane. A way to distract her from Quillian without jeopardising the exit strategy she offers for River and Nix. Instead, I have a still-burning belief that Claudius brought Nix and River here for good reason, a belief they seem to share so strongly they're genuinely prepared for whatever the consequences might be. And the knowledge that Quillian looked at them so differently than he does the prisoners – whatever their history, he certainly doesn't loathe them in the same way.

When I left Cortane the first time, I felt like I'd started to live two versions of myself. But, as I let my belief in Claudius, Nix and River, and my feelings for Quillian, expand in my chest, I can't help but feel I am already further across the middle line of those two halves than I ever would have thought.

Blossom's slowing breathing is soft next to me on the couch, mirroring the gently swaying sheer curtains that frame the night outside. As I let the sound of her sleeping wash around me, I feel no doubt in my decision not to give Cortane anything that could hurt Quillian. But, in the absence of that, I do need to offer her something.

But all I have is my own truth.

If I am brave enough to use it.

The garden is as quiet as expected when I cross, any gatherings here after the dinner well and truly finished, or moved to closer quarters. I'm faster at the crossing this time, wondering again why I've never seen any guards on this side of the prison. Maybe they don't have them. It's bright enough for all movement to be monitored but no one has picked me up.

Yet.

Cortane is waiting in the alcove as normal and I hope Blossom finds my note before she worries about where I am when she wakes. Cortane's shaved head shines in the light behind her, like she wears a halo.

'Well?' she asks, clearly having no interest in small talk.

I draw a deep breath, hoping she can't see the shaking of my fingers.

'I'm not going to give you anything on the new Warden,' I say, careful not to use his name.

'Oh?' her voice spikes in surprise.

I don't comment.

'I thought you wanted my help,' she says.

'I do. But I gave you information once and someone – at least one – ended up dead.'

I look at her while she assesses me.

'So he's gone, too?' she asks, and my chest compresses a little at the final confirmation that it was not Cortane who killed Aiten Gall.

Silence is my only response. Not because I think it's a good strategy, necessarily, but I don't know how else to quell the maelstrom that's building under my skin. Part of me knows I should feel bad about people dying. Should be angry that they were dealt with outside of our justice system, because that's not fair to them. But the injustice of people like Nix, River, and Quillian being forced to take action when our government won't, is what tears me up the most. The knowledge that there is nothing *fair* about what is happening up here and the fallout it is creating in our lives.

But I don't – can't – voice any of that. So I swallow and focus on the prisoner in front of me. This woman should be the enemy – she is in Vana, after all, where they put the worst of the worst. But Kasera was keeping child slaves and she was in my prison, living in luxury. Perhaps Aiten was equally as awful? And clearly the Warden wanted Cortane out of here – so similar to his desire to get me off the island as well. How bad does that mean she can be? Or did Vana make her this way?

And yet here I am, having tried to forge an alliance of sorts with her – still trying.

'You realise information on the Warden was part of the cost of my help?' she asks. 'Without which you and your friends can't leave.'

I try to swallow but my throat is thickening. Of course she would know 'the soldiers' we talked about previously are important to me, why else would I be here?

'Yes,' I say. 'But there is still the matter that you need me. Even if I don't know what for, exactly, I can see in your face you don't want me to walk away as much as I don't want to.'

She scoffs. 'I can walk away any time I like, Princess. Claudius sent you here so you could help me, maybe – yes. But it's *you* he sent here to prove yourself, to prove the colour of your soul. He might have thought you were on your way, but he left it to me to decide. So you can choose now – stop hiding, think for yourself, tell me something *real*, and I'll decide. If you're worthy, maybe I will get your soldiers off this island before they land in this prison with me.'

I don't bother trying to hide the long exhale that leaves me. Or the way I have to press my fingertips into my temples to try and quell the noise in my head.

Prove my worth—

The colour of what?

All I have is the truth.

I could lie, I suppose, but what would that achieve? Turning my gaze back to Cortane, I assess her flat, hazel eyes.

Not once did Claudius ever ask me to lie.

'I was supposed to be collected at the end of my duty,' I say wearily. 'But my collector turned up in the next intake, along with his brother. Claudius was expecting me to be on the mainland and them to be in Zanteera prison, not the three of us here together. He sent me to meet with you in place of one of them – less conspicuous for a concierge to get to you, maybe.' I pause, thinking back to that last conversation with Claudius in a slightly different light and seeing for the first time the desperate, but hopeful, look in his eyes as he told us of Cortane. 'I think, maybe, he also wanted us to meet, for me to gain your trust and help you find a way for them – and you – to get off the island.'

I catch the hardness in the line of her jaw, as if she's clenching her teeth. I watch her carefully as I tell the rest – that Traelen thinks I was extended and, officially, I am due to finish that extension and take up a recommendation in Parliament as a 'contact' for something I don't really understand. That I know the soldiers we have spoken of have tasks they need to do here – 'tasks' that seem to be assassinating particular individuals

– before they can leave, but I'm terrified Traelen will transfer them to Vana first and either they, or Cortane and I, won't be ready to get off the island.

I tell her that I understand Kasera wasn't a good person but that I truly believe Quillian is. And that, even with the knowledge I could be condemning Nix and River to a lifetime of Vana, I can't condemn Quillian to death.

'That's a lot,' she says eventually, letting the moment stretch between us. 'But I will honour your truth with a little one of my own – not all of that is news to me.'

I don't even feel an echo of surprise. 'I know this is all connected somehow, I'm just missing the links.'

'And you still don't want to tell me anything about the Warden? Even if it would give you the pieces you're lacking.'

It's not something I need to think twice about. Not because I care more for him than Nix and River, but because I still need them to care for me. But also because *I* still need to care for me. They are here, doing something they believe in, and I need to do what I believe in, too. And volunteering up a good man, despite Nix's anger at him, is not something I can do.

'No.' I drag myself to my feet, hunching in the small space. 'Thanks for your time.'

'It's done,' I tell Blossom when I appear back in our apartment as she prepares the tipples. 'I told Cortane I wouldn't give her anything on Quillian.'

She exhales heavily as if she understands, but doesn't necessarily agree with why I needed to have that discussion with Cortane on my own. 'Now what?'

I drop into a bench stool and let my head sink to the cool marble countertop.

Fuck.

I just saved one man only to condemn two. Those numbers don't add up. But it didn't the other way, either.

Banging my forehead on the marble as Blossom's question – *now what?* – screams in my mind, I groan and jerk upright. 'Shit, Bloss, I don't know. What did I do? What *do* I do?'

Shoving the stool backwards, I pace the living room. Cortane killing Quillian wasn't an option, I stand by that. Nix and River going to Vana is also not an option, I still believe that. But I've just blown the second by achieving the first.

Think, Luka, I scream silently clutching at the back of my head.

'Luka,' Bloss says gently, coming around the kitchen bench, 'we can figure this out. We know the brothers weren't going to go anywhere until they're done, anyway, and you've bought Quillian some time. What would Claudius have done?'

I stare at her, my hands dropping back to my sides. If he was here, what would he have done? Probably stayed on as Warden.

If not that ...

He would have left with Traelen via the receiving plane, or ...

'The portal in the Warden's residence,' I say, pausing my steps to look at Bloss.

She nods in agreement, her curls bouncing a little as her thoughts seem to be whirling like my own. 'Yes ... I think we might have to chance that.'

'How do we know where it goes? Where would they end up?'

'We don't. Nor do we know if they will be marked by going through it. That said, it's already an official portal so perhaps it's exempt from the wards already.'

Bloss stares at the floor for a moment, as if she's still absorbing the possibilities. The Warden's portal isn't new to us, but it's one I've never seen – nor have any idea how to use. Nor do I know if it arrives somewhere helpful, or somewhere full of Hunters.

'If it was that easy, though,' she says, 'how come he said we need Cortane?'

I blow out a breath, furiously hoping I haven't blown my only chance to get Nix and River off the island by not giving Quillian to Cortane.

'I don't know,' I whisper. 'If only one of us was a fucking Shaide.'

She watches me for a moment. 'Maybe ... you could see what information you can get from Quillian about the portal in the Residence?'

'I don't want to play him, Bloss,' I say, moving to the stool I left behind and dragging it back to the bench to sit down.

Blossom walks to the kitchen and places the three etched glasses in front of me on the white stone bench.

'I know,' she says, 'and I know it's not ideal to suggest you do. But you do need to tread carefully until you are *absolutely* sure what he stands for, and if it's something you can be on board with.'

She says it like it's something she's said, or at least thought, a hundred times before. I cock my head at her in question.

'And you?' I ask.

She places both hands on the bench, 'I will do the same,' she says, pointing to the tipples before us. 'Time to face what scares us.'

The tipples that represent so much of what we've given here, as well as the reality our work day is just beginning. And, until we know exactly how all the pieces fit together, including ourselves, we need to remain part of that picture.

After a moment, I pick up the first. Birth control.

Up. Throw back. Down. Clink.

I look at Blossom as I pick up the second, the immune booster.

Up. Throw back. Down. Clink.

She waits for me while I pick up the last, ready to start our day of work. But the bitter tipple of magic inhibitor stops halfway to my mouth. Slowly, I lower it back down without drinking.

Blossom watches me.

'Who will actually know if we stop taking this?' I ask.

Blossom and I smile at each other as I tip the contents down the sink and she follows suit. A secret rebellion just between the two of us.

We're slightly late and the room is already full of the concierge teams helping themselves to Koko's breakfast spread. Their voices buzz around me and, for the first time in a long time, I really pay attention to the happiness here. There's a soft sadness in some of the faces, the clear missing of their loved ones and lives back home, but the joy is genuine. There's a purposefulness in the air, a sense of achievement. And our duties are that much of the time – purposeful, relatively easy and, at times, fun. Genuine friendships, and sometimes more, are made here.

But Kasera, for all her primping around Claudius, and the superiority that exuded from her, was actually one of the worst kinds of people. Part of me wanted to believe it was a mistake she was here and not in Vana. But the fire in Quillian's voice when he told me of her was clear – her being here in this prison, that is far more like a resort, was no mistake.

Which not only opened the question of why all the others are here, something that goes around and around in my mind on an endless loop, but, more specifically, why was Aiten here and was that the reason for his death?

Quillian is standing at the board, at the far end of the room, and my breath hitches at the sight of his broad, muscled back. He turns towards the room as I watch, attention landing on me and then sliding away again.

Talk to him.

Blossom gives my hand a quick squeeze as I leave her to take my own place before the board, seeking out Janly on the way for her update.

'Davorous is chafing against the extra attention,' she says by way of greeting. She glances around quickly, lowering her voice as she walks beside me through the room. 'Finn is actually being quite helpful with that,' she says, looking sideways at me as if waiting for my reaction. 'He always seems to just appear whenever Davorous is asking about Bloss or looking for her.'

Her coarse, grey hair swings heavily around her jawline as she lowers her head towards my shoulder a fraction.

'It's a bit uncanny really,' she says, 'like he has some extra sense we don't know about.'

Emeris talks to Quillian and, from where he stands in my vision, the Warden seems to be doing the same thing as me. Watching without looking.

Face what scares us, Blossom had said. So did Cortane in a ... slightly more roundabout way.

'Blossom has talked of Finn too, actually,' I say to Janly. 'But we can't rely on another prisoner to keep Bloss safe. I'll talk to Quillian again. Also, what's the update on Aiten?'

'Aiten Gall,' she says slowly. There's almost a touch of bitterness in her voice as she repeats his name, but there's nothing on her kind face that confirms I heard it. 'The healers are working on identifying the cause of death but it doesn't appear obvious at this point.'

I can't help the uneasy sensation in my stomach as she confirms it again. Janly's words feel like they're being carefully chosen, but I immediately think of Claudius and what his next of kin would have been told about his death. He seemed so ... undisturbed.

'Jan,' I say quietly, my throat thick. 'Claudius, did they ...?'

Janly's eyes are gently lined with tears as she looks at me and swallows.

'No, dear,' she says, placing a hand on my arm. 'I know, unequivocally, there was no foul play there.'

I grip her hand, steadying myself against the rush of opposing emotions in my chest. On one hand, knowing he definitely wasn't murdered is a balm on the still burning pain of his loss. On the other, not knowing exactly what happened opens a pit underneath the wound that's slowly filling with all the things I don't know. Things I don't know but feel like are guiding me somehow.

The concierges start to quieten as my time to talk through the board draws nearer, but I stare at Janly before chancing one last question. 'Do you know why Aiten was here?'

She looks back at me, her features unreadable. 'You mean the announcements when he arrived?'

'No,' I breathe.

For a moment, the room seems to still around us and I wonder if I have made a mistake by raising this with her. But her grip on my arm tightens a little.

'Sex trafficking.'

My skin crawls. How many times did I smile at that man? Make sure he had adequate time in the playroom? Order him the finest bed linens? Spray his room with perfume before he retired in the evenings?

'What is happening here?' I ask, my voice no more than a whisper.

'Here? We are about to do our check-in. That's where you need to focus right now. Then you ask those questions of everything you see. Quietly.'

I mentally shake myself as Janly gently draws me closer to the front of the room, less than a handful of steps away from Quillian and Emeris, quietly chattering by my side.

'—they're trying not to let it show,' she's saying, as if that's the conversation we've been having, and I make myself look to the board, like I'm preparing for today. 'But the prisoners are skittish with these deaths. Traelen has been notified and will be along in due course.'

I try to clear my throat; I am in way over my head.

I feel rather than see Quillian's focus on me and I can't stop myself from meeting it head on. The gentle, but insistent, tugging between my breasts makes me look.

In a number of ways, he'd said he'd known Claudius.

Claudius was expecting Nix and River. Was he also expecting Quillian here? Was he expecting him as ... *Warden?*

The enormity of that possibility threatens to drag me under and I try to hold on to the sounds I can hear around me. But they all seem to fade away ... did Claudius purposefully die to make way for Quillian? For that to even have a chance of working, the organisation, the planning, the *steps* that would have needed to occur are staggering.

Sweat prickles my forehead as Quillian remains watching me. As if he can see what I'm piecing together and doesn't want to interfere. Like he's waiting again. For my reaction. My judgement. Just like he did when he declared his hand on his views of this prison.

'Luka?' Janly asks as we arrive at the board. 'Are you okay?'

Quillian's brow is etched in worry as he waits for me to work this through. As I search him for the answer I'm not sure I'm ready to hear.

'Luka?' Janly asks again, and the sounds around me slowly come back into focus.

'Yes,' I mutter, almost painfully dragging my gaze from Quillian's to address her. 'Yes, I'm fine. Just thinking about the deaths,' I say quietly. 'It's awful.'

The last bit is added as an afterthought but she just nods sombrely.

She goes on to list the issues and requests that have come from the prisoners overnight. New pillows, the week old ones now too uncomfortable. A different fragrance for their balcony – I happen to agree jasmine isn't the most wonderful scent, but hard to change all the plantings of the prison for one person. Exclusive use of the playroom for a particular threesome.

As she talks, listing the things that have been discussed, things we would normally do everything in our power to deliver on, my jaw clenches harder. My teeth pressing together uncomfortably.

How many of those requests had come from Kasera in the past? Aiten? How many did I personally see to delivering for them? The vision of the dart in Kasera's eye no longer makes my stomach churn, but an indignant burn takes place in my chest instead.

She should have been properly punished for what she did to those children.

Then ... perhaps she almost was.

Was Aiten?

Quillian watches me as he now also listens to Janly's handover from last night, every fibre of my body aware of his presence and its distance from me. Completely absorbed in wondering who Quillian was to Claudius for Claudius to have possibly gone to the most extreme lengths to get him here.

Why, if Claudius was also supporting Cortane, did she want information on Quillian?

CHAPTER EIGHTEEN

As check-in draws to a close, and Quillian bids them good day and thanks the night staff for their time, the concierges file out. I try to listen to what else he says, I really do, but watching his mouth form the words and his hands punctuate the points is what draws my attention. Second only to the care he seems to genuinely have for the concierges. Just like Claudius.

'Luka.' Quillian's voice is quiet and coats my skin like honey.

I step towards him, unable to resist the pull to be near. My whole body warms in his presence but burns with the need for answers. Even if they hurt.

He glances at Blossom, who watches him like she's doing the assessment we spoke of earlier and she's still deciding how she feels about him.

'Ready?' he asks, looking back to me, my skin starting to tingle under his attention.

'Of course,' I say as I exhale and follow him from the concierge room, looking back once at Blossom in an attempt to steal her strength.

We walk side by side through the halls of the prison, the warmth of the sun caressing the top of my head and shoulders. Several times, I feel Quillian turn in my direction but I don't look back. Not yet. Our knuckles brush, as if drawn together like magnets, and I can't help but wish it was as simple as being able to take his hand. That the action in itself would stop the maelstrom of thoughts and questions firing through me. Would centre me enough to focus on what's real. To work out what's real. What's right.

Many of the prisoners have scattered to do their various entertainments and the prison hums along in her quiet, steady rhythm. We pass one group on our way to Quillian's office, their voices a hushed whisper as they watch us. The coldness emanating from Quillian is palpable as he ignores them and I find I don't particularly care to soften their unease any more, either.

But, despite the increasing grating of its inhabitants on my spine, the prison building itself is still spectacular. If I had a choice in the matter, I would even live somewhere like this. It's the lack of choice that takes the shine away.

I glance around for Nix and River. They seem to have found their own rhythm here and I haven't seen Nix since the dinner I'd spent mostly with River. And Quillian. But his disapproval was clear from afar and I don't really feel like running into him now. As it stands, he is the only person that's directly warned me off Quillian, but the more I get to know him, the more I think that's a reflection on where Nix is at, and not Quillian. Cortane warned me not to get attached to him, but I had assumed that was because she wanted him dead, but I'm not sure anymore. It's clear there is history with Nix and River, but how does she fit into it all? How was Claudius connected?

'Would it be wise of me to ask?' Quillian says, breaking into my thoughts.

I glance at him, 'Pardon?'

'You seem to have a lot on your mind.'

Make absolutely sure you know what he stands for.

'I think we should partner Blossom with Emeris,' I say, choosing something we needed to talk about anyway. A topic that's a bit easier to discuss in the middle of the prison – easier than the questions forming in my mind. 'She's still getting too much unwanted attention and we talked about putting some security in place for her.'

'I did,' he says, 'and it will remain. But we can pair her with Emeris as well if you like. Juggle the prisoner allocations as you see fit.'

Reaching his office, he holds the door open for me and I step through.

'The security you speak of,' I say when the door is shut again, the soft whoosh of the timber sinking into its frame shuts out the quiet from outside. Making it even quieter in here. 'Does the prisoner Finn have anything to do with it?'

He stands still in the middle of the office, as if he's on alert. But the softness he holds when he looks at me remains.

'He has the perfect background, and was very happy to assist.'

'But you hate the prisoners.'

It's not a question, but I still expect him to respond. To explain why this is a situation that he thinks makes sense. *Face what scares us*, Bloss said. *Think for yourself*, were Cortane's words.

They're both right.

'Why is Finn okay to watch over one of your concierges when you clearly have no regard for the prisoners here? In fact,' I say, thinking of a better question, 'why are you here at all? You clearly loathe everyone that walks these halls.'

He walks to the window where he stands with his back to me. 'I came here to do a job, an important one. And I don't loathe everyone here, and I think you know it.'

'How come most of the concierges don't know why the prisoners are really here?' I ask, ignoring his last statement altogether.

Slowly, he turns back to face me, hands behind his back.

'Because there are few people who can be trusted to know what the system does not wish to be known. Only those that prove—' He cuts himself off.

There's a familiarity in his words I can't place. More than what Cortane said to me.

'Prove?'

'I trusted you with information about Kasera, didn't I?' he asks.

I nodded. 'You also know what Aiten did, then?'

Quillian drops his arms and rubs his face.

'You're getting very close to asking me things that will be hard to answer, Luka. Which will only make you want to ask them more – are you sure you're ready for the consequences of that?'

He cocks his head a little with the question and the light picks up his tattoo. I think I can make out the word 'prove', but it must be a trick of the sun. I've never been able to read it before.

'I'm ready.'

I walk over to the arched stone window near him and peer out. I've always loved this view. There's not as much of the island to be seen from here, but the severe drop into the sky seems so gentle. Like I could just fly off into the clouds. I try to ignore the prickle of jealousy that, with his Karaylia magic, Quillian can probably do just that. But perhaps, even as Warden, he's subjected to the wards as well.

I drag a deep pull of the fresh air into my lungs and turn, immediately captured by those deep green pools.

'I know why Aiten was really here. What I want to know is why he was here and not in Vana.'

'You sound like you're surprised.'

I am. I want to say. If the people here, who I have literally served for five years of my life, have committed crimes that mean they should in fact be in Vana – where the worst are supposed to go – then what does that say about my role in this system? Who decides what crimes can be exempt from what is supposed to be a sentence to Vana? Or is it not the crime that's important, but *who* commits it that warrants the exemption? Why does there seem to be a growing number of people around me that disagree with this system?

'I'm just trying to understand it,' I say.

Quillian stays standing next to me as we each look out at the sky.

'I think that's something that takes time. Honestly, I wish it didn't. I wish I could make everyone see what I see, know what I know, and understand why some of the choices of this government are so wrong. But all I can do is act on the understanding I do have, and hope, in time, others see the facts and come to their own understanding. Like you now know the history of both Kasera and Aiten. Know those crimes *should* have sent them to Vana. Instead, they were here. On what? Certainly not a sentence of any sort.'

There are no *charges.* River's words come back to me and I think on how the Academy would sometimes manage professors that didn't have the favour of some important person from time to time. If they weren't hung out to dry, they were simply ... removed from the spotlight for a period of time. But, the general public on the mainland doesn't know this prison exists.

I rub at the space between my brows. 'Why do *they* think they're here?'

'The prisoners?' There's an upward lilt to his question, like it's ballooning a little with hope. 'It varies, I think. Most would be very well aware of what got them sent here, even if they disagree. It's almost like the outcome of a performance management discussion.'

The silence feels expectant around us. Like it also knows Quillian has effectively told me he doesn't believe in his job as Warden, in this system, and is waiting for my response.

Like I could maybe ask him about using the portal and he wouldn't have me arrested for suspicious activity.

'Why are you here, then?' I ask, testing the waters a little more.

'Because—'

A knock rattles the door, and I take a quick step further away from Quillian's side as he calls for them to enter. Emeris, a load of fabrics in his arms, asks Quillian about the budget allowances for tailors, and if it can be extended for one of the new prisoners. At least I think that's what they discuss. I look between them as if I am following the conversation, but my vision has glazed over as I think about everything Quillian has said. And not said.

He didn't say he was worried about his job. Or that he is concerned about the comfort, or loss, of the prisoners.

All of which he should have said.

But he doesn't believe in the role like Claudius did.

Except Claudius sent me to Vana. And made way for Quillian by ... sacrificing himself.

Perhaps the two of them are more alike than I realised.

'Lu,' Emeris says from the doorway, 'Paulana isn't well and I don't know how to get ...'

I look between Emeris's flustered face and Quillian, who inclines his head, clearly understanding I am now required elsewhere. 'I'll be fine, thanks Luka.'

I don't follow Paulana's shift strictly to the time allotted for it. Instead, I spend the time reshuffling what I can of her load amongst the other concierges, and to her next shift when she'll hopefully be back. The rest I pick up to make sure we get through as much as we can. Which, unfortunately, means I spent most of my time sorting through concierge requests and complaints from prisoners.

Scrolling through the lists of items allocated to me from my team's various shifts – any they couldn't readily fulfil themselves – feels like building a wall in my insides. Every outrageous request, every completely unreasonable complaint, are like layering the bricks the prison is made of so high I can barely breathe.

Coffee imported from Coprath; a consultation with Nuntainia's best jeweller; milk from a remote farm near the Tae border; a physical paper from Klades delivered every morning because reading it online isn't immersive enough.

Around me, the concierge room is quiet as I gently run my finger over the seemingly endless list on my phone that mirrors the bottom right corner of the board. I update what I can action easily, what I need to add Quillian to on the task so I can get his approval, and note the ones we'll have to talk through first before noting any action in the system.

I arch my back as I come to the last few to sort through and prioritise, shifting in the hard seat I dragged over to the board.

Acid burns low in my gut as I absorb the next three on the board.

Playroom request: Blossom, Davorous has entered.

Pack of luxury paper notebooks, Aiten.

It could be a simple request, but my stomach turns over at the thought of what he might have wanted to record anyway.

Playroom rule amendment: guests to determine their playmates.

The last is from Zenaton Blake – one of the newer prisoners – and a drop of surprise finds its way into the turmoil rioting through me.

It's not an immediate rule change. He can't do that here. All requests like this have to be approved by the Warden and, if not him, Traelen. But Traelen acts on behalf of the Prime Minister and his sole goal is the smooth running of the prison. Which means happy prisoners. I know Quillian wouldn't approve this change, the same as Claudius wouldn't have. He'll stand by Blossom and others having a choice in what they do – or don't – in the playroom. But how long would Traelen hold that line if Zenaton went around Quillian?

Fuck. Right now, I wish nothing more than to be done with people like Davorous and Zenaton.

The day is starting to fade when I look around the board and out the large, arch windows, and I close my task list in disgust. I have no choice but to raise this with Quillian – to get in front of it somehow – but I am done with these demands for today.

Closing my task list both on my phone and the board, I drag the table back into place, wincing a little at the sound of its legs dragging on the hard floor. I'm not a prisoner here, but nor do I have the guest-like status of the prisoners, and I wonder now if the concierges are really the captives.

I sigh, a desperate wish that Nix had collected me and that, instead of sorting through thinly-veiled, disgusting requests from people who shouldn't even be in a position to make demands, we could walk along the riverfront at night. That sparkling, inky blackness that reflects Klades back to anyone who passes by.

But then even that doesn't feel like it fits now. Doesn't have all the people in it I want now.

Before I really register how far I've come from the concierge room, the doors to our garden are before me and I don't even think twice. Leaving the building that feels like its occupants are suffocating me, I gasp in the crisper, fresh air.

Wandering the various clearings and paths, I find the place where we held the mourning ceremony for the Warden. The edge of the island is so close here, so unobscured by buildings or forest, it's like a plateau I could just walk off. I missed the scattering of the Warden's ashes, and part of me grieves for not witnessing that gesture.

But not more than I mourn the loss of him. The inability to talk with him. To understand what was driving him. To know what he believed in so fervently to have taken this course - to have made way for Quillian and brought Nix and River here.

To leave me.

There were times we would watch the grey herons together as they dove off the island and through the wards. Watch as the wards sparked the slightest shade of gold, so easily mistaken for sunlight, as the birds plummeted through. We'd wait the fifteen seconds until the wards flashed back into place and I would smile, marvelling at both the beauty and the knowledge the island was as secure as ever.

Now, those gold nets that frame the island feel like they're tightening.

I sink into the cool grass and watch the sky darken slowly, the clouds bobbing around the island as night starts to fall, creating space for morning. Trying to remember a time when each new day felt like an opportunity. But I can't see past the monotony. The brief glimpse I had of a possible freedom, gone. Because Nix didn't come. And, then, because I couldn't make a hard choice.

But perhaps I made a harder one.

'Sorry,' Quillian's soft voice startles me from just inside the treeline behind me, my heart hammering in my throat for a moment, but it's also somehow comforting. 'I didn't think anyone would be here. I'll leave you—'

I breathe in time with the soft steps he takes away from me, back towards the prison.

'Stay,' I say as I turn my head as if I'm looking over my shoulder at him, but I keep my gaze on his black boots. The ones he wears under the navy pants of the Warden's uniform.

'You okay?' he asks as he draws near, the memory of the first time we met flooding my senses.

I will the tears not to come, but they're defiant.

Am I okay? Not really, but how do I articulate everything that's running through my mind? Is it even safe to do that with him?

There's a dull ache in my chest and I can't help but feel like I *know* I would be soothed by him. A need to be close to him that's like a soft hum just under my skin. Quietly, Quillian sits down next to me in the grass and crosses his legs, his left knee close enough to mine I can feel the heat of him through my uniform.

'You can talk to me,' he says gently, and I close my eyes.

I want to – so desperately. I'm bursting with the truths I want him to know. I know my judgement isn't off about Quillian, but telling him everything is still a very risky thing to do.

Turning to look at him, soft tears still on my cheeks, there's nothing but open concern in his expression. And what still looks like the word 'prove' on his neck. But perhaps that's just the memory of my conversation with Cortane playing on repeat in my mind. Either way, it feels right. I want to prove where my lines are – I've shown it to myself, made a stand for what I believe in. Now, I want people to know what they are. Including Quillian.

'I gave someone information about movements in the prison in an attempt to garner her help.' I look out at the sky as I tell him, my heart in my throat at what he will think. What he will do. But some unnamed part of me begs me not to stop now.

'And then Kasera ended up with a dart in her face.' I cringe at the lack of sympathy in my voice. 'I was ... having to prove myself trustworthy and the person I was hoping to help me asked for information on you.'

I wait, still looking at the dusky sky, and I feel him turn to look at me.

'And?' he asks carefully.

'I couldn't do it,' I whisper. 'I told her I wouldn't give her anything on you.' I turn to look at him again then but there's no emotion on his face. But nor is his complete mask in place. 'And now I have no way to save my friends.' A soft sob catches in my throat and briefly fills the silence that falls between us.

'The Kilroy brothers, I assume?' he asks, although it's clear he already knows the answer.

I watch him, waiting for the reaction – any reaction. Deep, forest-coloured eyes run over my face but I feel too raw to even look away.

'Why didn't you tell her anything about me?'

'Because I didn't want you to get hurt.' My voice is barely a whisper, my body flooding with relief he didn't condemn me for my relationship with Nix and River. Not yet, anyway.

He looks back out over the edge of the island – where Claudius's ashes were scattered – before propping his hands behind him and leaning back. The action making his shirt pull taut around his chest.

'More of me is grateful you made that choice than I should admit,' he says, talking to the open space before us. 'But I'm also sorry it was such a painful request for you.'

'Thank you,' I whisper, his acknowledgement warming me a little from the inside.

'You're confident they should get to leave this island?' he asks, but it feels like there's something else underneath his question.

The profile of his nose and lips catch the last rays of light, gently illuminating them in a silvery gold.

'Yes,' I say.

'Okay,' he says finally, drawing himself up to standing. 'Then we each have a day of prison work to complete and it seems like we're both going to need a drink to do it.'

He stretches out his right hand towards me and the air around us seems to thicken with a silent question. Placing my palm against his, I let him pull me to standing, bringing me so close to him we're almost touching.

'Let's make it two,' I say quietly, my cheeks burning. 'One for work, and the one we haven't had yet.'

CHAPTER NINETEEN

The walk back to the prison and Quillian's office is quiet but full. Like something between us took flight as we sat at the edge of the sky. Yet, the closer we get to the stone walls and the people in it, the more there is a sense of tethering – as if whatever has shifted between us shouldn't, or can't, be set free.

My head spins as we cross the concierge gardens in silence, heading for the door on the ground floor to the right end of the building. Glancing up at my apartment window, the lights are on and I wonder who, or what, it is that's making me feel like Quillian and I need to be careful. Blossom? Nix? The fact Quillian is still actually my boss?

Work. I need to focus my attention there. There are too many moving parts – complications – about my role on this island to jeopardise anything more than I already have. Quillian said we had a work day to finish and he's not wrong; the list of requests I need to talk through with him are burning a hole in my phone.

The halls are quiet as we make our way through, most of the prisoners and concierges at dinner, and Quillian doesn't speak so neither do I. The familiar twinge of pain in my centre as we come to the door of the Warden's office is now accompanied by a flurry of other activity, both of which I try to quash down.

Before I've even closed the door, Quillian is on the phone to Koko.

'A grazing platter is perfect,' he says in his deep, velvety voice. 'Thank you.'

My stomach gives a little rumble in response as he hangs up and he laughs softly.

'Right,' he says, all business. 'Let's get this first part over.'

As I talk through the various requests, Quillian's response is almost always a short 'no'. There are a few I push him on as we make our way through the generous platter Koko had delivered, giving my views about why we should grant them, whether Claudius would've done the same, and how much Traelen might scrutinise what we decline. He relents on most of those but the tension in his jaw increases with every one.

'You're not worried the prisoners will complain about you to the Prime Minister?' I ask as he takes a mouthful of the last of his whiskey.

He watches me from the opposite end of the couch we sit on.

'No. I'd welcome an opportunity to talk with the Prime Minister.'

My heart rate turns up a notch. It's clear he's saying one thing, but his expression is asking – telling – me something else, and I can't quite work out what.

I clear my throat. As much as I am growing desperate to unpack Quillian, there are still issues we need to sort out. Whatever else is happening between the two of us, we're still running this prison.

'Davorous has requested Blossom in the playroom again, and Zenaton has filed a request to have the rules changed – he doesn't want there to be a request process at all, and any requested concierge should be required to serve in the playroom.'

The words feel thick and spread an acidic taste in the back of my throat.

'Zenaton Blake,' he says, sitting forward and turning the bottom of his glass on the palm of his other hand. 'He *is* someone who could get an audience with the Prime Minister. He's held a number of roles in Parliament in his time. But my answer is still no. There are a lot of blurred lines up here, but protecting basic human rights isn't one of them.'

He drains the last of his drink and places the empty crystal on the low table in front of him. 'Can you reassign Blossom to areas of the prison Davorous is less likely to be?'

'Yes and no. She can work wherever I send her but I worry about having her more isolated from the rest of us if he finds her. On her current shifts, she sees him more but it's easier to make sure she's not alone,' I say, thinking of both River and Finn.

Two prisoners helping keep one concierge safe.

He makes a sound of agreement before twisting to me on the short couch. 'Is that it?'

I nod. 'That will do for today – I've processed them on here,' I say, gesturing with my phone. 'The team will be able to start to implement the ones that you gave the green light to in the morning. Anything else you need to do?'

Quillian's broad shoulders are completely turned to me and I try not to let my gaze too obviously travel along them as he places an arm on the back of the couch.

'I would like to say I am done Wardening for today,' he says slowly, 'but that is a hat I can't take off just yet.'

It's almost a cue for me to leave. Or is it an invitation to leave?

'So two drinks shouldn't become three?' I ask instead of giving any hint of leaving. Not yet.

I turn towards him and mirror his pose, one arm along the back of the couch, and tucking my legs up underneath me. Our fingertips almost touch where they reach towards each other. I feel the path Quillian's gaze takes as it trails over my legs, my torso, up to my face. Silently, he moves away and pours us each another drink, and I watch the way he moves to the bookcase and back.

Our hands brush as he hands me the cool glass and I take it in my left hand – the one not still reaching for his place on the couch – and take a long sip. Closing my eyes, I smile into the heat that races down my throat and into my belly.

'That's so good,' I murmur, opening my eyes again as Quillian sits back down, adopting the same position again. The intensity of his stare feels so tangible, I want to wrap myself in it.

Quillian stretches his left arm towards me a little, enough so that the pads of his fingers brush the backs of mine. My breath catches as sparks fly up my forearm and leave a tingling in my shoulder and chest that starts to travel downwards. I swallow and lift my glass to my lips again as he watches, grateful for the steeling quality of the drink. As I catch a remaining drop on the rim of the glass with my tongue, Quillian lets out a strangled sort of sigh. One that almost sounds like a groan, and my cheeks heat in tandem with the growing warmth between my legs.

Stretching his arm a little further again, he brushes the back of my hand. Lifting my own to meet his, our fingers slip between each other and he caresses mine gently as I can feel my eyelids get heavy.

'Yes,' he says quietly, 'I think two drinks needs to stay at two.'

I hold his heating gaze as our hands still gently explore each other on the soft fabric, my stomach tumbling over itself. Neither of us acknowledge the contact, as if it's happening completely outside our control. Maybe it is.

Not done 'Wardening' he'd said, and I use that thought to try to drag myself back from the direction every sense in my body wants to go.

Draining my drink in a much faster way than it is supposed to be enjoyed, I slowly unfold myself from the couch, unwilling to let go of his hand and waiting for him to release me instead. But he stands with me, our fingers still entwined, as he puts his glass on the table once more and then does the same with mine, gently plucking it from my hand. We stand like that for a long moment, me staring at his chest, hands still clasped as I try to slow the rise and fall of my breathing.

'I should go,' I whisper, wondering if he can feel my exhales through his shirt.

Quillian tucks a finger from his free hand under my chin and slowly tips it up until I'm looking him square in the face, my lungs emptying at the want there.

'Yes,' he whispers back.

He doesn't move.

A shrill sound cuts through the room and I startle, stepping even closer to Quillian who drops his forehead to mine as my phone rings. Sliding my phone from the almost hidden pocket in my dress, Shiloh's name appears.

'Shit,' I mutter, drawing my head away from Quillian's a little and taking the call. Hoping the healer can't tell how heavily I'm breathing.

Grateful she can't see how I'm a sliver of space away from being entangled in Quillian.

'Lu, it's Shiloh.'

'I know,' I say, clearing my throat. 'Everything okay?'

'Not really – I've got Freya down here.' Her voice is quiet and a note of alarm sneaks through the heat I can still feel pulsing through my body. I glance up at Quillian who looks back with a question forming on his face. 'She's got strangulation wounds from the playroom.'

I frown and take a step back from Quillian who lets my hand drop as I do.

'Okay, that's not entirely unusual,' I say, thinking of the various equipment and activities I know go on in there. 'What are you not saying?'

'She can't talk just yet, but I'm not convinced it was consensual,' Shiloh says quietly, and I can picture Freya lying on a bed in the wellness centre where Shiloh is. 'She seems ... frightened.'

'I'll be right down.'

'What is it?' Quillian asks before I've even put my phone away.

'Shiloh's got Freya in the wellness centre. It looks like she's come from the playroom with strangulation wounds and ... she's scared.'

Quillian's arms drop to his sides as he searches me for something. Or for something he might say. Instead, he steps forward and gently takes my hand again, this time without entwining our fingers.

'Thank you for the drink, Luka,' he says, before slowly dropping his face towards mine and placing a soft, *soft* kiss to my cheek.

But, instead of the heat that I would expect to race through me at the feel of his lips on me, my insides cool. Because that just felt like a goodbye kiss before we really said hello.

'She'll be okay – physically at least,' I tell Blossom as I shut the door to our apartment and lean against it, the events of this night finally starting to catch up with me. 'Shiloh's managing her pain and healed her throat but ...' I sigh. 'Fuck, Bloss. Freya was frightened.'

'Who was it?' she asks over the back of the couch where I know she's been waiting for me since I messaged her earlier. 'Come have some tea,' she adds, waving me into the room.

'It's been a really big day,' I say, sinking into our lounge and hugging my favourite green cushion. Between the requests of Davorous and Zenaton, my time with Quillian in the clearing and then in his office, and completely exposing my betrayal to him, and Freya in the wellness room ... I lean my head back against the soft fabric. 'Big day' feels like a big understatement.

Blossom frowns in confusion.

'I don't know who it was,' I say, answering her actual question. 'Freya won't talk and I get the sense that's not just about her throat. She hasn't even confirmed if it wasn't consensual – it's Shiloh's guess based on the frantic state she was in when she arrived and that she obviously didn't want to stay in the playroom and be seen by the healer on duty there at the time.'

'Does sound like she was trying to get away from someone ...' Bloss's voice trails off. 'Do you think ... do you think it could have been Davorous?'

My stomach sinks as she voices the very thought I have been turning over and over in my own mind. 'I mean ... it's definitely possible, right?'

She blows out a loud breath as she sits back on the couch.

'Quillian is never going to put you in the playroom, Bloss – we talked about the requests again tonight.'

Bloss's whole body is taut as she nods back at me. 'Will Freya be safe enough in the wellness room?'

'Quillian's got a Hunter coming up from the mainland to stand guard – he looped in Traelen on this one.'

'Okay,' she says, and we fall silent. Both of us seemingly aware that there's not much else we can say. Freya won't tell us anything, she's been healed and will now be under guard.

But it doesn't change the sick feeling in my gut at the possibilities of what happened to her.

'Why else was it a big day?' Bloss asks after a time, her steaming tea still in her hand.

I groan. 'I think I better update Nix and River at the same time.'

Within less than five minutes of messaging them both, Nix and River appear on our balcony. Even if I couldn't hear the soft slide of the door opening, I'd be able to tell by the way Bloss looks down at her hands and the slight dusting of rose lining her cheekbones. Her fingers are held together too tightly for her to be entirely comfortable with her reaction though and I stand, putting myself between her and the boys – just for a moment – so she can collect herself.

It feels like too long since I saw Nix and I wrap my arms around him and hold tight when he comes in before River.

'Hey,' he says, squeezing me back. 'What's this for?'

The weight of everything I need to tell them makes it too hard to answer and he nudges me away.

'Lu?'

'You better sit down,' I say, moving to the side so they can join Blossom on the couches.

River eyes me as he walks past but says nothing. When they're settled, the two men turn their attention to me. Blossom, as usual, looking between us.

'I'd prefer it if you just told us quickly, Lu – this is a bit excruciating,' Nix says, his brows lowering as he sits his elbows on his knees.

I glance at River, who nods in encouragement.

'You know I've been meeting with Cortane,' I start, and neither of them object. 'She's been asking me for information on different things in the prison to prove myself so she'd agree to portal you both off the island – the first piece of information ended with Kasera dead. Then ... she asked for information on Quillian.'

River looks to Nix quickly and back to me.

Nix stays silent, his presence starting to feel like a dark, wet cloud next to me.

'And I said no.'

I let the sentence hang as they absorb what I've said.

'Just to be clear,' Nix says, 'You declined to give her what she asked for because she wanted to know about Quillian?'

'No. I said no because I draw the line at offering up innocent, good people to be targets for someone just so I can *prove* myself.' My stomach goes in circles. 'But it came at a cost … she's no longer a way off the island.'

And it hits me. Not only did I not secure a way off the island for Nix and River, I failed in Claudius's task for me – to earn her trust. I rub at my breastbone.

'I also told Quillian,' I say when neither of them utter a word and Nix's gaze slides to me.

'Fuck me, he is really getting under your skin isn't he?'

I look straight back at him. 'Yes.'

Nix throws himself back in the chair, head banging softly before he jerks to standing. 'You know what this is, River,' he says, ignoring Blossom and me completely. 'I didn't want her involved. She's supposed to be *safe*.'

River stays seated, looking up at Nix, but I don't miss the way he angles himself in front of Bloss. Just a little.

'It doesn't change anything, Nix, you know that. We came with a job to do and it's getting done. You *know* why we're here.'

'Of course I fucking know,' Nix spits, pacing the living space. 'Which is exactly why Luka should have *nothing* to do with it. You know this, River. You know what they're doing. Do *not* make me explain it.'

I catch Blossom's eye and, for the first time, I see concern for Nix. Is that because she knows him better now? Or has she been talking to River about him?

'We have another way off the island for you,' I say, trying to break the thread of conversation between Nix and River.

They both look at me then.

'Cortane is supposed to be the only out,' River says, and I shake my head.

'No, there's a portal in the Warden's residence.'

'We don't know where that goes, Lu,' River says calmly as he shifts in his seat again now Nix's pacing is slowing. 'Or how it's tracked.'

'I can ask—'

Nix scoffs. 'If you don't know, he doesn't know.'

'And we still need Cortane,' River says gently. 'Our instructions were clear on that. We're either in Vana with her, or she's out with us.'

CHAPTER TWENTY

My eyes are gritty when I arrive in the concierge room. After yesterday, and last night, I barely slept at all. River's whispered comment as he left about not worrying about Nix's views on Quillian didn't help either.

The board tells me Paulana is still sick today so, with no prisoner allocations myself yet, and no meetings scheduled with Quillian, I take her shift instead – cleaning the concierge rooms. It's not glamorous by any means and, at one point in my time here, I swore I'd never clean another room again. But it also provides a perfect opportunity to be on my own and somewhere I won't accidentally run into Nix or Quillian. Or River – that man knows too much.

Today, I almost feel exceptionally grateful to do it. Just yesterday, I wanted off the island so badly. Now, when faced with the reality that Nix and River might not escape Vana because of my decision not to tell Cortane, I'd happily clean these rooms every day for the rest of my life if it meant they didn't get transferred to the worst place in the world. While we don't ever engage with the Vanan Hunters, we have seen the small group of workers stationed there on duty like us on occasion. And the only thing they have to be grateful for is that their roles don't always explicitly involve torture – unless some are that way inclined already.

One woman I met told me the sound of screaming doesn't ever leave her – not while she eats or bathes or is supposed to be off shift or sleeping.

Never. Just a constant stream of strangled noise in her head. Though I all but dismissed what I thought was an exaggeration of their duty at the time, now that I know what the people I've waited on day and night during my duty on this side are capable of, I'm not so sure. I'm not certain I'd be strong enough to survive a day in that place. Definitely not if I had to watch Nix and River in there, too. But won't it be worse if I am sent back to the mainland and have no idea what happens to them?

Collecting the brass trolley, I make my way to the concierge wing. Working from the furthest end of the hallway, I move through each of the rooms. All the concierges know this is cleaning day and so most personal effects are put away and tucked out of sight for ease of cleaning. But it's still, mostly, fairly easy for me to work out who belongs where, if I didn't already know. Like how Emeris never fails to leave a vest hanging over the back of his couch; and Shiloh has medical textbooks on her coffee table. Not all of the rooms are in use but I give them a once over anyway so they're ready.

Finding my rhythm quickly, I spend the day cleaning bathrooms and turning down beds. Mopping floors and tidying kitchens. It's not work I particularly enjoy but there is a certain satisfaction in seeing the spotless rooms.

The last empty room has two bedrooms and I check over the second bedroom first. Glancing out the window, the sun has gone down and I know I should have finished some time ago. But this is the last stop so I might as well finish it. I smooth the covers and fluff the pillows before deciding it's done and crossing the living room for the other bedroom.

The door opens and I let out a little squeal.

Quillian kicks the door shut with his heel as he spins to look at me, one fluid movement.

Fuck.

Our gaze locks, his as dark green as the forest we were in not so long ago. The thickness of the air shifts, pressing against me, the little hairs on my arms standing on end. He takes a step towards me, almost involuntarily, and his face darkens as he seems to realise our proximity. My skin prickles in response to the look on his face.

But I don't move away.

I should, I didn't choose to like him. Even if his bewitching eyes stalk my dreams and my mind constantly snags on the feel of his hands on my stomach as he stitched me up, the way he caressed my fingers last night … how it felt for him to lift my chin like he was going to properly kiss me. He's a complication I don't need. One that is clearly unsettling Nix as well. Not to mention the unspoken 'goodbye' in Quillian's kiss on my cheek last night. Or the fact that I blew the best way off the island for Nix and River for him. Chose him over Claudius's wishes for me.

Through the shock on Quillian's face, I can see the warmth that's in it whenever he looks at me. So different to the hardness he shows the prisoners.

I should definitely move away. But how do I do that when I can physically feel his presence in the room like a current dragging me closer? When he's able to draw a smile from my lips in times I would never expect? When, despite the things happening around us, he seems to focus on me so intently? Seems to want to make sure I'm okay? Even when he's kissing my cheek.

'I didn't know you were checking the rooms,' I manage to say.

'I'm not,' he says quietly, frowning. 'I'm … staying here.'

My gaze flies to his face but there's no joking there and I cover my mouth. 'Oh … shit,' I mumble through my fingers. 'I had no idea. I was—Paulana was—*is* sick. I was—I'll go.'

I make to walk past him, but he doesn't move. He raises his chin a little, looking down at me, hesitant but assessing. We're less than a hand span apart and I can almost feel the beating of his chest against mine. The pulse in his neck hammers hard, his dark-brown skin flickering in that spot where it beats in and out of the light, and on the other side, his sparkling tattoo runs along the side of his neck and disappears into his shirt.

My fingers twist a little in my dress as a sharp image of my fingers chasing the ink flashes in my mind.

Following where it leads.

Can't take off his Warden hat just yet, he'd said last night. *He's your boss, Luka*, I tell myself. *This isn't a good idea.*

'I really should go,' I make myself say, but I blush at the lack of conviction in my tone, it's breathlessness.

He nods shallowly. 'You should.'

Still, neither of us move.

I blink and he wraps his arm around my middle, palm on my lower back, pressing me into him. A cold rush of air tears down my throat as I gasp into the mouth that's now kissing me like I've never been kissed before. Even before my arms finish their journey around his tattooed neck, I know this is a kiss I'll never forget.

One I've waited for.

His lips are hot, his tongue is hotter as it finds mine and runs along my teeth. Large hands rove my back and pull me tighter, tighter; his callouses catching slightly in the delicate fabric of my dress. The hair between my fingers as I run them up the back of his head is short and surprisingly soft.

Something near my heart expands and catches alight, and I groan as I focus on the feel of his muscled form pressed along my front. I lean further into him, as if we could become one right here, and he sinks his teeth into my bottom lip. I trail my hands down his back. The shape of him is smooth and defined and, at least through his shirt, there is no indication of where his wings begin.

Stumbling back towards the kitchen as I try to make for the couch, I drag on the front of his shirt and he follows me step for step. The need to take as much as I can before we have to stop, consuming me. Finding my path to the couch blocked by the kitchen bench, I unhook my arms from his neck briefly to lift myself onto it instead and he grips my hips, helping me there. Running his hands up my legs he grapples with my dress and shoves it up towards my waist.

I pant there for a moment, looking at him, his face slightly flushed with desire. A moment's pause passes between us. As if we're both waiting for the other to put a stop to this rush of blood.

Reaching for his pants instead of the door, I let my heating body decide for me. Using the heels I have now wrapped around the back of his legs, I pull him closer again.

'Are you ...' he asks in a hoarse whisper.

I nod into the neck I'm kissing, his clean shaven skin soft on my lips. I bite him there, hard. He moans.

'In the tipples,' I murmur against him.

He exhales loudly before pulling my face back to his and taking my mouth once more. The need he's driving through my limbs and core blurs my vision and I let my head fall back, pushing the tops of my breasts into his waiting mouth as he leans down to meet them.

Another gasp escapes my throat as he frees my breasts from my dress, tugging the fabric down, and takes my nipples, in turn, into his mouth. I reach between my legs and guide him to me. Lifting my head, he looks at me one last time, eyes sparking. Another opportunity to say no – one I don't take – and then he yanks my underwear sideways, driving himself completely into me. Pressing my fingertips into the cold stone bench top behind me, I brace myself.

Quillian's movements are hard and fast, forcing all thought from my mind, and I tilt my hips up to meet his rhythm. Sweat beads on his forehead, and I suck on his tongue as a moan escapes him.

The building in my core starts much faster than I've experienced before and soon I can't help but call out as the feeling becomes too much, letting it consume me. Quillian drags his teeth over my neck as I tremble in his grip, head dropped back and chest heaving.

He thrusts into me again and again before he presses so deep, spilling himself into me, I think I might go over the edge so hard I'll never come back. His hands are tight on my hips where he holds me in place, before his head comes to rest on my shoulder, breathing hard down the front of my chest.

We stay like that for long moments, me raking my fingers in his short hair; his hands winding around my waist and holding us together.

I watch the dark, starry sky across his small living room and out the doors to the balcony, understanding, with a slow acceptance, that I don't feel like I should be anywhere else. Right now, I don't even want to be off the island if it means I'm without Quillian. And it's that understanding that shocks me the most.

But I know it's just for now – the post-fuck glow.

I think.

Slowly, Quillian eases himself from me, lifting his head from where it fell, and clearing his throat. He does up his pants without looking at me, and my chest tightens a little.

What did I just do? With my *boss*? The one who can't stop 'Wardening'. The one who might need to give me access to the portal in the Warden's residence, even if he's not staying there.

I slide off the bench, also not meeting his gaze, and replace the folds of fabric properly over my legs. The act of placing my breasts back in the front of my dress brings a rush of heat to my cheeks as it really starts to sink in what we've done.

Moving away from the kitchen, away from Quillian and his broad, brooding form and towards the door, I clear my throat.

He remains silent.

'Now, I really should go,' I say quietly.

He reaches out, quicker than I can react, and takes my hand. Looking back to him, it's there. On his face. The warmth and the vulnerability he shows to me. The wanting kindness that dances across his face. And it bathes my soul, my heart rate quickening again.

'Please,' he whispers. 'Not yet.'

He watches me carefully as he says it, as if fully expecting me to say no. I can tell by the sag of his shoulders and the cracking appearing in his eyes.

Silently, I link my fingers in his as a tightening in my chest takes hold, and let him lead me to the other bedroom – his bedroom. It's the same layout as mine but his bed linens are darker, a richer representation of the midnight blue of a sunset. He hasn't made it today – maybe he never does – and I glance up at him. At the intimacy of bringing me into this space that's dominated by the smell of him.

He pulls me close again. I don't object when he cups my face and kisses me again, slowly, deeply, and passionately enough my body starts to beg for another turn of him. Gently, he lifts my dress, this time taking it all the way over my waist, and I lift my arms for him to remove it entirely. His forest-coloured stare drinks me in as I slip my underwear off, letting them fall down my legs, and stand naked before him, his pants tightening as he watches. His face shows promises I'm now pretty sure he knows how to keep.

We're more leisurely this time, more exploratory, the thickness of the air having shifted again into something more vulnerable. Warmer, rather than scorching hot. Removing his uniform from him, I trail my fingers along every edge and muscle and scar I can see. The tattoo I've been so mesmerised by still holds much of my attention. Its shimmering lines and curves drop onto his chest where they explode in a rush of colours that blow out across the top of his stomach and wrap around his ribs on the other side.

I feel it all and I don't miss the jagged, scarred skin under the tattoo. But how much of it there is, or what all the words say, is harder to tell in the dark.

He lowers us into the bed and lifts me onto his hips where I rock to the rhythm he sets, his hands holding me on either side of my waist. His palms snake up my front, massaging my breasts as we come together. I lean forward a little and one of his hands comes higher, running up the side of my neck and taking my face again, slipping a thumb into my mouth. Running my tongue around it, he moans softly before finding my gaze again and we watch each other's undoing.

I lie on his chest for a moment afterwards, trying to digest why my own feels like it's grown three sizes in the time I've been here. And trying to find my resolve to finally leave this apartment where my senses seem to fail me. Or at least run amok in their own desires.

But as I roll off and land beside him, readying to get up, his arm wraps around my waist once more and tucks me in against him, my back to his chest as a deep slow breath leaves him. A contented one. I still. All intention of going back to my own room evaporating as if it never existed.

It's darker than normal when I begin to wake, but the chatter of birdsong tells me it's morning. Quillian's arm is still around my waist and I don't dare to move. Opening my eyes, it's immediately clear why it's dark.

I'm cocooned in a storm-grey wing, the feathers creating a cave around my head and shoulder.

I can't feel them against me, the edge must rest against the bed cover that's in place at my waist. Tentatively, I reach out to where the wing descends to the mattress in front of my face and run a single finger down one of the darkest feathers. My breath catches in my throat as I let more fingers trail the softness. Fully aware they could slice my skin whenever he chooses. Or flinches.

I allow myself to stretch slightly, my fingers still roaming, and I can feel his desire growing behind me. But he doesn't move and his breathing doesn't change from the sleeping tempo it was a moment ago. Before I traced his wing.

Then he shifts, stifling a waking groan, and leisurely kisses my bare shoulder.

I turn to face him, our bodies still flush against each other, and he blinks slowly at me. I watch as his sleepy, open face crashes with shadow. His green eyes, now worried and ... almost sad, run over my face.

'Oh, Luka,' he says quietly. 'I'm sorry. I—'

The sound is loud, harsher that I can bear, and I hold a hand up to stop those words, as if not hearing them will make it easier. As if it's no less painful to see them written on his face. As if they didn't create a fissure as soon as he uttered them. As if it's not screamingly clear I'm not wanted here.

'It's fine,' I say, still unable to move. The words are completely inadequate for the sense of singed falling that's currently swamping my system. Like I'm suddenly made of burning leaves. And nothing about the look on his face, and those words, while I lie skin to skin with him is *fine*.

'Fuck,' he says, as a rush of air chases his wing back into his skin, leaving me even more exposed. 'I shouldn't have—'

He gets out of the bed as I sit up slowly, clutching the midnight blue cover to my chest. Hating the compression that starts there, the way the back of my throat starts to feel like its aflame. Scrambling for his clothes, he heads to the door.

'I'm sorry,' he says again without looking at me and leaving his own room. A moment later, I hear the apartment door shut, too.

I stare at the spot he occupied. It's numbness I expect to feel, one that slowly creeps through my limbs. And it comes. Just not fast enough to drown out the sting on my cheeks that blooms as if I've been slapped, the beginning of tears clouding my vision.

My chest constricts further in its vice as I throw my legs over the side of the bed and gather my dress. The tears retreat, the warmth I'd felt only a handful of heartbeats earlier being replaced by something else.

I close the door to his apartment behind me quietly, checking there are no other concierges around. My heart sinks a fraction at the knowledge I will never set foot in that room again, will never do *that* with him again.

But I ignore that foolish emotion and don't look back as I walk away.

CHAPTER TWENTY-ONE

It's not until a few steps down the hallway I truly get my bearings, my head still spinning from the events of last night … and this morning. My room is only two doors away. Belatedly, I register I've left the brass trolley outside his room, but that will be a problem for later.

I shower and prepare the tipples, only two of them, for Blossom and me while I wait for her to rise. But I sit on the couch in my towel, unable to bring myself to put on another concierge's uniform. Idly, I muse at how quickly that change has taken place. As if a line in my capacity for serving my country was drawn the day I was supposed to be collected. The day I was supposed to go back to my own life and instead found myself trapped here.

And every day since then has been subtly testing the boundaries of how much more I can do. How much further I will go from following exactly what is expected of me, to questioning everything I can see.

Then there's Quillian, a man who could talk to Traelen about ending my extension, or push through another recommendation. A man – Warden – who knows I am constantly putting those I care about above my duty, and my country, regardless of the rules. Knows I am actively engaging with a prisoner from Vana to break them out of another Zanteera prison – an act that more than warrants my own transfer to Vana. A man who's just walked out on me after what was the most intimate night of my life. A man who literally holds the key to Nix and River's last way off the island. Even if I have to force them to go without Cortane.

And I've just slept with him. Blowing the door wide open for everything to go wrong. Which it did.

Nice. Professional.

Smart.

'Fuck,' I mutter as I slump on my side and drop my face into a couch cushion.

'Good morning to you, too,' Blossom says sleepily as she wanders into the kitchen.

I stay where I am, plastered to the couch and wishing the day would never come. The back of the cushion depresses a bit where I can feel Blossom leaning on it and then she's prying my eyelids open with her fingers.

'Do I need to be worried?' she asks.

I can only see part of her face with one eye open and the other pressed into the linen, but she's walking the line of concern and mirth.

'I slept with Quillian,' I whisper, the gentle scratch of the couch fabric reminding me of the softness of his lips against mine.

I drag myself upright and cover my face with my hands. Slowly, I hear Blossom walk around the couch and sit on the low table in front of me.

'You're going to have to repeat that,' she says gently. 'For a moment I thought I heard you say you fucked Quillian.'

Her mouth has dropped open when I finally lift my face and look at her, my wet hair falling around my shoulders.

'Oh,' she breathes.

I let out an exasperated groan as I lean back again on the couch, sitting this time, and looking at the wet patch my hair has left on the other side.

'Tell me everything,' she says, her voice teetering between worry and reluctant happiness.

It's the tiny sliver of happiness that calls the tears back and I let them creep down the sides of my face quietly. For one brief moment, I knew the rush of possibility. The 'what if' that came burning through our every breath, every touch. Just to have it snatched away, all the doors to a different future closed down. Along with the possibility of gently asking him about the portal in the Residence.

'Luka?' she prompts softly, concern lighting her features as she sees my tears. 'Please tell me what happened.' She takes my hand and threads her fingers in it.

'I don't know how—' I say, the memory coming hot and fast with no way to adequately describe how he made me feel. 'We were just ... standing there and then he kissed me. And I kissed him back and ... then I woke up there.'

I watch her face as I tell her my disjointed story, unable to voice how right it had felt. How, having someone who seems to see me – actually *see* me – touch my skin with his, who kissed me like he'd never kiss anyone else again, ignited a longing I'd ignored for so long. I don't tell her I don't know how to shut it off.

'Did you enjoy it?' she asks.

My skin flushes at the memory of just how much but I know Blossom means more than that and I nod, fresh tears warming a path on my skin.

'But he didn't,' I whisper.

Blossom's brow furrows and I take one of the brown curls that frames her face absently in my fingers. Absurdly, I think of the painting – the one of the woman draped across the lounge in the prison hallway. I was right, I think, that the image it portrays is ridiculous. At least for me to keep pondering her poise and beauty as I pass it by. Because this is my version – bedraggled and hurting.

'He said he wished we hadn't ... and he left.'

She sits up, back straight, and the curl pops from my fingers.

'Oh,' she says quietly. 'What does that mean for using the portal that's reserved for—'

The sheer curtains blow inwards suddenly, the air swirling around us. Ice slides down my spine as Cortane appears in the living room, her hazel eyes running over every surface, and then Blossom and me. She strides in and I press myself further into the couch.

'I've made up my mind,' she says in greeting. There's a strange buoyancy to her tone I haven't heard before.

She's much shorter than I'd realised, but her presence fills our whole apartment. The tight black pants she wears shine slightly in the sunlight that's now streaming in behind her, the sleeveless shirt was probably once white, or some variation, and is now an assortment of stains I don't want to identify.

She looks like the sort of person I would expect to carry a weapon, but I don't see any. Not that I really know where to look, I suppose. Slowly, my heart rate comes down. Just enough for me to properly understand that Cortane, a prisoner from the other side, is standing in my living room.

And I'm crying on the couch dressed in nothing but a towel.

Blossom stands and puts herself between us.

'You shouldn't be here,' she says.

Cortane cocks her head. 'That's true of just about everywhere I go. But not really the point right now, is it?'

'What do you mean you've made up your mind?' I ask. 'That was quite clear the last time we met.'

She studies us each for a long moment, my skin tightening uncomfortably under her gaze.

'You have an exit off the island, as long you don't fuck up your recommendation,' she says, pointing at me. 'The soldiers do not. They do, however, have a job to do. When it's done, I'll get them home.' She perches herself on the edge of the chair to my left, it's back facing the entrance to my bedroom. But there's nothing casual about the movement. She's a tightly coiled spring.

'There are preparations that will need to be made,' she continues.

'You can't just pop everyone off the island today?' Blossom asks. I can't tell how much sarcasm there is supposed to be in her tone, but it's dripping with it.

'Not without us either being fried on the way, or setting off every alarm in Zanteera with the tracking magic we'd be branded with on the way through the wards.'

She looks between us, just like she did when we first met in the alcove.

'A tea would be nice,' she says, leaning back and crossing one leg over the other. The pose is relaxed but I don't doubt she'd be able to murder us both in the blink of an eye.

Reluctantly, Blossom moves to the kitchen to prepare the tea and I take the opportunity to race to my bedroom and change into soft pants and a t-shirt, dumping the towel on my bed for the moment and ignoring my wet, knotty hair.

I feel compelled to not be killed while naked, but I don't want to leave Blossom alone for long.

'—know how to find them,' Cortane is saying when I reappear in the living room.

She turns back to me, shrewd assessment running them down the length of my body.

'Not sure that's a huge improvement, Princess' she says.

My teeth click shut, I have no idea how to respond to this woman. Blossom gives me an uncertain look before she pushes two cups across the kitchen bench. The steam curls out from the two of them and, trying to swallow away the trickle of fear that still grips the back of my neck, I take one in my hands. The warmth radiates through my palms where I hold the soft yellow cup, until it becomes a heat that's too hot and I shift my grip to the handle.

Cortane studies hers, a pink floral with a gold handle, where it sits on the bench. Something like sadness flickering across her face. Raising it to her mouth, she takes a savouring sip and her lashes flutter closed briefly.

'Right,' she says, her eyes flying back open, the moment of gentleness gone. 'If we're going to do this, we do it right.'

She moves back to the sitting area and takes a seat on the couch. There's no instruction to follow her but every move of her body suggests we need to obey her silent orders and join her.

'Do you know why I am willing to help you?' she asks.

'Because ... it's nice of you?' I ask, still trying to process that she's here and committing to help.

Cortane's eyes almost bulge out of her head as she stares at me. Then she laughs so hard tears dampen her cheeks and she clasps at her chest. The sound is hollow and raspy as if she's entirely out of practice.

'Claudius,' she says, steadying her breath, 'did not send you to me because he thought I was nice.'

That is a truth we both know and I am all out of smart-ass replies, so I stay quiet.

'He trusted me to make an assessment – one I have made – and now we move forward,' she says, glancing up at the sky out the large doors to the balcony. 'There is a lot that will need to wait until another time. First, we need to know we can actually get off. You two already have a mechanism. Luka, your extension will be up soon and you'll be collected. Blossom, your duty ends in what, two years, right?'

She waits for Blossom's confirmation before she continues. 'That timing isn't ideal. When I'm back on the mainland, I will organise for your duty to be shortened.'

'Hold on,' I say against the flaring hope that starts in my stomach. 'How can it be shortened?'

'You'll be stationed in Parliament – you will help me.'

Blossom and I stare at her.

'Like I said, much to be worked out when we're off the island,' she says.

There's a soft puffing sound that takes me a moment to place as Blossom's loud exhale. 'So, how do we do it right?' she asks.

'The wards around the island are legendary,' Cortane says. 'We won't be the first to try and portal out, but we'll be the first to succeed if we do. At least without being tracked and found in less than a day.'

I let my head drop on the back of the couch as the weight of what she's saying starts to settle.

'I just need to know how to portal through the wards, without being tracked.'

I watch her as she looks between us.

'If we're marked with trackers,' she continues, 'we're as good as dead and the soldiers would be better off in Vana.'

Little bumps breakout on my skin and I rub at the cold that's started to attach to my limbs. I start to wonder if this is such a good idea. I've never so audaciously broken the rules before, and these ones are here for a reason – to keep prisoners separate from Zanteera. To stop them hurting people. And now I want to send three of them back. One of whom I *know* is a murderer.

And I could be condemning both Blossom and myself to a lifetime of Vana in the process if we're found to be assisting the breakout.

Cortane watches my hesitation and she softens slightly, her body losing the tiniest amount of its rigidity. ' I know this is a big deal,' she says. 'Just keep being discreet in what you're doing. Traelen is the primary link between Zanteera prison and the Nuntainia mainland – keep him in the dark, and you'll be fine.'

'That might be a small problem,' I say, my voice thick with the sickness in my throat. 'Quil—the new Warden … I told him you wanted information on him, and that I refused to give it.' I draw a long breath. 'He knows I'm searching for a way off the island and for who.'

The look Cortane gives me is almost enough to turn me to stone.

But I don't tell her I know Quillian is far more than Warden of this prison. That I know he is connected to Nix and River and, at least by association, to her. How much he questions what he sees up here and how much it sits so badly with him. Cortane might be helping us now – and I have been so truthful with her in the past it hurts. But none of that means I can actually trust her.

'I'll deal with him,' she says, and my stomach turns over. 'But you tell no one else. Understand?'

I stare at her.

'Why do you need us?' Blossom asks, but I can barely hear her through the screaming in my head. 'Why not just leave on your own?'

Cortane's face is virtually unreadable as she looks between us, but her voice drips with condescension. 'I might not have a 'duty' the same as the two of you, but there is a creed I live by. As for you two, Claudius wanted my views – something I never got to give him – and I need information on the wards from the Warden's office,' she says. 'It's warded against my portals so I need you to get it.'

She looks back at me. 'You obviously have a relationship with the new one, use it to get the specifications on bringing the wards from that office. I need them to work out how to go through without being marked.'

I think of Nix and River and how badly they need to be done. The pain in Nix's face when he talks of his duty. The way his letters started to warp.

And how here, even when he should be focused and precise, his turbulent emotions are clearly running so closely to the surface.

'Also,' she says, 'it's clear you're on your own ... journey here, Luka. You need to work out how far down that road you're prepared to go.'

'I'll get the information.' I raise my gaze to Cortane's. 'But if you hurt him, I will spend my last breath getting you back into Vana.'

CHAPTER TWENTY-TWO

Blossom takes charge of selecting my uniform for the day, throwing a white dress with a long, full skirt onto my bed. I used to love this one, how graceful it made me feel. And a little seductive, like I could drape myself on a lounge like the lady in the gold-framed picture and be admired forevermore.

Now, I'd like to take that painting and throw it off the island for perpetuating stupid ideals.

Nothing happened between Quillian and me that we both didn't want. Really want.

But that doesn't stop me from feeling like a used toy. A dirtied one ... and one that is really struggling to comprehend being discarded. My chest twinges and I push away any question of what his explanation could be.

Although I can't push out the deep-rooted thought that sending me away like that this morning is not his style. That the explanation could be completely valid ... like I'm leaving and he's not ... or ... or like he's a Warden and I'm a law-breaking concierge. I smother the sting that remains from the fact he did it anyway, turn my other cheek as I've done countless times before when the other shoe drops and I'm, once again, not chosen.

Blossom and I are quiet as we leave our apartment and head for the concierge room. It's the first time in a while we've started work at the same time. As we reach the open air hallways, I can hear the gentle murmur of voices from our break room.

I draw a deep lungful of air—

'Luka,' Janly says, as she pops out of the doors we were about to go through. 'I've got this – the Warden has asked to see you in his office.'

My steps falter and Blossom takes my arm, Janly disappearing back into the room again. I watch the doors close behind her.

'I guess I was never going to be able to avoid him.'

'You can do this,' Bloss says.

'Get the information on the wards, not get him killed, and not feel like a fool at the same time?'

She gives me a soft smile.

'I'll be here when you need me.'

The white-panelled door gives me pause – a longer one than normal. How different would things be if Claudius hadn't made the decisions he did?

Quillian is standing behind the desk when I enter, watching the door. Professional. I can keep it professional.

'Good morning, what's on your list for today?' I ask, trying to keep my voice light – and failing – as I close the door and make my way towards the windows. 'I believe there's another intake coming in the next week. Janly is leading the preparation for that along with the ... removal of Aiten. I have a meeting with the events committees later today to—'

Quillian moves around the desk and takes a hesitant step forward, his hands fisted in his pockets, straining the dark blue fabric.

'I was hoping to talk about last night before we talk about work,' he says quietly. All the coldness that shields him as we walk the halls has left his features, and I curse the way it flares a warmth between my ribs.

'It's fine, sir,' I lie, 'you made a mistake, you said. We don't have to make this uncomfortable. There are many more things unfolding that require our attention. I'm sure we can keep this ... respectful.' Respectful, as opposed to professional. I think that fits. My current goal of breaking out three prisoners is hardly in keeping with a *professional* concierge.

I can't look away as he takes slow, deliberate steps towards me, closing the gap I haven't been able to. The seriousness in his stance radiates through his shoulders and across his chest. But still, he walks to me.

My breath hitches. This isn't what he's supposed to be doing.

He stops less than a step before me, and I lean against the stone wall, the rock cool through the back of my white dress. I press my hands behind me, finding the sheer fabric of the curtains beneath one of my hands.

'Please don't call me sir,' he says quietly. Gently.

If I didn't know better, I'd say hurt stained the pools of his eyes.

'Okay,' I say back, any other words failing me.

'I made a mistake,' he says, and my mouth goes dry.

I knew that's what this was about – I *knew* – and it's painful anyway, like he's scratched a line down from my collarbone to the dip in my dress.

'I know, it's fine,' I say, willing my voice not to break at my naivety.

He narrows his gaze at me.

'What do you think you know, Luka?'

'You made a mistake,' I repeat, willing a bit of steel into my voice. 'I get it, you're my boss and ... it's fine. That Warden hat doesn't come off, I get it.' There's more of a bite in my last words as I say them again.

His lips pull up at the side in a sort of grimace. The left side, showing just the tiniest hint of dimple. If I didn't know it was there, I wouldn't notice. He leans forward and rational thought starts to flow away.

'I did make a mistake,' he says, his voice tight. 'But not for the reasons you think.' I watch as he leans back a fraction and fills his lungs. 'I shouldn't have ... kissed you. I shouldn't have asked you for a drink that day in the wellness centre without knowing more about ... your connections here and what role Claudius might have you playing.'

I press a hand to my chest.

Asshole.

And we did a whole lot more than kiss.

'Then we're back where we started,' I try not to scoff. 'You made a mistake. I'm not sure how many times we need to repeat it, but it's fine. I have work to do.'

I push off the wall but he blocks me with his body, stepping further into my path so I collide with him. His hands slowly leave his pockets and land on my hips, just his fingers lightly holding me there, flush against him.

My head starts to spin, but I don't pull away.

'I shouldn't have kissed you, or let myself get so caught up in your goodness I thought I could share in it – just for one, non-work related drink, because that led us here,' he repeats. His actions and his words don't match and I can't keep up. I need to breathe. His breath fans my face as he drops his forehead to mine. I squeeze my eyes shut. 'But the mistake was leaving you like that.'

All the wind leaves my already flailing sails and I stare up at him. The vulnerability in his words cracking something in my chest. Ripping it wide open and leaving it waiting to be filled with something new. Something different.

'I'm sorry.'

I peer up at him but find I need a moment before breaking our contact. Just to absorb what he's telling me. I nod slowly, moving both of our heads with the action. Desperately soaking in his words. The fact that the truth of it is written all over his face.

'Why shouldn't you have done it then?' I ask, not sure I want the answer.

'It's ... complicated,' he says.

I pull back to look at him. He doesn't force me to stay so close but I can't move away, even when he's given a terrible answer.

'Because ...' I prompt, forcing myself to be still.

'Because it will hurt people we both care about in ways you don't expect and ... because I can't tell you why. I shouldn't have put you in the middle of something you don't completely understand – can't yet understand.'

'The magic binds?' I ask, unaware the role of Warden would be subjected to the same contracts.

'More like ... the binds of honour. And I have not upheld what I was supposed to.'

Tentatively, I raise a hand between us and place it on his chest. He looks down at it before raising his face again to mine, the heat in his eyes palpable.

'What if ...' I whisper, horribly conscious of the warmth racing across my own chest and down my centre. The words are far more vulnerable than I would like but looking up at his face, one that's really still very new to me, I can't stop how much I want to know it more. To know why he left like that, why he's looking at me like that *was* a mistake. How much he feels like ... *possibility*. Something different. I trail my fingers in loose circles over his shirt, my gaze tracing their path, finding them drawn to his collar, to his tattoo ...

He squeezes the fingers on my hips a little harder and makes a questioning sound in his throat, prompting me.

'What if the opportunity presented itself again?' I can't look at him as I ask. Instead I watch my hand on his chest, wondering what he'd do if I slipped it between the buttons on his shirt. If I told him everything about how my feelings about this prison and its people feel like they're being woken up. How I feel like I might not make it to Traelen's unknown ending of my extension. How desperately part of me wants to leave with Nix and River and take Bloss with us.

He wraps his hand further around my back, finally pulling me completely against him, and drops his head to my shoulder. A shiver runs the entire way down my body as he drags his nose up the column of my neck and puts his lips to mine so softly I think I might imagine it.

'That would be an opportunity I didn't think I would have. One I don't deserve. And one I would need to wait for.' His breath tickles my face.

'What do you mean?' I murmur.

He cups my jaw in his hands and looks at me, weighing up his response. 'I can't hurt those people like that again, Luka, you included. Even if I feel like it's going to kill me to stay away from you. I did not expect ...'

I stare at him blankly but he says no more and my stomach drops through the floor – he can only mean Nix and River. I can't find the words I need in this moment. I don't even know what the right ones are. Eventually, he removes his hands and steps back. Shifting to the desk he picks up a folder of papers and shuffles them around a bit.

Finally, he looks back to me, clearing his throat, and we hold each other's gaze as we make a silent agreement to let the moment go. Let the tension in the room subside. At least as much as we can.

'Shall we go through the list?' he asks.

The rest of the day is spent in a growingly familiar way. We work, we talk, and we dance around the unspoken words between us. Quillian is careful, never too overt with his touches or his looks. Just not careful enough for me to not notice him being so controlled. My mind frequently wanders the questions I have no answers to yet, the ones I should have thought of a long time ago – ones my father would probably be quite disappointed I haven't been asking.

Or would he have just expected that I do my duty, my service for my country, without further question?

Whatever the case, I know now I can't let those questions go. I want to know why all the prisoners are treated like esteemed guests when the acts they have committed mean they should by rights be in the true Vana. Quillian walks me to the door when the sun is setting, but there is no part of me that wants to leave.

'I guess I should go,' I say, willing the soft yearning to stay, to be quiet.

He nods. 'I have a few things I need to tidy up before our next check-in with Traelen, there's no point in you staying for that. You should ... enjoy your evening.'

The space between us goes taut but he reaches around me and opens the door. I step out into the hallway and he follows, just a step behind. Until we're both occupying the space just on the outside of the doorway, as if neither of us wants to completely leave the sanctuary of his office.

'I'll see you later,' he says quietly. 'We can talk more if you're sure you're ready.'

Our gazes come together and hold there a moment. For a wild heartbeat I want to lean forward and feel his mouth again. But doing so here, in the hall, wouldn't be right – especially after all of our discussion this morning. Nor do I want to give the prisoners anything to complain to Traelen about. So I breathe into all the spaces in my chest that I want to fill with something else and straighten my spine.

'You fucking bastard,' a low voice mutters.

A broad frame launches itself at Quillian, shoving me to the side and into the wall. The impact of my head on the stone pings around my skull and I blink furiously to clear my vision. Nix straddles Quillian and draws his fist back before slamming it into Quillian's face, blood spraying the door to the office.

Quillian covers his face with his arms but otherwise doesn't fight back. His wings don't make an appearance, and my head spins with gratitude that he hasn't already shredded Nix to pieces.

'Nix!' I shout, finally finding my voice. 'Nix! Stop!'

My heart races as I throw myself on Nix's back and try to grapple his arms into place by his sides. But he's too strong for me and the impact I have on pulling his punches is limited. I dig my fingers into his scalp and yank on his hair. His head jerks back as he curses but he still doesn't focus. Wrenching himself from my grasp, he leaves me staring at the dark red strands left in my hands. I slip off him as he pummels Quillian.

'RIVER!' I scream until my voice is hoarse.

Prisoners start to gather, mouths agape, whispering. Some of them cover their eyes but they don't walk away. At least one has a phone out.

All I can focus on is Quillian's face, the grunts of pain he makes as Nix makes contact. A surge of panic fires through my limbs – for Nix or Quillian, I don't know – and I throw myself at Nix again, screaming at him to listen to me.

He makes to dislodge me and smacks me in the side of the face with his elbow. The sensation in my cheek and a white hot pain lances through my eye socket and down my neck as the world tilts and I can't see.

The stone walkway greets me with another kind of hardness as I drop onto it, my arms falling out beneath me as I try to get up.

But the prison is getting too dark and the tears are hot on my face.

'Nix, please,' I whimper. 'Stop.'

CHAPTER TWENTY-THREE

A series of voices fades in and out of my mind as I try to focus, time slipping away.

'Luka, you in there?' River asks, and I groggily try to peel open my eyes. His soft blue ones fill my vision as I blink away the darkness.

'Quillian,' I mumble, pushing away from River.

'He's been taken to the wellness centre.'

'Oh, wow, that hurts,' I say, leaning my head back against the wall and cupping the side of my face. Opening my eyes again I glance around, making sure someone has dispersed the prisoners. 'Where is Nix?'

'Gone to cool off.' River's shoulders sag.

'Cool off,' I say, still trying to clear my vision. 'Cool *off*? He shouldn't have any need to cool off – what the fuck was that, River? He could have killed him.'

I look at him suddenly, a sickening feeling growing in my chest.

'Not dead,' he says. 'But he's pretty busted up.'

His brows draw together, his disappointment more apparent than his anger right now. 'As are you,' he says quietly. 'I ... Lu, I—'

I take the hand of the man who has always been a guiding presence in my life – one that was, and is, always so calm and stable in comparison to my wild best friend – and let him pull me to standing, leaning into him for support. I can see the heaviness in his features as he draws me near, shadowed under the weight of supporting Nix for so long, and I don't even know all the details of why. Not anymore. But it's so clear it hurts; Nix's duty has altered him in some way I might only ever be able to guess at.

The hall to the wellness centre is quiet as I make my way there with River, his bulky form shadowing mine. His mood is dark, darker than what seems right under the radiance of the sunlight, but it matches the turmoil under my own skin.

Nix beat Quillian. I want to say I don't understand, that I don't know why. But I do know. Nix's fists literally flew at the thought of Quillian and me together. What I don't know is why that would set him off – what that was a trigger for. The anger churning in my gut makes me feel sick.

'He had no right, River,' I mutter under my breath and glancing sideways. 'I've never seen him like that before, I just—'

I throw my hands up before noticing the prisoners eyeing us curiously, the rumours obviously having already whipped through the rest of prison. Even though it feels like every one of them was there, watching. Something I will have to try and deal with when my head doesn't feel like it's pounding to the point of explosion with every step I take. I groan when I think about how many of them are already contacting Traelen to give their version of events. Of the prison that is unravelling under the watch of Quillian and me.

'What the fuck is going on?' I ask.

River sighs heavily, as if the weight of the world pulls on his shoulders.

'It's been a messed up time for us, Lu.'

His downcast gaze and clenched fists paints a picture of complicated sadness when I glance at him.

'I'm not going to make excuses for what he did,' he continues, 'but there are—fuck, things I can't really talk about. Between our ... current situation and the fact some shit is just really fucking hard but ... our service is – was – fucked up. It's what brought us here. We were asked to do one too many things we couldn't live with. Appalling things.'

The anger in my gut directed at Nix starts to fizzle, leaving an uncomfortable sensation in its wake. I think of the prison on the other side, the torture I know goes on there but have never seen – never want to see. How many of the people behind those walls were never supposed to end up there? How many of the 'prisoners' here should be over there? Is the power deciding the fates of those of this prison-island the same one sending people like River and Nix to do things so awful on their duties that they can't talk about them? That makes them do … whatever secret, probably quite morally grey, activities they are now actively engaged in up here?

'What did they make you do?' I ask quietly, as we round the corner and the onlookers start to fall away.

River stops just before the entrance to the core of the peace and calm that emanates through the prison and I glance behind, taking a step back to him in the hallway. Gently, he takes my wrist in his hand.

'I'd tell you everything, Lu, but it will take time and there are things that are not mine to say. And some things are really difficult to say – or hear.'

'I can't help him if I don't know,' I say, confused tears trying to force their way forward.

'You can help more than you think, Lu – you doubt yourself too much.'

River's voice is so soft I can barely make it out, but it hits the same note he's told me again and again. As expected, the hope in his face that I can help is clear as day. It tugs at me, at the place Nix and I are connected. Pressing on the truth that I will help him no matter the cost. But it doesn't stop the fact there is another connection, one glowing with a warm light, that I will defend as well.

If I can prove to Cortane they are both worth saving.

'Do you know,' I say mildly, half wondering at how groggy I might still be, 'two people I know both have tattoos about "proving" something. I don't know what that means for them, but somehow I feel like I am constantly having to prove something to everyone. I just don't know when I've done it, or if I ever will.'

'After you,' River says after a beat, gesturing to the door to the medical section of the centre – the same place Quillian stitched up my skin.

'I'm leaving,' I hear Quillian grind out from the other side of the room.

He's roughly shrugging his shirt back on when we walk in, River only a step behind, and I hold my breath. Suddenly unsure if he would want me here or not. He spins, the front of his shirt covered in blood and undone. The air I'd captured in my lungs rushes out between the fingers I press to my mouth.

His gaze lands on my face immediately and he turns to stone. The only thing that moves after a long moment are his eyes as they narrow and slide to River.

River shifts on his feet once but says nothing, almost like he's waiting for punishment for Nix's actions.

Quillian stalks across the space to us, leaving the healer staring after him, a white cloth held limply in his hand. I remain frozen to the spot, my hands remaining on my mouth as I take him in, an uncomfortable sensation in my stomach. His face is still bloody and one of his brows has split open, blood leaking down his cheek and dripping slowly from his jaw. There are black, tacky bits of hair sticking to his face and part of the tattoo on his neck is obscured.

He doesn't bother with the buttons of his ruined, blood-splattered shirt, and I check what I can see of his torso, searching for more injuries, but it's hard to tell between his coloured tattoo and the blood.

Stopping less than a foot from us he looks at me, his forest eyes almost black in his expressionless face.

'If you *ever* drag me away from her when she's hurt again, I will not be merciful. Understand?'

The hairs on my arms stand on end but River seems to understand it's him that's being addressed, despite Quillian's stare not leaving my face.

'You were barely conscious,' River says quietly, and I swallow.

'Not an excuse.' Quillian finally looks at River again. 'He hurts her again – accidentally or otherwise – he forfeits all right to hold this against me. Leave us.'

River and I turn to each other at the same time, me searching him for any hint of confirmation of the understanding crystallising in my mind. What 'this' Quillian is talking about. How clearly he knows there is a dynamic between Nix and me and it's one that now involves him. How he ... orders River in a way that seems so different to a Warden/prisoner relationship.

I stare at him. Quillian *is* their commanding officer. The person who coordinated with Claudius to get them here.

Quietly, the medic takes his leave as well, and River gathers me in his arms. Kissing my forehead briefly before pressing me away by my upper arms, his gaze flicks over my face. He squeezes me gently and a warmth runs around me, strong enough for me to pull myself back into him and hold him hard once more, as the solidifying of what I'd suspected about Quillian becomes abundantly clear.

'I'm so sorry, Lu,' he whispers into my hair.

'I'm okay, this isn't on you,' I say, trying not to wince as I smile gently at him and pull away. A flash of guilt sparks behind my ribs at the weight of responsibility in his frame as he leaves the wellness centre. The large, frosted glass door swings silently after him. He isn't to blame for Nix's actions, but I now also wonder how much Nix is responsible – what was he made to do on his national duty that's damaged him like this? How much of it is because of Quillian's role as their leader?

I look at the opaque surface of the door several moments longer, even after River has left, trying to collect my spinning thoughts amongst the throb in my cheek. As I turn back to Quillian, my lips start to quiver as I desperately try to keep the tears at bay. But his face, battered and bloodied, drags a sob from my chest, and I cover my mouth again even as my mind whirls with questions. Trying to trap the emotions inside.

A tear meanders down the side of my face and I shake my head. 'I'm so sorry. I can't believe—'

He steps towards me, close enough his warmth starts to seep into my rapidly cooling body. His strong hands take mine and he gently pulls them away from my face.

'Hey,' he whispers, the coldness draining away from his face. 'Don't do that – don't cry. Not for me.'

I trail the side of his face with my fingers, so lightly his expression doesn't change. At least, not in pain. But his softness takes root.

'He deserves your tears,' he says quietly, 'and then your support. Don't waste them on me. But, shit – this—'

'I just – I don't know why he did that, he's never—' I sniff. 'He's not like that.'

He runs a thumb over my bottom lip.

'I know,' he whispers.

'Are you okay?' I ask, the band around my ribs loosening a little at the lack of fire in his tone about Nix.

He nods slowly.

'Yeah,' he breathes, still holding my jaw and one of my hands. A dark cloud crashes over him again as he scans my face. 'But I'm absolutely furious about this.'

'I'm fine, please don't make a thing of it. It's nothing compared to what happened to you. Or the depth of trauma I think it means Nix has been through.'

'I probably will be a little more colourful than you tomorrow,' he says. 'But that doesn't change my feelings, Luka.' He points to his face. 'Most of this was deserved.'

I frown, but he cuts me off before I can ask, images of the way he didn't fight back flashing in my mind.

'That,' he says, turning his finger to me instead, 'was not. No matter how traumatised he is.'

'I need to talk to him,' I say, 'I need to understand.'

His hand drops away from my cheek slowly, the tingling staying even after his skin has left mine.

'We also have a lot of explaining to do for Traelen. I had the security team shut down external comms for a while so we can try and get ahead of it, but that won't last long.'

The relief I feel is instantaneous. Today feels like all the balls I'm responsible for have been thrown into the clouds and I have no idea how to catch them all. Or which ones should be caught first. Mentally sorting through the things we need to do feels like wading through mud.

'First, we get ourselves patched up,' I say wearily. 'Then Nix, then the prisoners and Traelen. But after that, Quillian'—I wait until he looks back up at me—'you are going to help me understand every tiny thing that is happening here, got it?'

☀

At Quillian's behest, the previous healer returns with his more magically gifted team leader, but Quillian refuses to be seen to first. So I watch him, watch me, as I perch on the bed and Shiloh attends to my face. Asking me questions and tilting my head backwards and forward, pressing on my jawline and cheekbone in different places.

I wince when she touches my cheekbone, and Quillian clenches his fists harder in his pockets, pulling at the fabric. His shirt is still undone and it takes more concentration than I'd like to admit to stop my gaze dipping below his busted face.

He cocks his head slightly when he catches me looking but I can't look away, despite the blood I can feel rushing across my collarbones and flushing my skin. When Shiloh finishes her healing magic on me, Quillian reluctantly takes my place on the bed. Virtually scowling.

'Most of our Wardens don't look like they've been brawling,' I tell him and he grunts, half-amused but still resistant to the help. 'Shiloh is one of our most talented Arkanans. Let her work her magic,' I say, my face still tingling slightly where she's healed me as best she can – setting my body up to do the rest on its own. The dull ache will likely last a while longer but at least the splitting pain has subsided.

In the back of my mind, a little voice reminds me I haven't been taking my magic dampener. It's been a short amount of time but I haven't noticed a single change, and with each day that passes and there's nothing new ... well, it seems more and more certain I have pushed down for good on whatever that was going to be.

'I'm tougher than most Wardens,' he says, eyes flashing in my direction. 'Not all, but most.'

A soft smile appears on Shiloh's face as she glances back at me. Her fiery red hair piled into a high collection of strands on her head, keeping it out of her face as she works. But her uniform is like mine, an ethereal dress. Not very practical for our healing staff, but it upholds our image.

Just like that blasted painting.

Beautiful, artful, but a false reality all the same.

Just like the one I have been living – a prettily dressed concierge on a pretty island with pretty things.

Yet, now, I feel like the paint's been scrubbed off and I'm starting to see the actual shapes underneath.

And they're definitely not pretty.

The tension in Quillian's face softens slightly as Shiloh lets her healing run over the surface of his skin, but he remains watching me. She won't erase the damage completely, only Nuntainia's most skilled healing wielders can do that – none of which we have here right now – but she'll greatly soften the visible components and pave the way for a faster healing process by our own bodies. I still haven't looked at my face but I can tell from the amount of tingling that she has significantly reduced the damage. Quillian had a quiet conversation with her before we started and, looking at his still-wounded face, I have a suspicion he's asked her to use more of her energy on me than him.

I stand behind Shiloh, watching her work on him, but the space between Quillian and me is almost a visceral thing. Like I could reach out and pluck its strings. My fingertips itch to do just that.

Shiloh finishes and I help her clean up, ferrying the cloths and small brass bowls to the long timber bench. Popping them into the large, square, white sink, I run the faucet and ready to wash them. She comes next to me and bumps me lightly with her hip.

'I can do this, Luka,' she says, looking at me sideways, a sly grin on her face. 'I can totally see why you're into him,' she whispers. 'That broody tension is enough to give *me* goosebumps!'

I can't help the laugh that escapes my mouth.

'No comment,' I say, despite what my smile clearly answers as I wipe my hands on the stone-coloured linen towel. 'Hey,' I say on a whim, 'what did it feel like when your magic was coming in?'

'Gosh,' she says. 'I haven't thought about that in a long time.' She goes quiet for a moment. 'I suppose it's like what we'd wish puberty was like ... there's this gentle warmth that spreads through your limbs each day, building until you feel like you might have sparks coming from your fingertips. And, as it dissipates, you're left with a sense of ... fullness. Like, on the inside, you've grown into the shape you were supposed to. It's easy. Right. At least, it was for me.'

I smile at her, a weight settling in my chest. One I don't think will ever dislodge.

I shouldn't have asked.

'Ready?' Quillian says as I meet him at the door.

He glances down at my hands where they hang by my sides and, for a moment, I think he will take one in his.

'How you manage this will be important for your ... stability as Warden. We're going to need a pretty solid story.'

My heart compresses at the look on his face but I can't read it.

'Let's go,' he says, pushing the door open.

I stay a step behind him as we walk through the halls, avoiding the gazes of the prisoners around us. Finn strides down the hall from the other direction and nods almost imperceptibly at Quillian as he passes.

'Sir,' he says, his voice as quiet as the first time I met him.

Reaching the hall to the office, we make a turn and my stomach flutters uncomfortably at the blood that still stains the timber door frame. My concierge habits are hard to break though and I immediately text Emeris to get a cleanup crew to the Warden's office.

Each step as we approach seems to echo with the things we need to do – things I need to do. Sort out Nix, get a story together for Traelen, reschedule my events committee meeting, check on Paulana, and find out more about the wards and how to go through them or use the one in the Warden's Residence. As if I could possibly forget that Nix and River need an out and I am the conduit to get them to it. Hopefully without fucking up my own exit in the meantime. But every moment we don't have this situation completely contained is another one of the prisoners could be reaching out directly to Traelen.

I groan internally. I'm very confident things would not be this messy if Claudius were still here to guide us all through. Because that's what he would have done – helped all of us, Nix and River, Cortane, Quillian, and Bloss and me – to each do our part of the bigger picture he saw for us.

The details of the wards are something he must have known about, information I could have just asked him for. Or he would have just told me so I could share it with Cortane on his behalf.

I glance at Quillian. I haven't asked him outright about the wards which, by now, I'm quite confident I could. But not in the middle of the hall we walk down. But, when I think on his comments about what he was told when coming here, I think Nix is probably right – he's unlikely to know anything more than I do.

'Luka!'

Blossom's fierce whisper has me spinning on the spot. Quillian pausing beside me. There's murder on her face as she looks me over, only once nodding in Quillian's direction to acknowledge him.

She's not surprised, River has obviously found her and filled her in, but I don't have the energy to explain right now. Certainly not in view of the prisoners who still linger in the walkways.

Finally, she looks at Quillian again.

'We need you,' she says, no emotion in her voice. 'There's another body.'

I want to throw my hands in the air and swear. Instead, I give myself a moment and tell Bloss to lead the way. As she does, I find I am less worried about who it might be. And more hopeful it was someone who deserved it. Like Kasera. Like Aiten.

Like who knows how many more of them up here.

Including Davorous.

CHAPTER TWENTY-FOUR

The walk through the prison is long. Every step towards the most recent death feeling harder than the last. I used to love this building. Let myself believe I was up here doing something good because the government required it of me. But there's no way the government – the Prime Minister – doesn't know who they are really sending here. And it brings a weariness to my bones that's hard to shake.

'Who?' I whisper to Blossom as we each smile inanely at the prisoners that pass us by, wishing I had a touch more compassion in my tone.

'Traelen needs to get his Hunters up here,' I hear one of the prisoners say. 'Deal with whatever is happening that our staff clearly aren't.'

She slides her gaze to me quickly, before returning to watch where she's going, and I try to breathe past the pressure in my chest.

'Miana,' she says, quietly.

I frown, mapping out the prisoners in my mind.

'Fleur's friend?'

'Yup.'

The friend of the woman Nix spent the night with after the dinner. My tongue burns with the need to ask Blossom if she knows where he is, if River found him. But the prickling presence of the prisoners around us keeps the words from spilling out. There's an almost pulse-like quality to the air around us, the prison itself almost eerily quiet. As if it – and the prisoners – wait for something. My mind screams at me to be careful.

On the surface, the prisoners have accepted our bland explanations of the passings and mournings and otherwise redirection to other fanciful activities – with the help of copious amounts of Silver Sparkle, of course. But there's a gnawing at the base of my skull now that tells me believing that is naive. For these people to be among the highest ranking officials in Nuntainia and be hiding things like child slavery and sex trafficking means they are not the dim-witted souls I have allowed myself to believe.

Every step I take towards where Miana has been found solidifies my understanding that we are not the only ones playing games up here.

Little bumps breakout on my skin.

We reach the prisoners' wing and I force myself not to look too long down the hallway, desperately looking for any sign of the brothers.

Quillian pauses at the doorway, no other concierges in sight.

'Who found her?' he asks.

'Paulana's partner – Kristoff,' Blossom responds and I nod, at least that bit makes sense.

'Have you been in here?'

Blossom visibly shudders as I look to her for her answer.

'No chance,' she says. 'I just came to check the door was locked and then came to find you.'

Her deep teal eyes dance over my face as she says it, and I know it's not quite the truth. She's spoken to River in the time between coming here and finding us.

The white door has a gold handle and I watch as Quillian's brown hand engulfs it. He pauses and looks back at Blossom and me.

'You don't have to come in,' he says softly, looking between the two of us.

Blossom and I look at each other, a wordless agreement passing between us – we've come this far. I meet Quillian's gaze and he turns back to the door, pressing his other palm next to the handle as he does. The door swings inwards, straight into the plush living area.

It's the same as other rooms, just with Miana's individual taste layered on top, her abstract paintings so different to the romantic ones in the public spaces of the prison, the geometric throws she has covering the pale lounge suite.

'In the bedroom,' Blossom says quietly, waiting for Quillian to take the lead.

We follow him across the living room, past the sage-green and grey marble kitchen and towards the bedroom; but when Quillian strides towards the body – Miana – on the bed, Blossom and I pause. Neither of us seem to want to cross the threshold into the bedroom where the thin, cold weight of death is growing in the corners of the room.

Quillian looks down at her, holding a hand above her body, a tiny look of concentration on his face. Nothing happens between his hand and her body that I can see and I watch his face. I've read so much about Arkanan abilities, even trace ones like it appears Quillian has, but I've never been in the room with one and a dead body.

'She's definitely gone,' he says, looking back at us.

Blossom exhales.

'Just how many more of these are we going to have to deal with?' she asks.

My stomach turns over. Cortane can clearly go wherever she likes, at least on the island, and Nix and River have unrestricted access to this entire prison. I want to refuse the thought that either of the Kilroy brothers could have done this themselves. But Miana's stiffening and cold body, tangled in the sheets in front of me, makes me less disturbed that this could have been one of them, and more sure that she must have had something she was due to pay for.

'Blossom,' Quillian says without looking at me. 'Do you mind asking Emeris to prepare her for moving? I'll notify the family. And start the paperwork.' He turns to me, belatedly tucking the shirt back into his pants. Not that it will hide the blood that's still on it and the swelling that's clear on his face. 'Luka, will you join me? We will need to work through the messaging to the prisoners and concierges. Blossom, please don't talk to anyone other than Emeris about this until we can properly brief all the teams.'

Blossom doesn't move and the three of us watch each other, Miana's presence like an uncomfortable weight in the room.

'Quillian,' I say quietly. 'I want to help, you know that, but this ...' I glance at Blossom, who seems a little pale. 'There are limits on what we can ... clean up when we don't know exactly what it is we're involved in.

Traelen could be one message away from storming this place with Hunters and we're all up for Vana whether we know anything or not.'

He studies each of us so long I can't help but think he's considering the implications of sharing information with us. How many other things is he involved in?

Eventually, he nods and I take it for what I hope it is – an agreement to let us in.

Following him into his office, where I feel like I am spending most of my time lately, he comes to a stop so abruptly I almost collide with his back.

'Traelen,' he says, a tiny bit of ice in his voice.

'Quillian,' Traelen returns.

I shut the office door and step beside Quillian, completely unprepared for this conversation. *Answers* is what I wanted from coming here – answers from Quillian and on how to go through the wards. Not Traelen. Not lying about something I don't fully understand.

'Luka.' Traelen inclines his head to me. Just.

'Sir,' I say, the awkward tension in the greetings stretching between us as Quillian waits, seemingly unruffled by Traelen's sudden appearance.

Traelen looks at us for a long stretch of time, the thoughts whirring behind his eyes, and I resist the urge to step away from Quillian.

'What exactly is happening up here, Warden?' he asks, a subtle emphasis on Quillian's title as he takes in Quillian's bloodied torso.

'I was just coming here to discuss it with you,' Quillian answers smoothly, stepping around Traelen in his crisp white suit and moving to the bookcase. Pouring three glasses of gold liquid from a decanter, he holds one each out to Traelen and me before collecting his own and gesturing to the red couches. My gaze catches on the frame next to the decanter, the one with the pencil drawing of the prison Claudius loved so much, and I wonder if this prison was ever as simple as a line drawing.

I don't mean to sit next to Quillian but perhaps I'm repelled from Traelen and the questions he's about to ask.

Or I'm drawn to Quillian like a magnet.

'With respect, Sir,' Quillian continues, his voice tight, 'this prison, and the people it contains are ripe for unrest. We both know the announcements that are given when the inmates arrive are simply used to try to distract from the truth. The reasons underneath might be 'unpalatable' to the government but what's real is that you've given me a cohort punctuated with individuals who – at their core – are evil.'

Quillian shifts forward in his seat and I can barely breathe. How far is he going to take this with Traelen? In front of me?

'I'm sure the prisoners have told you themselves, but it's true I have a different style to Claudius. I believe his death has been the catalyst for the prisoners to feel even more liberated to behave exactly how they please, consequences be damned, for there *are* no consequences.'

Traelen swirls the drink in his glass, staring into the golden pool. 'That wouldn't have anything to do with the beating you took today, would it?'

So much for getting the external comms down before any prisoners could use their existing connections. Not that Traelen wouldn't have worked that much out just by looking at him. Quillian considers his answer as Traelen looks between us, again he doesn't show the faintest flicker of surprise.

'Anything else happening I should know about?' Traelen asks.

I don't move.

'Not all the prisoners here are enjoying a break from true repercussions, Traelen,' Quillian says, his voice low. 'Some of them have genuine trauma. I'd suggest what happened today is something that occurs when that trauma isn't dealt with.'

'Wonder what set that off?' Traelen asks lazily, but it seems very clear he doesn't care about anyone's 'trauma'.

He places his glass on the table between us, not having taken any sips. Standing, he looks down at Quillian and me.

'That can't happen again, Quillian – trauma or not – this is a place people come to for time out. To recover from their ordeals, not experience more.' He pauses for a beat. 'The Prime Minister expects his ideal to be upheld here, but the volume of contact from prisoners has gotten extreme. All communications from them will be channeled directly through me. Meaning, whether you like it or not, those prisoners you are supposed to be serving, are controlling your narrative. I'd think carefully about what that means. It is your *job,* Warden, to keep this pot from boiling over.'

Quillian studies him, unmoving, while my mind turns to static. *Their* ordeals? Not the children's? Or the people being sold as sex slaves? The 'narrative'? What the fuck is happening here?

'I should like to see the body,' he says.

Quillian stands slowly. 'By all means,' he says.

The two of them walk to the door and I try not to draw attention to myself. I don't know if they intended to leave me here but I can't see why I would need to go. And I'm happy to spend as little time with Traelen and the dead as possible. And I need my own information. As I watch the back of Traelen's white jacket, he pauses. Turning his head back to us, Quillian directly behind him and me still on the red couch.

'I assume you know there are prisoners here who should be on the other side,' he says. 'I am preparing them for transfer as a priority. Particularly given the circumstances. If I find anyone is playing an underhanded game here, they will be added to my transfer list without further question.' He pauses. 'For the record, I don't believe in 'luck' – good or bad. But you, Luka, might. You've done well supporting Quillian and gaining his endorsement – he gave you a glowing review yesterday and signed off on Claudius's original recommendation with no changes. So I'm ending your extension. I'm arranging to have your friend ... Vale, I think, collect you. You should be home in less than fortnight – after the Kilroy brothers have been removed,' Traelen says with a touch of a smile.

Everything stops as Quillian looks at me, his face completely unreadable. Is he ... sending me away? I feel like I'm hollowing out on the inside. I'll be sent back to the mainland with nothing, and no one, and Nix and River are being transferred to Vana.

I press my hand against my stomach.

'Thank you, sir,' I whisper. But all I can think about is the wards, and Cortane. If I can go with them.

'Also,' Traelen adds, 'I have addressed the prisoners – assured them you know what you're doing up here.' I glance to Quillian but there is no sign of irritation on his face. Despite that Traelen is now actively going around him. 'They're getting fearful. Fearful people make impaired decisions. That is not a situation we want up here. I want you to give the prisoners a gala. Immediately. Let them drown their fears and move on.'

I watch the door close, not telling him I think *drunk*, fearful people would make worse decisions, before I let my head drop into my hands, pressing my lips closed. But it's not low enough to stop the spin and I drop it between my legs instead, my braid dropping back over my head and almost reaching the floor.

Forcing the air in and out my nose, I count my breaths until I'm ready to stand. Willing the turning of the room to stop; I have information I need to find. The thoughts in my head tumble as I move around the room methodically, just like I would have done at the Academy. Wondering where the previous Warden would have kept files on the security of the wards, but not wishing to disturb anything too greatly. Wanting Quillian to come back, on his own, so we can sort through the knotted threads of information that are tightening in my gut.

My heart slams as I scan the bookshelf but nothing leaps out at me as instructional on how to break wards.

But then it probably wouldn't, would it? I curse at myself.

The drawers on the desk are heaving and full, one of them still containing the file that told me what room Nix was staying in. I stare at it a moment, it feels like just yesterday I was in here looking for that information, and the realisation steadies me.

I can do this. I've done it before. I just have to trust that Claudius wanted me to find the information. He wanted me to connect with Cortane and this is something she needs. I don't examine how much has changed since then, how much *I* have changed. And I certainly don't think on the fallout I will be leaving behind with Quillian. Something lodges in my throat at the thought of leaving him behind at all. At the same time, he doesn't feel like a Warden – or person – who will let the prisoners get away with everything which is perhaps exactly what they need.

Flicking through the files in the drawers isn't fruitful and I make myself go through them twice. Reading each label, but they're mostly files on the concierges themselves. Our start and end dates, next of kin.

Shutting the drawer again, grunting slightly at the weight of the one at the bottom, I walk out from behind the desk and turn my back on it. My gaze falling on the framed, hand-drawn design of the prison that sits on one of the bookshelves. Making my way back to the dark timber shelving that takes up the entire wall, I stand on my tip toes and pluck the frame from where it sits.

Help me Claudius, what am I missing? How do the wards work?

Blowing off the dust, I squint at the lines of the prison in my hand. Below the prison is peaked like an inverted mountain, the top half covered in grey and white foliage. The artist was incredibly detailed on the points that show the way back to the mainland and the landscape in which the prison sits.

Vana is the only building I can see, the drawing obviously either being done before the warden's residence and the other prison were built, or choosing not to capture them. Below the island, cupping the entire drawing, is an upside down arc that must represent the wards and the delineation between us and Nuntainia.

But there's nothing on how to bring the wards down, even temporarily.

Keeping a normal pace through the sun-drenched halls is almost impossible, and the muscles in my legs quiver with the desire to run. Finding Blossom or River are the highest priorities on my list. Hopefully they can fill me in on what's happened since Nix's altercation with Quillian so I can prepare myself for that encounter. Because Nix is second.

Then, I need to tell them we have less than a fortnight for them to be off the island.

'Luka!' Emeris says, as I poke my head into the concierge room looking for Blossom. The handful of other concierges turning to look at me. I keep my focus on Emeris as he rushes over to me.

'What the fuck happened?' he asks, eyes wide.

I stare at him having no idea what to tell him about my injured face, or Miana's death that took priority over everything else.

'I honestly have no idea,' I say.

He shakes his head at me in disbelief. 'This place is ...' he sighs. 'I mean, Janly warned me, you know? But ... a bit wonky isn't it?'

I laugh with little humour. 'Wonky is definitely one way to put it. Have you seen Bloss?'

'No,' he says, 'last I heard she was helping the Warden with something but I haven't seen her since.'

Thanking Emeris as I squeeze his hand, not looking at the others who still watch us, I message Blossom.

I'm panting a bit by the time I get to the room I share with her. Not having found her in the wellness centre or the kitchens, and still waiting for her to respond, I make my way to our apartment.

'Blossom!' I call out.

But it's Nix I come face to face with, standing in my living room, attention glued on me. Nix who watches me with Quillian's blood still on his knuckles and dried over his fingers, splashes on the back of his hands. I breathe in, hard, while I stare at his face, unable to stop the glare I can feel on mine. Waiting for any semblance of calm, I take another breath.

It doesn't help.

Shutting the door behind me, the hot rage that burns through my limbs and races up my chest is quickly overtaken by the cool rush of relief that he's here.

'Why?' I grind out.

He just looks at me as I face him.

'Why, Nix?' I ask, more quietly this time. 'What the fuck were you thinking? You *hurt* him,' I say, my voice losing its edge altogether and finding a sad tone instead. 'You hurt *me*.'

He drags his bloody hands down his face, his shoulders shuddering behind them.

'There's no excuse for what I did, Lu,' he whispers.

'I need to know why, Nix. Quillian said some of it was deserved, I know this isn't just about me getting to know him.'

He sighs heavily, uncovering his face and looking up at me again, pain swirling in his eyes that grips my heart.

I sink down to the couch in front of him and wait.

CHAPTER TWENTY-FIVE

The look Nix levels me with is heavy as he, too, takes a seat.

'Quillian and I,' he says quietly, 'we ... know each other.'

'That I know already,' I say. 'I know you said he's the reason you're here and ... I know he's your commanding officer – the one you said knew Claudius.'

He blows out a breath that puffs his lips out, as if the things he's holding on to are finally ready for escape. 'My last service was on the front. I was one of the soldiers sent to Tae to bolster their numbers.' He waits while I let that sink in.

'Tae?' I frown. Tae. Where Aiten Gall was buying people to sell. A country bordering Nuntainia that I've barely thought of and has now come up in two separate conversations in a matter of days.

He nods as I stare at him, willing my mind to connect the pieces I'm not sure I can see.

'But ... that's not our fight. Tae and Coprath are at war, not us.'

'Nuntainia has a vested interest in Tae maintaining control of the Rite Gorge. You know Tae gives Nuntainia access to the Gorge and open trade. According to Nuntainia, Coprath is highly unlikely to allow the same liberties. And so the government bolsters Tae's numbers to keep Coprath forces at bay, and away from the Gorge.'

I press my fingertips into my temples, listening to what he's not quite saying. 'You've been *at war* these last five years? *Active* war?'

His gaze searches mine for understanding. In it I can see the weight of everything he can't seem to say. At war. My country isn't even supposed to be *at war*. Not anymore. Soldiers, I knew – they said that. But I thought that meant training, doing peacekeeping activities – *preparing* not *doing*.

'So Quillian was, too,' I say, thinking out loud. 'That's how he's become Warden. He served well on behalf of Nuntainia and this position is his reward – a cushy Warden role in a beautiful location.' My stomach tightens. 'And that's where things went wrong between the two of you – in Tae.' My tone is question enough and Nix dips his chin in confirmation. 'Fuck, Nix, I – I don't know what to say.' Suddenly, his behaviour towards Quillian doesn't seem so out of place. How many horrible things has he been required to do? A bitter taste builds in the back of my throat. 'Will you ...' I start tentatively, 'tell me what happened?'

Nix reaches out to take my hand but there's something reluctant about it, as if he's not sure he wants to burden me with whatever it is.

'I've come to understand that he didn't know the full ramifications of his decisions – or perhaps made the least horrible decision available to him. But the cost was the same.'

'Tell me,' I whisper.

Nix's hurt is almost concealed in his voice. But the set of his jaw, the way the fingers on his free hand grip the soft cushion, give it away. And an awful sense of foreboding tightens in my chest as I watch him.

He looks away, out of the window across the living room.

'There was a ... need, for someone to charm the local villagers. To make sure they never made the connection between Tae and Nuntainia, and to encourage them to fight for Tae – without the appropriate resources or time to have them all sign the contracts that allow compensation.' He swallows. 'Most of the younger boys couldn't wait to start. We ... people like me,' he glances sideways at me. 'People good at fighting were paraded in front of them. To show them what a 'hero' looks like. To get them to strive for that ideal.' He scoffs. 'Fucking *heroes*. That's what they wanted us to convince them they'd be. Heroes and not fodder. Heroes instead of predators.'

He turns to look at me fully then. 'They were mostly in their early teens,' he says. 'Boys and girls desperate for the glories of war. Because of the bullshit that was spun to them.'

I don't ask if he was the only one doing this, or maybe leading it. It doesn't actually matter which, his involvement is clear. A lump grows in my throat and the pictures of Zale's and Akira's children spring unbidden into my mind. I know they are miles away from this conflict but they become the faces of the children who deserve better. Living in a country I thought would protect them because we knew better – the only one of our continent not at war.

Nix's face changes then. Even as I watch, it gets softer. Sadder, rather than angry.

'I'd been searching for a way out,' he says. 'But the contracts can be so hard to work around, particularly while they're live. And then I met someone.'

The foreboding I'd felt in my stomach a moment ago takes on a physical weight as it settles in my gut.

'Someone I ... someone I loved, Lu.'

My heart starts to ache. There is no happiness, no joy, in Nix's tone. I'd been right. His letters had changed. Because he was watching the very worst of what our country was asking children to do. And because he fell in love with someone in the midst of all that darkness.

'I wanted to tell you, Lu. So bad,' he says, his voice soft. 'But I couldn't bring myself to write the words. The contracts we were under made them hard to form and I—' He looks away. 'Now, I wish I did, maybe it would have made the good things real. And the ... others, different.'

I blink. Several times. But I don't miss the 'were' in his statement – somehow, they've found a way out of the contracts and just let me believe they were still under them. But that's not important right now – not in this moment. I clear my throat, my mind whirling with everything he's said. What he's endured.

'What happened to her?' I ask.

He leans back on the couch, brushing his dark auburn hair off his face, exposing the plane of his clear forehead, and stares at the ceiling for a moment.

'We – the Nuntainians – were ordered out of the village. By Quillian. I knew it was off,' he says, sitting forward again. Like he can't bring himself to sit still. 'But still, I left. As instructed. And the village – her village – was blown to pieces.'

I watch as he stands, placing his hands behind his head as he starts to pace the room.

'He'd known. Quillian knew it was coming and got us out.' His face darkens impossibly as he drops his hands and looks back at me. 'But didn't give us the opportunity to save anyone else. None of those who were actually worth saving.'

A tear leaks from the corner of my eye as I stare at Nix. Slowly, I stand and walk to him, taking his hands in mine.

'I'm sorry,' I say, knowing how hollow the words sound in the face of his grief.

He pulls me to him and I embrace him back, hard.

'I shouldn't have hurt you, Lu. I'm sorry,' he says into my hair. 'But I can't watch him take away someone else I love. I know – I know he's not all bad but I ... I just can't do that again.'

In an instant it makes sense. Nix's pain, his anger at Quillian, and why seeing me with him would trigger such an ... explosion of a response. That he did love someone like I think we all want to be loved. Only to lose her. And I know, had he been there, there is nothing that could've stopped him from saving her.

At the same time, I can't imagine Quillian knowingly putting him in that position. He'd said the beating Nix gave him was deserved, and I assume this is why. That Quillian didn't know something he feels he should have. But I know how hard it can be to get Nix to open up and so I'm not at all surprised he didn't tell Quillian about this woman. Why would he have?

'Nix,' I start gently.

'Do you hate me?' he asks, cutting me off.

I can't help the confusion that drags my brows down. 'Why in the world would I hate you?'

He takes a deep breath. 'Because I just pummelled the shit out of your ... boss, and someone I can tell you care about'—his face flashes with emotion—'and put you in the wellness centre.' He pales as he says it.

'No,' I breathe. 'But I need you to get some help to work this through. You'll never forget her, or stop loving her, I can tell. But you can't carry it around with you like this, Nix. Don't let that love become a poison.'

He cries then, for how long I don't count. My heart breaks for him and this woman I will never know. I have always been so envious of Akira and Zale for the lives, and loves, they have. Now, I am only grateful they get to hang on to them, not like Nix.

Eventually, his quiet tears stop and he releases me, an emptiness taking their place.

'Would you tell me about her?' I ask.

He closes his eyes briefly before we sit again, a tiny, sad smile playing out on his lips, and he starts at the beginning.

'I am not at all in the mood for this,' Blossom says as we dress for the ball.

Me neither, I think as I reflect on my time with Nix. How the pain in my face is nothing to the soul wound he's been delivered. There's a shadow of that pain sitting in my own chest, a smear I imagine will remain for as long as he hurts. The same as part of me aches for Blossom's loss.

But Traelen insisted we throw an event for the prisoners – to distract them from the death that seems to be around every corner at the moment and convince them we have everything in hand. That their stay won't be adversely affected by the bodies that keep cropping up. I think – I hope – death would have always worried me. Especially when it's come at such short intervals. But now I can't help the irritation that surfaces at the priority that is given to the prisoners.

Somewhere along the way in my service, I stopped caring what they were here for. Stopped wondering why 'prisoners' were treated so well. Now it's starting to chafe against my skin. And now I have to face that and Quillian, who seems suddenly keen to have me off the island. I press down on the hurt that he didn't even talk to me about it first.

'I'm worried about Traelen looking into these deaths, Lu,' Bloss continues as we stand side by side in the bathroom mirror. She is better at making me look presentable than I am, so I get ready in her bathroom for many of these events. 'Even putting aside the fact he's currently negotiating with the Vanan Warden, who I know sits outside Traelen's direct influence – although he *is* the Prime Minister's Chief of Staff – the brewing unrest of the prisoners will surely be enough for some sort of fall out. What if it impacts everyone's recommendations? What if ... they bring Hunters here to question us all?'

Fuck. That is *not* something I'd considered.

The heaviness that appeared beneath my ribs when Kasera died squeezes a little tighter. We did that. Blossom and me. And it's only a matter of time before Quillian is under enormous pressure to tell Traelen he knows who's behind it.

And yet, despite the fact he's sending me away, I can't help but believe the little voice in my head that tells me to trust him. Trust in his obvious disquiet about what's happening here.

Because mine's starting to match.

I put the brush down on the sink with a little more force than necessary and Blossom looks at me in the mirror.

'He's signed off on my recommendation,' I say to her reflection. 'Traelen's organised Zale to collect me within the fortnight. After Nix and River are gone.'

Bloss's eyes go wide, filled with more hope for me than I want to see – but leaving her here with this mess isn't something I can do. The way her mouth falls open gives away the conflict in her. She both does and doesn't want me to leave, too.

'I don't know why he didn't ask me first,' I say, hoping she knows I mean Quillian, 'but he – and Traelen – have just given us a deadline. We have to get Nix and River out before Traelen transfers them, before Quillian's forced to completely jeopardise his standing in the government and ...' My stomach churns. 'What would Traelen do to him for that? If he knew how they're all connected? Send him to Vana, too? Are we all just going to end up there together?' I draw a deep breath to try and control the hysteria I can hear rising my voice.

Bloss's mouth presses into a thin line and I can just about see the thoughts crossing her mind. That given the hurt he's inflicted on me, I shouldn't have any concern at all for doing the same. But I also see when she recalls the conversation in his office I told her about. When he apologised. When he talked about the realities he wished people could see.

When I told her he's their commanding officer and about the war they've been fighting.

She twirls the last curl around her face in an attempt to wrestle it into submission. It bounces back to its original position when she drops her hand to look at me instead of talking to my reflection.

'Quillian hasn't stopped you with anything so far,' she says carefully. 'I think he's less of a risk than Traelen and the Hunters. It's time for us to chance it – get a message to Cortane and tell her to be ready to portal. Ask Quillian about the one in the Residence – if we can't get to it easily, we go with the boys to Cortane.'

I lean my hip against the pale stone counter.

'You think we should be ready to all go with her? Through the wards?'

Her chest rises and falls as she seems to stare at the gold taps for a moment. 'I think ... in our hearts we've started making choices we can't articulate yet. The things we know about up here but are bound not to voice and what we've learned since you weren't collected have taken root in each of us and we need to see this through. You taking Traelen's portal is the best option for you. The boys go with Cortane as a first preference, but through the Residence portal if absolutely necessary. It's also likely it will be able to detect unauthorised access. As for me ...'

A fist grips in my torso. Claudius told her not to be here for the next collection, and she's not even due to leave then. Cortane said she could reduce her time from below, but what does that mean we'd be leaving her with up here in the meantime? Davorous?

Acid burns in my gut.

'Bloss—' I start but she shakes her head.

'Let's focus on finding out how to bring down the wards for Cortane. Then we'll go from there.'

'I still don't know how to bring down the wards,' I say.

'Then find a way. Tonight – we'll go to the office tonight.'

The grandroom is a feast for the eyes when we arrive in time for me to check the venue before the prisoners arrive. Platters of fruit and cheese are nestled between layers of flowers and leaves, punctuated by tiered stands full of decadent, colourful canapés.

Low lighting frames the ceiling, hanging bulbs dotted in the stone arches that look out over the island and into the depthless night sky beyond. This is my favourite time to visit this room. When it's not filled with people I need to please, with a smile forever on my face. As soon as I am confident everything is in place – and my previous visits to the kitchen and the musician's rehearsal room tells me that it is – I normally have a moment to breathe it in on my own. Or almost on my own. There are a number of other concierges arriving, carrying last minute decorations or fulfilling the wishes of our guests in some way.

Tonight, I can't shake the weight of Nix's admissions. The memory of the hurt that was written all over his face as he talked about her. The woman he loves. I promised myself I'd get him off this island. I wish I could promise him we'd find her instead. That I could heal that hole in his heart. Fulfilling the first is something I will do everything in my power to do. But healing him ... I know that's beyond what I can offer.

The conversations of the concierges get fractionally louder before they dip away again, a sign the last of them are just about here. The last minute jobs are urgently communicated and then they fall silent, waiting for the Warden to arrive moments before the guests.

My breath catches as Quillian strides in, the deep navy of his dress uniform complementing his rich brown skin. I blink away the vision of his wings over his shoulders. Now I know they're there, how they feel when they're soft, it's impossible to drive them from my mind completely.

He smiles and greets the other concierges warmly before he finds me. It could be how the lights catch in his eyes but they almost seem to sparkle as he takes me in, pausing to run his gaze the length of my body. The little hairs on my arms prickle under his attention, a warming starting below my belly button. Unable to stop the lifting of the corners of my mouth, I watch him walk to me.

There's a gracefulness to how he moves, as if he's gliding through the air despite not using his wings. There's also a ... disappointment? Maybe regret?

'Evening,' he says when he's close enough for me to touch if I wanted to.

I make loose fists with my hands and keep them by my sides, pushing away the memory of how his bare shoulders felt under my fingers.

How his face looked the last time I saw him.

'You look ... exceptional,' he says quietly, and the room starts to fade away around me at the low timbre of his voice.

'You look quite impressive yourself,' I reply, unable to stop myself.

I jump slightly as someone clears their throat beside me.

'Traelen's incoming,' Bloss says with a look full of knowing. 'You might want to pick this up later.'

CHAPTER TWENTY-SIX

Quillian shifts to my side as the other concierges fan out in all directions, roughly spaced around the grandroom so the prisoners can easily find assistance at any time. The exact positions change regularly during the evenings as we are required to do different things, including entertain the prisoners who request it, but we must always be accessible.

Traelen enters through the large timber doors that lead to the internal courtyard, greeting each of the prisoners he passes with a handshake, or a kiss on each check – or both – before making his way to Quillian and me, the taupe suit he wears making his skin look golden in the light.

The conductor of the band glances at me as Traelen takes his place and I duck my chin to give him the go ahead to start the music. As the violinist lifts his instrument, he cocks a brow and looks pointedly at Quillian. I suppress a smile when his face cracks into a broad one and Quillian shifts on his feet next to me. My smile freezes as his knuckles brush the soft folds of my dress, pushing the fabric along my skin.

The gentle weight of his hand dances along the side of my thigh as we watch the prisoners help themselves to the food and mingle, chatting with each other. As they begin to approach the concierges and the first wave of food has been consumed, my teams start to relax with their stations, but there's still a slightly stilted feel in the room.

'Dance,' Traelen says.

I glance sideways to where he stands on the other side of Quillian to see who he's talking to, but he's looking straight ahead. One of the prisoners, Fleur – the same one Nix was with at our last dinner, Miana's friend – approaches Traelen, my palms starting to sweat. Just before she draws him in for a conversation, he turns to Quillian and me.

'I'd like you to get the dancing started. You two need to be on the floor. Now.'

He takes the drink Fleur offered and guides her away, a hand on the small of her back, so they can talk away from us. Away from the staff. I remember Claudius doing something so similar, many times in the past, when prisoners requested his time. But it felt so different – I never doubted that he was one of us. Traelen, though, he definitely doesn't consider himself part of this team. At the same time, there's a distance between him and the prisoners that feels familiar.

I stare after him.

The thought of being that close to Quillian again sparks a little fire in my belly. Right where the heat started when he walked into the grandroom tonight. But doing so, so publicly, also creates a tightness in my jaw. I haven't seen Nix arrive and I'm not sure he will be up to it. But, despite the assurances he gave me that it wouldn't happen again, his wounds are so raw it's a risk I'd prefer not to take.

The conversation we had after he beat Quillian was open, and heartfelt. But I don't believe that means he's ready to think he can lose me to Quillian. Not to mention there is still a lot unresolved between Quillian and me—

'Shall we?' he asks, holding out his arm.

'Of course,' I say, trying to force any uncertainty from my voice.

I place my hand in the crook of his elbow, the shape of his bicep – just the very bottom – under my fingers, and let him lead me to the space between the large stone arches and the food table. The concierges barely bat an eyelid, used to this routine of the staff helping the prisoners warm up from time to time. In my old life, I was very rarely first onto the dance floor, and if I was, I'd had more than a few Flaming Georges under my belt to help me along. But while most of my teams don't even bother to look our way and remain focused on their jobs, I don't miss Janly's curiosity. Or the slowly growing warmth in Blossom's expression.

Turning into Quillian, it's impossible for my breath not to catch at his proximity. His face gives little away but there's a tiny, fast flicker at the base of his jaw that belies his composure. '—*that prove*—' is written on his neck, his tattoo shimmering before it dips under his collar, and I remember where it fans on his body. But the memory of the sting when he walked out is pronounced, even now, after his apology, and it helps me gather myself under the watchful gaze of Traelen. Helps me remember he wants me off the island and back on the mainland, something that feels so at odds with the closeness we shared.

Smiling politely, I stop my perusal of his broad chest and face. The full mouth that trailed between my—

My heart hammers. I look over his shoulder as we take up our dancing position and he begins turning me around the floor. His hand is warm where it envelops mine and we keep a respectable distance between our bodies.

But the weight of his hand on my hip is hard to ignore. The way he holds me there with just enough pressure to be straddling the line of polite and familiar. We move at a moderate speed, our dancing not intended to be a display, but an invitation for others to join us. As we glide past Traelen his attention follows us for a moment, before he turns his back and resumes his conversation with Fleur. Some of the tension in my gut releases at the loss of his attention and my body feels like it moves more readily over the floor.

My fingers curve around the top of Quillian's shoulder, not quite reaching his back, and I try not to get lost in the memory of just how muscled that back is. But the memory of our night together takes me with a low burning that builds at the very bottom of my gut, a warmth racing up my chest and carving a hot path up my neck and across my cheeks. As we move around the floor and I attempt to regain control of my wandering thoughts, I wonder if this really will be my last time at one of these events. The last time I thought that – let myself believe it wholeheartedly – I ended up crying on the floor of the collection room.

And intricately involved in things I'd never even considered before.

Quillian inhales deeply, almost like he's noticed any awkwardness from touching him so publicly fading from my steps as I sink into rhythm with him. A tickling at the back of my neck runs up the side of my face and over my head, and I catch the lights of the music in their own dance, streaming above and out from Quillian and me. They rapidly create a gentle whirl around us and the two other pairs that have now joined. White and yellow blinking lights that imbue the essence of the music.

A soft laugh bubbles in my mouth and Quillian tugs me forward a fraction. I can't see his face properly without pulling back to look at him, but his nearness makes me tingle and I can't help but wonder what his face shows.

'Did you talk to him?' he asks quietly.

It's my turn to suck in a steadying breath. But the conflict between Nix and Quillian is a mountain I haven't completed getting over yet. Nix may blame him for his loss, but they have been through some of the darkest things together.

At the same time, the kernel of disappointment that Quillian has arranged for me to go back to the mainland without talking to me won't dislodge.

Part of me thinks I should be wounded that Quillian didn't tell me he knows Nix. There was certainly enough trust on my side for me to confess things to him. But he did openly admit that the beating Nix gave him was deserved. So he didn't hide it, either.

I think on my conversation with Nix. About how he admitted he doesn't think Quillian's all bad, but Quillian still made a decision to save him despite the pain Nix would ultimately endure. How much of that operating style is in effect up here?

Is that what he's doing? Does he think he's saving me by sending me away?

'Yes,' I breathe, 'I spoke to him.' It's an effort to keep the genteel smile on my face as the music, and the dance, continues when all I want to do is drag him away so we can talk.

Quillian doesn't immediately respond. Whether that's because knowing we spoke is all the answer he needs, or he doesn't know what to ask next, I don't know.

'So you know why I said 'shouldn't' the other night, then?' he asks, his voice still a whisper as we move around the timber dance floor.

I let my head lower a little, conscious not to rest it on his shoulder despite the pull to do just that.

'I know,' I murmur. 'And Nix knows you did the best you could with the information you had at the time.'

He's quiet for a moment, the music dying away around us as we move. The sound of our breaths like our own beat.

'Sometimes what you know in the moment isn't enough,' he says roughly and it feels like he's talking about more things than I can possibly know right now. 'I signed off on your recommendation ... before ...'

His words trail off and I wonder what 'before' he means. Before we were intimate? Before we grew closer? Before he shared thoughts and feelings with me that could easily be taken as traitorous to Nuntainia?

'I wanted you to have options,' he whispers. 'This is ... messier than I had expected.' His fingers tighten around my side.

I try not to exhale too heavily. Or lean into him too far.

'Which bit?' I ask, still smiling my concierge smile.

'Bits I'd really like to explain. Things I regret not being able to tell you earlier.' His voice is quiet but serious and I can't help but feel like there's truth there. Like he genuinely wants to let me in but between our jobs and Nix and Traelen and all the deaths, we haven't really had a chance to talk properly. Not when there seems like there's so much to talk about.

Our steps slow as the piece comes to an end and I catch Nix's narrowed gaze in the crowd of prisoners, his fists clenched as he watches Quillian and me in the final stages of the dance. Blossom approaches him and he bumps her shoulder as he spins and walks away.

Something pinches around my insides but I still don't let go of Quillian. I give Blossom a beseeching look and she sighs but leaves the room after Nix. The song ends and Quillian guides me back to our station.

'I do expect that explanation, Quillian,' I say quietly as we now take in the other dancers before us. My waist still warm from where he held me.

He turns to look at me again but one of the newer prisoners, Zenaton, dressed in a simple grey suit with his white shirt open to the navel, approaches from across the dance floor. His focus is firmly on Quillian who, when I glance sideways at him, is struggling not to keep the usual disdain from his features. He told me once that Zenaton had particularly good connections to the Prime Minister. I swallow. With both he and Traelen here, in a sea of prisoners who have seen death after death, the likelihood of someone asking the wrong – or right – question seems suddenly very high. If those answers got back to the Prime Minister ...

I still as the back of Quillian's knuckles brush mine for a moment before he looks back to the approaching prisoner.

'Lovely event you've put on,' Zenaton says as he reaches us. 'Much grander than when the last Warden was with us.'

I stifle a grunt. Given the teams that have organised the events under both Wardens are the same, I find that very hard to believe. Although I suppose Zenaton hasn't been with us that long.

'How fortunate you get to partake in all the festivities,' Quillian says and gives a tight smile.

'I was thinking,' Zenaton continues, gesturing to Quillian with his scarlet filled glass, tiny pink bubbles bursting around the rim. 'A glass platform could be nice.'

'A glass platform?' I ask, meeting his dark, hazel-blue eyes.

'Hmm. For our next event. You could put it up near the edge of the island and then we'd be able to literally party in the air.'

Quillian turns to me, a little wide-eyed at the request, but I don't miss the tension that creeps back into his shoulders. It's an outlandish request, but when I would have once laughed it off, this evening it makes me bristle. I might not know what Zenaton has done to be here, but I know he is not merely on holiday in Nuntainia's most fabulous resort.

I glance at Traelen, still in deep conversation with some of the prisoners. For all I know, they are planning what they will do when they each get out, and Traelen is completely unconcerned with what they've done to be sentenced here. Or are they giving him their account of the strange things that have been happening around them. My skin itches. I don't actually know what he thinks of all of this and I do think his priority is the Prime Minister – perhaps the prisoners here are just part of that ecosystem and not a priority in their own right.

But giving Zenaton anything to complain to the Prime Minister about is another piece of attention we don't need right now, and so I make myself smile widely.

'We'll add it to our list,' I say to Zenaton. 'Thank you for the suggestion.'

He nods in acknowledgement before he turns and scans the room.

'Ah! Davorous,' he calls as the large timber doors open and Davorous slips in.

Quickly, I glance around the room myself, but there's no sign of Blossom and I'm quietly thankful I sent her after Nix. I watch as Davorous scours the room himself. His predatory gaze searches all the concierges – I can only assume it's for a particular curly-haired one. My skin starts to crawl at the thought of what he'd like to do to her. Because there's no doubt in my mind that it is *to* her that he wants to do things, not *with*.

I keep one eye on him as I monitor the prisoners. A number come to me with requests or suggestions for improvements; my frequent position at Quillian's side having obviously been noted. I dutifully make a note of them, knowing I'm unable to outright dismiss them. Indeed, some of them I will need to make happen so their satisfaction of the stay remains high.

Finn offers me a small smile as he stands not too far from me, quietly observing the prisoners. Just as I am. I still haven't seen him engage a lot but Janly confirms he is present enough and I suppose being here at our busiest event is testament to him having a reasonable time at least. Sometimes it's the quietest ones who need the most careful watching to make sure they're enjoying themselves. The loud ones make their own fun.

But, at least according to Traelen, we need excellent client reviews from them all.

Quillian engages, mostly, with the prisoners that come to talk with us, but otherwise doesn't leave my side. Despite that I would normally wander the room and check different details, I find myself hesitating to leave my spot next to him as well. I peek at Quillian, his face like stone as he watches the celebrations. Celebrations that are for nothing more than frivolous enjoyment.

'The details for the transfer are complete.' I try not to jump at Traelen's voice which appears out of nowhere. 'I'll have a team of Hunters up here in the morning to make sure nothing goes ... awry ... in the meantime. I've also shut down the portal in the Warden's Residence for safety. I do not need any rogue prisoners turning up in Parliament.'

I stare at him, hoping I've misheard.

'The transfer?' I ask. Quillian gives nothing away. *The portal?* I don't ask out loud.

'To Vana Prison,' he says.

'Who do we need to prepare?' Quillian asks blandly.

'The Kilroy brothers.'

Traelen's face blurs before me and I try to blink.

Nix and River Kilroy.

'I'll be back in two days to facilitate the transfer – the Warden over there can be a bit prickly,' he says, face blank. 'I'll need to do some more negotiating, but it will go through as planned.'

Phantom screams fill my mind as I imagine what the inside of that prison will be like. Cortane herself said the innocent scream the loudest. Once, I would've argued that's exactly what River and Nix are. Now, I know they're not entirely 'innocent'. But what does 'innocence' mean in the face of the things they were made to do under government direction? How do their actions under orders compare to the other choices they've made, leading them ... here?

Standing still while I watch Traelen walk away takes more of my strength than I expected. It's all I can do not to run from the room and straight to Cortane. But having her portal them off without knowing how to bring the wards down will only mark them – for a lifetime. They will be tracked and hunted by the best bounty hunters of Nuntainia – the same Hunters that Traelen is bringing here.

Maybe they're not innocent, but I'm starting to understand there are degrees of guilt and innocence, and that seems to depend on who's making the judgement.

And when I think of what Nix has lost, what they were asked to do—

'I need some air,' I say to Quillian, my voice barely there. I don't look at him or the large stone arches that face directly into the sky and head across the grandroom. Davorous has a satisfied smirk on his face as I pass him, gloating about something to Zenaton, and I hurry past so I don't have to hear what it is.

Two days.

I have two days to get the information on the wards and organise Cortane and her portal – and River and Nix have two days to complete whatever it is they came here to do. I refuse to think about the possibility that they'd choose Vana over escape, duty over life. But, then, it's no longer a duty for them – any of them. It's honour.

A creed, Cortane called it.

CHAPTER TWENTY-SEVEN

The doors are heavy as I shove them open, gulping the air into my lungs. I cross the stone hallway and lean over the banister. But I crane my neck upwards so I can look at the sky instead of the courtyard and the garden below. If I can free Nix and River, even if they're marked, wouldn't that still be better than being in the prison on the other side? It might not be freedom, but it's closer than being sealed inside Vana.

The stone is cool under my hands and I gently lower my forehead to the rail, bending in half. I might be committing them to a life on the run, but at least they'll be alive.

I now have a firm way off the island with Traelen ending my extension. I can go to Parliament and do what Claudius needed from there.

But ...

I'd be without Nix. Or River. Blossom. And Quillian.

Everyone I've been working to keep safe.

What good is being in Parliament as their contact if I can't contact them while they're on the run? Can't be with them in some way?

'I'm sorry,' a muffled, familiar voice says from further down the hallway. My skin starts to prickle uncomfortably. Drawing myself back to standing, I turn to where I expect to find Nix whispering with someone down the hallway. Instead, he's crouched over something on the floor.

He's blocking half of it with his body where he leans over, but the legs that lie sprawled on the stone are horribly familiar.

Stumbling in my dress skirts, I run.

Her blue dress is pulled up high around her thighs, Bloss's flawless bronze skin exposed in a way that makes my palms clammy. I slow a couple of paces away, suddenly unsure exactly what I will find.

'Bloss?' I ask.

Nix barely spares me a glance, anguish all over his face, before a knife drops from his grip and he presses both hands into her side. My head goes fuzzy at the blood that oozes between his fingers and I look back to Nix. A tight moment passes and I'm dimly aware of my lack of motion. Action. But Nix's words play on repeat. *I'm sorry,* he'd said.

A knife fell from his hands—

'Get River,' he says, his voice all business. No trace of the anguish that was there a moment ago. 'Now, Lu,' he barks.

I flinch and race back to the grandroom. I can't believe he would do that to her – to me. But Quillian's battered and bruised face is still fresh in my mind. How I felt when Nix slammed me into the wall. Accidentally. It was an accident. But he'd lost control all the same.

And he'd just now seen me dancing with Quillian.

I sent Blossom after him.

My stomach rolls.

The timber doors loom before me and I take a shuddering breath, entering the grandroom once more. My throat thickens – I don't even know if she was conscious. River. *Where are you?*

Frantically, I search the room and spot him talking with Finn in a corner. I push my way through the people to get to him on the other side of the grandroom, but someone gently catches my elbow.

'Luka?'

I spin into Quillian's chest, unintentionally gripping his arm. Scanning his face quickly, I look back to River. Nix doesn't trust Quillian. But I do.

'I need your help,' I say, feeling my stomach falling away at just how badly.

'I said River,' Nix grinds out.

'What happened?' I ask, ignoring him and the pounding of fear in my limbs as I drop down next to Blossom, cradling her head. Her skin is cool and slightly sticky where I brush the hair out of her face.

'Can you hear me, Bloss?' I ask.

I can't bring myself to look but I think Nix's hands are still pressing into her side.

'We need to move her,' Quillian says. 'My skills aren't enough for this, she needs a full Arkanan.'

'That's why I said bring River,' Nix snaps and my stomach clenches. Of course, they're not taking magic dampeners either.

'River's in the grandroom,' I say, feeling stupid and aware of Nix's gaze on me.

'There's no time now, let's get her to the wellness centre.' Quillian directs Nix to keep his hands on the wound and scoops her up, grunting slightly as he pushes himself to standing. Nix walks backwards awkwardly, keeping the pressure on the stab wound in Blossom's side.

I run ahead and have to suppress an overwhelming need to cry as I find Shiloh on shift tonight – Blossom is going to need every bit of her skill. A moment later, Quillian places Blossom on one of the beds and I almost feel like I am watching my own experience with him as an outer body memory.

But this is worse. Much worse.

Blossom's head lolls to the side on the white sheet, her skin seemingly paler than it was moments ago. I stand by her side and hold her hand, her fingers limp in my grip. Swallowing the queasiness in my gut, I make myself look. The blood is slowing between Nix's fingers but her dress is soaked – a large, dark red splotch on the pale blue fabric.

'Maintain the pressure,' Shiloh says as she runs to the closet and returns with a large, white case. Dropping its lid open on a brass trolley next to Bloss, she removes a pair of large scissors and immediately slices through the fabric across her belly.

'I got it,' she says and Nix slowly removes his hands. Blossom's blood coating his palms and framing his fingernails.

'River will want to know,' he says quietly as he straightens and turns to Quillian, leaving Shiloh to focus on her tools and her magic.

I watch one of Quillian's brows quirk in question but Nix just stares back at him, letting Quillian draw his own conclusions. But when he looks to me for confirmation I nod. River will want to know. And I don't think Blossom will object.

'Unfortunately, you're not the only one at risk of compromising us all,' Nix mutters into the space between them.

Quillian watches him for a moment before he turns and walks away.

I look to Bloss and the moments start to blur together as Shiloh cleans the wound, completely absorbed in her work. She closes her eyes and hovers a hand over the hole in Bloss's side. A faint shimmer in the air between her hand and Blossom's skin is the only indication she is doing anything. But slowly the bleeding stops until no more runs out.

Shiloh takes a moment to wipe her brow on a towel, the use of her magic clearly taking its toll.

'Bloss?' I ask quietly, squeezing her hand.

Ever so gently, she squeezes back and uninvited tears push their way down my cheeks, the crash of relief more than I can contain.

'What happened?' I ask Nix for the second time as he dries his hands where he's washed her blood off.

He stares at me for a long moment.

'I didn't do this, if that's what you're asking.'

I try not to let my exhale show and I grip Blossom's hand tighter, flicking my gaze back to Shiloh briefly, who's started stitching her up, a faint shimmer accompanying every loop.

'Why were you apologising to her?'

'Because that's what you do when one of your friends is hurting,' he says.

He sighs heavily, letting some of the tension drain from his body. But the shadows remain in his features.

'I didn't see what happened,' he says. 'But Davorous was walking away when I found her. I would have gone after him if I didn't know she needed immediate help.'

A cold sickness winds its way through my veins. The force of the anger that follows is enough to take my breath away. I want him killed. *I* want to kill him.

'Quillian was supposed to be having her watched,' I say quietly, still watching Nix's whirling, champagne-coloured eyes.

I expect the statement to make him angry. Another thing to hold against Quillian. But instead, he softens a fraction.

'It's hard for any of us to be everywhere at once,' he says.

Blossom groans and I immediately let her take all my attention.

'Hey,' I whisper. 'I'm here.'

'Luka?' she asks.

'Yeah. You're going be okay,' I say as I look at Shiloh for confirmation. She nods without looking up. 'I expect that's going to hurt for a bit but you're going to be okay.'

'I thought I was going to die.'

The tears resume their path down my face. 'No, Blossom. Not on our watch, okay?'

She tries to smile but still doesn't open her eyes.

'That's her done for now,' Shiloh says. 'She's done well. It was lucky she was found when she was, and the pressure has been applied consistently. She'll need plenty of rest but I think it best she stays here for the night. Perhaps tomorrow or the following day she can return to your rooms.'

'Shiloh,' I say, 'can you work with Janly to make sure no one is on their own tonight? I don't want any concierges unattended – no exceptions.'

She agrees solemnly, with a long look at Blossom, before taking her hand towel with her and hurrying away.

Turning at the sound of the door, I find Quillian. River just about walking on his heels to get into the room. His entire body somehow filled with worry as he looks to me.

'She's going to heal,' I say quietly when he reaches us.

He stares down at her, taking in her dressing, but he doesn't move to touch her.

'Shiloh's good at what she does,' I say, and he purses his lips as if he's not convinced she's good enough. As if he would have preferred to do it himself.

'You hurt?' he asks without looking away from Bloss.

'No,' Nix says. 'Davorous is about to be though.'

'You're fucking kidding me? That's what happened?'

'Think so, yeah.'

Nix's gaze slides to Quillian, who is still standing a step or two back from the rest of us.

'We doing this now, then?' he asks.

I look between them, an element of dread seeping in. But also … another measure of relief. That someone is taking responsibility for the atrocious actions of the prisoners. Taking care of Davorous. Blossom sighs, her body seeming to give in to the pain relief Shiloh gave her, and River watches the rise and fall of her chest.

'We can,' Quillian says slowly, 'but it would likely mean giving up the rest. He's not on our—'

'Wait,' I blurt out and Quillian looks at me, his eyes so dark in the low light they're almost black.

They're a team, I know. In the war I didn't even know we were fighting in. And they're still fighting. My mind starts to spiral, honing in on the details I know and connecting those tiny specs of information.

'What list?' I ask Quillian, sure that's what he was going to say.

His whole face shadows and a thought I never want to have presses in on me.

'Quill,' River says, 'if you're going to explain it to her, now's as good a time as any.'

Quillian's expression is pained. 'Involving innocent people was not—'

Nix laughs, but it's not entirely cold. 'Taking your pants off didn't exactly help there, did it?'

'Nix!' I scold as my face heats.

'She can read your tattoo,' River sighs. 'Claudius involved her well before we got here, and continuing to try to leave her in the dark is only going to get her hurt.'

Read his tattoo?

That prove. The words on Quillian's neck dance before me, but I don't know what the rest says – I haven't seen him with his shirt off since …

The Warden had a similar one I recall … or were the words the same? The room is quiet for a long moment, the only sound Blossom's gentle breathing. I use her rhythm to steady me, slow down my thoughts.

They're a team. With the same goal – the details of which I'm not sure I can grapple with right now, not as Blossom lies in a wellness bed with healing magic in her system. Good things, but not what was supposed to be happening to her. I've given them time to do what they needed here. I've given them as much space as I can and literally helped clean away the bodies. Whatever remains on their 'list' now takes second place to my goal – keeping them safe.

'Right,' I say to the silence. It feels like breaking a wall somehow. For so long I have been the second in charge, aways deferring to someone else. Always looked over for someone else. But, in this room, and some outside of it, are *my* people – my responsibility. 'We have two days before you're transferred to Vana. I don't know exactly what you're doing or how far along you are and, frankly, right now I don't want to know. My contact from the other side is ready to portal you two'—I point to Nix and River—'off the island.'

Quillian opens his mouth but I cut him off. I'm good at plans and I have stepped back from taking charge for too long. I glance at Blossom. I no longer have the luxury of waiting to be included, of living just outside of understanding, even if it takes me somewhere unexpected.

'Finn – can he be trusted with shadowing Davorous? And *only* shadowing Davorous?'

They all nod, but if they pick up on the dual meaning in my question, they don't say. While the anger burning through my veins at what he's done to Blossom makes me feel like I can't breathe, having someone else turn up dead won't help us. Instead, it would be the fastest way to get the Hunters here, questioning and watching everyone and every move. Right now, I can't examine the worry that he left Blossom, even for a moment, but now River is with her and I know he won't leave her side for anything.

'You have one day – you will be portalled off this island before any transfer can take place. River, you're on Blossom watch until I say otherwise. Nix, you finish as much of whatever you started as you can. And Quillian, you're going to help me work out how to get the wards down.'

This time, Quillian trails me to the office. As I march through the halls, the night breeze gentle on my skin, I search the faces of any prisoners we pass. Like I could find their sins if I just look hard enough. Davorous's though, I don't need to search for – but I do want to find him. I remind myself, again, that Blossom will be safe with River. That my focus needs to be on finding the key to bringing the wards down so Cortane can get these three men off Zanteera Island. Not once has anyone said Quillian needs to go as well, and I have certainly been working on the basis that he would need to stay. Seeing them in that wellness centre though, there is no way he won't be implicated somehow if River and Nix leave without him.

A small lump appears in my throat as I consider what all of this will mean for my collection. By Zale, not Vale, as Traelen mistakenly called her. Can I really pull this off without being implicated myself?

Unlikely. It's too far known throughout the prison now that I have some sort of connection with each of them. Even if no one knows about Cortane yet, making the link won't be hard once they all disappear.

It also leaves Blossom up here with Davorous.

Perhaps, him, I can talk to Traelen about – get the system to work as it's supposed to.

But it doesn't answer the question that's vying for attention amongst the chaos in my mind: do I even want to be collected? To be separated from this group and the light I think they can shed on what's created this vacuum of consequences on Zanteera Island, at least in this prison? Do I really want to be in Parliament House ... alone?

Taking the door handle in my hand, I realise Quillian having been in the Warden's position would surely mean he's been looking for information on the wards already. But if so, why would Cortane ask for information on him, like she did Kasera?

That prove ...

Unless that task was a test for *me*?

If so, did I pass or fail?

'So, you've found nothing so far?' I ask when the door has closed behind us again – sealing us back in this space that now feels like 'ours' and no longer the former Warden's.

I pour us the drinks I'm sure we both need tonight, the engraved glass slightly rough in my palm as I pull the stopper on the decanter. Just for a moment, I let my gaze fall on the line drawing of Claudius's, wishing it could give me the answers I need, and then I face Quillian, drink in hand.

'No,' he says, 'nothing. I have searched every inch of this office and there are no records anywhere – not even hidden in the books. Before she was sent to Vana, Cortane scoured every digital file she could access in Parliament House, and nothing. Not even on who created them. If there are records, they're up here, or in the archives underneath Parliament House.' Quillian gives me a heavy look. 'We haven't been able to get anyone physically in there yet.'

'Have you tried his residence?'

'Finn and I both went through that – nothing. I've had the team walk the perimeter multiple times too – also nothing.'

'You never thought about just taking that portal? Even before Traelen shut it down?'

'No,' he says. 'Not when we had no idea where it goes. Now Traelen has confirmed it goes directly to a receiving room in Parliament House, that would be somewhere that would be hard to ... fight our way out of. Shaides can also normally detect if people come and go through their portals, and Cort didn't create that one.'

A shudder runs down my spine and I shove away the thought of those ramifications. The questions his comments raise.

'So ... how do we know there is actually a way to take the wards down? What if they're permanent?'

His chest broadens for a moment with his inhale and he runs a hand through his hair. 'We don't, not really. It's mostly based on a theory that anything built, or created, can be undone.'

I try to piece that logic together but it doesn't quite fit for me. Can things that are created be undone? Sure. But does their shadow or memory remain? Yes. So does that mean they are actually 'undone'?

A weariness starts to press its way over my body, starting with the top of my head, making me feel like it weighs too much all of a sudden.

'I think, after all of that, we need to start working on a plan that includes going through the wards – not taking them down. As I think it through,

I can't actually imagine Claudius leaving that information somewhere for anyone to find. He was much more considered than that,' I say.

Quillian doesn't seem fazed at all and I can only imagine how many times he has been required to pivot a plan in his time. Like when Nix's girlfriend was killed.

'Going *through* the wards means being marked with tracking magic. One the Hunters have direct access to. The longest I've heard anyone being able to out maneuver them is three months, give or take.'

In that instant, my life seems to be broken into chunks of time – time I have to work through just to get to the other side. Five years of duty. Two days before Traelen's deadline. One day before I send my friends through Cortane's portal instead.

One day before I decide my own fate.

One day to find a way to not abandon Blossom, while not condemning her to a life half-lived.

Three months of borrowed time for Nix and River. And maybe Quillian.

Right now, having that additional time for them seems like a small blessing. What's the point if it's only going to lead to heartache and pain? But at least they have an out, even if it's not perfect. Blossom, though ...

'There's no way to get the tracking removed?' I ask, heart twisting at the thought of more harm coming to Bloss.

'None that have been successful so far, but there are always things to try.'

I think of the herons Claudius and I would watch dive through them, how gracefully they would fall, their wings—

'Wait,' I say. 'Can you fly through them?'

I have no idea how that would help anyone else but, it seems worth the question at this point. His shoulders flex, like he's thinking about what it would be like to fly away; I certainly am.

'No, unfortunately. It's the presence of magic that triggers the tracking magic. Listen, Luka, you know you don't have to be in this, right? This isn't your mess.'

I look at his tattoo – one I'm now very keen to read the rest of. But I can still see that it says something about 'proving' over the top of his collar and, while strictly speaking some could say he's right, there is also a liberation of sorts in choosing what I am responsible for. Even if I could emotionally walk away from any of them, it's not something I would ever be able to live with. For better or worse, these people *are* my mess.

And I *want* to prove it myself – that I can do this. I can right this. I can make people like Davorous pay for their crimes.

'I think they – and you, to be honest – are going to have to take their chances with the tracking magic,' I say carefully, my throat seeming to thicken as I do. 'I need to talk to Cortane, and then I want to see Blossom.'

CHAPTER TWENTY-EIGHT

Cortane wasn't happy about the ward situation, but I think she understands it's the only shot we have. Claudius wanted her out of that prison for a reason and I intend to make it happen for him, whatever the consequences. Blossom is awake when we return to the wellness centre and some of the knotting in my stomach starts to release. Her deep blue eyes have lost a little of their lustre when she looks up at me. I feel like I have aged in the hours I have been away from her.

'How are you feeling?' I ask as I sink onto the narrow bed beside her and take her hand. Her warm skin releases more of the tension from my shoulders.

She flicks her gaze to River, who sits in a chair across the room – as if he's giving her as much physical space as he can bear. A little spark of gratitude lights in my chest. I'd told him to take it carefully with her, and he's nothing if not respectful of both of us.

'Like I'm floating on a cloud,' she says in a voice full of whimsy, and I laugh as she looks around the room.

'That will be your pain meds.'

She drops her voice to a mock whisper I don't think is purposeful. 'Are there actually several stupidly attractive men here, or am I dreaming?' she asks. 'Wait. Are *you* here?'

I grin at her as her eyelids start to droop.

'I am, but I'm going to leave you to sleep,' I say, the pull for my own bed suddenly making itself known. I glance at River, who is clearly settled in for the night, and he nods at me. 'River will stay here with you and I'll be back first thing, okay?'

She lets her eyelids drop closed with the slightest nod and I press a kiss to her forehead. Standing, I look at River.

'Anything changes,' I say, '*anything*, and you call me.'

'Of course,' he says.

Nix mutters something to Quillian as I walk back to where they stand by the door. There's a long pause as we all watch each other, a sudden awkwardness tingling my skin. Nix clears his throat.

'He'll walk you up,' he says carefully. 'I'll keep Riv company for a bit.'

My heart beats in time with my aching footsteps as we get closer to my door. To where I will say goodnight to Quillian. Before I can work out what to say to him in the wake of Nix's seeming ... approval, we've reached my apartment and I turn to face him. His face has the softness I have come to expect when he looks at me, with no trace of the fierceness he holds back in the presence of the prisoners. Or even Nix. It's like it's a look he reserves just for me and my cheeks heat at the thought.

He scans my face and opens his mouth to speak.

'Do you want a hot drink?' I ask before he can say the night is over. Despite its horrors, I'm not ready for him to leave yet.

A faint smile graces his mouth, the dimple just beginning to show on his left side.

'I'd love one.'

My apartment feels at once too big and too small when we enter and, belatedly, it occurs to me it's his first time here, in my space. It feels like it's been full of visitors recently between the former warden, Nix and River, and – of course – Cortane. But this is the first time the tall man before me has been here.

I make a fist to stop myself from reaching out and head for the kitchen. Collecting two mugs, I place them on the bench as I prepare the tea. It's a mixture Blossom has made up from different ingredients she sources both from Nuntainia and the island itself; purple flowers float in the hot water I pour into each cup.

Quillian joins me in the kitchen and leans back against the counter, placing his hands on the bench on either side.

'How are you holding up?' he asks.

I let the question really sink in as I allow my gaze to trail over his blue uniform.

'My feet hurt,' I say.

A wicked grin graces his face. 'I can help with that if you like.'

Little flurries of warmth skitter through my belly at the sight of the spark in his eyes.

'I might take you up on that if you're not careful.'

He watches me as he slowly picks up his tea cup and blows across the top of the liquid before taking a sip. The movement of his mouth captures my attention and I have to force myself to look at him properly.

'What did he say to you?' I ask. I don't have to say when. It's clear he knows I'm talking about his moment with Nix in the wellness centre.

He draws a deep breath. 'That if I was fucking with you, he'd fuck me over in return.'

I swallow.

'But he didn't need to warn me, Luka.'

I can feel my brows start to furrow. 'What do you mean?'

Quillian's shoulders drop as he sighs, placing his cup back down and resuming his hold on the bench behind him. 'This wasn't part of the plan,' he says. 'I – none of us – were supposed to create attachments. Not here. Not anywhere. At least not to anyone but each other.'

His words settle over me. There's something comforting in knowing they all know each other. Even if his relationship with Nix is a complicated one. And it increases the intensity of the tug I can feel towards him. But I'm still not totally willing to declare my hand. Not on my own. There are a lot of leaps I am taking at the moment, a lot of risks to my heart, and this one …

'And are you forming an attachment?' I ask, heart pounding.

He scoffs a laugh. 'I know I acted like an asshole the other night, but … it hasn't been mixed messages, Luka.' His voice is almost a whisper now. 'I'm just terribly bad at not breaking things. I should have been honourable enough to not go there at all.'

'Are you referring to me or Nix?'

'Take your pick. But staying away is proving … more difficult than I'd hoped.'

'So you opted to have Traelen end my extension? Effectively sending me away?'

Quillian holds my gaze, the space between us heating.

'You needed to have that as an option – you still do. Do I want to send you away? No. But nor will I trap you here, or with us, against your wishes or your best interests.'

'Will you tell me what's really going on? Fill in the blanks for me?'

He's quiet a long time. 'Yes,' he says eventually. 'If you're okay that you can never not know. Once you know, you'll be bound to us in some way. Forever.'

I stare at him but there's no jest on his face. Waiting for the hesitation to creep in brings nothing, just a solidifying knowledge that this is my path. For good or bad.

'Even if it's just to keep our secrets,' he adds softly. 'But, for full transparency, people who know our secrets, and are not with us, are generally considered loose ends.'

My ribs expand with a deep inhale, and I try to keep my eyes from widening.

'I would do everything I could to keep you from harm,' he continues. 'But I'm not completely infallible. If you're not sure, it's best you just don't know. Not officially. The connections I can see you've already made on your own make you enough of a risk to our cause – you know too much. Blossom, too.'

I place my teacup on the kitchen counter and take a moment to absorb its details. The way the pale green vine winds its way around the rim and dips down to circle the bottom. How the white flowers decorate the vine, their naivety threatening to strangle the delicate cup.

Quillian's hand still grips the edge of the counter beside his hip. The brown skin of his knuckles is marked in several places, and I wonder how many times he's split them. He doesn't move. Doesn't even shift a finger. But I can feel the heat in his stare as he watches me.

The rhythm of my heart is fast and loud in my ears as I slowly lift my face and meet his gaze. A jolt of heat rushes through me, starting in my cheeks, sparking in my stomach and landing low in my core.

'And if I don't want to know,' I say, 'I'd be expected to just walk away?'

'I'd insist on it. For both your safety and Blossom's.'

I lean the side of my body against the bench near him, the stone pressing into my soft flesh. He looks down at me, almost over his shoulder. I'm close enough to him I could run my fingers over the muscles in his arm that are filling his shirt. If he turned to face me, we'd be almost chest to chest.

The thought takes hold and I can't dislodge it.

'I know you can't see the whole picture from where you are now, Luka,' he says, his breath just reaching my face. 'But you've seen and learned so much – now you're standing on a precipice.'

'I do know that much.'

'But you don't see how deep the drop is.'

'What if I decide tomorrow?' I ask, a voice in the back of mind telling me I've already made up my mind.

He closes his eyes briefly. For a moment, I think he's disappointed. But when they open again, they're full of opportunity. Of desire.

'Then it would be impossible for me not to ask what you want to do now – before you ... decide.'

'I want to believe you didn't mean it when you said "you shouldn't have". I want to believe you don't regret spending that night with me.'

He exhales heavily, pieces of my hair dancing away from my face.

'I was right when I said I shouldn't have.'

I suppress a flinch and start to draw back but he takes my hand and I still, his skin hot on mine.

'Because,' he says firmly, 'I shouldn't have brought you any further into this. Part of me still wishes Claudius hadn't, and I stand by that – in addition to his grief, I can see why Nix wanted you far away from all of this.' He pauses. 'But, then, perhaps I wouldn't have met you and I certainly can't regret the time we've spent together. I am *grateful* for that night. For what you reminded me of.'

My fingers twine between his of their own accord and I look at where they join. 'Which was?'

'What it is to have something worth fighting for.'

I suck in a quiet breath as I look back to his face. At the seriousness there. Lifting our joined hands between us, I move to stand in front of him. Our hands at shoulder height, our arms press against each other to the elbow.

'You want to fight for me?' I ask.

'Yes. But only if you're absolutely sure you want to be part of something other than what you see here.' He lifts his eyes to the door to indicate the prison and, I assume, the wrongness here. 'I would never force you, Luka.' He lifts his other hand to my face, sliding his fingers along my jaw, and into my hair until I press my face into the palm of his hand. Tingles of sensation running down my sides, my toes curling. 'But we agreed to decide all that tomorrow.'

'We did,' I say, my voice betraying the heady tension that's warming me from the inside. 'So I suggest you kiss me before I combust.'

I can't help the small groan that escapes my throat as his face cracks into a hungry smile, his dimple on full display. Slowly he lowers his face to mine, stopping short of my mouth and resting his forehead against my own. His skin is warm and his breath hot on my lips.

'I didn't mean to hurt you, Luka.' His voice is so quiet I can barely hear him over my expectant heart. 'Please, forgive me.'

There's a desperation in his voice that chips at me. I can't help the corner of my mouth lifting slightly at the knowledge I'm not in this on my own. Quillian is leaping as much as I am. I let go of his hand and take his face in both of my hands.

'Done,' I say. I press my lips to his, softly. He almost sags against me, the tension leaving him, only to be replaced with a different kind.

Wrapping my hand around the back of his head, I bury my fingers in his short hair and move to kiss the side of his neck. I brush my lips across his ear.

'Forgiven,' I say. 'But expecting you to make it up to me tonight.'

'Hopefully not just tonight,' he says into my neck where he drops his head, trailing his lips along my throat. I tip my chin back, exposing the most sensitive skin. The slight drag of his mouth along my jaw deepens the warmth spreading through my limbs. I open my mouth to take his kiss but instead he bends and drops a line of kisses down the middle of my chest and over the top of each breast. All without even moving my clothing.

It's so much slower than the first time we were together but the subtle throb in my body gives away how ready I am for him. He wraps his arms around my back, one sliding down to hold my ass and pulls me against him. Finally his mouth finds mine and it's soft, and gentle, and wanting.

It sets fire to the need that's building between my legs.

I tug his shirt from his pants and slip my hands up his taut sides, the contours of his stomach running under my thumbs.

I can read his tattoo, River had said, the memory warming alongside the building heat of my body. As if those two things belong together.

Slipping my hands up and over his shoulders, I slide his shirt off and down his arms, letting it fall to the floor before I trail kisses along his collarbones. Shifting to his right side, I brush the explosion of colour with the pads of my fingers, little bumps breaking out on his skin as he stills. Waiting.

Seamlessly woven in the different patches of colour that overlap and bleed into each other is a line of text that starts just behind his ear before winding down his neck and across his right pectoral muscle. His brown nipple hardens as I trace the letters and words, putting it together.

For those that prove the colour of their soul.

I stare at it for a moment, the understanding that this is what Cortane said to me – must have been what Claudius had tattooed as well – slams into me. Slowly, I pull back to look at him and am almost swallowed whole by the depth of emotion swimming behind his eyes. As we stare at each other, my hands still on his body, my legs and hips pressed against him, I find I don't know what to say. How to articulate what feels like the cementing of a fundamental shift that's been occurring in me. One that's partly to do with Quillian, and partly not.

But one that his tattoo seems to symbolise in a way I can't explain.

So I take his face in my hands again and kiss him in a way that I hope tells him instead, opening myself up to everything he can show me as his lips crush mine in return. Dragging my hands back down his body, I slide my fingers in the front of his pants, eliciting a sharp inhale from him. I grin into the kiss, nipping his bottom lip between my teeth before breaking away and leading him by the pants into my bedroom.

I was hyper-aware of his presence in my apartment when he first came in but here, in this room, it feels like it was made to accommodate the two of us. Leaving my door open, he closes in behind me, removing my hand from his pants, and crossing my arms carefully across my chest as he presses against my back.

Gently, he takes the hair that hangs down my back and scrapes it over one shoulder, blowing softly on the patch of skin he's exposed. Skin that prickles when he runs a finger down the top of my spine, towards the zip in the back of my dress, and slowly drags it down.

The shoulders of the silky fabric loosen first, slipping to the sides, the sheer pieces bracing the tops of my arms until Quillian slides them off. My breasts are suddenly heavy under their own weight as the dress skims my hips and drops to the floor.

His large, brown hands wind around me from behind, cupping a breast in each one and I lean further back into him. Kisses land on my neck as he pinches my nipples between his fingers, forcing my head to drop back on his shoulder and my legs to press together in an attempt to abate the aching between them.

I press my ass into him, his clear need doing nothing to simmer down my own desire. Not wanting him to move his hands unless it's to claim me further, I tuck my fingers into my underwear and let them fall, kicking them to the corner of the room.

Quillian groans loudly as he firmly runs the flat of his hand down my stomach and grips me between my thighs. Molten heat surges through me and I arch into him, gripping his arm. He circles his fingers just at my entrance and I push against him, creating friction against the heel of his palm as his fingers pulse just inside me slowly, so slowly.

'More, Quillian – I need more,' I beg.

He pushes half a finger into my swollen core, teasing. 'Like this?' he asks against my ear, voice husky.

It's there – the ledge I want to go over. Close enough for me to almost see it with my eyes shut. But he's keeping me so far from it.

'More,' I demand, clutching his forearms.

More fingers drive their way inside, suddenly filling me, and I cry out. He applies pressure when his fingers find a place that makes me see stars, my knees going weak as he pulses in a circular pattern. Holding me to him with one arm across my chest, he keeps up his relentless rhythm.

A rhythm that drowns out all thought other than chasing that ledge.

I clench my thighs around his hand and suddenly the ledge is flying at me. Fast enough for me to shudder, unable to catch my breath before it slams into me. A cracked sound tears from my throat and he kisses my neck and the side of my face where I turn into him.

'I got you,' he murmurs. 'I got you.'

CHAPTER TWENTY-NINE

Quillian is already awake when I stir just before dawn. He's sexily mussed in the morning – his eyes hooded and sleepy, all guardedness gone from his features.

'Morning,' he says almost shyly when I blink up at him.

A flash of heat races across my cheeks as I take in where I'm nestled into his chest, his arm behind my neck. But I don't move. Instead, I let my fingers dance gently on his skin. Feeling the dark hair he has there. The scars.

'Morning,' I echo, enjoying the memory of last night. Of how he almost brought me to my knees with only his hands. How I'd pushed him back on the bed and tasted him until he swore, and then rode him as I watched the tendons in his neck strain. How he broke, throwing me back over that ledge, too.

'I wish we had more than today,' he murmurs, absently stroking my arm that rests across him.

I swallow.

But I know what I will be facing. What my choice is. And there is nothing that can keep me here, in this prison that I now know is literal and metaphorical. At least for me, even if it's more a luxury resort for the prisoners. But I won't walk away from Nix and River. And I certainly won't walk away from Quillian and the things he's willing to help me

287

understand. Blossom has said that she goes where I go, but we both need this to be her choice as well.

Even though I know having all the answers won't necessarily be easier, I have lived in this false haven for too long.

Quillian holds my hand over the top of his heart where I can feel its gentle beat. 'Luka,' he says softly, 'we need to talk about last night. What it means.'

I wriggle forward a fraction until I'm completely flush with the front of his body. 'Tell me you want more,' I breathe.

'I want everything. But you shouldn't rush to give it, and I–I don't even know if I am in a position to take it.'

His lips are softer this morning – if that's possible – when I kiss him in answer, but his tongue is just as hot and inviting as it was last night. Sucking his lip into my mouth, I can't help but sink my teeth into it gently. I sense his smile, but it feels tinged with sadness.

Drawing back, I let the seriousness of what I am actually going to agree to bring me out of this beautiful daydream, putting aside the flutter in my chest as his words 'I want everything' echo in my mind.

'Last night,' I say, 'you told me I was heading towards a precipice with you. One I didn't know the depth of, and won't before I commit to joining you, regardless if I like your secrets or not.'

'Doesn't sound like a good deal, does it?' he says.

'But it's the reality, I know.'

'What are you saying?'

'You're fighting for good. To fix whatever has gone so wrong in Nuntainia that people like Kasera, Aiten, and Davorous end up here and not in Vana.'

It's a statement I knew in my heart to be true. Yet, to see him nod in confirmation brings a rush of relief I hadn't thought possible.

He gently drags his fingers through the ends of my hair as he seems to consider his words. 'Nuntainia is our continent's most powerful country in terms of wealth, military might and size. But, instead of using that position to help Tae and Coprath, it is at secret war with Coprath using mostly Tae resources.' My scalp tingles where my hair pulls gently, but my skin runs cold as I think on what Nix told me – what this war has cost him. 'And, yet, I'm not sure that war is the worst of it. It's almost just the end product of systems, decisions, *choices* that enable them to so effectively keep Tae down.'

'So you really are fighting a whole country?' I ask, the words seeming to fill the room. My head starts to pound at how close to the discussions and recommendations of such systems and policies my father could have been. But I know he was striving so hard for good in our country – good *for* our country. So where has it gone wrong?

'Yes,' Quillian says simply, gaze burning down into mine. 'I am fighting a country, for a country. We're all here for different versions of the same thing. I fight for Tae,' he says, hand sliding all the way into my hair to cup my head, 'and I really do want to fight for you. But you need to think about what you want too. You wanted to go home – to create a life.'

A softly beating stillness settles over us as I think about the version of me that did so desperately want to go home. To Klades and Akira and Zale. But now none of that feels like mine. And Klades is the capital of Nuntainia – the place our government sits and seemingly condones the actions of the prisoners here. At least enough to keep them in luxury and not Vana. How many of the decisions Quillian is talking about did these very people make? And how can that be where I belong now?

'I want to know your secrets, Quillian. But we save our friends first. Then ... I want to know where home is.'

The light has returned to Bloss's eyes when she spies me creeping across the wellness centre. River's still in his position in the chair. For all the world, he looks like he's asleep, but there's an awareness about him somehow that tells me he's noted my presence. He doesn't stir.

'How are you feeling?' I ask Blossom when I reach her side.

'Tired,' she says, lifting herself to sit in the narrow bed.

The mattress squeaks a little as I sit beside her, placing a hand on the covers over her knee. 'Can you tell me what happened?'

Her face is full of hatred when I look at her, an expression she so rarely wears. River's awake state is given away when his breathing stops momentarily and fingers grip the arm of the chair. Blossom looks over to him and he slowly opens his eyes, meeting her gaze. I wait for her to ask him to leave. Instead, she addresses both of us.

'Davorous wanted to take something I didn't want to give,' she says. 'When I refused – clearly – he thought maybe his blade would convince me.' She looks away. 'I guess he didn't realise I'd rather die.'

An oily, sour feeling coats the inside of my stomach. I study Blossom's profile in the silence, awed by the fierceness under her soft exterior. Not for the first time, I wish I was more like her – openly standing for what is true and important to me. No matter the risks or what others may think. The fact people like Davorous assume they can steal the goodness of people like Blossom burns the back of my throat. That people like Davorous feel it's their right to take what they will. With no regard for what they break in the process. Because I can tell the woman before me has changed since last night. No matter that, in his view, he may not have succeeded, he has still robbed her. Stolen some of the light she wields.

I take her hand and she grips it back harder than her now faraway look would suggest.

'We'll find a way to make him pay, Bloss,' I say quietly, glancing at River. He nods solemnly. As if he and I have just made a vow. I look back at Blossom. 'We'll make him pay.'

Blossom clears her throat and looks back to us, lingering a little longer on River.

'But today,' she says, 'we have other things to do.'

I exhale, my mouth puffing out. Clearly she has done some talking to River because today is the last day before Traelen returns to transfer River and Nix to Zanteera prison, condemning them to a life of torture and isolation for a lie.

'We need to talk about that first, Bloss,' I say.

'Yes,' River says, sitting forward.

Blossom watches him as he draws himself to standing and stretches his legs and back. Crossing the room to stand beside her bed, he drops into a crouch, eyeing us both.

'There are things at play here that neither of you understand yet,' he says.

He looks at me. 'I assume Quillian has been clear with you about what happens if you do know?'

'He has.' Or close enough. Being a 'loose end' to people who are capable of killing Nuntainia's politicians in their secret hiding place can only mean so many things.

'And what did you decide?'

'I know what I want to do, River. I understand what's at stake. But I won't make the call until Bloss does, too. Until we can talk it through together.'

'Sell it to me, then,' she says wearily.

I listen as River takes Blossom through essentially the same discussion Quillian and I had. Minus the attachment part. Listening to River gives the words a different weight to when I talked with Quillian. That conversation was more personal. More charged. While I care for River deeply, it does bring an objectivity to what we're being asked to do. To agree to a side of an argument we haven't been a part of. To fight in a way that brings an unknown cost.

But as he talks, I visualise the connections I've already made: Quillian's insistence that I find ways to learn why they're really here. The jarring differences between those reasons and the ones Traelen announces when they arrive. The conditions the prisoners are entitled to here. The relief on their faces when it's clear it's not the infamous Vana Prison they have arrived at, but the secret, exclusive one with no real name.

Only places people aren't supposed to know about have no names.

Now I wonder if the magical, contractual binds aren't designed to protect us – the concierges completing their service – but the people who decide where we end up. And the prisoners that end up here and the reasons for their 'sentence'.

The enormity of what's starting to take shape in my mind pushes into my temples. A dark shape I can't see the edges of yet. A shadow that's not making my understanding clearer, but far more complex. Worrying. About the decisions being made, and who is making them.

'It's never a sensible proposition,' Blossom says with a heavy tone before frowning at River. 'You're asking us to trust you implicitly. To hand our lives over to you based on what? Patchy information at best.'

'We're not asking, Blossom,' River says. 'We won't ever ask. You're either all in on the basis of your own experiences and observations and desire to make Nuntainia a better place, or you walk away. You need to look at everything you see here – and what you don't – and decide for yourselves if you think it's just. Think about the things Nix and I have been instructed to do as part of our *duty*, at least the things you know, what that cost has been, and not just for Nix. Then, you need to decide what you do about it.' He stands again, looking down at each of us. 'Which brings us back to the options: join us because you believe in something better, or you walk away. From everything.'

'Even from stopping your transfer?' I ask, willing the fear to stay out of my voice and not only for River's benefit. If I think too long on the risk, I may crumble under the weight of it.

He pauses, giving me a long look as he thinks it over.

'Not necessarily,' he says. ' But that would be it, Lu, that's a huge risk to be associated with if you're not under our protection as it is. We weren't even expecting to have this time with you – finding you here was a huge surprise. But there'd be no more once we leave, you can't run with us if you're not *with* us.'

Blossom gives me a long look. 'I don't want you to miss out on what I have,' she says before looking at River. 'Get everyone together.'

'Hey Bloss,' Emeris says as we pass him in the hall on the way to our apartment. 'You left early last night.'

His smile is so warm but still mine falters a little. He'd mused about how 'wonky' this place is not long ago, now I think it's almost completely bent, breaking, like it's preparing to be remade into something else.

'Just Luka keeping me on my toes, as usual,' she says and keeps walking, her hand held lightly at her side where I know her dressing lies.

Emeris nods in acknowledgement of River where he trails behind us. Despite what we're about to meet to discuss, my blood heats a little at the thought of seeing Quillian again. In my apartment.

'What are you really thinking about all this?' Blossom asks under her breath when Emeris is out of ear shot.

My heart swells unexpectedly with an anticipation I haven't felt in a long time. An anticipation for something bigger.

'I know it seems crazy,' I whisper. 'But it's so clear now there is something very wrong with who our government is sending here – why this place even exists. Something that needs to be stopped. And what if ... I don't know, this is what we're meant to do?'

'We don't even know what *it* is.'

'No ... not entirely, that's true. But we do know they're good people. We know they're prepared to risk their lives to bring people who abuse their power to justice – people who we've been blindly waiting on hand and foot until now. And what's the other option? Stay here so Davorous can finish what he started?' My chest pinches at the words that fly out before I can reconsider. But they're not wrong. Seeing Bloss prone on the stone floor, Nix leaning over her with the knife, is still so raw ... She can't stay, not within reach of him.

'Sorry, Bloss,' I say at the flash of terror that spikes in her eyes. 'I just ... I know in my bones these men are good people who are trying to make things better. And we both know the people we serve in this place are anything but good.'

The thought of staying here – forced to live and work amongst these people, treating them as though they're above everyone else despite their festering sins – is almost suffocating. The idea of working in Parliament with them, where they have free rein to abuse their power, feels worse. Blossom has a different perspective, I know that. She's endured a pain that means she understands better how to be grateful for every moment. To not constantly be searching for something more. An outlook I'd thought I'd mastered up here. Now, I wonder if I was just being naive to what's really happening in the world. And finally I have an opportunity to have my horizons broadened.

We reach the hallway to what is 'home' in this farce of a prison and she pulls me to the side, pain pinching her features.

'I do know they're good,' she says. 'I do.' She brushes a large dark curl out of her face. 'It's just ... this isn't the first time someone has tried to pull me into this world, Lu. And then he died.'

'I'll give you a moment,' River says, heading towards the door but loitering just out of earshot, half turned to us. Instinctively, I glance up and down the hallway but there's no sign of Davorous. Not that I would expect him in the concierge quarters, but I don't want to take any chances.

Blossom's gaze doesn't return to me but remains fixed on River.

'It's just ... terrifying.'

I frown, looking after River again, fairly certain we're not only talking about what Frank was involved in before he died. 'Which bit, Bloss?' I ask gently.

Her eyes are full of silver tears when she looks back, still not meeting my eye. 'I'm not supposed to be attracted to anyone.' My head almost spins at the direction she's taking, but I know better than to say anything. Not yet. 'I shouldn't be contemplating anything that takes me too close to ... that.'

The breeze blows through the courtyard, bringing with it the strong scent of jasmine. When she finally meets my gaze, I know she's ready to hear what I have to say.

'Bloss.' I wait until she acknowledges me. 'I think we might be talking about two different things.'

'What if taking this leap is one and the same for me? That to do what I couldn't before means I am putting myself right in the path of something else I can't do?'

'Then, and only if you also think hearing their story is the right path, I will be there to collect you at the bottom. Whatever comes.'

She nods slowly.

'If you take River out of the equation, what are you thinking?'

She sighs heavily and seems to give it considerable thought. 'That ... Frank was right. He knew about people with tattoos like the one on Quillian's neck.' She pauses, as if waiting for my reaction – the realisation that she can read it too, that that's probably exactly why she was wary of him in the beginning. But I know there's more to Blossom's uncertainty than my understanding of that connection, so I say nothing. 'I'm thinking ... there are too many hidden injustices that shouldn't be allowed to continue. Things that people like Frank and those with the tattoos were – are – fighting against. That it's going to be hard and ... dangerous and ... that maybe there is a legacy I can try to fulfil. That I think there's something ... honourable on the other side. And I want to be honourable.'

CHAPTER THIRTY

Our apartment feels tight with all of us in here. A small shiver runs over my bare arms as it sinks in what we're about to do. Even if I don't know all the details, I know enough to understand I am leaving whatever remains of 'concierge Luka' behind today.

Maybe more than that.

Nix is seated on the couch, one ankle propped on his knee, his checked shirt open to expose the top of his chest. The tension in his shoulders betrays the hesitation he's trying hard to cover up. When his golden gaze finds mine, I know he's just biding his time before he makes us all very aware of his thoughts.

I listen to the door close behind River, who held it open for Blossom and me. The sun is now completely in the sky above us, the sitting area bathed in light from the windows. My mind tugs at the memory of what happened in here last night, just to my left. It takes a lot of effort to stop the blush racing across my cheeks as I watch Quillian turn from where he was looking at the view and face us.

His gaze meets mine first and my heart skips. The softness I search for in his expression isn't quite there but it's somehow more comforting that it's not. Today, my entire focus is how to get us off the island and if Quillian should come, too. With Cortane willing to help, our first port of call will need to be working out the wards – providing she's not *really* planning to do anything to harm Quillian.

I don't think about what either option means for him and me.

Nix gives Blossom a careful once over and she smiles gently back. A moment of something passing between them as we all watch on. Seeing her, sitting with us and engaging, as well as Nix's now blood-free hands, eases another piece of tension in my heart. But the desperation for her to be safe, and away from Davorous, just moves further into its space.

The only way she will be that, is off this island.

'Where should we start?' River asks.

Quillian releases a wearied sigh. Like he knows this will be hard.

'Traelen will be here to transfer you two tomorrow,' he says. He glances at Blossom and me before looking back to Nix and River. 'There are ... things you can still achieve over there. But that is admittedly more of an end of the road situation.'

'One we were going to take if needed,' Nix says.

My mouth drops. 'You mean you were *expecting* to go there?'

My question hangs for a long moment but it's Nix I look at.

'Not for sure, no. Claudius gave us the job of getting to Cortane and, at that time, we didn't know you were also assigned as the contact for her. We also didn't know if you were going to be successful in gaining her trust and getting her or us the information needed. Traelen transferring us was not the only risk if we failed up here, Lu.'

'But you succeeded,' River says to me.

I look at Quillian, but I know I have to be the one to tell them.

'I didn't, actually,' I say. 'I haven't found anything on how to stop the wards.'

'Well that puts a bit of a dampener on things, doesn't it?' a new voice interjects and I whirl back to the windows, where Cortane casually leans against the wall. The air rushes from my lungs and I hesitantly step between her and Quillian, giving him my back, with literally no idea how I can defend him against her – or if that's what I need to be doing. Did I pass or fail that part of her assessment?

'That's cute,' she says, her cool gaze running the length of my body. 'It's good to know my team has been effective.'

I've lost the ability to put my thoughts together, so all I can do is stare.

She takes a step towards us and I mirror her movements, not prepared to relinquish whatever position I have between her and the new Warden she wanted information on. Not until I know for sure what she intends to do. I wish I knew if River had his knife with him, the way she cocks her head makes me sure we might need it.

Her eyes narrow and she seems to take a second, deeper, look at me.

'Are you going to step aside, or are we going to make a mess of your pretty dress, Princess?'

Her tone is not unlike when we first met, colder than the last time I saw her. When she agreed to help me.

'Cort—' Quillian starts.

'That depends,' I say. 'Are you here to help, or hinder?'

A lethal smile slowly stretches across her face.

'I think I sort of like you,' she says and shrugs. 'But I guess you should already know that. I definitely don't make a habit of helping people I don't like.'

Nix laughs. A real and open sound that bursts from him. Dragging my mind from the blankness, coating it in something crisper.

'What is going on here?' I grind out, not taking my focus from Cortane.

She stills, clasping her hands in front of her. She tilts her head to the other side and a shiver runs through me. 'You're not cleared to know that.'

'Luka.' I jump as Quillian appears at my side, his gentle fingers on my elbow. 'Seeing us all together, knowing how we're all connected ... that's a lot for us to be declaring. For now.'

Slowly, I turn to face him. The depth of his dark green eyes seems suddenly as bottomless as the other side of the precipice he talked about.

I place a hand on his chest and he leans into it slightly. 'She asked for information on you ...' My voice is so quiet, even to me, as I process my thoughts out loud. I don't know how he can possibly hear me.

'And you didn't give it,' he says, just as quietly.

My fingers flex where they lie on him and he gently places his hand over mine.

'So it *was* a test?' I ask, ready for them to admit it out loud.

'One Claudius demanded,' Cortane says.

'We can talk logistics about getting off the island with you, and enough to give you an idea of our intent, Lu,' River cuts in. 'But that's all. It will be a strange conversation and there'll be a lot of gaps we can't fill in. Not one of us is going to try and push you in a particular direction.' I hold Quillian's stare as I listen to River, the room spinning slightly, but I don't tell them how much Quillian has already shared. 'But there's a hard limit on what we can share – everything we are, have done, and are preparing to do, are hanging by a thread here.'

'For the record,' Nix says, leaning back and throwing an arm across the back of the couch. 'Under no circumstances do I agree to Luka joining us.'

I slide my gaze to him. 'I don't think you get to decide that.'

Quillian gives my fingers a gentle squeeze where they still lie over his blue shirt before he lets go and I drop my hand.

'I wish I did,' Nix says. 'But I can kill—'

A weight appears on my chest, surrounded by a hot, simmering anger that suddenly burns.

'What?' I ask. 'Who—'

'That's not helpful, Nix,' River cuts in, shaking his head slightly.

'You'll kill only the people I tell you to,' Cortane says and my knees start to lose their strength.

Blossom murmurs something under her breath and River looks worriedly at her but I look at Cortane. Quillian is the brothers' commanding officer ... is Cortane his?

'What I *can* tell you,' Quillian says, 'is that we are a group of people that have, for one reason or another, been exposed to the underside of the Nuntainian government. Been on that side, seen or experienced the horrors, and decided to take a stand. But, being in this group does two things. One, it allows access to highly sensitive information we will *never* share with anyone who is not sympathetic to our cause. And two, while those in the group will protect each other at all costs, an association with us will still expose you to the full might of Nuntainian law, including sentencing to Vana.'

Even though it's merely confirmation of what I've come to know, a carousel of thoughts and questions spins in my mind as the room falls silent for long moments.

'Right now,' River says into the quiet, 'my feeling is that the conversation around each of you joining us long term or not is too big. So let's just focus on our immediate challenge.'

'Which is that you failed on the wards,' Cortane says, cocking her head at me.

I sigh, trying to drag my focus to the task at hand even though part of my mind is snagged on a conversation I've had before. Zale and Akira talked of a vigilante group. Could this be ...

My skin prickles under the attention of the room. 'I have no ideas other than you, Nix, and River being marked with the tracking on your way down. Any other suggestions?' I ask.

'I wish,' she says, looking at Quillian. 'Looks like we'll get to experiment a little more.'

'I want to know what the ground rules are here,' Blossom says, fixing Cortane with a steely stare.

'Ground rules,' Cortane says slowly, leaning against the arm of the couch. 'Quillian.'

Quillian rubs his forehead briefly before dropping his arm back to his side.

'In an ideal world, you would swear allegiance to ... us, before ever getting this far. Right now, I think the best we can do is take your word for it. But it means we will be careful with any details we give you. You need to appreciate the significant risk that we're taking should you decide to expose us, and understand if we feel that risk is rising – and no longer worth the return – that you will be ... taken care of.'

'That'll win them over,' Nix says sarcastically.

But he didn't see the depth of truth in Quillian's face when he said he wanted to fight for me, too. Doesn't know the relief I've felt when I've discovered the crimes of those who have died – not relief that those crimes existed to ease any grief, but relief they'd died. Doesn't know how much I now want to see actual justice done, and how I feel I can no longer stay here and watch it be perverted.

I give Blossom a moment, wishing I could read her mind, but she just looks steadily back. Nix was so unlike himself when she first met him, and it took me too long to understand why. Too long to ask what was happening with him.

'Why, Nix?' I ask gently. 'Why don't you want us to be part of this? Do you not believe in what you're doing?' I ask, and everyone else turns to him as well.

Nix's brows lower as if he wishes I hadn't asked him that question. 'Of course I do. But I'm here – River is here – we can fight the corruption in our government on behalf of the three of us. Listen, Lu'—he shifts in his seat—'there is no guarantee we will succeed in having any impact on the government and the skewed choices they make. But, if you join us, I can guarantee your life will never be the same. Outside of this room, of this *prison*, you can live the life I know you've always wanted.' He glances sideways at Quillian. 'Think about what we used to write about – you can live alongside Akira and Zale, your children could grow up together. You could study. You could ... contact your father. You could have a *life*.' A lump forms in my throat and he tries to smile at me. 'You could track down Hugo and have a boring husband to help you make as many of those children as you like.'

Quillian seems particularly still in the periphery of my vision but I don't dare look at him.

My throat thickens with tears for the life I did think I would have, the one I wanted – minus the 'boring Hugo' bit perhaps. But Akira and Zale don't need me to have children alongside them, they've already done that. And this prison doesn't need me to keep up its pretense. Not to mention I don't think I could keep up a false life of my own now, knowing what I do. How would I genuinely 'live hard', as Bloss said to me the day I was supposed to be collected, when I know what lies underneath?

But more than that, I'm not sure I am that person who only wanted all of those things anymore. Now, I'm someone who *has* seen more of what's beneath the surface. Who knows there is a decision-making trail that leads back to someone, or multiple someones, back in Parliament House. Who understands that this prison is a symptom of something running much deeper in Nuntainia.

I am someone who feels on a precipice and I'm ready to find out what's on the other side.

'Outside of this room, Nix, I have nowhere else to be.' The honesty in my words cracks something in me. It's both true and not true – Akira or Zale would have me, so would my father if pressed. But in all of those places, at some point I would be just another guest. Another complication they have to work around. The thing they have to accommodate. The 'almost' that pulls them up short from those perfect lives. The thought of my father reminds me how desperately he wanted social equity in Nuntainia, how hard he worked with the government to achieve that. Perhaps this is a way I can help him with that?

Nix grips the back of his head before dropping his arm back to his side. He rests a fist on his knee and a small patch of jasmine on the balcony outside fizzes, turning black as it withers under his earth-wielding Clayti magic.

'Then it's done, and you've been warned,' Cortane says. 'Luka, you will take your collection as planned and get into the House.'

I press down on the objection that I don't want to go to Parliament House, the want to ask if there is literally anything else I can do that will keep me with them. But I know that's my role. If I am going to get to the bottom of what's happening and help them put an end to it, that's where I need to be.

'Blossom,' Cortane continues, 'you will remain until I change your collection date in the system. At worst, you've got a little under a year until the next one.'

I can feel the blood drain from my face. 'No—'

'It's the only way to keep her from being tracked,' Quillian says gently, 'that doesn't put her at risk of being found by Hunters and sent to Vana.'

'But—' I look at Blossom, who also seems a little pale.

'Finn will stay with her,' he says, and I have to close my eyes for a moment. 'And I will be here.'

'No,' I say again. 'Tracking or no tracking, Bloss will only be safe when Davorous is dead.' My heart slams in my chest at the conviction in my voice. Conviction that's pounding in my veins. 'Given we can't do that yet, the next best thing is for her to leave.'

River shifts in his seat. 'I agree.'

'Bloss?' I ask – plead.

Her gaze is watery when she looks up at me from where she sits next to River. 'Yes,' she says quietly. 'I want to go.'

I blow out a breath and look back to Cortane, giving her a curt nod.

'We go on dusk tonight,' Cortane says, without missing a beat. 'Right as the sun is setting – it will make it harder to see. Do what you need today, make any final attempts for information on the wards, and meet me on the other side of the gardens here.' She jerks her thumb towards our window. 'But we go today without fail. If you boys get transferred tomorrow, it will be almost impossible to get you out. The magic suppression in Vana isn't a game – I don't know how much longer I can work with what they gave me when I arrived, even with the lack of ongoing treatment thanks to Claudius. It's certainly impacting the size of the portals I can create already.'

She walks to Quillian and embraces him, hard. 'See you in a few, *Warden*.'

Until now, I hadn't really let myself think about what it might be like to say goodbye to Quillian as well. Even if I can't think how we can see each other while he's here and I'm on the mainland, I know I'm not ready to give him up. Blossom takes my hand and I don't stop her. Instead, I thread my fingers in hers and squeeze them tight. To hell with trying to show my strength to Cortane. Right now, as I prepare to send three of my best friends to likely be hunted for the rest of their lives, and say goodbye to Quillian when I am collected, I need Bloss's strength.

I make myself look at Quillian to find him already looking at me.

'Shall we take one last look?' he asks.

We spend the next half an hour searching the office for anything that talks of the wards, only to keep coming up empty-handed. The office is quiet, only the sound of rustling papers and books being opened and closed filling my ears. An increasingly sinking feeling spreads through my body. Every page I turn shows nothing useful. Nothing.

I pick up the pencil drawing of the prison again, trailing a finger along the glass. It almost winks at me in return, mocking my inability to see how to break through the simple line framing the bottom of the island, almost the shape of a tea cup. If only I could smash it like a cup. Quillian joins me at the bookshelf and I turn to him, resisting the temptation to press myself into him.

'It was special to him,' I say, gesturing with the small frame. 'But I don't know why. If only it could talk to us, right?'

'We'll figure it out,' he says.

He tips my chin up with the side of his knuckle and I inhale deeply, trying to keep my eyes dry. But my lip trembles when I meet his gaze and take in the gentleness in his expression.

'I need you to promise me this isn't just about Nix and River,' he says softly.

The band that feels like it's squeezing my chest winds tighter.

'It's not just about them.'

He presses a soft kiss to my lips and I press into it slightly, a tear running down my cheek.

'I know you want to save them – us – and that's ... more incredible than I can explain. But it also needs to be about you and your—'

The door knob rattles and we break apart abruptly. Blinking, I look back to the door to find Traelen. Dressed in a charcoal suit today with an inky black trim. Two Hunters on either side.

'Traelen,' Quillian says without missing a beat. 'What brings you back today?'

Traelen remains silent but jerks his head in Quillian's direction. The two Hunters move to flank him and Quillian doesn't even look at them. Just keeps his eyes on Traelen.

'Quillian O'Daire,' Traelen finally says. 'You're charged with treason and will be transferred to Vana Prison immediately.'

My gasp is audible and I flounder for words.

'Luka,' he says, 'I trust you can keep things running up here until I find you another Warden. I have someone in mind – the transition shouldn't take long.'

My throat starts to thicken and Traelen's brows twitch downwards.

'O–of course,' I say.

The Hunters march Quillian towards the door and I grip my hands to stop from reaching out for him.

'Keep the prisoners inside today, I have another team of Hunters sweeping the premises for the brothers as we speak.'

It's all I can do to keep breathing.

'You're taking them all today?' I ask.

Traelen nods, taking a step away.

'What should I tell everyone about ...' I try not to look at Quillian. I fear if I do, everything will be given away on my face. But I need to keep them here for a little longer. To try and—

'That the Warden was a traitor, a murderer, and perpetrator of war crimes.' Quillian's shoulders tense at the last words. 'Tell them Nuntainia doesn't abide traitors and their lives will be better without him.'

'Yes, sir,' I say dully.

'It's a shock, I know,' Traelen continues and I want to scream at him to stop. 'You've been an exceptional concierge, Luka,' he says. 'I'll re-write your recommendation personally. It would be best not to have Quillian's name on it where you're going. Hale will come for you this week – just after I've transferred the Kilroy brothers so a Warden can have a fresh start. Janly will take over from you then until I appoint the new Warden.'

The edges of my vision start to blur with the effort of keeping my face neutral. I see the breadth of Quillian's shoulders drop where he's held just outside the doorway, his back still to me. His arms are twisted behind him, wrists bound so tightly a rivulet of blood drips into his right palm.

'Thank you, sir,' I breathe, and I watch them walk away.

CHAPTER THIRTY-ONE

The day was impossibly long. Full of concerned glances from the other concierges, none of whom suspected Quillian of any wrongdoing. And countless conversations, going over and over and *over* what happened with Traelen.

But none longer than the grilling from Janly.

'What time did they leave?' she asks.

It's the first different question in some time, as well as the most inane. We've gone over and over Quillian's arrest. Who were the Hunters with him, what did they look like, how did they bind him.

'Jan,' I say on an exhale. 'What does it matter?'

She flicks her gaze around the interior courtyard where we stand, watching the Hunters patrolling the area. The acidic taste in the back of my throat turns my stomach. I haven't seen them take Nix or River – yet – but that doesn't mean they won't find them. Or that they haven't already and Traelen has just ordered the Hunters to stay.

A chill runs down my spine, the thought of any of them stuck in Vana Prison for the rest of their lives pressing in on me from all sides. But it's the knowledge I will be here, so close to them but unable to see them, help them, that makes me swallow hard and hope I won't be sick. Until Zale comes to get me, and then I will be completely out of reach.

'I know you care about him,' she says, 'and he you.'

I snap my attention back to her.

'Trust me when I tell you, you have to find a way,' she says. 'Quickly.'

'What?'

A Hunter lumbers towards us and Janly draws herself up straight. 'I'll do what I can,' she says before walking away. I stare after her before snapping my attention back to the Hunter. Just how much does she know?

'How can I help?' I ask the broad, bearded man before me.

'Traelen said you're in charge up here for now?'

I nod, trying not to look too disappointed. Heartbroken.

'My men will need rooms for our stay,' he says. 'We can eat separately to the guests – prisoners – if you can set us up somewhere to eat together.'

'How long do you think you'll be here for?'

He runs his hand along his jaw, scratching gently at his full, red beard. His face is kinder than I would have picked for a Hunter. But I know enough about them to know what they do. They're not military in the same way as Quillian and his team, but Nuntainia's elite law enforcement. And I don't want them here. Or anywhere near my friends.

'Indefinitely at this stage,' he says. 'The transfers Traelen wanted done are complete—'

My chest feels like it's cracked. 'How – how many were there?'

'Transfers? Three.'

'And they're all on the other side?'

'They can't worry you anymore, ma'am,' he says, a tiny crease between his brows. 'I'd put them out of your mind.'

'Of course,' I say, smiling tightly. 'I'll organise to get you set up.' I turn to walk away, a hot restlessness starting to burn in my feet and running up my legs.

'Holland,' he says.

'Pardon?' I ask, looking over my shoulder.

'My name,' he says. 'For when you need to find me.'

'Sorry,' I say, giving him a small smile that probably distorts my face. 'It's been a long day. Nice to meet you, Holland.'

The glass of water Blossom hands me is cool in my hand when I take it and gulp it down. Washing away the taste of vomit.

'We're fucked, Bloss,' I say, pressing the glass against my forehead and leaning back on the tiles of my bathroom wall. 'I should've got them off sooner. I—'

'Had no ability to do that,' she says frankly.

Turning to her, I knock the back of my head against the grey marble instead.

'Why did it have to be so hard to find anything on the wards?' I ask. 'And now it's too fucking late.'

'They're still alive, Lu.'

'But they'd be better off not.' I close my eyes as another wave of nausea takes me. 'They'll never be the same once the other side gets started on them.'

Blossom slowly sinks to the floor beside me, a hand holding her side as she does. The pink dress she's wearing pools around her bare feet.

'I should have called them out long ago,' she says quietly, 'when I first saw Quillian's tattoo. Now they've gone, I feel like a door has closed. One we should've gone through.'

I turn my head on the tiles to look at her. 'Me too. But Cortane will still take you, I'm sure that won't change. I imagine she won't like it, but they will be better off with at least one of them out of reach of Vana. She will go and she will take you.' I don't know how to form my thoughts around the fact I am now also leaving the island while three men I love are in Vana.

'Yeah,' she breathes, 'I think you're right. She's kind of ... cold. But I don't think she'll abandon us.'

'Janly was asking me strange questions today,' I say after a while. 'Like she wanted me to give her their itinerary.' I laugh hollowly and shake my head. 'I couldn't bring myself to tell her what they'd be facing – surely she knows what happens over there.'

Blossom's brows start to furrow.

'She could have a point, actually,' she says. 'There'd be a process they have to go through. Same as here when they get announced, assigned a concierge and all that. What if ...'

'What?' I ask, too impatient to give her space to think.

'Well … they're going to have a magic suppressant of some kind over there right? There's no Claudius to intervene like he did with Cortane. What if they haven't had those yet?'

'I don't know why that's—'

'What are they?'

'Nix is a Clayti,' I say. 'River's Karaylia with strong Arkanan abilities. And you know Quillian's Karaylia, too.'

'River has wings?' Blossom's brows are now shooting for her hairline and I can't help but smile. 'You know, I always thought Clayti were supposed to be a bit more … grounded – pun intended.'

I laugh softly at her small joke at the earth-wielders' expense.

'But that actually makes a lot of sense – Nix's … intensity, and River's gentleness.'

'I guess so, but what does that do for us? They'll still be held over there and there are still the wards we don't know how to bring down.'

'No … but Cortane can still get in and out of Vana, right? The three of them, and me, could be a lot for her to portal at one time … we need to go see them. I have an idea.'

River is on the other side of the alcove when Blossom and I skid to a halt at the exposed bars. My immediate reaction is relief – that someone was here waiting for us. But seeing his face on the other side does something to the inside of my chest. Hardens it somehow. Another blow to my view of Nuntainia.

'I don't know if I'm pleased or disappointed that you're here,' he says. 'But I'm not surprised.'

'You *were* waiting for us,' Bloss says.

'Always. But I don't have long – I'm supposed to be in the food hall.'

Her cheeks deepen in colour and she looks away.

'Can you get the others?' I ask, not wanting to ask the question that's really burning on the tip of my tongue. 'Can Cortane—'

'Not easily, but we can get messages to each other – so far,' he says.

My stomach sinks, an unfulfilled need to lay eyes on Nix and Quillian taking root. I squeeze my fists closed for a moment, taking the small sting of my nails on my palms to bring me focus. I look at Blossom, waiting for her to explain. When she looks back to us, it's me she focuses on, not River.

'How strong is Nix?' she asks.

My mouth drops open to tell her it's been too long for me to really know, but River fills the gaps.

'Very,' he says. 'We were all chosen for our service based on our strength and skills.'

'So it was more than his charm?' I ask, remembering what he told me about being a liaison for the villages.

River scoffs a laugh, but it's missing all of its humour.

'There was never just one thing they wanted,' he says. 'Why do you ask?' He looks back to Bloss.

Her looks between us, suddenly uncertain. 'There's a portion of the island that's been fenced off because it's too unstable for general use – Emeris told me he found it one night with one of the guards from here.'

River's gaze starts to narrow as he tracks her idea.

'If Nix could sever it from the island,' she continues, 'with us on it, he could move us beyond the wards.'

'But we don't know exactly where the wards begin and end,' I say. But as the words come out, I wonder if that's true.

'No. But we've already agreed that marked is better than dead, so—'

'We could go over the wards,' I say, staring at her. 'The picture – the wards – what if they don't go all the way around?'

I blow out a breath and River closes his eyes.

'It's … not a terrible idea,' he says, opening them again. 'But you said "us". That is a bad idea. No one knows of your involvement yet, Lu – you're in the clear to go to the House.'

River's still wearing the clothes he was in when I last saw him, not that that's completely surprising. But suddenly I can't think of anything other than those being the last clothes he'll ever wear. How often do they get replacements here? Basic hygiene? The thought that Quillian might die wearing the uniform of a government that has betrayed him sends an angry chill snaking between my ribs.

'That may be so,' I say. 'But it's too dangerous to stay here now. The Hunters Traelen brought over are staying—'

'Shit,' River mutters.

'—and I'm sure it's only a matter of time before our involvement in everything comes under greater scrutiny. I doubt there is a prisoner over there'—I jerk my thumb behind me—'that hasn't noticed some sort of connection between me and the rest of you. And there is certainly not a single person who will believe I have no idea why Blossom is suddenly missing.' I think of the events where Traelen has quietly watched me work with her. 'Definitely not Traelen.'

'You need to go back,' he says. 'I'll talk to the others, but if we're doing this – regardless of the wards – we need to move quickly. Tomorrow night.' He looks between us and Blossom breathes in deeply. 'There's no going back from this though, you know. If you change your mind before then, no one will hold it against you.'

'Except us,' Blossom says, taking my hand.

'I need to see them,' I say to River, squeezing Blossom's palm against my own.

River glances around behind him, into the light filled space before the building begins.

'I'll see what I can do. If no one's here in fifteen minutes, you need to leave.'

Blossom and I don't talk while we wait, sitting on the rough concrete and dirt that's been chipped away. The metal bars are old and I wonder how many times visits like these have taken place, who carved it out away from view of the guards.

My mind drags itself back to the wards and I rest my head back on the cold, curved slab that hides us from view. Running over all the things we found and searched in the Warden's office. His desk, the files, the shelves. Nix even checked under the rug and the base of the couch. But nothing talked of the wards.

Little stones and bits of dirt skitter through the bars as Quillian skids to a stop. He grips the bars to steady himself and lifts his gaze to mine, all the air whooshing from my lungs.

'I'll give you some space,' Blossom says quietly. She's gone before I can stop her and I watch, heart in my throat, as she races across the open green space without me. I can't see where she's stopped, but I hope she's waiting in the tree line for me.

The uniform I'd worried about Quillian wearing is torn across the front, his coloured tattoo exposed across his ribs. There's an angry red mark across his face, but the skin's not broken. Not there, at least.

He reaches out to take my hand. 'Don't look like that,' he says softly, 'it's fine. We're all fine.'

I search his eyes for any hint of a lie but he seems mostly concerned for me and my chest tightens at the generosity, but unfairness, of that. How long has he gone without being able to have any real concern for himself?

'Blossom and I – we're both coming. You're getting off and we're coming.'

'River told me your plan,' he says. 'It's so crazy, it might just work. But, you know, without being able to bring the wards down, we are very likely to be marked as we cross them – there is no guarantee there is an 'over'.'

I nod.

'And you still want to go?'

'Yes,' I breathe.

He pulls me closer, until I'm standing as flush with him as I can be with the bars between us. But it's still enough to feel the heat of his skin in places.

'It needs to be about you, Luka,' he whispers. 'You have to really want to fight a broken system. But to do so means you'll be on the wrong side of it.'

I slip my hand into the rip in his shirt, sliding my palm around his side and Quillian sighs.

'I want to fight,' I say. 'I can't stand back and watch this happen to you. Or live in ignorant luxury over there while it continues to happen to other people. I can't do anything about the ones I was naive to before. But I can make a stand now,' I say.

The intensity in his face when he meets my gaze sends warmth running across my cheeks.

'It ... might also be a bit about you,' I say. His exhale is loud and his breath reaches my face. 'How would you feel if that was the case?'

'Like I was being set up. Like I met you too late,' he whispers.

A sharp pain digs into my breastbone. 'Why would you think that?'

'Because it's not supposed to be this way, Luka. *I'm* not supposed to have attachments in this way.' His face shutters. 'And I wonder what it would have been like if we'd met long before all of this.'

We watch each other for a long, quiet moment. My hand still in his shirt where I can feel the movement of his breath. 'Well,' I say, 'we can "suppose" all we like, but this is where we are and we're getting off this island. Together.'

He stretches an arm through the bars and around the back of my neck, pulling me to him and claiming my mouth. There's a desperation in the kiss. One that entwines itself with the desire running through my limbs. His fingers slip into my hair, sending a shiver down my neck, and I press against him harder, the bars biting into my flesh.

'We can do this,' I say, short of breath. 'We can do this.'

Quillian kisses me again, his tongue finding mine and his teeth dragging over my lip as he breaks away.

'I hope so,' he says.

CHAPTER THIRTY-TWO

Janly's expression is dark as she goes over the board, updating me on the events of last night and anything I need to know about the concierges in her team. My eyes are gritty and it's hard to focus as the words and photos on the large board start to run together. Blossom and I made it back a couple of hours before dawn, but sleep wasn't something either of us could manage – so we lay awake together instead, each lost in our own thoughts about what will come tonight.

Part of me knows I should rest before we go. But I also know there's no point even trying.

Whatever it costs my energy, I need to make sure Traelen's Hunters, and Traelen himself, think Blossom and I are here, running the prison as requested.

'Finn's keeping a low profile – as he should,' Janly says quietly, still looking at the board, and I blink several times to try to focus. There's something lying under her words.

'Jan,' I say carefully, 'why did you tell me to find a way to get him?' I glance around as I drop my voice to a whisper, but we're alone in the concierge room. 'Why do you keep bringing up Finn?'

Her gaze is shrewd when she turns to me fully, her short bob swishing slightly around her jawline.

'Because ... up here it's good to know where people's loyalties lie,' she says, her voice low. 'As for telling you to get to Quillian, I know Traelen –

sort of. And if Traelen has organised for Quillian to be out of reach – it was for a reason.'

I stare at her, words trying, and failing, to form in my mind.

'What do you know of the wards around the island?' I ask and her eyes widen before she smiles. I don't think Janly would do anything to harm me, not after that confession. And I suddenly wonder if the warmth I've always felt towards her was because we unknowingly, at least to me, share similar values.

She glances back to the door as Emeris and a small group of other concierges start to filter in. 'Perhaps we should retire for a cup of tea after the briefing? Emeris is okay, but I don't know about the others.'

My phone vibrates gently.

Zale: Luka! Are you ready?? I'm coming to collect you so soon. I promise, with everything I have, I will be there x

Shit. In all my planning, I haven't even thought about what to tell Zale. How crazy would she think I am if I told her I've taken Teddy's dream of running away with the vigilantes? I pocket it as the concierges are in place, noticing Holland take a place at the back of the room, complete attention trained on me. I try not to look at him as he watches me take the teams through the events for the day: a seminar with one of the leading academics from Nuntainia – someone my father would know; lunch in the gardens; and an afternoon meditation by the pond. The wellness centre also needs a concierge to assist with stocktaking their medical supplies before they are replenished from the mainland, and Koko wants to start mapping out the events and menu for the next few weeks. It's me that will have to do this last one, and I try not to feel sad I won't be here to see her deliver on the plans – or bitter that her delicious creations are part of the cover hiding what's really here and she probably doesn't even know.

'When should we expect the Warden back?' someone calls out. I don't see who and it's probably better that way.

But my gaze is immediately held by the Hunter who watches with unwavering attention.

I swallow.

'The Warden ... has been charged with crimes warranting his arrest and placement in Vana Prison,' I say, looking out at the concierges, hardly believing this lie I have to tell them.

'I don't believe it,' Emeris says, brows furrowing. I give him the briefest glance, hoping it can convey everything. Janly said he's okay. I am learning I need to trust my instincts here and so much less what I am told. But I know it will never be enough.

My skin starts to itch where I can feel the Hunter's gaze still tracking my reactions. My words. My movements. I grip my fingers in front of me as the quiet disbelief ripples through the room.

'Traelen is sourcing us a replacement,' I say. 'I will let you know as soon as I do when they will be arriving.'

It's those words that wipe away any doubt I am doing the wrong thing. There is nothing in me that has any interest in meeting and serving another Warden. Perhaps it's short-sighted, but the thought of seeing something else – *being* somewhere else – makes my heart swell. And to do so while I get to spend my time with the people I care about the most, doing something *good* – even if we're all being hunted – is more than I could ask for right now.

There's a small, but intense burning under the skin at the front of my chest that quietly asks me to examine that further, what it is I really want to do off this island. But I squash it down. I don't have time to focus on it yet. And so it remains a smouldering ember.

Janly stays with me for the rest of the discussion, where we spend much of the time talking about the glass platform Zenaton suggested and how we could make it work – or someone else could make it work, because I have no intention of being here. Still, the ridiculousness of entertaining the idea creates a pounding in my temples. While I stand here and talk about the parties the prisoners want, Quillian and the others are counting down the minutes until their magic is suppressed and their torture begins.

The Hunter, Holland, approaches as the concierges file out after the primary topics have been talked through and settled. The prisoners won't stay unattended for long. And I guess none of us will now, either. Does that mean Traelen already suspects my involvement?

'All seems to be in hand here,' he says. His beard covers most of his mouth.

'I didn't realise we were being assessed.'

His eyes narrow momentarily. 'Not at all,' he says. 'Merely admiring your work. It's an ... interesting operation up here. Most of us are stationed at Vana at one point or another, but this – this is quite different.'

I make a non-committal sound, squashing the urge to beg him for information on Vana, and turn to Janly.

'I'll meet you in the office for our next meeting,' I say, before walking out of the concierge room, the Hunter following behind.

'Your rooms are ready,' I say over my shoulder. 'I moved some concierges around so you are all in one section of our wing. There is also a room there we have converted into a breakout area of sorts. One you can eat and rest in as you like.'

'Thank you, Luka,' he says.

We pause in the hall, overlooking the internal courtyard, and he turns to me. Something flickers across his face but I can't catch what it is, if it's something I should be frightened of. But it's definitely not something I trust.

Janly takes longer than I hoped to meet me in the Warden's office; I systematically move through the room once more while I wait, cataloguing every drawer, desk surface and shelf, including everything we have already checked. There is only one explanation – Cortane is wrong, the information is not here. While I wait, I go over the prisoner files of those who died recently and one thing is very obvious – they were all part of a defence committee. The one that, I assume, made the decision to send our people to Tae.

The discovery is both surprising and not. In the back of my mind, I knew there had to be a connection. That one – or more – of my group were systematically taking out select prisoners. Now I know why.

The most surprising bit is that I feel happier than I thought I could about that fact.

But the shadow I'd felt earlier is only growing in its dark intensity about how Nuntainia operates – and raising questions about how just it is. If it's 'just' at all.

The framed line drawing of the prison catches my eye again and I wonder why the Warden spent so long looking at it. It's like its mysteries captured him like the painting of the woman on the couch did me.

The weight of the frame is now familiar in my hands and it shimmers as a knock on the door sounds.

'Just me,' Janly says as she pokes her head in.

'Thanks for coming,' I say. 'Anyone with you?'

She takes a subtle moment to look behind her, down both ways of the hallway before entering the office and shutting the door behind her with a shake of her head.

'But we should be fast, those Hunters are like a rash,' she says.

'What can you tell me about ... what we discussed?' I ask, conscious Holland could decide to position himself outside the door at any moment.

'Just what Claudius showed me,' she says, her voice thick with sadness. 'But if your intentions are as they should be'—she eyes me meaningfully—'it will be enough.'

She takes the frame from my hand and wipes her thumb across the arched line underneath the prison.

It disappears.

'What,' I breathe, snatching the frame from her. 'What does this mean?' I examine the drawing, twisting it every which way in the light. But the line doesn't return. Janly reaches over and swipes her thumb over where the line was and it returns once more.

'I don't know how long it stays like that on its own, or if it sends a message anywhere to alert that it's been done. But that's what he showed me.'

My mind slows and I try to wade through the different memories and thoughts. The Warden tried to help me, but he also wanted to help Cortane. And, somehow, he maneuvered to get this team here.

'Jan,' I ask, afraid of my own question. One I've been shying away from, even in my mind. 'Did Claudius … did he know he was going to die?'

Something in her face fractures. 'He chose it, Luka. To make way for Quillian.'

The air whooshes out of me and I find I have to sink onto the couch. His couch.

'What were the two of you going to do?' I ask.

Her brown eyes rise slowly to mine, the intensity in them making me hold my breath.

'Further the revolution,' she whispers.

Despite everything I have learned and the layers I have peeled from my vision these past few weeks, I still gape at her. Janly. The most committed, hard working concierge we have. Apart from me.

'Don't look so surprised,' she says. 'I gather you know a bit more now about the people here and what they're escaping? And yet our most talented people are sent to a war no one is supposed to know we're supplying fodder for. And if you try to expose those secrets, you end up in Vana Prison – often even if you don't. Aid those that continue the sham, and you end up here for any *perceived* wrongdoings by the public. At least until the news cycle forgets about you and moves on to the next thing – then you get your life back like nothing ever happened.'

'But, I still don't—' I cut myself off. I think I actually do now understand, but my brain is still catching up and the thoughts haven't crystallised enough to say out loud yet.

'We deserve better than to be whisked away from our own lives, bound to never talk about the details, subject to go wherever they deem fit. All the while, our government does what it pleases. Not once looking at the betterment of the country or its people. Instead, they subject innocents to the horrors of war while secreting away the worst kind of people to stay in luxury resorts for their sins.'

'What were you planning?'

She glances back to the door and I follow her gaze, suddenly hyper aware we are almost openly talking treason. Something that would see us in Vana Prison, too.

'There's a woman,' she whispers. 'Someone he needed to get out of Vana. But I couldn't get to—'

Footsteps sound in the hallway and we freeze. But I don't need her to continue, she can only be talking about Cortane. Hearing it from Janly adds fuel to the fire burning behind my ribs. How many others did the Warden try to mobilise? Try to get to see a different world by revealing the truth of the injustices of this one? And yet he never forced his views. Always gave me the time to figure it out myself.

'Who else knows?' I ask.

'A couple that I'm suspicious of, but we don't talk about it. Definitely Emeris.'

'Why risk raising it with me?'

She gives me a long look. 'Because how you feel about those men is written all over you.'

Heat blooms through my centre. 'But—'

'It's a good thing, Luka. I'd heard of Quillian,' she says, but her face is sad, 'from Claudius. But it seems I wasn't the only one – Traelen knows the threat he poses.'

I think of him behind those bars, in his torn and filthy uniform. The quiet sadness in the set of his mouth.

'They thought this was the end for them.'

'That doesn't surprise me,' she says. 'Sometimes, to make the biggest impact you need to sacrifice yourself. But Quillian can't be sacrificed, do you understand?'

I blow out a loud breath.

'I wanted to burn it all down when I worked out what was going on,' she says.

I nod, now only partially listening.

'You'll come?' I ask abruptly.

'If you can take me.'

My palms sweat while I wait for Janly once more. Dusk is about to descend, the time the world feels like it's coated in magic. I tick off all the things I needed to make sure were in hand in the prison before we leave, part of me cringing that I have still taken the care to do that – to leave them with a smooth running sanctuary when that courtesy is not extended to those who actually do make sacrifices for others. But I also need them to not look for me yet – and the longer things run without my involvement, the better.

The event schedules are set and the committees are briefed on their next steps. Koko and I have confirmed the menus, and the musicians have new pieces to learn. The wellness centre is restocked and the most recent team of concierges is as up to speed as they're going to get on my watch.

'We'll be fine,' Blossom says from the balcony doors. But either she doesn't notice the shake in her voice or she just can't hide it.

For the second time today, Janly knocks. This time, though, I answer the door and check the hall myself. As I turn back into my apartment, I know I am going to miss this room. Both its magnificent view and the memories I have with Blossom here.

Against my temptation to clean everything before we go, Blossom suggested we leave things as if we've just popped out for a moment. So the cushions remain scattered over the couches in no particular order. Our tipple glasses are in the sink, Blossom making sure to include three for each of us even though neither of us are taking the magic dampener anymore.

That thought is like a barb catching in my chest. I haven't been taking the dampener and yet nothing has changed. I feared being here, under this contract, would mean I missed my magic coming in. And it appears to be true. Quillian asked me once what I am. Without any magic, I suppose that means nothing?

I drag my eyes from the crystal glasses and look at Blossom. She's still pale, and moving too quickly pains her side. She watches me as I pull my phone from my pocket.

Luka: You won't believe this, I write to Zale and Akira, fingers trembling. *I've been extended again. Another short-term one, I hope. I'll check in when I can. Love you x*

I have to bite my teeth together to keep my composure, desperately hoping I didn't just send a goodbye text without telling them.

Gently patting my hand over where the framed drawing now rests in the pocket of my dress, taking up far too much room, I take a deep breath. It's perhaps not the best hiding spot for it, its corners constantly poking out, but we agreed not to change from our uniforms to not draw attention to ourselves. It will be easier to say we have been working late if we are questioned by any of the Hunters. In a strange way, while I know what side Quillian is on, it makes it easier not to have a Warden wandering around as well.

The crossing of the staff gardens is the most terrifying, with the Hunters set up in our wing, in apartments that overlook this space. At the time, I'd organised it that way as a reminder that the moment we left our apartments we needed to be officially on duty – we couldn't let our guard down. Now, as I imagine any one of them looking out of their windows and catching us sneaking to the other side of the hedges, my heart seems to beat in my throat and I feel like I might choke.

But we get across without incident and make our way through the dark forest, only the lights on our phones to guide us. Blossom leads us first towards Vana and then cuts away to the right, following no path I can discern in the dark. I can only hope the instructions Emeris gave her on how to find the unstable portion of the island were detailed.

Now, after talking with Janly, I think I know why he told her about this place.

'Just here,' Blossom says, after several moments. Moments in which the quiet of the island drags out around us. A sound I have always found so peaceful. But now it pulls on me, counting down until it's shattered by something I can't see coming.

But I can feel it. The dread inching its way along my limbs.

The trees start to thin slightly here, a part of the island I've never ventured to, but I can see the inky blackness of the sky where it meets the drop of the land. It always looks different just along the horizon than looking up for some reason. Like, between the stars and the faint lights of the city below, there's a band of blackness that's hard to penetrate.

Soft voices start to filter through and my heart rate kicks up a notch at the sound of them. Janly said how I feel about these men is written over my face and she's probably right. There's nothing I wouldn't do to keep them and Blossom safe.

My phone vibrates in my hand but I ignore it.

A louder voice reaches my ears from up ahead and I freeze.

'Well, this is rather an entertaining turn of events.'

CHAPTER THIRTY-THREE

Blossom takes a step back, gripping the flowing skirts of my dress. Janly crowds me from behind and we huddle like that for a moment, trapped in the in-between.

'Wait here,' I whisper, my feet moving before my head can catch up as I push myself past Blossom gently. Quietly.

She clutches at my arm and I expect her to try and stop me. But when I look back, the fear in her features isn't only for us. River is there, too. I can see it in how her gaze keeps flicking towards where we're supposed to meet them. As she reaches for the phone in my hand and turns the light off, I breathe a shuddering exhale. Letting my eyes adjust to the new dark, I gather up my skirts close to my body, the frame digging into my thigh, and creep forward, heart in my mouth.

Davorous laughs softly. 'I don't know why you really thought you'd get away with it.'

I can see their shapes now, dark masses against the night sky, the stars above them illuminating the space ever so softly.

'Granted,' he continues, 'it took me longer to work it out than I would have liked, but here we are.'

'Here we are,' Cortane repeats, 'about to leave. But it's been so lovely chatting with you.'

'By all means,' Davorous says. 'You know as well as I do, portalling through those wards will only make you easier to find.'

Quillian's face is hard when I can finally make out their features. Nix, River, and Quillian are focused only on Davorous. Cortane leans her shoulder against a tree, looking completely bored.

'Only if we don't take you down first.' She shrugs. 'And who says we can't disable the wards?'

Davorous glances over his shoulder, back towards me. The action gives away his doubt and I duck behind the tree I've been standing against, holding my breath against the slim hope he didn't see me.

'Come out,' Davorous says with more certainty than I'd like, and I press myself harder into the slightly damp bark.

But if I stay, he'll come looking and I can't risk him finding Blossom and Janly in this halfway place between the prison and escape. So I suck in a breath that tastes of the island forest and step into the small space they occupy.

Quillian's gaze doesn't leave Davorous but his shoulders tense when I'm in view.

'You need to learn to say no, Lu,' Nix says gruffly, 'even if it's silently.'

Davorous's eyes widen and then roll. 'I should have fucking known. What is it about Karaylia women find so irresistible? They're good for one thing only. Those wings will cut you down as quick as they'll caress you, you know. Is your friend with you?'

I say nothing. I'm not even quite sure what's happening. But the distance between Blossom and Janly starts to feel far too close to Davorous, and yet too far from the others. From where someone could protect them better than me. A sharp breeze whips my face as Davorous appears before me faster than I can blink. Cortane flashes between us, her back to me.

Quillian draws a sword I hadn't seen him carry and Nix palms his knives. Weapons I can only assume were easier to get here than guns.

I stumble back a step, my heel catching in my dress, and Davorous pops into the space before me again, leaving Cortane behind. A surprised scream catches in my throat and I trip, slamming into the earth underneath me.

He's a Shaide.

'You won't bring the wards down—' he starts, teeth gritted.

I scramble away from him in the dirt, the sharp pain in my thigh giving away what's happened to the small frame in my fall.

Tall, dark bodies crowd around us but all I can see is Davorous's face. His dishevelled, pale hair falling across his forehead.

'You have one second to step the fuck back,' Quillian grinds out and I stop moving.

'I'll die before I let you loose down there again,' Davorous says.

'Okay.'

Hot liquid sprays my face and throat, dripping down my front.

My breath comes in short bursts, the sensation cold on my nostrils as they fill with a metallic scent.

Davorous's mouth drops open and his eyes roll back in his head. I watch as, in slow motion, his knees start to fold and his body gives way, toppling him to the ground. Wet, gargled noises fill the space. White starts to press into the sides of my vision but I can't look away from Davorous's dying form.

River ducks to me, dropping to his knees, and takes my face in his hands.

'Deeper, Lu,' he says. 'Breathe deeper.'

Slowly the white recedes from my vision and I shift my focus to River's face. I nod, answering the question there, and he steps back towards Blossom and Janly, who I can see have joined us and now watch with wide eyes. I let myself stare at Quillian's black boots for a long moment as I try to collect myself. Gradually taking in the black pants that are fitted in the thighs, the belt that's covered in things I can't comprehend, and the tight, short-sleeved shirt he wears. The top of his tattoo on full display across the side of his neck. The sword still hangs in his hand, blood coating its blade, and I look quickly back to his chest.

He stands completely still.

The others talk quietly, filling in Bloss and Janly, but I'm conscious of Nix's watchful gaze as I finally allow myself to look at Quillian's face.

But whatever I was expecting to see – was frightened to see – it's not there.

My chest twinges to find he still looks like him. His face is the same when he looks at me. But a sharp pain radiates along my ribs at the hint of vulnerability. Like he's waiting for my judgement. Again.

Slowly, I hold out my hand for him to help me up, and he snatches it from the air, lifting me to my feet, tugging me against him. He drops his head into the crook of my neck and inhales deeply.

'I'm sorry,' he whispers.

Winding my hands up the back of his neck and into his hair, I shrug my shoulder so he lifts his head up to face me. His eyes are almost black in this light but I wonder how much of it is something else. Softly, I press a kiss to his lips before breaking away. The throb in my leg reminding me we have other things we need to be focusing on.

'We found how to bring the wards down,' I say, digging into my torn dress to find the pocket. 'But it may not be worth anything now.'

A trickle runs down my thigh as if to confirm my suspicions and I tentatively pull out the broken frame. I shift my weight off my injured leg. Quillian tracks the movement but I ignore him, carefully collecting the broken shards of glass in my palm before depositing them in a pile on the ground.

'Jan,' I say quietly as I remove the drawing from the shattered frame, its paper thick between my fingers.

I hold it out to her and she gasps as she takes in the gash in its centre. Carefully, she runs her thumb backwards and forwards over the parchment but her face falls.

'I–it's broken,' she says.

Nix curses and a weight settles in the bottom of my stomach.

'Okay,' Blossom says. 'We knew this was a strong possibility. Tonight doesn't change. There's no going back – we need to leave.'

I could swear a small smile dusts River's face, but somehow he still looks sad at the same time.

'You shouldn't be coming on the run with us,' Quillan says, still looking at me.

Nix throws his hands in the air, knives still held in his palms.

'You're joking. *Now* you want to see sense? *Now*? She's just seen you in action. Knows who we all are, has probably burnt the fucking bridge between her and that fucking *prison* to the sun and back, and *now* you're suggesting we leave her here to deal with all of this bullshit on her own? I don't—fuck. I don't even have the words for that, Q.'

I look between them for a moment, stunned into silence.

'Nix,' I start. Somehow I always start with him. Calm him down and the rest will follow.

'No, Luka,' he says. 'Don't fucking placate me. You—' he draws a big breath. 'You deserve better than any of this. You all do,' he says looking at Blossom and Janly.

'So do you.'

I glance at Janly who's quietly taking us all in, and a little memory creeps into the back of my mind. But it's the thought of all the choices taken away from us that starts the building of pressure in my head. The family I wanted to have before I was summoned to duty. The time I could have spent getting to know Akira and Zale's children. That, instead, I was tasked with spending this time serving people who should barely be surviving for the things they've done. The magic I imagined would be my own, only to be literally fed something to stop me reaching my full potential. Now, I have to believe that the decisions that have led me here have been the right ones.

I have to believe that I can ease the pain Nix and Bloss have seen and give them a brighter future. To ease the burden River carries of looking after Nix. That Claudius didn't choose death for nothing. That Quillian can be free of the weight of responsibility for everyone around him.

I know I will die trying to make all of those things true.

'The Hunters will likely be out soon,' I say, clearing my throat and hitching my dress so I can look at my thigh. I pinch the piece of glass that sticks out, Quillian moving forward to tear some strips from the already torn fabric of my dress. The glass is smooth between my fingers and the pressure intensifies the throb. I don't think it's too deep, but that doesn't stop the uncomfortable flop of my stomach. I grit my teeth, breathe hard out of my nose, and pull.

'Fucker,' I mutter as I let the glass drop to the ground.

Quillian kneels before me.

'Riv, can you—'

'It's now or never,' Cortane says.

In response, Quillian wraps the pale dress fabric around my thigh and I watch the care with which he ties the ends together.

'Let's move,' Cortane says.

'Wait,' I say, thinking again of my earlier conversation with Janly. 'I have an idea. If I'm not back in half an hour – go without me.'

Quillian and Nix protest at the same time and I ignore them – despite the tiny warming that at least they're on the same page now – and turn to Blossom instead. She narrows her eyes at me.

'I'm not waiting here,' she says.

'Please, Bloss,' I say. 'I need to know you're okay. Stay with River.' I glance at where he watches us, a tiny dip of his chin the only indication he's heard me. That he will protect her against whatever is to come.

'And I don't need to know the same about you?'

I look at her, pleading.

'I'll go with you,' Janly says and Blossom glares at her. 'We'll come back.'

'You're not leaving me here, Luka. I'm not going anywhere without you,' Blossom says, firmer this time. 'The Hunters will—'

'They won't find me – won't know we're up to anything. I promise.'

She sets her jaw in the way I know nothing I say will change her mind. But I can't take the three of us back and guarantee we'll all get out again. Only Blossom, Janly, and I have any chance of getting in and out without drawing the attention of the Hunters. But we can't fight them anyway, so we don't need numbers. I need stealth. And to not be worrying about Blossom, who is still nursing the last of her wound. I cringe internally about what that says of my feelings for Janly. I don't want anything to happen to her, either, but it's Blossom that will break me.

I look at River again and his face darkens with regret as he moves behind Blossom and I step backwards. She lunges at me and he grabs her from behind, a hand over her mouth. Turning away from the betrayal on her face, I run – Janly hot on my heels.

'We won't wait!' Cortane calls after us and a coldness coats my skin at the truth in her words.

We crash through the trees and the undergrowth, paying no heed to quiet, the pain in my thigh shooting through my leg. There's no time for it. Now all I have is a tiny hope we don't come across any Hunters.

Reaching the stairs to my apartment, I all but drag myself up them. Gasping for breath as I collapse at the top.

'For all ... the good ... in this ... world, Luka,' Janly gulps in air. 'I'm not as young ... as you. Explain.'

It takes me longer than I would like to catch my breath enough to talk with any sense. But, sprawled on the stone of what was once my balcony, I tell Janly my last hope.

'You said something about burning it down,' I say. 'We're doing that. Our magical contracts are anchored to here, right? Maybe the wards are the same. And, if not, none of these prisoners should be able to remain here at least.'

Janly blinks at me, her mouth still open and dragging in air, sweat in her hairline.

'It's all I've got,' I say.

'Hunted forever,' she says, mostly to herself.

'But we've made our choice, Jan. And I've realised ... I can't leave them here.'

Janly shakes her head at me, not understanding. 'We're not—'

'The prisoners. They're slavers. Child abusers. Women abusers. I don't even know what else. How is it fair that we go on the run, marked for life, and they stay here?' I gesture around us. To the jasmine-covered stone pillars whose scent cloys my senses. But I know she gets my meaning. Knows the luxury this stone contains.

A wicked smile immediately appears on her face, her white teeth glowing slightly in the moonlight, and I can't help but mirror it. Their time here ends now.

'We need to get the concierges out,' she says and I nod. 'I'll find Emeris. Get him to spread the word and get them to a safe place.'

'Tell him ... subtly if you can, what we're doing. Anyone who wants to join us can come.'

She raises her brows at me in question.

'Cortane mightn't like it, but I'm not leaving them here with no options. The others ...' I trail off. 'The prisoners,' I say quietly. 'I don't know if they all deserve to die, and I don't want to be their judge.' Janly makes a sound of reluctant agreement. 'So we'll set the fire alarm off early.'

She exhales. 'We better move.'

I try not to look at my apartment again as we make our way through and out into the dark hallway. It's quiet. Everyone here, and not on shift, is likely already asleep. Hopefully not for long. I glance back at Janly once before she gently closes the door to my old apartment and we creep down the hallway towards the Warden's office.

At the end of the hallway that will take me to his office, we pause and I stare at Janly.

'I–I don't have anything to start a fire,' I stammer, belatedly realising how stupid this plan really is.

Janly doesn't miss a beat. 'Bottom drawer, right-hand side, there's a lighter. Use the books. I'll meet you on the other side of the hedge.'

She takes off in the opposite direction, towards the concierge room – I assume so she can check what shift Emeris was on today. Without giving myself time to reconsider, I run down the hall and smother the urge to slam the office door behind me, closing it with a painful slowness until I'm on my own.

Sprinting to the bookshelf, I drag everything down in great handfuls. Armfuls. Anything I can get my hands on goes into a pile on the rug. With any luck, it will catch alight as well.

The lighter is exactly where Janly said it would be and I turn it in my palm briefly. The smooth, gold surface cool on my skin. Taking it to the pile of books, it sparks on the second try and I lower the flame to the pages. As the flame grows, I catch the engraving on the side of the lighter. *Love J*, it ends with.

The flames lick the edges of the bookshelf now; the heat starts to warm my legs and a dull throb beats in my chest. This office holds so many memories of Claudius. Of Quillian. Of Bloss and me. And I'm destroying it.

For good reason, I remind myself. I want to stay and see it take, just to be sure, but I don't have time. The smoke is starting to make my eyes sting, but this feels right. Maybe something better can be made from the ashes of this place. And maybe I won't be marked for the rest of my – potentially short – life.

I could also be branded a traitor ... and as I watch the flames, their blue and orange heat beginning to devour the books around me, I can't think of a better way to describe how I feel right now. I've moved beyond my quiet rebellions with Blossom and our tipples. Right now, the fire in me is mirroring the one building around me. I'm going to bring it all down.

I move to the door and reach for the handle.

It flies open, slamming into my fingers and making them bite with pain.

'What the fuck are you doing?'

CHAPTER THIRTY-FOUR

Bile rises in my throat as Holland stares at me, knife in hand. His pale eyes flick between the fire and me. The flames illuminate part of his bearded face and plunge the rest into darkness, making his expression hard to read. He takes two steps into the room and closes the door.

My feet won't move.

I scream at myself to move. To respond. To do *something*. *Say* something.

My head pounds in time with my heart as he lifts his blade and points it at me.

'I can only hope you have a fucking good explanation for this,' he says.

He blocks the door and I know I have no hope of getting past him that way. The window Blossom and I have snuck in before is behind me. I can't see how many paces without looking away from him, but it feels like an eternity away. My leg throbs harder at the thought of trying to make it even that far.

Smoke fills my next breath and I cough, the crackling of the flames getting louder.

With a last look at the fire to make sure it's as caught as I can get it to be, I spin and make for the window.

It's too far.

But I dodge around the corner of the desk anyway, my thigh barking in protest.

Holland curses and I hear him move the same time I'm tackled to the ground, my head slamming into the floor. The room turns around me and Holland crushes me with his weight.

I try to buck my hips, to drive my elbows backwards, to dislodge him in any way, but I don't make contact. Drawing a deep breath to scream, my lungs fill with smoke and I cough, choking on the thick greyness that's now pouring through my chest. My eyes stream with tears and I let my head drop to the floor. A defeated sob wracks through me. I won't be able to get him off.

Cortane will make the others leave without me.

As she should.

'If you're finished,' he says roughly, 'we need to get the fuck out. And I'd suggest the garden underneath that window – where the rest of my crew are gathering for the search for the missing Vanan prisoners – is not where you want to go.'

I can only cough in response. But a tiny sliver of relief creeps in.

'I'm going to get up now,' he rasps through muffled coughs. 'Don't scream.'

The heat in the room builds and soon the smoke will be billowing out the window and door. Instead of standing, he rolls off me onto all fours.

'Stay low,' he says, 'and follow me.'

Following him is the last thing I want to do. But if he's telling the truth about the Hunters, my options are limited – and I don't want to burn alive today either. The office is getting darker as I drag myself after Holland, my ribs and thigh aching. Every breath sends a sharp pain spinning around my sides and back.

Reaching the door, he runs his hand up the timber, reaching for the handle.

'Get out as quick as you can – the smoke will raise the alarm in the hallway,' he says. 'We'll need the few extra minutes to get away.'

He opens the door and the flames surge higher, the heat intensifying against my skin. We scramble into the hallway and he slams the door. I stare at him a moment, pulling myself into a crouch. Pushing aside the pain in my body and preparing to run.

'Holland!' a voice calls and another Hunter races down the hallway to us. 'What's going on?' he asks when he reaches us, eyes flicking to the door.

'We need to get out,' Holland says, 'it's time.' He nods at me. 'Help her – she's got an injured leg and possibly some busted ribs.'

I stare at them. Time for what?

My eyes still sting from the smoke, but I have no choice but to let the second Hunter help me stand.

'I'm fine,' I say, pushing him away when I'm on my feet.

'You have a lot of explaining to do, Hol,' he says.

'I'm not the only one,' Holland replies and we take off back down the stone hallway.

I flounder at the end, unsure which way to go. I can't stay here, but I can't fight them off either. And I certainly can't lead them to the others. I just need to stall them long enough for Cortane to insist the others leave.

I flinch as the high pitched scream of the fire alarm ricochets through the prison, bouncing off the stone. The flames have now devoured much of the door to the office and lick the stone, leaving dark marks in their wake.

'That stone won't catch,' the second Hunter says, 'but it's going to spread through the rooms. What's the plan?'

As he talks, smoke starts to billow out from the other doors that dot the hallway.

'I think we're in Luka's hands right now,' Holland says, dark brown eyes fixed on me.

My heart squeezes.

Trust me, his face seems to say, but I can't rely on that. I took a chance with Janly but I've known her a lot longer than I've known this man.

There's only one way to find out. I've lost track of the time I've been in here. Now, I will either make it with their help. Or, I'll be able to create such a distraction with the Hunters that the others will go on.

I try to run, but it's more of a fast hobble between my left leg and my ribs, but the two Hunters stay just behind me, letting me lead. Taking us along the stone hallway, past the internal courtyard, I catch a glimpse of a group of concierges heading towards the kitchens and my heart sings. They know there's an exit back there. Janly – or Emeris – got to them in time.

Turning away from them, I lead the Hunters back towards the concierge gardens where I need to meet Janly. Downstairs, where the rest of the Hunters are said to be gathering.

I hope I'm not running headfirst into my own stay in Vana.

Holland grips my elbow as we reach the wide, timber door that will take us straight out onto the lawns.

'Sure you want to do this?' he whispers fiercely.

'I need to cross the garden,' I say, pulling my arm from his grasp. 'This is the fastest way.'

'And the deadliest,' the second one mutters. 'Damn it, Holland – a little warning would have been good.'

I leave them to their glares and inch open the door, slipping into the dark garden. In the corner, under the balcony, a large group of Hunters is gathered. The lights from that part of the building illuminate the tops of their heads. Glancing up, closer to where I stand, I can see the burning office, flames spewing from the window almost in time with the blaring alarm.

Most of the Hunters are turned away from us, making a semi-circle around a Hunter that points and shouts directions.

My veins hum with urgency.

The distance between here and the hedge where I hope to find Janly, and then hopefully Cortane still waiting with the others beyond, stretches in my mind. An impossible distance to cover in time. The seconds feel like they scratch my skin as they leave. I take a steadying breath and yelp from the pain it produces in my side.

Cursing myself, I push off the wall and turn to the two Hunters behind me.

Holland's gaze flicks between me and the group of Hunters at the end of the building. At any moment they could turn their attention to us.

Holland's companion just stares, dumbfounded at the two of us. 'I'm not really following what's happening here,' he says. 'But I'm going to go out on a limb and say you don't want to be noticed by that crew.' He jerks his head towards the dark-uniformed men.

I nod.

'I don't want to get you in any unnecessary trouble,' I say. 'But if you could not follow me, that would be greatly appreciated.'

Holland laughs softly.

'You've got balls, that's for sure,' he says.

'I don't need them.'

His brows lift in surprise and a slow smile splits his red beard.

'Noted,' he says.

My time is either out, or almost up, and the Hunters start to move towards the far corner of the prison. Around which the kitchen exit will come into view. I skim my hand over my thigh, fingering the fabric Quillian tied there. One last run, I tell myself, then I'll work it out from there. If I make it, I know Quillian and the others will take care of these two on my tail. They haven't killed me yet, I can only hope they won't do so before I make it.

But I know with a surety I haven't felt in a long time, I'd rather die trying to get there than stand here and give in.

I don't bother looking at Holland and the other Hunter again before I take off across the garden, my nose filling with the soft scent of burning jasmine, to where I will scream at Janly to move – if she's still there. The grass is damp and it licks up my feet where my sandals sink into it, my ruined dress streaming behind me. Sharp, shooting pain in my side darkens my vision but I push on, over the gently lit grass and towards the hedge. Towards—

'Hey!' a male voice shouts from somewhere to my right.

I keep moving. I just need to get close enough to Jan to make her move. Or be sure she's not there waiting.

'Luka!' the voice calls and I almost hesitate. Until I remember most of the Hunters are likely to know my name now.

My hobbled running slows.

'Are you okay?' he asks again, a voice I don't recognise.

The hedge is filling my vision now – I'm almost close enough to touch it. My thigh groans as I land too heavily on that side. Flinging myself at the gap in the hedge, thin branches whipping at my hair and face, I start to softly call to Janly.

'Go,' I say. 'Go, go, go.'

But instead of Janly, Zenaton stands before me, grinning. The last time I saw him was in the grandroom, when Davorous was sharing a story. Just after Blossom had been attacked. The blood in my veins turns to ice and my body comes to a stop, my jagged breath still sending pain radiating around my torso.

'Go where, pray tell?' he asks.

I keep my mouth shut.

He makes a show of looking over his shoulder, in the direction I so desperately want to go. 'I wouldn't go that way, if I were you. Rumour has it the Hunters are just about to apprehend some escaped prisoners from the other side. Dangerous people.'

'Dangerous to who?' I ask.

His gaze narrows a little as he slowly takes me in. My torn, bloody dress, the limp. The way I'm trying to carry my side. He glances behind me and his face drops in admonishment.

'The prison is on fire, Luka,' he says. 'Shouldn't you be helping us – your *guests*? Not out here ... running?'

He takes a step towards me, a hand reaching for my arm as Janly bursts from the bushes and crashes a rock into his temple. Zenaton drops to his knees, head in his hands, and cries out. Janly drops the rock, a touch of blood on its corner, to the ground.

'Run,' she says, true fear trembling in her voice. As I lift my eyes from Zenaton, I find she's not looking at me, but over my shoulder. Spinning, Holland and the second Hunter move through the hedge, Holland's gaze landing on the moaning, bleeding, prisoner.

'Go,' I say, turning back to Janly. 'I won't be fast enough.'

She doesn't have time to respond before I shove her. 'Run.' Janly turns away and stumbles into the forest as I sink into the dirt. 'Tell Blossom I'm sorry,' I whisper.

'None of that,' Holland says, lifting me to my feet. I wince as I sag against him. Too tired, too overwhelmed, to fight him. Knowing the longer I keep them here, the more chance Janly has to make it to the others is the only ray of light I have. And so I use it to warm me from the inside. They'll get off the island. They have to.

Zenaton groans from the ground and glares up at me.

'You'll pay for that, you bitch,' he grinds out. 'I'm so sick of concierges that think they're better than us.'

A scream builds in my chest and I curl my lip at him.

'And what are we, Zenaton?' I grind out, moving to stand over him. 'Tools to be used? Toys to be played with and discarded? Or just vessels to be fucked and destroyed at your whim?'

Something flashes across his face, but it's not regret.

He grabs my ankle and I go down – hard – cursing myself for not learning my lesson from Davorous. Don't get too close to dangerous men.

A sharp whisper slices the air behind me as Zenaton rolls to the left and a sword pierces his side. Blood oozes from the wound as I follow the blade to its handler. The second Hunter looks back at me. We stand there, looking at each other, for a long moment as Zenaton gasps shallow breaths on the ground beneath us. Dimly I notice the Hunter has a large gun of some sort as well as his sword. But there seems to be nothing either of us can say about what's unfolding.

'Where were you headed?' Holland asks as if they drive blades into guests every day.

I bite my lip as he collects me from the ground once more, and I can't stop the whimper that escapes my throat. I look between them again, the second one sliding his sword back into the holder at his side.

I glance back at Zenaton, who seems to be losing consciousness.

'Leave him,' Holland says gently, wrapping an arm around my waist. 'It won't be long anyway.'

Throwing what could only be described as a prayer to the sky, I let him take some of my weight.

'This way,' I say.

The walk through the forest is quiet, only the sound of our footsteps and my breathing marking the space. But behind me is the scream of the fire alarm, the loud pop of flames as they engulf half the building, and the cries and screams I can only hope are of the people watching, and no one trapped inside.

A weight grows in my stomach the closer we get to where I will find an empty patch of land – or, rather, no land if Blossom's idea was successful. Is it better to get to say goodbye or not? There was so much potential in what I shared with Quillian, something I'm definitely not ready to let go of. But it's the hurt on Blossom's face when I deviated from our plan that will haunt me.

The second Hunter realises we're getting close the same time I do and he draws his sword as we slowly make our way through the thinning trees.

In an instant, we're surrounded. Five swords pointed in our direction.

Holland pulls me closer to his side and Quillian's eyes flare. He stalks forward, blade out, and I gently push myself off the Hunter. Beside me, he raises his hands slowly, taking in the group before us.

'Careful, Quillian,' Nix says, not unkindly. 'Your possession is showing.'

CHAPTER THIRTY-FIVE

I hold my side as I move towards Quillian and the others. His gaze flicks to my hand and back to Holland.

'They with you?' he asks, no hint of disbelief in his voice.

I look back at Holland and the one whose name I don't know – the one who stabbed Zenaton as I watched.

I nod slowly. 'I think so, yeah.'

'I definitely can't portal this many people,' Cortane says, some of her swagger gone. 'And we're really fucking overdue here.' She rounds on Quillian. 'I waited. Now you can choose who is left behind.'

My heart lurches into my throat and I find Blossom's gaze. It's still hurt. Angry. But at least she's looked for me, too.

'You know we're not leaving without everyone here, Cort,' River says gently.

'They're not part of us yet, asshole,' she replies. 'Until then, I can leave whoever the fuck I like.'

Nix looks at me like he's torn between being proud and wanting to kill me. When the light catches in his auburn hair, I realise how close to dawn we are.

'If that blood on his blade isn't Luka's,' Nix says, pointing at the second hunter. 'Then I think it's safe to assume they've all done enough to prove they're with us. For now.'

A crashing of foliage nearby makes me jump. The others simply turn in that direction and raise their blades again. The Hunters included.

'Are we too late?' Emeris calls through the trees.

I almost cry with relief but a garbled laugh bubbles from my throat. Blossom throws herself at him and he hugs her hard as he breaks the treeline. His finely muscled forearm squeezing around her back.

Finn emerges, silently followed by three other, terrified looking, concierges – Shiloh, and Koko, and the violinist, who throws me a wink. I can't help but laugh at him, even as the rage that flooded my body when confronting Zenaton hasn't quite subsided. But it's making way for something else as well. Something a little like hope.

Cortane turns slowly on her heel, the fire in the distance reflected in her eyes.

'Any more strays you wish to bring along?' she grinds out.

'No,' I say, grinning. 'I think this is all of us.'

I watch as Blossom and River start talking animatedly to Nix and pointing along parts of the ground where we stand. The warm touch of Quillian's fingers on mine draws my attention away and I turn into him.

'You waited,' I say, all trace of a smile gone from my face. Instead, a surge of cool relief so powerful that I almost sob races through me. But I try not to examine what powered it.

'I didn't have a choice,' he says quietly.

I deflate a little.

'Nix or Blossom?' I ask.

He laughs a little, the darkness in his green eyes receding a fraction.

'Well, they were both pretty adamant. But, no,' he says as he takes my hand and raises it to the middle of his chest.

Holland clears his throat and I look away from Quillian, cheeks aflame.

'I take it there is some kind of plan here?' he asks.

Quillian's fingers tighten around mine but it's Blossom that responds.

'Yes,' she says.

Cortane mock bows at her, throwing her arms wide before she rises and pins Quillian with a glare.

'We need everyone over here,' Blossom says, pointing to the very edge of the island. 'You'll need to be seated and with enough room around you that you can move a bit. We don't want anyone getting bumped off.'

The blood drains from the other Hunter's face and he mutters under his breath.

'Alright?' Holland asks, a touch of laughter in his voice as he slaps the second Hunter on the back.

'You've led me blindly into this with zero warning,' he says. 'And if we're about to do what I think we are ... no, I'm not fucking alright.'

'It wasn't quite zero warning,' Holland says. 'We've talked about this shit enough to take a leap – and the opportunity presented itself.'

Blossom ignores him as she directs the other concierges to the space, Emeris on the outside, the sheer drop illuminating his face with seeming glee. She directs the nervous Hunter to the middle of the group and Quillian and the others make a ring around us, with Nix closest to the rest of the island.

Nix drops to his knees and I do a quick head count, catching River's gaze and finding him doing the same thing. Blossom moves into place as she casts her eye over all of us and he subtly positions himself between her and the rest of the island ... what is about to become the edge of a much smaller island.

'Sit,' Blossom commands. Something only the Hunters and concierges obey. I hold tight to Quillian's hand, unable to step away.

The ground starts to shudder underneath us, and I look back at Nix and the island beyond. The flames of the prison now caress the pink sky where the sun is starting to rise, washing the island in a pastel glow.

'How do we know if the wards are down?' I ask Janly.

She looks up at me, her brows furrowed. 'We don't.'

'Nix is going to take us as far as he can at this height,' Blossom adds, not looking at me. 'We'll try to go over them.'

I glance at the sweat already running down Nix's neck, the veins pulsing in his forehead under the strain.

He pushes hard into the ground and a deafening crack makes me cover my ears, pressing my palms against my head, until the tiny piece of land we're on tears away from the main island and starts to float in the sky, away from the prison.

A slow exhale leaves my lips. And I'm not the only one that stares back at the island, a gaping wound now in her side where we used to stand. I've never seen it from this perspective before, and the inverted dip of her base, all dark soil, exposed rocks and trailing roots, gives me pause. Above, she is blues and greens and the red of my favourite flowers. The forest diminishing in size as we drift further away.

It's hard not to think of Nuntainia as I watch her disappear. Of how much darkness is underneath our pretty exterior.

Nix grunts as he holds our height and pushes the piece of land along.

'He can't hold this for long,' I whisper to Blossom who has ended up beside me.

I glance around. The Hunters now both have their eyes tightly shut while the concierges are looking around in wonder, and it's clear now how much the open-air receiving plane has prepared us for this moment. All that practice of being on a platform in the sky.

'Jan,' I say, watching Nix's shirt soak with sweat and his muscles tremble. 'Are you sure there's no way we can tell about the wards? We need to be able to drop down, now.'

She shakes her head at me, still looking at Nix. 'Not unless someone goes through them.'

We're silent a moment, perhaps all of us reflecting on how unfair that seems after everything. I could reconcile it before – when it was just me, Blossom, and the others. People who made a choice. People who knew we were likely to be marked. But Emeris, Finn – who I now know was part of the group all along – the concierges they brought here. Even the Hunters that got me here in the end. None of them deserve that.

'I'll go,' Quillian says beside me.

I spin to him.

'What?'

'I'll go. It's the right move.' The last part he says more quietly, as if it's meant just for me – to reassure me. I stare at him.

'It makes the most sense, Lu,' River says. 'Wards or no wards, he can come back and tell us. It's best we have a healer on hand, just in case.'

Nix breathes heavily and River runs his hands through his hair.

'Can't you help him?' I ask.

'Not in any real way. Not yet. This chunk of dirt is too big for me. I wouldn't even be able to push it along.'

'But you said you were elite,' I say, knowing full well I am clutching at straws.

Holland smiles grimly, even with his eyes closed.

'They are, sweetheart,' he says. 'But even the elite have limits. And this island would be heavy as fuck.'

Quillian and Finn share a look.

'It's okay, Luka,' Quillian says, and the pain in my ribs suddenly seems so manageable compared to the one racing between my breasts.

'You'll be marked,' I say.

'Which will only make my position in this world more formal in their view. I already know what side I'm on. Who I am.'

I drop his hand and step away, sucking in the cool air to help me focus. I search the island for another way. But Nix's drooping shoulders, Cortane's arrogant stare, both tell me there is no other way.

My palms start to tingle and I press them against my chest as I turn on the spot. There has to—

'Lu,' Bloss says quietly, and I meet her gaze, finding the anchor she gives me. Her ocean coloured eyes are several shades darker than the expanse of sky we drift through. I don't know if anyone else sees what's written on her face, but I do. It's the look she gave me when we first agreed to stop taking our magic dampener tipples. Meaning we are the only ones without magic currently running in our veins. The only ones who have a shot at getting any of us out of this with a chance at freedom.

Perhaps there is a blessing in having no magic after all, just like the herons.

River knows there's something being decided here, even if he doesn't know what, and he looks between us.

'Here's to honour,' she whispers.

I swallow.

Without another word, we link hands and look out into the dawn. Quillian moves behind me and kisses my neck, a shiver running down my spine.

'I'll be straight back,' he says, turning to Nix and saying something I don't bother listening to.

'See you soon,' I say and grip Blossom's hand.

The air whips around my face, my hair long since free of its binds. What remains of my dress is tattered and torn, ruined in a way that will never be fixed – much like my views of Nuntainia. And our government. And the *prisoners* we left with no refuge on the main island.

For those that prove the colour of their souls.

I look into the wide, open sky that's always called to me and take one last breath before Blossom and I swan-dive into the unknown.

AMBER WOLF (DRIARN DUOLOGY, BOOK 1)

FRIEND. GUARD. ORPHAN.
Lish Taylor thinks she knows who she is.
But when her tactical team begins to investigate a series of abductions,
the haunting questions she's carried since her mother's murder come
flooding back. With the case growing increasingly suspicious, Lish leaves
her climate-ravaged city to seek answers, even after she's ordered to stand
down—only to be abducted herself.
Captured by the brutal General Siosal, Lish is determined to free not only
herself, but also the General's other victims. With the enigmatic cell-guard,
Lochlain, as her unexpected ally, Lish's escape catapults her into the hidden
world of the Calahi, where magic pulses through the land. But, even with
its incredible differences, Lish can't ignore that this world is also suffering.
The threads of her investigation soon draw Lish into a war for a dying
kingdom. To survive – and reclaim her future – she must bring those she
loves together and prove that healing a broken world begins with standing
in your truth.

*Amber Wolf is an adult, dystopian fantasy with forced proximity, found
family, fated mates, climate themes and hidden worlds. If you love family
secrets, slow burn open door romance and epic magic, this is for you.*

BLUE POINTED STAR (DRIARN DUOLOGY, BOOK 2)

A new queen must save the Realm.

But those who would deny her the crown are strong.

Lish Taylor knows that she is the rightful Queen of Airlie. But, before she can officially claim the throne, she is accused of murdering the previous queen – her mother. Forced to retreat to a neighbouring court, the shadow of regicide at her heels, Lish's only chance to regain her throne, and prevent the collapse of both the Human and Calahi lands, is to reassemble the shattered pieces of the Blue Pointed Star.

Underground assassin, Aeyva Kaylneau, is one step closer to fulfilling her lifelong dream of becoming a Sentinel to the Queen. But Aeyva's past allegiances threaten to jeopardise everything she has worked for, and the secrets she keeps have the potential to not only push away the woman she loves, but bring the entire Court of Airlie to its knees.

As the Human and Calahi realms crumble around them, Lish and Aeyva must unite a network of allies across rival courts and the boundaries of magic, to expose a sinister conspiracy that imperils the very fabric of their worlds. As Queen and her Sentinel, they must show that the future belongs to those who fight for more than power.

Blue Pointed Star is the final book in the Driarn duology (sequel to Amber Wolf). Lovers of fated mates, slow burn open door romance, sapphic romance, found family and becoming who you were always meant to be will adore this thrilling conclusion.

WHEN SECRETS BECKON

Every secret has its price...

Rubilena Lanmiere can barely remember how it felt to live life for herself. Or what it feels like to live a life in the open. Raising her daughter in a world where it's dangerous to be noticed, her days are spent selling forbidden remedies in her grandfather's shop — and paying her brother Theo's debts in an underground fight den.

When their absent mother returns to gift Theo a mysterious medallion, Rubilena and Theo find themselves fleeing their home in Koamah, hunted by the entire Kingdom and its enemies. With the secrets of the medallion painting a deadly target on her brother's back, Rubilena is forced to seek help from a man who once broke her heart, and her trust.

In search of the mystical witches who can free Theo from the medallion's claim, the group find themselves wrapped inextricably in the tendrils of a prophecy. But as the fight for the ultimate knowledge intensifies, the weight of secrets already between them threatens to tear Rubilena and her allies apart.

And they can't be sure if the medallion is seeking to fulfil a deadly prophecy, or save them from the encroaching darkness...

*When Secrets Beckon is a standalone adult, dystopian fantasy with an epic second chance romance, siblings, clashes with royalty, prophecy, witches and a single mum FMC. If you love your fantasy with forced proximity, touch HIM and d*e, and open door romance, this one is for you.*

TRAITORS' CREED (TRAITORS DUOLOGY, BOOK 1)

Truth makes traitors out of even the most dutiful.
Zanteera Island has a secret: it has two prisons. Vana, the one the world knows and fears, and an unnamed compound lined with comforts. Serving her National Duty at Vana's secret counterpart, Luka Brideoake doesn't question the unorthodox disciplinary system, or the VIP status of the criminals. But when the Warden offers her a prestigious new assignment in Parliament, she starts to see the prison and its inmates in an uncomfortable new light.

Then, her childhood best friend and his brother show up sentenced to Vana, and   Luka is forced to go against every rule she's upheld to seek a dangerous new ally. All the while, the Warden's cryptic advice suggests a political web far bigger than Luka could have imagined.

As inmates start to die and the authorities move in, her path intersects with a man as enigmatic as he is powerful. But how much of the life Luka thought she wanted is she prepared to trade...for the truth?

Traitors' Creed is an adult urban fantasy with an epic slow burn romance. If you like your love interests cold to everyone but the FMC, with wings as sharp as blades (literally) and a touch of forced proximity and forbidden romance, this should be your next read. With political intrigue, high stakes and a found family that will sacrifice everything to save each other, you will love Traitors' Creed.

Traitors' Promise (Traitors duology, Book 2)

Even the greatest escapes don't guarantee freedom.
With the gilded facade of Zanteera Island's prison smouldering in her wake, Luka Brideoake prepares to make her status as a traitor official. But nothing could have readied her for a summons to a second National Duty. This time, in the heart of Nuntainia's poisonous corruption: Parliament House.

Tasked by Quillian with finding the evidence needed to expose the political tyranny, and armed with an invitation printed with government ink, Luka has no option but to report for duty. Alone.

But as the net of her government's lies closes in, Luka risks returning to the island and the prison she didn't burn—Vana. This time, behind bars. With neither time nor magic on her side, Luka will discover just how much she can endure to reveal a truth that will unseat the highest powers.

Traitors' Promise is the final book in the Traitors duology. Full of an epic romance, open door spice, friends to die for, political intrigue, rebellion and high stakes, this is an adult urban fantasy not to miss.

FIND YOUR NEXT READ

All of Lauren's books can be found here, www.laurenparkerrhodes.com/buy, or at all good bookshops and online platforms.

To stay up to date with all new releases (and inside stories...) subscribe here or at www.laurenparkerrhodes.com

Loved this book by Lauren Parker Rhodes?

I'd love you to leave a review wherever you purchased from or on Goodreads! Just a sentence or two, or even just a star rating, will go a long way to supporting this duology and it would mean the world to me.

After all, without readers, stories go unread and unheard.

Acknowledgements

This book, Traitors' Creed, challenged me in ways I didn't expect and I am so very grateful to you for getting this far and I hope you have enjoyed the ride (and aren't hating on me too much because of the ending!). I can't wait to share the rest of Luka's story with you.

To family, literally none of this would be possible without your support. By this point, I think that's clear!

A huge thank you also to my critique partner, Erin Ogilvie. The appreciation I have for you is hard to put into words. Our books are side by side on my bookshelf and I wouldn't have it any other way!

To my beta readers – Erin Thomson, Katherine Turner, Cerys Lloyd and Bron Swasbrick – thank you so much for all your glorious insights and help to make Traitors' Creed the best I possibly could. Your time and energy is truly valued.

To my editor Danikka Taylor of Authors Own Publishing (https://authorsownpublishing.com), you are a seriously valuable partner in this writing process and this book, my writing, and my author career would not be the same without you, my friend.

Escaping to fantasy worlds is a specialty of Lauren's, either creating her own or reading other people's – providing there's a strong romance, Lauren is all in. Living in semi-rural Australia with her husband and two little wildlings, Lauren tries to teach her children of the wonders of nature. About the impact of all our tiny decisions and that, sometimes, it only takes one person to make a difference. When she's not living vicariously through her characters, or kid-wrangling, Lauren can be found at her second home, the coast; feeding her coffee and chocolate addiction; or trying to fit in a yoga class...even though Archie the labrador would much prefer a walk.

Instagram: @laurenparkerrhodes
www.laurenparkerrhodes.com